D0375106

Walking the Lions

STEPHEN BURGEN

Constable · London

Constable & Robinson Ltd
3 The Lanchesters
162 Fulham Palace Road
London W6 9ER
www.constablerobinson.com

First published in the UK by Constable,
an imprint of Constable & Robinson Ltd 2002

A copy of the British Library Cataloguing in
Publication Data is available from the British Library

ISBN 1-84119-448-4

Printed and bound in the EU

For Daniel, Louis & Ruben

Acknowledgments

As always there are too many people to thank, but above all thanks to Sarah Davison for her forbearance, encouragement and loyalty. I am also much indebted to my agent David O'Leary for his patience and good advice and to Krystyna Green, my editor at Constable & Robinson. And finally, muchísimas gracias to Mary and Mariano for the loan of their *celda* in Carrer d'Ataülf, where I first starting writing this. Most of what I wrote there ended up in the bin but that's my fault, not theirs.

Author's note:

Placenames and street names are rendered throughout in Catalan, as is once again the custom in Catalunya. The village of Sant Martí Dels Moixoness is fictitious, as are all the characters. Any resemblance to anyone living or dead is entirely accidental.

1

The engine note dropped as the plane banked before making its final approach. Alex looked out the window. From the air the city looked trapped, like a grey lava flow stopped by the sea and the surrounding hills. It hunched into itself, the way old cities do; it didn't reach for the sky like New York. A stewardess came down the aisle with a bowl of boiled sweets. Her pink lipstick was fresh, ready for landing and the crew's ritual goodbye at the cabin door. It was curiously old fashioned, like the way the pilots still dressed as naval officers. She reminded Alex of a Sondheim song, a simple duet between an air hostess – who has to leave for work – and her lover:

' "Where you going?" '

' "Barcelona." '

' "Oh." '

' "Do you have to?" '

' "Yes, I have to." '

' "So." '

He didn't want a sweet but he took one anyway. Something about air travel made him compliant, afraid perhaps that any sort of non-cooperation might jeopardize the flight, that the black box flight recorder might reveal how, moments before the plane plunged into the hillside, the passenger in 26B had said no to both tea and coffee. In that respect at least he was like his father, who made a virtue of assimilation, of fitting in and avoiding the immigrant trap of living in one place while dreaming of another. His father was honest, scrupulously honest, or so Alex had always believed; obdurate as a string of mules, but honest. Which was what made it so hard to believe that all his life he'd lied about his sister being dead. Why? His father was quite specific: he didn't say she disappeared or they lost touch, he said she died of TB at the end of the Civil War. But Alex had a letter in his pocket which said she died six months ago, nearly sixty years later, and furthermore that he, Alex Nadal, was the sole heir to her farm. Why pretend she was dead? What could a girl of sixteen have done that was so terrible it made his father pretend she no longer existed? For Alex that was question number one. Number two was what to do with this farm. What did he know about farming? Absolutely nothing.

2

Alex's point of contact in Barcelona was Miguel Montero, the lawyer who had executed his Aunt Anna's will. Montero sent a brief letter explaining that Anna Nadal i Sunyer, sister of his late father Ignasi, had bequeathed him Can Castanyer, a twenty-five-acre farm south of Barcelona, near the village of Sant Martí dels Moixoness. On the phone the lawyer said it would be best if Alex didn't go to the farm alone and should come and see him first.

'Why's that?' Alex said.

'There's a slight complication. I'll explain when you get here.'

Alex intended to comply with Montero's request but the moment the plane landed he decided to go straight there, just to take a look. He was wheeling his bags over to a car hire office when he heard over the PA: 'Alex Nadal, just arrived from New York, please go to information.' First in Spanish, then in English. But no one knew he was coming; more to the point, there was no one to know, except the lawyer, and even he didn't know which flight Alex was on. He scanned the terminal for the information desk. The woman behind the desk had wide-apart brown eyes and dyed blonde hair tied back in a short pony-tail. She wore full make-up, the way women in the airline business always seem to. A big, well-dressed man with bulbous, sad fish-eyes leaned against the far end of the desk.

'Alex Nadal,' Alex said, raising one eyebrow.

The information woman's face said: 'And what of it?'

'Alex Nadal,' he repeated. 'You paged me.'

The fish-eyed man went outside and stood smoking with his back to the glass wall of the terminal.

The information woman looked puzzled. She turned to her companion, another brown-eyed assisted blonde.

'I'm sorry, there doesn't appear to be any message,' the second blonde said. 'We received a phone call, asking us to page you. That's all. Is someone expecting you, sir?'

Alex looked through the glass wall but the fish-eyed man was gone.

'Not that I know of,' he said.

The woman in the car hire office wore a small gold badge with the name Reyes stamped on it. She had pale skin and black hair and spoke with a slight lisp. Next to the Visa machine there was a little blue flag with the words *Felicidades*, *Felicitats*, *Zorionak* printed on it.

'What's that for?' Alex asked, pointing at the flag.

'The royal wedding,' Reyes said, swiping Alex's card through the machine. 'The Infanta Cristina, the king's daughter, she's getting married next month. Here in the cathedral in Barcelona. To a Basque. That's Basque for congratulations,' she added pointing to the word *zorionak* and laughing. 'It's the only Basque I know. Everyone's very excited; it's the first royal wedding in the city for seven hundred years, they say.'

Alex liked the matter-of-fact way she said that: seven hundred years. Seven hundred years ago the Cheyenne and Pawnee and the Aztecs and the Incas still had three or four centuries of relative peace and quiet ahead of them before the white man arrived in America. But here you could talk about a royal wedding in Barcelona cathedral seven hundred years ago, as if it was seventy years or seven thousand or last week, it didn't much matter. He liked that; the idea that, compared to America, what Europe lacked in space it made up for in time.

Outside the terminal building, the heat took him by surprise. He hadn't expected it this late in September and wished he'd asked for an air-conditioned car. He took the slow road down the coast, through Castelldefels and Sitges. After the Atlantic, the Mediterranean was placid, a house-trained sea, and the sky was closer and smaller than the American sky. Alex told himself not to make comparisons, not to anticipate. As usual, his mother had done her best to fill him with dread. She believed in misfortune the way other people believe in God or reincarnation. Misfortune was everywhere, invisible, but more like a virus you tried not to catch than a god you strove to placate. Misfortune was the natural order of things, the norm: anything else was extraordinary good luck.

'Alex, I wish you wouldn't go,' she said after he received the letter from Montero. 'I have a bad feeling. There's nothing there but bitterness and bad blood.'

After they found his father she went a little crazy. She came home from the morgue and opened her wardrobe and said, 'Whose clothes are these? Who put these hideous clothes in my closet?' And the next day gave every stitch of her clothing to a charity shop. But when Alex took her out to buy new outfits, the things she chose were indistinguishable from what she'd thrown out. Also from that day she stopped speaking English. She always spoke Spanish at home but now she spoke it to everyone, even the next door neighbours, who were Vietnamese, and the building superintendent, a Ukrainian Jew. When the letter came about the farm she said she didn't want Alex to go, but she did. So did Pepa, his sister, although she tried to dissuade him. They said don't go but they meant the opposite. No one in his family ever said what they meant. Before he left he had lunch with Pepa in Chinatown. She drank green tea, he drank Tiger beer. Pepa didn't drink or smoke or take drugs, ever. 'I just don't see the point,' she said, missing the point. She inhabited a Pepacentric universe in which the world was understood only in the way it affected her. If eating, say, pig's feet, disgusted her, then it was disgusting, not just to her but per se. Or if someone related some unpleasant story to her, what happened to the protagonists in the story was less significant than the effect the story had on her. So when a boyfriend persuaded her to go with him to see *Schindler's List* she was upset – by the film, of course – but more that her boyfriend had deliberately taken her to see something so distressing. He didn't last long.

If Pepa was a bit of a control freak, she did at least have one gap in her defences, a very big gap indeed. The name of the gap was Greg. Alex could never decide whether it was perverse or inevitable that his sister – who imposed on her world as much order as was humanly possible, whose home, despite a full-time job and two children under ten, was as immaculate as a show house – should fall, and fall is the *mot juste*, for a waster like Greg. Greg couldn't have survived in a world without women. Only women, with their propensity to mistake promises for promise in a man, would give houseroom to a man as useless as Greg. It wasn't that he was bad or violent or dishonest or a drinker. He was just useless. And this uselessness was rooted in the conviction that he was made for finer things than getting up in the morning and going to work. He was constantly coming up with schemes – not even scams, scam implies a degree of success – which would generate a large amount of money in return for an immeasurably tiny amount of effort. The most interesting thing about Greg was that he was prepared, driven even, to put so much effort into avoiding something of which he had no experience – work.

And yet Pepa, who herself embodied more work ethic than South Korea, believed in Greg, she had faith in him. She let him live in her house and sleep in her bed; she bore his children and worked hard so that he didn't have to. And she defended him: against her mother's dismay and her father's silence and her brother's contempt and against a world that didn't see the Greg she saw, a world blind to his potential. But all good things must come to an end, even for the Gregs of this world. Whatever void he'd been filling in Pepa's psyche was one day suddenly full and she told him to go. No fireworks, no tears; just go, please go. She let him see the children, when he could be bothered, believing they needed a father, even one as ineffective as Greg, but other than that she never mentioned him. For a long time Alex thought she hadn't got over him, then he realized it wasn't that at all; she simply couldn't remember what she'd seen in him in the first place, let alone why she'd spent seven years of her life on him.

Pepa sipped her tea. A party of eight young Chinese men came in. As they sat down each one took out a mobile and put it on the table. Like in a Western, Alex thought, where everyone hangs up their gunbelts when they enter the saloon.

'Don't you think it's weird that Dad said his sister was dead when all along he must have known she was alive?' she said, spearing a paper-wrapped prawn.

'Well, yes, of course I think it's weird.'

Pepa was angry with their father, as though he destroyed his life simply in order to make her feel bad. She said it was typical of him to do something so selfish. Which wasn't fair, he wasn't a selfish man, he was closed. Emotionally, he was like a private club that isn't taking any new members. Pepa's need for certainties made her a touch moralistic, unshakeable on the subject of good and bad, right and wrong. Alex wasn't close to his father; there was no such thing as being close to the man, he didn't permit it or, perhaps, couldn't cope with it, but Alex was more attuned than his sister to the dark forces that drove his father, and so was less inclined to judge him.

'Something awful must have happened for him to make up a story that his own sister was dead,' she said.

'Obviously something did happen.'

'And you're on a mission to find out what?'

A broad-faced, flat-chested waitress brought him a plate of scallop dumplings. She had the brusque manner of Chinatown, perfunctory, just this side of rude.

'I'm not on a mission. I've been left this farm and I'm going to take a look at it, that's all.'

'I wish you wouldn't go.'

Which was what his mother said, but neither of them meant it.

'You don't know anything about farming, Alex,' Pepa said.

'Come on, you've seen *The Waltons*. It doesn't look that hard.'

A mile south of Torredembarra, the village of Sant Martí dels Moixones was signposted off to the right. The road wound up through a wide valley lined with vines, olives, almond trees and vegetable plots. The farms were small, he couldn't imagine they provided much of a living. The village was plain to the point of austerity, with a Presbyterian feel that was incongruous in the hot southern afternoon. It was spread up one side of a hill. An old woman in a floral apron swept the pavement in front of her house. On a shoulder of the hill the village levelled out into a small square with a fountain in the middle. The fountain was dry. One side of the square was taken up by a plain brown stone church topped by a bell tower with a wrought-iron cupola. It supported a single bronze bell, streaked with verdigris. Opposite the church was a bar with no name, with a single table and chair on the pavement. Next to it a bakery, again with no sign, but with the smell of bread wafting through the red and yellow plastic strip curtain across the doorway. Just off the square was a small shop with a rusty *El Periodico* paper rack outside. There were no papers in it. An old woman crossed the square and a small boy ran out of the shop clutching a bag of potato chips.

He parked outside the church and switched off the engine. For a moment he sat in the car, arms outstretched, fingertips on the steering wheel, swaddled in the thick silence of the hot afternoon. He could hear a baby crying in an upstairs room and the distant hum of an airplane. Nothing else. He had that sense of dislocation air travel produces, when the droning tedium of the journey evaporates and suddenly it's as though it never happened, that only a moment ago he was in New

York and now here he was in a different world altogether. He went into the bar. It was tiny and dim, six stools and a fruit machine and a tortilla on a glass-domed cake plate. Behind the bar there were a couple of tarnished trophies and a faded football club pennant next to an equally faded team photo. The barman was alone, watching a game show on a TV above the bar. He was a short, bald man with a greying Errol Flynn moustache.

'*Bon dia*,' he said, in a way that suggested he wasn't really open for business but in any case would see what Alex had to say. Alex said he'd like a beer. The barman poured him a beer then shifted his attention back to the TV. An unmuffled two-stroke bike racketed through the square. Alex was thirsty after the drive and drained the glass.

'I'm looking for a farm called Can Castanyer?' he said.

The barman gave him a sideways look.

'Can Castanyay,' he said, half in inquiry, half as a correction to his pronunciation. 'Carry on up the hill, past the cemetery. When you start down towards the sea you'll see a house all on its own with a big chestnut out front. That's it.'

Alex stood in the square, blinking in the white light of one p.m. From the day he opened Montero's letter he barely paused for thought – he put his New York life on hold, bought a ticket, rented a car and now here he was. Up until now it was all about the journey, about getting here, but now he was here, he'd suddenly run out of certainties. The steel-chain fly curtain shushed in the doorway of the village shop. He went in; he could allow himself a little procrastination. The small shop was crammed to the ceiling with everything you could need aside from food and drink: writing paper, exercise books, pens, Sellotape, toys, baby clothes, needles and thread, cards of shearing elastic, wrapping paper, disposable razors, watch-straps, make-up, cigarettes and newspapers. In the magazine rack Alex was surprised to see half a dozen porn magazines, gay and straight.

The woman behind the counter was in her mid-forties, very neat, and discreetly but thoroughly made-up. She wore her hair in a bronze bob, with a small gold cross around her neck and a pair of gold shell earrings. She gave Alex a pleasant smile and asked, in Catalan, how she could help. Everything about her said shopkeeper. Whatever else she was or whatever she thought of you was concealed under this patina of retail respectability. Alex tried to imagine buying a porn magazine from this woman. Did the guys pull up in their tractors to pick up the latest issue of *Legal Age* or *Dirty Boys*? He couldn't picture it. He didn't know what he wanted, or rather he didn't want anything, so he introduced himself instead.

'Anna Nadal's nephew,' she said, in heavily accented Castilian. 'My, my.'

That 'my, my' was impossible to read.

'And you've come all this way.'

That, too, was unreadable. What was she saying? You've come all this way for what? For nothing? To make trouble?

'I never met her. Did you know her well?'

The shopkeeper looked down for a moment, as though she wanted to think about that. On a shelf above her head there were three videos: Disney's *Alice in Wonderland*, *Terminator* and a third entitled *Fantasias Lesbianas*. Alex started to adjust some preconceptions about village life.

'Your aunt was a very private person, kept herself to herself. Apart from going to mass, she scarcely left the farm.'

Whatever she thought about his Aunt Anna she wasn't about to tell him. She gave him an expectant look which said quite clearly that if he wanted to come in and chat he'd have to buy something too. He cast around for a moment then pointed above her head. She turned and reached for the *Terminator* video.

'No,' he said and her hand froze and she half turned towards him. 'I'll take *Alice in Wonderland*,' he said, adding inexplicably, 'It's for a friend.'

Can Castanyer was one of those old stone houses that seem to have risen unplanned from the ground, extended upwards and outwards as the need arose, without the aid of builders, and certainly without an architect. Like the village it was austere and unembellished, aside from a pink rose and a rosemary bush that flanked the front door. The doors and shutters were locked. Alex peeped in but it was too dark inside to see. He went round the back. Vines and hazels and tomato plants stretched in neat rows towards the almonds that marked the edge of the property, my property, he reminded himself. It was odd; he'd pictured the place overgrown and run to ruin but it was well looked after, as though someone was living there. Ducks and chickens clucked and snuffled in the dust. He took a deep breath; the heavy air was green with the scent of olives and thyme.

He became aware of someone behind him. He turned to see a small, unpolished man of around sixty, with two tufts of grey sticking out from the sides of an all-weather face. Alex held out his hand.

'Alex Nadal,' he said.

'Jaume Sabadell,' the man replied, letting out a loud goatish laugh like someone who's just delivered the punchline to a risqué joke. He ignored Alex's outstretched hand and looked him over – the new Timberland boots, black chinos, expensive white T-shirt damp with sweat. Alex had a friend from the Tennessee backwoods who claimed he could tell the weight of a pig just by looking at it; now he felt weighed in the old man's eyes.

'The prodigal's return,' Alex said with a shrug and a half smile.

Sabadell fired off another alarming laugh.

'Like a dog to its vomit,' he said, then turned and walked away.

3

Alex delivered the hire car to an office off Plaça Catalunya and immediately succumbed to Barcelona's ardent and malodorous embrace. He dragged his bags through the labyrinthine gloom of the Old City and breathed deep the odour of seafood, drains and cheap cologne that pervaded the noisy, narrow streets. After his grim reception in Sant Martí, the bustling indifference of the city seemed almost welcoming. In his head he sang, 'What are you doing the rest of your life, the north, south, east and west of your life?'

It wasn't his first time in Europe, but it was the first time he had a chance to see anything other than hotels, train stations and clubs. A couple of years ago he was in the band that accompanied the singer Ellie Zinegyi – a Lilliputian Jew into whose tiny frame nature had misfiled a deep dark bass clarinet of a voice – on her two-month European tour, but in order to make it pay they played a gig every single night, and each night in a different town. So what was on the itinerary as five nights in Paris turned out to be one night in Paris and four nights in satellite towns nearby. The same in Rome, Berlin, Madrid and London. They set up the gig, played it, went back to the hotel to sleep, then next morning got on the train to somewhere else. It was like being introduced to a succession of fascinating people and never having a conversation with any of them.

Alex chose a cheap hotel in the Carrer de la Princesa. He could have gone to a Holiday Inn, where he'd be sure of a decent shower, but one Holiday Inn was much like another. They guaranteed a world without nasty surprises – or nice ones either. Always the same, wherever you were. Maybe that was the great American achievement, that uniformity. You could sit in your room in a Holiday Inn anywhere in the world and wash your Whopper down with a Diet Coke and you felt safe. You felt at home. But Alex was prepared to risk a malfunctioning shower and a saggy bed in exchange for the prospect of a little local colour. The pension was across the street from El Rey de la Magia, a shop that supplied tops hats, scarves and whoopee cushions to the conjuring trade.

Reception was on the second floor. There was a vase of plastic freesias on the desk with a little blue flag with *Felicidades, Felicitats, Zorionak* sticking out among the flowers. The concierge was a wide-chassis, low wheelbase woman of around fifty with dyed auburn hair and grey-green eyes set in a broad, rustic spade of a face. She succeeded in being prim and flirtatious at the same time, and Alex liked her immediately. She wrote down his passport number. Through an open door beyond the reception desk he could see the back of a chair and the plump arms of someone sprawled in front of a TV game show.

'I can't place your accent,' the concierge said.

'No one ever can. It's sort of Cuban-American plus whatever my father's accent was. He was from here. Well, not from Barcelona, but Catalan.'

'Cuban and Catalan,' she said, widening her eyes. 'You must have the rumba in your blood.'

She raised her arms above her head and moved her feet and hips to a rumba beat.

'The rumba was invented here,' she said. 'Right here in Barcelona, *la rumba catalana*.'

'Is that so? I thought it came from Cuba. My mother can

rumba. I'm not much of a dancer myself, though if I thought I'd be any good I'd take up the tango.'

The concierge clucked dismissively.

'The tango's for faggots and assassins,' she said with finality, then added brightly, 'You can call me Lluisa.'

The double 'l' rang like a brief trill on the threshold of her name. She handed him the room key.

'Xavi,' she called over her shoulder into the TV room. An overweight boy of about sixteen appeared in the doorway wearing a Public Enemy T-shirt. His eyes had a dull, Nintendo sheen.

'Seventeen,' Lluisa said, pointing to Alex's bags. Xavi sighed but didn't complain. He picked up the bags and slumped up the stairs with Alex in his wake. Xavi's large soft body gave off an adolescent odour of sweat and masturbation.

The room was painted cream. A sacred heart of Jesus hung above the limp, creaky bed. There was a TV on the wall and a remote control chained to a steel staple beside the bed. Alex unpacked and put a small framed photograph of his father on the dressing table. He wondered what his father would have thought about him bringing his picture along. Would have – the tense for loss. Pepa, who taught English to new New Yorkers whose vocabulary would otherwise be limited to Budweiser, home run and motherfucker, told him it was the conditional perfect. Very conditional and not at all perfect, he thought. It was the tense for unrealized potential, a would have been station on the way to a terminal was. The memory played in his head for the 10,000th time, like a film clip, like the Zapruder sequence of Kennedy being shot. Always the same few frames, always in sequence. His father's disappearance, his mother's wild and wilder theories of what might have become of him, Pepa neurotically cleaning the clean apartment, her anxiety laced as ever with anger, and then the ring at the door, a cop in uniform. 'A body's been found,' he said, pausing to let the bare fact speak for itself.

Alex pulled off the hot, too-new boots and took a shower. The shower was half-hearted, like standing in light, warm rain.

14

He lay on the bed, still damp, and thought about Jaume Sabadell's disarming laugh and his crack about a dog returning to its vomit. He got up and opened the window and the room filled with noise. A van was unloading in the street below and everyone stuck behind it had their hands on their horns. A man in the car at the front of the jam leaned out the car window and shouted abuse, egged on by the drivers behind him. The men unloading the van answered in kind. The good-natured aggression of the exchange reminded him of New York. Further down the street, men were digging up the road with a jackhammer. A young Arab pushed a trolley of orange butane bottles which he beat with a spanner to let potential customers know he was passing. In a room across the way Bruce Springsteen's 'Hungry Heart' was playing at full volume. Then Alex noticed a large man leaning against the wall next to El Rey de la Magia, smoking a cigarette; it was the well-dressed, fish-eyed man from the airport. Alex threw on some clothes and ran downstairs but when he got to the street he'd gone. The only trace of him was a half-smoked cigarette, still smouldering on the pavement outside the magic shop.

4

The jet lag woke him early. It was a new experience; Alex wasn't familiar with the hours between four a.m. and noon – he worked late and slept late. Lluisa the concierge was up and when he inquired about breakfast she directed him to the Meson de Cafe a few minutes away in the Carrer de la Llibreteria. It was a tiny place, with barely room for half a dozen stools between the bar and the wall, but the coffee was divine; so strong it tickled his inner ear as it throttled across his synapses. He took out a small notebook and added to his short list of Catalan words: *bon dia*/hello; *adeu*/goodbye; *llum*/ light; *Dimarts*/Tuesday. In the front of the book he started a list: Phone Montero; Phone coroner; Bookshop. Alex was methodical, persistent. That's what his first piano teacher said to his mother when she asked how he was getting on. 'The boy is persistent,' he said. Which was faint praise but true. Alex did all his exercises, following his teacher's dictum that expression is the child of technique, and passed steadily if not meteorically up the grades. Not that he was without talent, but it was his doggedness that saw him through.

There was no sign of fish-eyes when he went back to the hotel and he asked Lluisa if he could use the phone. She made a show of busying herself with bits of paperwork in order to eavesdrop. First he phoned Miguel Montero, the lawyer, and arranged to meet him after lunch, which Montero explained meant four thirty. Then he called the coroner, who referred him to the coroner's office in Tarragona, where he spent forty minutes being passed to a succession of people who were unable to answer his question. Finally, a man with a thin, quavery voice like the upper register of a bassoon informed him that a verdict of accidental death had been recorded in the case of his Aunt Anna.

'She died after falling down stairs,' he said. He paused before adding in a tone of respectful apology: 'She had apparently been drinking.'

'Forgive me, but I couldn't help but overhear,' Lluisa said. 'Do you always call the coroner when you go on holiday?'

Alex explained that his aunt had apparently died in 1938 and now again in 1997 and naturally he was curious to find out the truth. He said she'd left him her farm.

'You don't look the farming type, if I may say so.'

'I'm not, I'm a pianist. There isn't a lot of work for farmers where I come from.'

'Are you famous?'

'No,' Alex laughed. 'But sometimes I play with people who are.'

Alex realized early on that he wasn't a genius, or even an innovator. He was a good musician who had the respect of other musicians and especially singers, who sought him out as an accompanist. He was good enough to make a living doing what he liked best and not many people could say that. But he wondered from time to time whether it was only cowardice that separated mere talent from greatness, whether he was simply too lazy to test his full potential, or too afraid that the ruthless singlemindedness that seemed to characterize the greats he'd met would leave him isolated, unloved and unlovable.

Lluisa's son Xavi appeared in his dressing gown. He kissed

his mother and gave Alex a sly look over her shoulder before disappearing through the door. Alex saw him point the remote at the TV as he lowered himself into an armchair.

'I worry about that boy sometimes. He has a heart of gold but,' and she tapped her forehead, 'but no *seny*.'

'*Seny*?' Alex asked. She pronounced it like the English word sane.

'The Catalan for commonsense,' she said. 'But not just that, a combination of commonsense and guile. The boy needs *seny*, he's too trusting.'

Alex added *seny* to the list in his notebook and went out and for the next few hours he followed his feet around the Old City. He felt curiously at home, like when you meet someone and you just click and it's as though you've known each other for years. Maybe his father bequeathed him a gene with the word Barcelona etched in amino acid. He walked around the Barrí Gotic and across la Rambla into el Raval. In Carrer de Balmes he found a bookshop with several histories of the Civil War in Catalunya, all of them in Catalan. Sant Martí dels Moixones wasn't listed in the index of any of them.

He sent postcards to Pepa and his mother and lunched on rotisserie chicken in Pollo Rico until the grease ran down his chin and then he walked some more, taking in things as they came to him – the Boqueria market, Gaudí's Palau Güell, the strangely camp monument to Columbus – all the time feeling he was on the cusp of something new. It was an uneasy feeling. He found himself in Barceloneta. New York is on the sea, but it doesn't feel like it, not unless you take the train all the way out to Jones beach, and then it doesn't feel like New York any more. But in Barcelona the sea is right there. Alex strolled past the yachts in Port Vell and crossed the broad boulevard into Barceloneta and there, at the vanishing point of the dark, washing-draped, fish-wafted streets, was the Mediterranean. He stood on the promenade above Barceloneta beach. The sea looked old, as though worn smooth by centuries of trade. Below him groups of noisy old men, shirtless and sun-blackened, smacked dominoes on rust-puckered tables. They joked and argued and swore, fuelled by glasses of coffee laced with Pujol rum. Their wives sat apart from them on folding chairs; small, round women held in shape by bright patterned one-piece bathing suits, chatting and knitting baby clothes. Like the men, they had the mahogany skin of people who spend their lives in the sun.

Alex followed the promenade as far as the hospital then took the steps down to a beach bar. He sat, half sun, half shade, under a parasol and ordered a beer. He liked it there in the little outdoor bar, with the city at his back and the sea before him, but he couldn't escape this feeling of premonitory unease. After a few minutes he became aware of someone standing over him. He looked up to see a woman shielding her eyes with one hand and gesturing to the chair opposite with the other. There were plenty of free tables but if she wanted to sit with him, that was fine. This isn't New York, he told himself, deciding she was too well dressed to be a psychopath. He gave her a nice but not flirtatious smile and gestured that, of course, she was welcome.

She set a slim brown briefcase beside the chair and sat down. Alex did an inventory: pale skin, hazel eyes, a little mascara but no eye shadow; thick brown eyebrows, lightly plucked; dark brown bob, dyed presumably and expensively streaked with auburn; quiet lipstick. She had a fine-boned face, nicely proportioned with a hooked nose. Her face was a little, not sad – sad was too bittersweet – there was something else there, disappointment, perhaps, or regret. She wore a light-weight pale lilac suit over a white blouse. Her nail polish toned perfectly with the suit and Alex restrained an urge to look under the table to see if her shoes matched the rest of the outfit. She sported a wedding band and an old-fashioned diamond engagement ring. Low to mid-forties, turned out just so, very much the professional woman, but not prim. In the right circumstances, her manner suggested, she could produce a fair amount of heat. As distinct from warmth.

She ordered a *vermut negre* and the waiter returned with a sweet Martini. Alex took out his notebook and under *seny* added: *vermut negre*/Martini Rosso to the list. He looked out to sea and saw her out of the corner of his eye take a cigarette from her handbag and light up. They sipped their drinks and their eyes met over the rims of the glasses. She had nice eyes, not fall in and drown eyes, but nice enough. *Ojos que hablan*, as they say; eyes that talk. He looked away, conscious of his tendency to stare, though his stare was usually more of a looking beyond than a gazing in, the eyes at anchor allowing the mind to drift. But it was a bad and sometimes a dangerous habit. People didn't like it if you looked at them like that, at least they didn't in New York.

'So how are you enjoying Barcelona, Señor Nadal?' the woman said. Her Spanish was clotted with a thick Catalan accent, all glottals and fricatives.

Alex set his glass down slowly and looked past her towards the spindly palms along the beach and the swaying masts in the marina beyond. He sidestepped the obvious question.

'I like it fine,' he said. 'Great buildings, terrific coffee, lovely people. Everyone acts like they already know you. Are you a native?'

The question seemed to surprise her, threw her a little off course.

'I live here but I'm from Terrassa, it's near Montserrat, about half an hour from the city.'

She spoke matter-of-factly, as if this were a perfectly normal conversation, an almost wistful smile drifting across her face, as though she was recalling some happy episode from her girlhood days in Terrassa.

'You already know my name, what's yours?'

'Cases. Montserrat Cases.'

'Montserrat from Montserrat.'

'Terrassa,' she corrected, a little tartly. 'Señor Nadal . . .'

'Oh please, Montserrat, do call me Alex, you know how we Americans hate formalities.'

'Almost as much as you love sarcasm,' she said, this time in perfect English.

'Well, please forgive me,' Alex said, sarcastically, and in

Spanish. 'I read something about Montserrat in a guide book. Isn't it the place with a shrine to a black virgin?'

'In the monastery, yes,' she said, reverting to Spanish.

'Was she really black? I mean, African?'

'There's a lot of debate about her origins. Certainly the statue of her is black. But . . .'

'I know, you didn't come here to chat about virgins. I suppose I could ask you how you know my name, seeing as I don't know a soul here.'

'You may not know them, but there are people here who know you're here and why,' she said.

She delivered the words in a pleasant, even tone and Alex thought about the big man with the sad fish-eyes. She was very cool in the professional sense, but knowing in a womanly way. It was a disarming combination, and she seemed well aware of it. She smiled at him.

'Shall we get to the point?' she said.

Alex shrugged, as much to say, It's your show. Montserrat drew on her cigarette. She smoked with the languor of a forties screen goddess.

'You have inherited a farm called Can Castanyer.'

He could have said yes, or that's correct or how do you know, but there didn't seem much point. He looked her in the eye and waited.

'I am a lawyer. My client has instructed me to buy the farm from you. The deed of sale has been drawn up, it's a good offer. All you have to do is sign.'

She picked up the slim briefcase, laid it across her lap and snapped the catches.

'What makes you think I want to sell?'

It felt like the sort of negotiation he was often forced to have with club owners, where you agree a fee then, after the gig, the owner tries to pay you less, some stupid excuse about the set being too short or the bar bill too high, something he's just plucked out of the air. You'd like to tell him to shove it but you can't, you want to work and there are only so many clubs, even in New York. So you stay nice and in the end you get less than you agreed but more than the owner's offering. It was a stupid game but you had to play. Alex knew he needed to play Montserrat Cases with care, but at the same time stand his ground. She said that people knew he was here and they knew why. What kind of people? Well, for a start, he thought, the kind who hire a well-manicured lawyer to run their errands.

'It's the sensible option,' said Montserrat. 'You should understand that there are a lot of complications when foreigners inherit land here. You'll need a lot of papers.'

'I know how to get papers,' Alex said, more sullen than he intended. 'We have a bureaucracy in America too, you know.'

'I doubt that it could compete with ours. Believe me, however many papers you have, there is always one more you haven't got.'

'It can't be that difficult. My father was a Catalan after all, so it's only a generation away.'

'It's not that simple. It can take years. All sorts of objections can be raised, the bureaucracy is endless. Selling is by far the best option.'

'There's a will that says it's mine. How complicated is that? And if it isn't, or if as you say it's going to take years to establish that it's legally mine, how can I sell it to you?'

'You wouldn't need to worry about that.'

An ambulance passed on the road above. A seagull perched on the railing turned towards it and imitated perfectly the sound of the siren. Montserrat and Alex exchanged amused looks, a confidential moment aside from the business in hand.

'I see, so all those difficulties you were talking about could, in the right circumstances, be made to vanish. So my situation is either terribly complicated or wonderfully straightforward, depending on the point of view. If I take your point of view and agree to sell, it's smooth sailing; if not, I can expect a rough ride. Have I got that about right?'

'Essentially, yes.'

She had a doctor's bedside manner, soothingly pragmatic. The way a doctor can say, 'Yes I'm afraid it's throat cancer, but we'll do our best to cut it out and who knows, within a year or two you may even be able to speak again.' And you find yourself saying, 'Thank you, doctor.'

'How much?' Alex said.

She took a document out of her briefcase and glanced at it as though to refresh her memory, although he doubted she needed to. She told him the price in pesetas, which was millions of course. He started doing a conversion in his head but she'd already thought of that and told him what it was in dollars. It sounded a lot but what did he know? The farm could have been worth ten times that.

'I'd have to think about it,' he said. 'But just out of curiosity, what if I said OK, I'll sell at double that price?'

Her violet nails drummed quietly on the lid of the briefcase.

'It's a generous offer already,' she said, then added after a short pause, 'I do have some leeway, I'd have to make some calls.'

'Of course, to Mr Mystery Client. But we're talking hypothetically here, Montserrat. Just you and me and a seagull that thinks it's an ambulance. I said double the price, I notice you haven't burst out laughing. So, just hypothetically, double the price doesn't strike you as completely ludicrous?'

'I'm not in a position to comment on that.'

'Good, that's settled then.'

She raised an eyebrow, but her face brightened a little, there was even the distant possibility of a smile.

'I won't sell,' Alex said. 'Not at any price, at least not now and not to your client. I'm sure you think I'm stupid because I'm American, and it's well known that there are a lot of stupid Americans. But one thing even stupid Americans know a thing or two about is money. And if someone is so desperate to buy my little farm it must be worth something, almost certainly more than you're offering. So I'm afraid you'll have to tell your eager client the bad news: no sale. And while you're at it, you can tell him or her or them that I don't like being told what to do. It has the effect of making me want to do the opposite. Childish, I know, but that's how it is.'

The lawyer sighed. She closed her eyes and sighed again and sat with her hands folded and her eyes shut for a full twenty seconds, as if awaiting divine guidance. When she opened them she looked right into Alex's. Again he saw that sorrowful thing, regret or whatever it was.

'Señor Nadal, please take my advice. Sell. Sell now, you'll have to eventually, believe me.'

'Are you threatening me?'

'I'm a lawyer, a messenger. I don't make threats.'

She snapped shut the catches of the briefcase, left some money in a saucer for her drink and stood up.

'I'm afraid this isn't the last you'll hear of this,' she said.

'I suspected that might be the case,' Alex smiled, raising his glass. 'Until next time.'

She turned and click-clicked away on her narrow heels. Her shoes were brown; they matched the briefcase, not the suit.

5

Carmen Montero knew Alex Nadal was in town but she didn't attach any importance to it. To her he was just someone she helped track down so that her brother Miguel could settle a will. But she had an urge to meet him, not for any good reason; she just wanted to see what he looked like. She sat in a side office at *El Mensajero*, the Barcelona daily, with her feet on the table and a notebook on her lap, watching a video of a recent interview with Salvador Oriol on TV3.

The grand old man of Catalunya was getting an easy ride. The interviewer asked him questions like, 'For many of us you have come to symbolize all things Catalan, to embody as it were the Catalan nation. How has this come about?' Oriol considered each question as though he was being asked it for the first and not the thousandth time and was giving great thought to his replies. He pursed his lips, he stroked his chin, he wrung his hands and then swept them up and combed his fingers through his over-long grey hair. He gushed platitudes and puffed himself up with phrases like, in all modesty, and, with great humility. He was an illustrious absurdity, like Gloria Swanson in *Sunset Boulevard*, except Oriol wasn't all washed up yet. Far from it. The reporter wrapped up the interview with the old chestnut, 'What does it mean to be a Catalan?'

25

'Well, firstly of course it is the language,' Oriol said, pushing his hair back and stealing a quick look at himself in the monitor. 'I cannot see how a person who doesn't speak Catalan could call themselves Catalan. Language is the bed-rock, the soul of identity. But there is so much else: our music and dance – above all, our beloved *sardana* – our distinctive architecture, our artists, our cuisine. I think to be a Catalan is to take pride in all these things, to love and nurture and protect them, and ensure that they are never again corrupted or overwhelmed by outside forces.'

Then he said he had a special announcement to make. To mark his forthcoming eightieth birthday he was going to make a bequest, a gift to the nation, as a gesture of thanks and as a mark of his faith in the people and the culture. But for now it had to remain a secret, all would be revealed soon. The interviewer applauded this wonderful news; even the crew could be heard clapping off camera.

'He's a show, isn't he?'

Susana, the paper's environment correspondent and Carmen's best friend, leaned against the doorway. Carmen stuck her fingers in her mouth and pretended to vomit.

'The man's got a master's degree in vanity,' she said, silencing the TV with a flip of the remote. 'The paper's doing some big brown-nose, grand-old-man-of-Catalunya special to mark his eightieth birthday. My job is to remind the nation of his incalculable contribution to the arts.'

'Which has been what exactly?' Susana said.

'Which has been exactly not very much. Usual big shot patronage – Liceu opera, Palau de la Música – not much else as far as I can tell. And now this bequest he's just announced, which may be connected to the arts, I've no idea. Frankly I shudder to think. Still, at least it gives me a news angle, which makes it slightly more interesting than recycling his cuttings. More to the point, this assignment's keeping me off the royal wedding coverage.'

'Lucky you. You know we've already done a front page dummy for the day after the wedding. Banner headline: "Princess of Barcelona". Everyone's gone mad. It's like we're all living in *Hello!* magazine.'

'I know, I don't get it. Normally people here spit if you so much as mention Madrid. Now the Infanta wants to get married here and everyone's thrilled senseless.'

'Including the inestimable Salvador Oriol.'

'Of course, the inestimable, the extraordinary, the magnificent. You ever hear anyone say anything bad about him?'

'What kind of bad?'

'You know. Any dirt? I thought maybe I'd do a little digging, make life a little more interesting.'

'Oriol's untouchable, isn't he?'

'No one's untouchable. Spain's a democracy now. Haven't you heard?'

'A democracy? My God, has anyone told the editor?'

It was through Carmen that Angel Domènech learnt of the existence of Alex Nadal. He found out by chance. Angel didn't like chance, it smacked of incompetence. He was sitting up in bed, smoking a Marlboro and watching Carmen get dressed. Until that day he'd watched her as he had so many other women, with the serenity of a man who has just made love with a woman he isn't in love with and who isn't in love with him. A clever, sexy woman who seems to want exactly what he does and nothing more, that is, to meet once a week or so to make conversation, eat seafood and have sex. A woman who doesn't ask about his business or his marriage. Up until now, Carmen had been perfect. Now there was a complication; he was starting to like her – a lot. Which wasn't part of the plan.

Angel and Carmen were in his flat in the Olympic village, a gift from a grateful property speculator. The lead-up to the 1992 Olympics was a boom time for Angel. The city was desperate to have everything ready on time and was prepared to cut any corner to prove to the world that Catalunya isn't Spain, that in Catalunya *mañana* means today. It was a time when a man of Angel's talents barely had time to sleep. His business card described him as a financial consultant. That was one way of putting it. The only other information on the card was a mobile phone number; that was his office.

Angel and Carmen were both Catalans but the Domènechs were *Catalàs de sempre*, Catalans from way back. Angel liked to say that Domènechs had been in Barcelona since the Earth was cooling, that when the Romans arrived a Domènech was there to welcome them with a glass of *cava* and a plate of *esqueixada*, the local salt cod salad. Domènechs were respected, if not respectable, and like most Catalans, they knew how to make money. What they hadn't grasped was how to keep it. Money blew through the family like an offshore breeze, leaving each generation to start all over. But the real family legacy wasn't money, it was people; the Domènechs knew everyone.

Angel was a fixer. His line of work was based on two simple premises: everyone has a dream and everyone has a secret. Find out what they are and you're in business. Angel made things happen, he removed the obstacles that lay between people and the thing they desired. As a rule, what they desired was money: more than they already had, generally more than they needed, though that wasn't for him to judge. They were grateful to Angel and showed their gratitude in the way they knew best, with money. On the rare occasions when a client failed to express the agreed level of gratitude, Angel would tell them a little secret, one of their own, something they hoped was not in the public domain, and Angel would assure them that it wasn't. Yet. People said a lot of things about Angel, good and bad, but everyone agreed he had *seny*. Like his father, who in the Civil War became a black marketeer, ensuring that he was sought after and despised equally by all sides, Angel had *seny* in spades.

The flat above the marina was a little thank you from a prominent member of Opus Dei who had felt it his civic duty to build a 300-room hotel in time for the Olympics but discovered that part of the chosen site was occupied by a tumbledown building of no importance. The building was occupied by people of still less importance except in that they refused to move out. Angel had been instrumental – indirectly, of course – in removing this inconvenience. He came to the flat by the marina a couple of afternoons a week, with Carmen or whoever. It was furnished with a bed, a chair, a fridge and a tray of glasses. Nothing else. A maid came once a week to clean, change the sheets and restock the fridge with *cava*.

Angel had cultivated the nonchalance of a man who walks on air but the truth was he felt the dull pull of gravity more than most, and lately more than ever. He'd always relied on the fleeting pleasures of the table and bedroom as a counterweight but recently they'd failed to buoy him up. Even the frisson of making deals was beginning to pall. Angel was forty-five. When he took a good long look at what his life was, it didn't seem to add up to forty-five years' worth. It lacked meaning, whatever that meant. That's what he kept saying to himself, it lacks meaning, the way he'd say of a soup, it needs salt.

From the bed he could see the tops of the masts of the yachts in the marina bobbing against the blue-green curve of the sea. He watched Carmen fish for her underwear among the pile of clothes on the room's solitary chair. The sight of a woman dressing excited him almost as much as undressing her did. It fascinated him to see the naked woman, in a few quick movements, transform herself into the public woman who presents herself to the world, walks down the street, rides the metro, catches or avoids your eye; the woman other men imagine naked. A naked woman is just that, naked, an accident of nature, a throw of the genetic dice. What you see is what you get. But there's nothing accidental about the public woman. A woman fully dressed is the result of a hundred thousand choices, decisions, experiments, mistakes and regrets. Angel watched the naked Carmen – compact, funky, dark skin, thick black hair. Then zip, flick, snap – this brilliant artifice – like a conjuring trick that never lost its magic.

Carmen knew Angel was watching her, and knew how. He was that kind of a man, a man who gourmandized women. She'd had lunch and sex with him on half a dozen occasions now and he approached both pleasures in exactly the same way: with relish, knowledge and enthusiasm. She knew he wasn't to be relied on, that he was married and a womanizer. That was fine by her. If she was looking for Mr Right she knew better than to call at Angel's address. The only danger with a womanizer is when a woman gets it into her head that he thinks she's special. Carmen had no such illusions. She suspected that Angel wanted her first and foremost because she was a woman, that at a certain, fundamental level, any half-decent looking woman would have done. She also knew she'd been chosen out of curiosity, the way at lunch that day Angel had chosen, out of simple curiosity, an obscure Basque wine. Not because it was recommended, but because he'd never had it before. This was what made Angel refreshing, because he wasn't interested in control, just pleasure. He didn't see her as a threat to be neutralized, she was a pleasure to be enjoyed. OK, it was limited, but he was good company – intelligent, cultured and handsome in the old-fashioned, con-quistador style, like Cortés in an Italian suit. And he did really like women, which made a change. But she decided to quit while she was ahead, before the thing lost its shine. This was going to be her last visit to the flat above the marina.

She sat in the chair in a white T-shirt, barelegged, her feet planted wide apart, with her back to the light, doing her eyes in the lid of a fake tortoiseshell compact. She looked past the mirror at Angel.

'Do you know Salvador Oriol?' she said. 'Personally, I mean.'

Angel had a bad feeling, a sensation that here was a good day turning bad, even before she introduced the subject of Alex Nadal. He looked across the room at Carmen. She snapped the compact shut and dug a pack of cigarettes out of her bag. Angel tossed her the lighter. She swung her legs over the arm of the chair and padded over to the window. Angel liked the way she moved, always within herself, assured, comfortable. Women tended to fall for him and he supposed that on some level he wanted them to. But Carmen wasn't falling, which kept him interested, too interested, if he was honest. He felt an urge to walk down the street with her, arm in arm, to see the I-wish-I-was-in-your-shoes look in other men's eyes. He reminded himself that she was a journalist and she was asking questions.

'Oriol? No, not really.'

'I thought you knew everyone.'

'Who told you that?'

'I think you did.'

'I wouldn't say I know him. I mean, we're acquainted, we've been in the same room on a few occasions, you know, civic functions, that kind of thing. Exchanged a few words, I suppose. Why?'

'Nothing really, just if you knew anything about him, anything behind the mask. I have to interview him. His eightieth birthday is coming up and we're doing a big spread, you know, grand old man of Catalunya, all that rubbish.'

'You don't seem to have a very high opinion of our beloved Oriol,' he said. 'Look, do you have to go back to work now?'

Generally by now – fed, fucked and flattered – he was quite happy to part company. But he wanted Carmen to stay. He also wanted to change the subject.

'How clean would you say he was?' she said, sidestepping.

'Now there's a question,' Angel laughed. 'Everyone's clean until they get caught, aren't they? You know the joke about the honest president of Catalunya? No? Well, this guy needs a big favour from the president so he goes to the Generalitat and offers him five million pesetas if only he'll grant him this favour. The honest president tells him indignantly that he's not for sale and orders him to leave. The next day the guy comes back and offers ten million. Again the honest president says he can't be bought and orders him out. So the next day the guy goes back and says he'll give him twenty-five million if only he'll grant him this favour. The honest president flies into a rage, grabs the guy and throws him down the stairs. The guy picks himself off the floor and says, "Why did you do that?" The president comes down the stairs, seizes him by the throat, and says angrily, "Because you're getting near my price."'

Carmen laughed, but she sensed that Angel was uneasy and wondered why.

'Oriol's got this big reputation but I don't know what for,' she said.

'Best kind to have. And the hardest to lose.'

'I hate the way everyone calls him the old man, you know, like he was some kind of paterfamilias. Big Daddy Catalunya, especially when he's so ridiculously short.'

'Well, every nation needs one, a Churchill or a Gandhi or a JFK. We've got him, Salvador Oriol, patron saint of Catalunya.'

'But what's he ever done? What is he?'

'I guess you could say he's a self-made man, in every sense. As far as I can tell he made himself up and we bought it. He got locked up in the sixties for some sort of language protest. Didn't do much time but it did the trick. He became a martyr to the Catalan cause. Of course he made his pile under the Franco regime but who didn't? Are you working now?' he asked her again.

'What? When, now?'

Angel was breaking his rules. Never ask a favour, his father used to say. Make them offer. Make them think that giving you what you want was their idea.

'I've got to look in at the office and I'm working tonight. Got to do a review. Lorca's *House of Bernarda Alba* at the Sala Beckett. Apparently it involves a degree of nudity, which I don't remember from the text, but so what. Why?'

'No reason. Just fancied a stroll by the sea, stop for a vermouth. Dish of snails maybe. Afterwards I could show you where my restaurant's going to be. Did I tell you I'm opening a restaurant? Fish and seafood mainly. Bit of steak on the menu to keep the Americans happy. I think I've found a chef, too. From Montpellier, a French Catalan would you believe.'

The restaurant was part one of Angel's attempt to give his life more meaning, somewhere he could kick back and play the patron, not just the bon vivant but a purveyor of the good life. He had found a place on the edge of the old city, in the Carrer Ample, near the basilica of La Mercè.

Carmen smiled at the invitation, but didn't say anything. Her black hair was cut short, emphasizing her best features: her curved-for-kissing lips and her black, almost Arabic eyes. Dark elliptical mirrors; when you looked in all you saw was yourself. She had a playful, mischievous look that men often mistook for girlishness. Her skin was dark, not Gypsy dark, but a dusty Gauguin cocoa brown. Her lips were almost mauve, a shade lighter than her nipples, Angel noted, which were the colour of ripe figs. And she had a whole repertoire of smiles: ironic, teasing, incredulous, coy, dismissive, sardonic, affectionate, enigmatic. Her smiles were protective, they were like Wonderwoman's bangles: harmful things bounced off them. The smile she gave Angel was of the 'well, what have we here?' variety.

'Did I tell you I've been playing detective?' she said, changing the subject.

The bad feeling hung there, but it was as if they could keep joking around maybe it wouldn't matter. The white T-shirt looked ultra-white against her dark skin. He wanted her to undress, rewind the tape. Maybe then whatever this thing was he thought was coming would just fade away.

'Detective eh? Why not come back to bed and teach me how to play. I could be your prime suspect.'

'I'd probably have to slap you around a bit.'

'I'd call my lawyer.'

'That's just it,' she said, zipping up a short black skirt of some shiny sharkskin-like material. 'Did I tell you my brother is a lawyer?'

'Your brother's a lawyer and you've been playing detective. Are these things connected?'

'Well, my brother had to handle this old lady's will, an old woman from the country, a village down near Torredembarra, on the coast. In the will she left everything to her nephew. But the address she gave was in New York and it was no good, I mean the nephew had moved on. So Miguel, that's my brother, calls me and asks if I can use the paper's contacts to track this guy down. "You're a journalist," he says, "you know how to find things out." Oh sure, big joke. Carmen Montero, the great investigative journalist. Everyone thinks it must be great being an arts reporter, free tickets and all that. But you wouldn't believe some of the crap you have to sit through. Did I tell you about that *Hamlet*? Four hours long and set in present-day Los Angeles. Hamlet's gay, of course. He delivers the "To be or not to be" speech in a leather bar. And all in Catalan, because the Generalitat won't give you a grant for anything that's not. So Hamlet's speaking Catalan in a leather bar in LA – I believe that's what in theatre is called suspension of disbelief. It's times like that when I say thank God I'm being paid to sit there. Anyway, I found him, the nephew. Super-sleuth or what? He's here.'

'What's his name?' Angel said. He got out of bed and wrapped a towel round his waist. He shouldn't have asked, shouldn't have shown any interest. He knew the answer anyway. He took a deep, slow breath.

'What's whose name?'

All the humour had gone out of his face. Without it, he looked older, worth every one of his forty-five years.

'Nadal,' Carmen shrugged. 'Like the football player. Alex Nadal.'

Angel looked at his wrist with a 'time's up' gesture. His watch was on the bedside table.

'Sorry, I've got to run.'

'Of course you do, you're a man,' Carmen said with good-humoured sarcasm. 'And just when I was coming round to the idea of a dish of snails.'

She kissed him lightly on the lips.

'See you around, Angel.'

Angel's mobile was on the window sill. A strong breeze – the Xaloc or Tramontana, he could never remember which was which – had made the sea choppy and brought the windsurfers out. He picked up the mobile and called Salvador Oriol.

6

After a day's walking around the city Alex's clothes were dank so he went back to the hotel to change before his meeting with Miguel Montero. Lluisa's son Xavi was lounging in reception looking like a hormone that had learned to dress itself. He was wearing shorts and an LA Lakers shirt and had one plump thigh draped over the arm of his chair.

He was an odd-looking boy, a bit simple perhaps. Perhaps that's what Lluisa meant about him lacking *seny*; she was probably too blinded by mother-love to see that the boy was just a bit dim. When Alex left the hotel ten minutes later Xavi gave him a lazy-lidded look, the sort you'd get from a sleepy dog on a hot afternoon. And hot it was. The streets drooped under a bleary September afternoon as Alex crossed town to the lawyer's office. Only La Mercè, poised like Mary Poppins to take off from her basilica, looked like she had any energy.

Montero's office was in Poble Sec, behind the Apollo theatre on Paral.lel. The office was small and neat. There were the usual things – books, papers, telephone, files, framed diplomas, a PC, a box of floppy disks. And then there were Miguel Montero's eyes, dark sorrowing pools that drew you giddily in. It was like looking down a stairwell and thinking how easily you could fall. Or jump. He was slightly built and about Alex's age. He held out his hand and lit up a big smile, a sunny yin to balance the melancholy yang of those eyes. He motioned Alex to sit down. Alex wiped his brow with the back of his arm.

'Is it usually this hot so late in September?'

'Not as a rule, no. They say it's El Niño. Once it was the wrath of God, now nature is punishing us. Fornication or greenhouse gases, either way, it's our fault. Beer? Mineral water?'

'Thanks, a glass of water.'

Miguel took a bottle out of a small fridge in the corner of the office and filled a glass. He had a loose-limbed manner but his actions were very precise, economical. The way he poured the water, the careful way he screwed the cap back on the bottle, the way he set the glass down on a coaster. Everything was just so. He folded his hands and looked at Alex as though to say, How can I help? Alex's instincts told him to trust him; his radar told him he was gay. He got straight to the point.

'You said on the phone there was some sort of a problem,' Alex said. 'Were you referring to whoever it is who's trying to muscle me off the farm?'

Alex studied Miguel's face. His reaction – total incredulity – seemed genuine, though it's one of the easier sentiments to fake.

He told him about the fish-eyed man and the encounter with Montserrat Cases.

'I'd like to speak to Señora Cases again, if indeed such a person exists. And I'd like to find out who her client is. Would it be a breach of professional ethics to tell me where I can find her?'

'Of course I can find out for you,' Miguel said. He shook a cigarette out of a soft packet and tapped it on the blotter. Alex noticed that no one here asked if you minded them smoking. In the States smoking was up there with homicide and child abuse.

'I don't know what to say,' Miguel said. 'That is, I really

37

have no idea what this is about. No one has approached me about buying Can Castanyer.'

Again he seemed genuine, but again, if you're going to wear a mask, a profession of total ignorance is generally a good fit.

'So what was the problem you referred to?'

Miguel gave him a long look, like he was thinking how to answer that. Alex had trouble returning the look; the lawyer's eyes gave him vertigo.

'It's a stupid thing. In fact, to be honest, I don't really know what it's about, but when I went out to the village, after your aunt died, I encountered a certain degree of hostility to the prospect of your arrival.'

'Like a dog to its vomit.'

'What?'

'That's what my neighbour said, a man called Sabadell. I went out there – sorry, I know you told me not to.

Montero laughed. '*Obedecemos pero no cumplimos*, as we say here. We obey but we don't comply. You'll obviously fit in well.'

'Anyway, when I suggested to this Sabadell that this was some sort of a homecoming on my part, that's what he said, that it was like a dog going back to its vomit. What's all that about?'

The lawyer looked ill at ease. He took a deep draw on his cigarette then took a long time over stubbing it out. Alex waited.

'It seems that the Nadals are not well liked in Sant Martí. It seems your father made himself unpopular.'

'By doing what?'

'It seems, at least this is what they claim, that your father betrayed some people, people on the republican side, to the fascists, a few months before the end of the war, and these people, young men, very young actually, were executed as a result. This is what they say, I don't know the details. I don't even know if it's true, except that the men – three brothers – were shot. There's no doubt about that.'

Alex didn't say anything for a while and Miguel didn't

break the silence. This was the first time he had caught a glimpse into what lay behind his father's reticence. All along he imagined his father had been wronged but maybe it was the other way round, maybe his father fled in disgrace. Maybe it was shame, not indignation, that had sealed his father's lips. He was the original man of few words. Talk was like money to him: he spent what he had to and saved the rest. He thought about what Miguel said. He tried to picture his father – he would have been about eighteen at the time – turning the three young brothers in to the fascists. He couldn't see it.

'I don't believe it,' he said.

'Of course,' Miguel said, sympathetically, fluttering a hand like a fan. It was a nervous gesture, and rather camp.

'No really. It's not just that I don't want to believe it, it's just not him. Look, my father was a very stubborn man, stubborn and loyal. And he hated bullies, whether in the schoolyard or the government. If anyone tried to bully him it just made him more stubborn. So when I try to picture him doing what you say he did, I can't. It doesn't fit. His whole attitude would have been – over my dead body, that's what he was like.'

'Perhaps the dead body option was the one that was presented to him. As I said, I've no idea how true this story is, only that it's what they believe in Sant Martí. But you must remember this was wartime and people often behave out of character during wartime. And in civil wars they can act out of all recognition. What does your father say about this?'

'My father wouldn't talk about those times and he hasn't said a thing since he threw himself off the George Washington Bridge early last year.'

The lawyer was too startled to speak. Alex, too, was surprised by his own vehemence.

'I'm sorry, I didn't mean it to come out like that. My father didn't speak about the war. His parents died in 1937, he said; his sister – the same one whose will you are executing – supposedly died of tuberculosis the following year. As far as anyone knew he had no family here. The story he told was this: the fascists rolled north and he fled south, which would be typical of him, to go south when everyone else was running north trying to escape to France. Somehow he made his way to Alicante. There was a ship in the port. He snuck on and wound up in Cuba, where he did the only thing he knew, farming. By the end of the 1950s he had his own tobacco farm and a young wife, my mother. Then in 1961, after the Bay of Pigs, the Fidelistas came to his farm and told him that from now on he had to give two thirds of the crop to the state. My father asked if he had a choice. When they said no he turned his back and went into the house. The next day he told his wife to pack their things, they were leaving for America. Then he set fire to the house, the drying sheds, the crops. Over twenty years' work and he never even looked over his shoulder. That's how stubborn he was, and that's all I know. We weren't allowed to utter Franco's name in the house, nor Fidel's for that matter. My father wouldn't have betrayed anyone to the fascists. Not out of political conviction – he was no lefty – not even because he was brave. He was just too stubborn.'

Miguel lit another cigarette. 'Perhaps we should get on with reading the will,' he said.

'He left a note,' Alex said, apparently not listening. He took out his wallet and unfolded a piece of lined paper torn from a spiral-bound notebook. 'On 16 June 1938,' Alex read, 'Captain Guillermo Morín, officer in charge of the nationalist forces that captured Sant Martí dels Moixones, in one afternoon destroyed and saved my life. I can no longer endure that life. Forgive me. Ignasi Sunyer i Nadal, 23 March 1996.'

'The poor man,' Miguel said with feeling. 'The poor, poor man.'

'I want to know what happened. I want to know what drove my father to this, and I want to know why he pretended his sister Anna was dead. His suicide has practically destroyed my mother, she feels she should have been able to save him from his despair, she feels a failure, although she's nothing of the kind.'

'Misfortune can often appear like failure,' Miguel said, almost to himself. 'People say you make your own luck, so it's easy to believe the reverse must be true, that you're the agent of your own misfortune. Psychologically speaking. Objectively, of course, it's complete rubbish. The victim is not to blame.'

'Even if I discover the most terrible things about my father, I want to find out. I want this laid to rest.'

Miguel tilted his head back and blew a stream of smoke at the ceiling fan.

'That, if I may say so, is a very American way of looking at things – the idea that you can lay something to rest by digging it up.'

'Most things are better out in the open, don't you think?'

'Perhaps, but by tradition we're more inclined to the private than the public confessional here. And these days we tend to avoid both.'

Alex restrained an urge to ask the lawyer for a cigarette, although he hadn't smoked for six years. Miguel untied a folder and took out Anna Nadal's will. His raised his eyebrows in inquiry and Alex nodded. The will was short and to the point and said simply that she left everything to Alex. Then there was a codicil. Miguel translated from the Catalan: 'Dear nephew, all my life I've kept myself apart from other people as they have kept apart from me. The nearest thing I have to friends – or children – are Victor and Núria Sabadell. All I ask is that you do right by them. Victor is a good soul but Núria – wherever she is – is troubled. She knows too much.'

'Sabadell? Any relation to Señor Dog and Vomit?'

'Son and daughter. Victor's the reason the farm's still a going concern, he's looked after it for years. Núria's a different story. She doesn't live in the village and the family is very cool on the subject. I got the impression she's a bit of a black sheep.'

'Núria knows too much. What's that supposed to mean, I wonder. Any idea where I'd find her?'

'I did the usual checks. I found a Núria Sabadell who's the right age. She has a record.'

'For?'

'Possession, mostly. Also conspiracy to supply. Heroin.'

'Great, I've inherited a smackhead. Does she have an address?'

'I'm afraid I don't have her current address.'

Alex looked the lawyer in the eye, which wasn't a good idea, not if you wanted to think clearly.

'Forgive me for asking, but how is it my aunt didn't pick a lawyer a little closer to home?'

'You have to remember your aunt lived in almost complete isolation. People were civil to her in the village, with that rub-along-together rural hypocrisy you find so often, but as she says herself, she had no friends. But I get the impression she wanted it that way, that she turned her back on the village as much as the other way round. Anyway, it so happened that I once represented the man who delivered her butane bottles; there's no piped gas in the country, not a lot in the city either. She relied a lot on people from outside the village, the postman and so forth, for human contact; sad really. So when she told him she needed to draw up a will, the butane man recommended me.'

'I spoke to the coroner's office. They said she was drunk and fell downstairs. Was there an investigation?'

'The police were called, of course; the verdict was accidental death.'

'Do you happen to know the name of the investigating officer?'

Miguel raised an eyebrow but said nothing. He shuffled among his papers until he found what he was looking for.

'A Detective Foix led the investigation,' he said. 'Tarragona police.'

'It's a bit of mystery how my aunt knew I existed. How did you find me?'

'I didn't, my sister did. You can ask her yourself. I'm meeting her for a drink when we're finished here. She's keen to meet you, to put a face to the name, if you like.'

'Sure, why not. What about the inheritance, the farm? Is it

true what Cases said, that there are a lot of complications, being a foreigner?'

'It's tedious rather than complicated. Spain is a very bureaucratic country. Not because we love order, heaven forbid, but it keeps a lot of people in work. Actually, work is the wrong word. It keeps a lot of people employed. Most of them don't have enough to do, so when something comes up they like to spin it out, to justify their existence. You have to be patient, that's all, and try to see the funny side. Otherwise you'll go crazy.'

'So what do I need?'

'Primarily a certificate of non-residence. You get it at the municipal government office, down by the French station.'

'What if I want to be resident?'

'You have to register as non-resident first.'

'That doesn't make a lot of sense.'

Miguel laughed. It was low, throaty laugh.

'OK, one more question. Any idea what it's worth, the farm?'

'Hard to say. Not a huge amount, but not bad. It's not really my area but I could find out for you.'

'What about the land itself?'

'You mean as development land? Nothing. It's zoned as agricultural. After the way so much of the Costa Brava was ruined the rules have got much stricter about what you can do, especially on the coast. There are very few exemptions; politically it's a very sensitive issue.'

Miguel had to drop some papers off near the maritime museum on the way to meeting his sister so they walked down Paral.lel to where it meets the Columbus monument.

'They say if you set off the way he's pointing you'll end up in Libya,' Miguel said.

'What's he doing here? Didn't he sail from Seville?'

'Cádiz. But there was a fashion here to claim him as one of our own, as a Catalan. Complete crap, of course. It's like gay people insisting all their favourite movie stars are gay. Wishful thinking, that's all it is. Not that we're short of famous people

43

– Miró, Dalí, Albeniz, Pablo Casals, Gaudí, of course. Even the man who murdered Trotsky was a Catalan. We turn our hand to most things.'

'Is it true the rumba was invented in Barcelona?'

Miguel burst out laughing. He had one of those whole-hearted laughs that makes you want to laugh along with him.

'That's the funniest thing I've heard all week. Who told you that? The rumba? The only dance we invented is the *sardana* which is, how shall I put it, not quite as sensual as the rumba. The rumba's from Cuba as far as I know, Barcelona used to trade a lot with Cuba. Most of the *rumberos* here are Gypsies, Catalan Gypsies if you like.'

They walked up la Rambla against the flow of tourists, rolling down to the port on a polyester tide of bumbags and too-bright clothes. As they passed a news kiosk Miguel stopped and pointed at the headline on a sports daily. It read: 'Nadal's nightmare in Europe.'

'Football,' Miguel explained. 'El Barça has a player called Nadal. They had a bad night in the European Cup.'

Alex looked nonplussed.

'I wouldn't worry too much about all this,' Miguel said. 'These people leaning on you, I mean. It's probably just someone trying to hustle you into a quick sale. Nothing more sinister than that.'

7

At six p.m. precisely, Montserrat Cases, the lilac-suited lawyer from Terrassa, chose a corner table in the bar of the Hotel Meridien. She'd walked from Barceloneta and was uncomfortably hot. Her armpits were damp and, worried that it might show through her blouse, she kept her jacket on, which made her hotter still. Señor Williams who, like her, made a virtue of punctuality, arrived less than a minute later. A waiter approached the table with a five-star glide. What Montserrat wanted more than anything was an ice-cold beer but she was sure her client would disapprove so she ordered still mineral water. The American ordered the same.

'Kind of warm, isn't it?' he said, in English. She'd heard him speak Spanish to the hotel staff and he spoke it well enough, but to her he only ever spoke English. She prided herself on her near-perfect English but unless it was completely necessary she avoided saying his name – Williams was almost impossible to pronounce properly, the W followed by the double l. It was humiliating. She practised her Ws in the shower. 'Whispering Williams went wild with white women,' she repeated aloud, but still she stumbled on his name.

'Yes,' she said. 'It's not usually this hot so late in the year. They say it's El Niño.'

Something about Williams unsettled her. It wasn't sexual, the way with some men you know they're saying one thing and thinking another, because there was nothing sexual about him at all. You couldn't even say he was cold. What unnerved her was the way he was so functional. His function was to represent his client; hers was to represent Williams on the client's behalf. It was as though they weren't really people at all and life was just a set of contractual obligations.

The waiter brought the drinks and Williams looked at her with a face that said, 'OK, that's enough small talk.' Montserrat took the hint.

'Señor Nadal won't sell,' she said. 'He seems pretty adamant.'

'What happened?'

'He doesn't respond positively to pressure,' she said, apeing the sort of circuitous construction favoured by Williams. 'And I'm afraid your client's eagerness to buy aroused his suspicions.'

A barely visible tremor in his face told her she was talking out of turn.

'I'm not suggesting there was necessarily another appropriate course of action,' she added defensively.

She preferred not to work under these conditions. She didn't know who the real client was and all she knew about Williams was that, his name, and not even his first name. As a lawyer, she disliked mystery, but if a client was secretive, that was their prerogative; it didn't automatically make them a criminal. Besides, in her situation she couldn't be too choosy about what work she took on.

'He seems a little pig-headed to me,' she went on, sensing that he wanted more information. 'And he seemed to think it was all a joke. When I tried to impress upon him the inevitability of a sale it just made him, well, flippant, flirtatious even.'

She immediately regretted saying that; it sounded so unprofessional. She needn't have worried; flirtatious wasn't in Williams' vocabulary.

'Is the price the issue?'

'Not in my opinion, no. He appears to see it as a matter of honour or pride or principle.'

Williams' body language said that he now had all the information he needed and that their meeting was concluded. That was the sort of thing that bothered her, this no frills manner of his. She'd delivered her report and now she was dismissed. It was dehumanizing.

'Thank you for your efforts,' Señora Cases, he said, rising to his feet. 'Please send your bill to me here at the hotel.'

'If you would like me to try another approach. . .'

'Thank you, we'll be in touch if we need you. But it sounds like we may have to explore some other avenue.'

8

Salvador Oriol looked out from the terrace of his house on Tibidabo and reflected on the nature of destiny. He never doubted that this was his destiny, to be above the crowd, the man who cast the shadow, not the one in the shade. And when you've made it big, when you've hauled yourself up from nothing, it's easy to forget all the small fry you left in your wake, but they don't forget you. The past is enemy territory, a gun at your head loaded with all the nobodies who think they helped you get where you are. And when you're a somebody the fear never leaves you that someone or something might pitch you back where you began, something you hadn't dreamt of until it happens, and then when it does you see clearly it was the thing you most feared all along.

Salvador Oriol was a somebody. He swam in the same water as the President of Catalunya and the mayor of Barcelona and the boss of el Barça, the city's great, this-is-so-much-more-than-a-football-club, football club. They were all self-made men, all big fish who fed on little fish on their journey upstream. In a few weeks Oriol would deliver a speech at a banquet where Catalunya's self-made men, and some old money too, would gather to celebrate his eightieth birthday. In the speech he extolled the virtues of the Catalan nation, its culture and creativity and above all its iron resolve, tempered down the centuries, not to bow down to oppression. And he contrived to suggest that he, in his humble way, had striven to emulate, even embody, these qualities. He'd given many such speeches, each with its built-in ovations. In this one he concluded that the curse of Spain was fatalism. But we Catalans, he would declare, we Catalans don't believe in fate, we believe in destiny. But Oriol didn't believe in destiny either, he believed in power, because power gave you some say in your destiny. That was the whole point of power – to leave as little in God's hands as possible.

He sat at the blue-tiled table, all Barcelona at his feet, and looked over the city, grey under a brown day. The late September air was thick and still, even here up on the hill. His nephew Narcís joined him on the terrace.

'Angel Domènech is downstairs. He says you're expecting him.'

Oriol gestured that Narcís should show him up. Narcís turned to go, then paused.

'So what about the American?' he said.

The old man looked up at his nephew. Narcís was loyal and hardworking, though not too bright, and not much troubled by subtleties. Oriol remembered him as a child, a spiteful boy always catching people out with malicious tricks. The boy imagined this showed how clever he was when all it proved was that people continued to underestimate his capacity for unpleasantness. He hadn't changed much.

'Do you want me to deal with him?' Narcís said. He liked action, he liked to cut to the chase. His uncle was too cautious, he thought, he'd lost his edge.

Oriol shook his head.

'Just keep an eye on him for now. And I'd like you to pay a visit to our friend Busquets from the land registry, just to be sure he stays onside. You can't trust that type, you know, the ones who want to do everything by the book. They scare easily, so we'd better scare him before someone else does. And there's someone I want you to check out, a journalist. Her name's Carmen Montero, from *El Mensajero*. She's on the arts side of the paper, probably harmless, but I'm giving her an interview so best find out what she's made of. There's a news editor there, Enric Luna, who used to work with her. See what he's got to say. Now you'd better show Domènech up.'

The old man motioned Angel to a chair but Angel stood at the balcony rail instead. Narcís took up a position a few feet to Oriol's left. Angel got straight to the point.

'How long have you known about this American?'

'Not long. I assumed you knew, too, you usually do, where it affects your business. You must be slipping.'

Oriol sipped a glass of *orxata*, an opalescent drink made from tiger nuts. He affected what men of his generation still thought of as the English style: tweed three-piece double-vented suits, herringbone hunting jackets, safari suits, brass button blazers. He had all his shirts and ties imported specially from a shop in Jermyn Street in London that had a warrant to make shirts for the English royal family. Angel stood at the rail and looked out over the city. He tried to find his house in Gràcia, tracing his path from the sea, up along the green gash of la Rambla, to the Plaça Catalunya, but the haze and pollution were too thick to see any detail. Oriol eyed the *orxata* with curiosity, like he'd never seen such a thing before, took a cautious sip and then a longer one. A linen napkin lay on the table. He wiped his mouth on the back of his hand, then dried his hand on the napkin. For all his grand affectations, his peasant origins clung to him like burrs to his Saville Row trouser cuffs.

'Clearly there is a problem, a new problem,' Oriol said. 'But no problem is insurmountable. And certainly not for a man of your abilities, Señor Domènech. I'm sure you'll find a way.'

Pompous old fool, Angel thought. Everything about the old man was phoney. Man and myth, you couldn't tell them apart. His gestures, the way he spoke, it was as if he was always on camera. And the hair, the trademark silver hair, swept back and a little long for a man of his age, and always that little bit dishevelled, as though he'd just conducted the Berlin Philharmonic through a hectic allegretto. It was as if he'd created himself to be viewed from a distance, on TV or on a podium addressing a crowd. There the grand-old-man pose didn't seem so ridiculous. But close up it was absurd, a burlesque, like wearing full stage make-up in the street.

'Why don't you just buy him out?' Angel said. His father had a saying: Money before muscle, money makes less noise.

'That option has been looked into.'

'And?'

Oriol took another sip of his drink but said nothing.

'So what do you suggest?'

'I propose that you do what you're famous for – remove the obstacle. Make him disappear.'

'I take it you don't mean literally. I'm not a gangster.'

'Of course not, nothing so vulgar.'

Angel caught Narcís' eye and half smiled. Narcís was generally regarded as a bit of a joke, a dandy with a flair for violence. Angel knew the type well: vain, impatient, not smart enough to know their limitations. Everyone knew it was Oriol's sons who ran the business, a pair of dour accountants with a knack for making money appear when required and disappear when not. They were as sharp as they were dull. Narcís, blinded by resentment, thought he could run things better.

'He could have an accident,' Narcís said, riled by Angel's air of contempt.

'Well, Lord above,' Angel snorted. 'Listen to Al Pacino here.'

Narcís looked to his uncle for support. Oriol ran his finger round the rim of the glass.

'We don't want anything messy,' he said. 'Nothing that attracts attention. In an ideal world he would just vanish, like smoke.'

'I take it this is what Williams wants,' Angel said.

Oriol looked startled.

'What do you know about Williams?'

'Slightly more than I did ten seconds ago,' Angel said, turning away. At the edge of the city, the ferry was pulling out from Drassanes, bound for Palma de Mallorca. Angel could just make out the black diesel smudge from the funnel against the blue-brown haze. Before all the car pollution blotted everything out they said on a clear day you could see Mallorca from Tibidabo. That's how the mountain got its name, because of the view. When Jesus was fasting in the desert Satan took him up a high hill and said: *Haec omnia tibi dabo si cadens adoraveris me* – All this will I give you if you will fall down and worship me. Tibidabo – I give to you. Christ declined Satan's generous offer but Salvador Oriol said, 'Thanks very much, I'll take everything you've got,' and had this castellated monstrosity of a mansion built as high up the seaward slope of Tibidabo as zoning regulations and bribery would permit. Angel hadn't been to Mallorca for years. Maybe he could talk Carmen into coming with him for a few days. Go some place on the west coast, away from the tourists. Get some good clean air, eat *tumbet*, swim in the sea, fuck outdoors. He pictured Carmen, naked in the hot shade of an olive grove, dark skin shiny with sweat. The daydream woke his slumbering cock; it stirred. He turned and looked at the old man: papery skin, cold-water eyes, *orxata* moustache. His cock went back to sleep.

'I've done my bit,' he said. 'You wanted Oscar Puig on board and I did as you asked. The rest isn't my affair.'

'Don't be ingenuous, it really doesn't suit you. Yes, you got Puig, and you were well paid for it. But I have a lot riding on this and a number of other people have come aboard, some of them – and I know this for a fact – on your advice. They believe they have boarded a ship that's taking them somewhere they'd like to go, not one that's going to be sunk by an American before it even sets sail. People took you at your word. What if it got around that Angel Domènech doesn't deliver, that Domènech's deals are full of holes, that his word isn't what it was? You could find it very hard to do business.'

'I'll survive.'

'This is what I've been hearing about you, but I didn't believe it till now,' Oriol said coldly.

'What? Didn't believe what?'

'That you've lost it, got no stomach for it any more. No balls either. I can't believe what I'm hearing. I'm not going to let some American ruin everything, someone who probably couldn't find Barcelona on a map until last week. You used to be a proud man, formidable. Is this what you've come to? We have a deadline and we're going to stick to it: the Infanta's wedding – I, of course, am invited,' he added, never able to resist an opportunity to show off. 'That gives us less than two weeks.'

'Like I said, with all due respect, this isn't my problem.'

The old man started shaking with anger. He stood up and lunged at Angel, as if he was going to hit him, but he merely grabbed the wrought-iron rail and put his face close to Angel's. Saliva gathered in yellowish bubbles at the corners of his mouth. Angel could smell the *orxata* on his breath. He wondered why Oriol was so obsessed with pushing this through. As long as there was no public announcement he wasn't committed, he could cut his losses and wait for another opportunity. There had to be something else that made the old man so fixated on this particular deal. Maybe it was the American, Williams, maybe he had him in a spot.

'A deal's a deal. You're in and you're staying in.'

Angel could feel the old man sucking him in, telling him, 'If I go down, you're coming with me.' Angel needed leverage. Everyone has secrets, and Salvador Oriol had plenty. But Angel didn't know what they were. That is, he heard things but he didn't have anything he could use. Oriol's fondness for publicity didn't extend to his business affairs, which he kept at arm's length and out of the public eye. It was impossible to say exactly what he did or how he made his money: the business all happened at one remove, his signature was never on anything, nor were his fingerprints. Angel held Oriol's gaze until the old man calmed down and shuffled back to his chair at the blue-tiled table. He stroked his chin and looked at Angel.

'I hear you're planning to open a restaurant.'

There's the jab, Angel thought. Now here comes the uppercut.

'That's right, in Ample. Right by la Mercè.'

'Lot of problems with planning applications down there right now. Who covers that area? Noguès, isn't it?'

'Yeah, but he's OK. Noguès owes me.'

Oriol squinted a little into the light, a little more than he needed to. Everything he did he did for effect.

'Noguès owes me too,' he said.

Another jab; Angel waited for the big punch.

'I see your boy's in trouble again,' Oriol said quietly.

He was good, Angel had to give him that. It was a good shot. Angel's sixteen-year-old son Josep seemed bent on wrecking his life, apparently in order to punish Angel for his unnamed but evidently numerous failings as a father. Right now he was having to pull a lot of strings to keep Josep out of jail.

'From what I hear he's more or less exhausted the court's patience,' Oriol said. 'They've been pretty lenient with him so far, but this time he could get a longish stretch, and not in some bad boys holiday camp either. Probably be La Model this time. Tough jail, that one. Tougher than your Josep I expect. The judges are really cracking down on youth crime. Lot of public pressure. I doubt you'd be able to keep him out.'

Oriol was telling him: 'You have good connections but I have better ones.' It was true. Angel's big fish would be scared off by Oriol's bigger ones and he'd be unable to keep his son out of jail. The boy acted tough, he talked tough, but it was all show, all from the movies. In La Model he'd meet the genuine article; they'd tear him to pieces. Angel dropped his cigarette on the balcony, although there was an ashtray on the table. It was a feeble gesture, when someone's got you by the balls, to drop litter on their balcony. The old man noted it but what did he care, he didn't do the housework. Angel was trying to contain his anger. He'd delivered some low blows himself in his time but there were some things he wouldn't stoop to and threatening people's children was one of them. Besides, it was none of Oriol's business what went on between Josep and him. His own father had taught him never to show anger. Show it in your actions, not your face, he used to say. Angel flicked the cigarette butt off the balcony with his toe and covered his anger with a look of resignation.

'OK,' he said to Oriol. 'I'll see to it.'

9

Miguel and Alex waited for Carmen at an outside table in the Plaça del Pi. To Alex, the new kid in town, the square epitomized Barcelona: cafe chic, a fourteenth-century church, bad drains and beautiful women. He was prepared for the city's fabulous architecture, but no one told him about the women. Good-looking women crossed the square – funky, slinky, elegant women, and every now and then a woman of such palm-sweating, tongue-dragging gorgeousness it made his eyes swim. Miguel was watching him.

'The men aren't bad either,' he said.

The centre of Plaça del Pi was raised, like a stepped dais. A girl in her late teens, her pale moon-face half-hidden behind a curtain of stringy hair with bits of coloured thread woven into it, sat on the steps with her dreamy eyes fastened on a boy around her age who strummed the same two minor chords over and over on a cheap steel-string. He moaned wordlessly above the chords. He was pale, too, and with his long mousy hair, wispy goatee and pained blue eyes he reminded Alex of the gaudy print of the Redeemer under whose sorrowful gaze he grew up. The girl was mesmerized, as though she'd stumbled into the Angel Gabriel's rehearsal room. Alex laughed at the tired old pose.

'Pathetic, isn't it?' Miguel said. 'A latter-day Jesus and a mousy Mary Magdalen. It's seems that any dreamy middle-class boy who gets himself up as an understudy for the *pietà* will find some fey girl only too anxious to clutch him to her bony breast. The music you hear in the street gets worse and worse. This square especially, it seems to be a magnet for the kind of musicians who only practise in front of the mirror. The patron saint of Plaça del Pi must be Our Lady of the Most Meagre Talents.'

Above the strumming boy Jesus, the square was noisy with talk. Everywhere in the city was; more so even than New York, Alex thought. When he passed a bar at lunchtime the noise roared out the door, everyone talking above the level of the TV, above the clatter of plates, the ding-ding of pinball and the hiss and splutter of the coffee machine, above the noise of everyone talking.

'People talk a lot here, don't they?' he said.

'Talk is the national pastime,' Miguel said. 'It's why we don't read, we read fewer books a year than anyone else in Europe; it would eat into our talking time. Of course no one listens – they're too busy talking.'

'In America we pay people to listen. It's called therapy.'

'That's catching on here too, but I've noticed a lot of the therapists are foreigners. They have to be, it's almost impossible to find anyone in this country who will listen in silence, whatever you pay them.'

'Do you think people in Sant Martí will talk to me, about what happened, I mean? Or this Captain Morín, if I can find him, the man my father says saved and destroyed his life?'

Miguel studied him, with the look of someone who isn't going to say anything until they're absolutely sure of their words.

'This Morín must be eighty years old at least, that's if he's still alive. And he could be anywhere. Just because he fought in Catalunya doesn't make him a native, he could be from wherever.'

'Don't try to put me off. I've made up my mind.'

'I see, so it's a mission. Well, let's say you do find him, what are you going to say? Excuse me, señor, would you be so kind as to tell me what role you played in the Civil War? Did you perhaps witness or take part in any particularly memorable atrocities?'

'You think I'm naive.'

'I scarcely know you at all. What I do know is the Civil War isn't a popular topic of conversation.'

'But it was sixty years ago.'

'Sixty years may be a long time in America but here it's nothing – look at Sarajevo. The thing about a civil war is it's personal. It's not like fighting Napoleon or Hitler. There are no heroes and villains; it's a neighbourly thing. You're at war with people you know, maybe you've known them all your life, maybe they're your cousin, your brother even. And you do the same terrible things as are done in any war, despicable, unforgivable things. Except at the end of it, when the dust dies down, the army doesn't retreat, because it's not a foreign force, it's from right here. The war ends and everyone has to go on living together, victors and vanquished, knowing what's been done and knowing that the other knows. So people don't talk about it. They keep silent, they have to. They're afraid. When people start talking, you get Sarajevo.'

'But if there wasn't the silence, if people had talked about it more, sooner, maybe that wouldn't be the case,' Alex said, wondering whether the lawyer really was trying to protect him or if he had some other agenda.

'Spoken like a true American.'

'Meaning?'

'To an American there's an answer to every question, it's just a matter of finding it; to us there's only the question. The real difference between us is that you Americans truly believe you're free but we Europeans know for certain we're not. Of course we talk about things, but we don't believe in talk's cleansing power the way you seem to. This idea that you can talk everything through. What makes you so sure there is a through? Where does it say everything shall be resolved?

58

People live with what they can bear. Truth isn't always an option.'

'You begin to sound like my mother.'

'A wise woman, no doubt. Look, here's Carmen.'

The moment he saw Carmen in her short black skirt and honey-brown skin, coming towards them with her loose, easy stride, Alex's chest tightened and he felt a rush of nervous excitement he hadn't felt in a long time. As she neared their table she broke into a big smile. Miguel stood up and the two of them exchanged kisses.

'My sister Carmen,' he said. 'Carmen, this is Alex Nadal.'

Alex got to his feet. He held out his hand to Carmen. She took it then leaned across the table and kissed him on each cheek. He caught her scent, no perfume, just her woman smell, a good smell, like her pheromones were getting regular work. Her eyes were even darker than her brother's, but while Miguel's gave him vertigo, hers gave him butterflies. They twinkled, if something so black can twinkle, but they were guarded too. If Miguel's were a dark vortex that warned, Abandon all hope, you who enter, Carmen's were a mirrored door with a sign that read, Authorized Personnel Only. She had kissy-kissy lips and crooked teeth. Alex liked that, it was a nice touch. Crooked teeth were illegal in America.

'I hope you're having a better week than Miguel Angel,' she said.

'I'm sorry?'

'Miguel Angel Nadal,' her brother explained. 'You remember the headline I showed you? He plays for el Barça, God's own football team.'

A little smile fluttered across his face and for a moment he looked exactly like his sister, the same light smile, rippling across his lips from right to left, a fleeting parabola of amusement, then gone.

'It's like a religion here,' Carmen said. 'It's quite something, even if you aren't a football fan. A hundred thousand people all going berserk. It's great theatre. I go when I can. You should come some time.'

She surprised herself, inviting him out when she'd barely said hello.

'I'd like that,' he said without thinking. Their eyes met. Alex held her gaze. What might have been a knowing smile twitched at the corner of Miguel's lips, then Alex looked up to find the moon-faced girl with the stringy hair standing at his shoulder with a velvet cap in her hand. He blanked her with a not-me face honed over the years on the New York underclass. Miguel looked up and shook his head. The girl's well-practised Deirdre of the Sorrows pose was no match for Miguel's authentic air of melancholy. Deirdre looked hurt, though that too was probably a pose. She was turning to the next table when Carmen picked up the small change from the saucer and tossed it into the cap. Alex raised his eyebrows and Carmen shrugged.

'Why not?' she said. 'It's only a few pesetas.'

'Bad music shouldn't be encouraged,' Alex said. 'Any minute now her friend will start playing the theme from *The Deerhunter*.'

'Of course, you're a musician,' Carmen said.

'A piano player.'

Carmen sized him up. People – men – said she was aloof. They complained that she was remote, but she was just wary. For two years she went out with Antoní, a reporter with TV3 news. They were happy, they were in love, there was talk of getting a place together. Then she discovered she was pregnant. She was confused. On the one hand she was angry, she hadn't been careless and here she was pregnant and it didn't seem fair. Worse still, it looked incompetent, and there were few things she resisted more than incompetence. On the other hand, she was pregnant by the man she loved, and that knocked the lid off a box she'd barely even peeped into before. The lid was soon back on. The day after the tell-tale blue line lit up on the home pregnancy testing stick she found out, by chance and via a third party, that Antoní was seeing another woman. And had been for some time.

The iron entered her soul. What might otherwise have been a lifetime's drip-drip of hurt and disillusion, Carmen got all in one dose. She didn't tell anyone anything. She made the necessary arrangements, told the necessary lies, and flew to London. The woman next to her on the plane was six months pregnant; they'd been trying for years, she said. Carmen took the Tube straight from Heathrow to Brixton. The streets were jammed with mothers and babies. Brown babies and pink babies. Babies in prams, in pushchairs, in slings. Carmen saw them and didn't see them. She marched herself and her over-night bag – one change of clothes and the heavy duty sanitary towels the clinic told her to bring – up Brixton Hill. The waiting room was full of young and not so young Spanish and Irish women like herself, spending their savings, women who had also told the necessary lies. Carmen didn't allow herself any feelings of solidarity. Not that she didn't care, but she'd agreed with herself to feel as little as possible, to treat it the way she did a visit to the dentist: this was happening, but not to her. When it was over she stayed one night in an expensive cheap hotel in Pimlico and was back in Barcelona by lunch-time. Problem solved. That evening she went to Susana's. She told her everything and sobbed so uncontrollably she threw up. She didn't tell Antoní. When he called her she said, 'I don't want to see you any more.' When he said, 'Why?' she said quietly, 'You know why,' and put the phone down.

So, two years later, Carmen wasn't looking for love. But she still liked sex. The bed was, paradoxically, the one place where she felt it safe to relinquish power and give up the unending and tedious struggle with men. Men were a disappointment and they were disappointing with a depressing predictability. It was as though whatever the description on the video box, when you took it home and pressed 'Play' the movie was always the same. But there was something different about Alex. She looked at him and Alex felt her appraising gaze. He noticed that people here looked at you very directly and made no secret of the fact that they were checking you out. Maybe his habit of staring wouldn't get him into so much trouble here.

'So what are your plans?' she said.

'Plans? I'm sort of making it up as I go along. Up until a few weeks ago everything was just taking its course the way it does, one thing following another, you know. And then I don't know what happened, it's like I went out one day and left my life ajar and, well, here I am. Your brother thinks I'm going to get myself into trouble because I ask too many questions.' Her presence excited him. He wanted to move his chair closer to hers and breathe her in. He wanted to touch the dark down on her cheek.

'Actually he thinks you're already in trouble,' Miguel said. 'Someone appears to be following you, someone has sent their lawyer to snap at your ankles. This is not my idea of the perfect holiday.'

Carmen leaned towards Alex, her curiosity aroused.

'He thinks it's some unfinished business from the Civil War,' Miguel said. 'And that there's someone out there just dying to get the story off their chest. I have to go now, I'll leave Alex to explain everything to you.'

Miguel and Carmen exchanged a look that Alex couldn't read because it was in sibling code.

'If you're free tomorrow I could take you out to the farm,' he said to Alex. 'You can meet Victor Sabadell, the guy who looks after it, and decide what you want to do about the place. Late afternoon all right for you?'

'Sure, that would be fine. By the way, what does it mean, the name of the village, Sant Martí dels Moixones, Saint Martin of what?'

'Moixones,' Carmen corrected him, pronouncing it Moshoness. 'It means little birds, St Martin of the Little Birds.'

For a moment after Miguel left they were like two people on a first date who realize they have no idea what to say to each other. There was a clumsy, almost adolescent silence.

'You seem pretty blasé about all this,' Carmen said. 'This trouble you may or may not be in.' She lit a cigarette and, sensing his eyes follow her hands, offered him the pack.

'No thanks. And no, I'm not at all blasé. I'm a musician, not some kind of action hero.'

62

'So what are you going to do about it?'

'Find out who's behind it.'

'And?'

'And tell them to leave me alone. Easy, really.'

'It might take a little more than irony. What's all this got to do with the Civil War?'

Alex told her about his father's suicide and his supposed betrayal during the war.

'Not really our favourite subject, the Civil war. Nor the rest of our history, for that matter. We still lie about things that happened a thousand years ago. We're still trying to come to terms with being conquered by the Arabs in the eighth century, never mind what happened in the thirties.'

'Your brother's already given me a lecture, thanks.'

'I expect Miguel is afraid you'll put your foot in it.'

'There doesn't seem to be anywhere else to put my feet.'

She gave him a warm smile, first with her eyes, then with her crooked teeth. She seemed to be offering him reassurance. She clasped her hands behind her head and her T-shirt rode up, exposing her navel. Her stomach was brown and she had a slight pot. Alex liked that; like her uneven teeth, it was refreshingly real after all those overwrought New York gym bodies.

'I don't know why but I feel like my aunt has cast me as some kind of avenging angel.'

'Has she?' Carmen looked past him across the square.

'Something like that. Seen someone you know?' he said, turning to see who she was looking at.

'No, don't look round. There's a guy two tables away who keeps staring at us. When I catch his eye he looks away.'

Alex waited a moment then turned around slowly. He expected to see the big fishy-eyed man but the man Carmen was looking at was much smaller and younger. He had a pinched face and a day's growth of black stubble and despite the heat he was wearing a black leather jacket.

'He's got junkie eyes,' Alex said. 'Maybe he's sizing us up, figuring out if your handbag's worth snatching.'

Carmen looked at her watch. Her gestures had a certain compact grace. She was – Alex searched for a word – fascinating. That was it, he was fascinated by her. On the edge of the table his left hand shaped the opening chords of 'Embraceable You'.

'I have to go a meeting at the Generalitat,' Carmen said, 'in Plaça St Jaume.'

'It's on my way to the hotel, I'll walk with you.'

I'm not going to ask her if she minds, he thought. If she does, she does. If she doesn't, fine. She led him along Santa Eulalia and he asked her about her job and about the music scene in Barcelona. There was something between them – chemistry, electricity, some sort of energy he was sure wasn't coming just from him. It was there, palpable, like a force field between them, as though their bodies were a couple of dogs they'd taken out for a walk, straining to get at each other. He told himself it was only his imagination. As they passed a shop selling ornate lace fans she took his arm and turned him towards the shop window. His pulse quickened at her touch.

'I think the guy from the plaça is following us,' she said, pointing to a fan in the window.

Alex looked slantways down the street. Fifty feet behind them there he was, taking a great interest in the window of a shoe shop. Carmen kept her hand on his arm and led him up the hill until they arrived at the flank wall of the Gothic cathedral in the Carrer del Bisbe. She looked over her shoulder.

'Come on,' she said, hurrying him down the steps into the cool shade of the cloister. It was a serenely eccentric place, a cross between a sub-tropical farmyard and a crypt. The centre was lush and green with giant palms and ferns and lilies while the perimeter was lined with saints and virgins lit by memorial candles, flickering inside red plastic cylinders. Among it all roamed a squawking flock of geese.

'What a wonderful place,' Alex said, sitting down on a stone bench and checking the door for a black leather jacket. 'Just absolutely wonderful. Like a Gothic jungle. But why the geese?'

Carmen sat beside him, just touching. Cool stone, warm skin, Alex thought, hearing it as the opening line of a song. He tried writing songs but it was harder than he thought.

'The geese have been here for centuries. I think the Romans used to keep geese in their temples for some reason. Maybe it dates back to then. I seem to recall there was a temple on this site and then they built the church on top of it.'

'It's mad, but sort of sublime as well. Eccentric. Earthy. And no one here seems to think anything of it, they think it's normal. I like that.'

'You're right, I'd never really thought about it before. So you like Barcelona?'

Alex nodded. No one in a leather jacket entered the cloister. Tourists read aloud from guide books and took pictures of each other in front of the saints.

'So, in an ideal situation, what would you do? I mean if no one was hassling you about the farm.'

Alex tilted his head back and looked up into the green lusciousness of the palms.

'An ideal situation? Now there's a thing. Ideally, I would find this Captain Morín I told you about and he would give me a signed confession exonerating my father from whatever terrible thing he's supposed to have done and your paper would devote a double-page spread to the story, one page rehabilitating the Nadal family name and the other nailing the true miscreants.'

'I could try to find out about Morín for you, but I wouldn't hold out much hope.'

'Of course, you're the great detective. How did you find me?'

'The musicians' union. There was only one Nadal registered in New York, along with several Naidoos and numerous Nadels. Then I had to get your current address; the one your aunt had was out of date, on Avenue B. Why Avenue B? Couldn't they think of a name?'

'I still don't understand how she even knew I existed.'

The geese squawked and the tourists swished and shuffled

past like mourners at a gaudy funeral. The junkie had either lost them or wasn't following them in the first place.

'So you clear your father's name and then you sell the farm and go back to New York, is that the plan?'

'I don't know. I'm not in a rush, and like I said, I like it here. And then there's the farm. I guess I could try farming.'

They looked at each other for about five seconds then both burst out laughing. She gave his shoulder a friendly squeeze.

'I don't think so,' she said.

He put his hand on hers.

'I like you,' he said.

She smiled – defensively, he thought – and then gave a little snort of a laugh and moved her hand away.

'You don't know me.'

'No, but I think I'd like to.'

'How can you know that?'

'You look for clues to see if a thing is worth pursuing. Besides, I need a friend, Carmen.'

He liked the taste of her name on his lips.

'I've got to get to this meeting,' she said, giving his hand a light squeeze as she got to her feet. In the street a guitarist sat on a low stool playing traditional flamenco. Alex tossed a couple of coins into the open guitar case. The guitarist nodded her thanks. A Japanese tour guide held a stick with a blue sign above her head and barked her flock of pensioners into line. Alex and Carmen walked the few yards to Plaça St Jaume in silence. They stood at the corner of the Generalitat. A group of elderly people were dancing the *sardana* to a wind band in a corner of the square. The instruments all sounded out of tune. Carmen fished in her handbag.

'How do I know there isn't a Señora Nadal and three little Nadalins back in New York?' she said, as though she was thinking aloud and not actually asking him.

Alex tried to shut out the music. Not only were the instruments out of tune but the drummer couldn't keep time. It was like Bedouins trying their hand at free jazz. He looked as far as he could into her black mirror eyes.

'There's no one,' he said.

He couldn't tell from her face if she believed him. She handed him a business card. 'OK, you need a friend, let's see if we can do that. That's my work number and my mobile.'

'Could we meet tomorrow?'

'Tomorrow you're going to your farm and I'm going to a funeral.'

Alex said he was sorry, about the funeral. She said it was all right, he wasn't to know. They kissed in the conventional way, right cheek then left. She kissed him a little lower on the cheek, a little closer to the corners of his mouth, than she kissed him that first time in Plaça del Pi. Or that's what he told himself.

He went back to the hotel. The air in his room was stale so he opened the shutters and leaned out into the street. The junkie in black was leaning against the shopfront of El Rey de la Magia, flipping a Zippo lighter open and shut. He looked up then looked away, trying to act natural, but he wasn't much of an actor. Alex was too weary to rush back down to the street to confront him. He lay down on the bed and turned on the TV. He watched half an hour of *Rambo: First Blood*, dubbed into Catalan. As a Catalan primer it wasn't much help, it was mostly grunts and gunfire and he would have got the gist of it in Algonquin. He dozed off and dreamt he was sitting on a bench in Central Park, beside the boating pond. A man with mournful eyes came up to him and said in a language he'd never heard before, 'Got any change?' 'Who are you?' Alex asked. The man smiled a smile of pure melancholy. 'I'm Martin of the little birdies,' he said. 'God's own football team.'

10

Early the following morning Alex sat at the tiny bar in the Meson del Cafe over a brain-tingling *cortado* and a cheese roll. He added a single entry – *tancat*/closed – to his Catalan lexicon and turned to the list of tasks at the front. He'd phoned Montero and the coroner and found a bookshop so he crossed them out. Alex knew that the art of list-making was to include things that were easy to achieve. So if a list included difficult challenges – Quit smoking; Be more assertive – it was important to leaven it with more readily achievable tasks such as Wash kitchen floor or Pay parking fine. Alex's new list began: Find Morín; Find Núria, Phone Detective Foix, and continued, Check land title; Get certificate of non-residency. Whoever he was up against, he needed to show them he meant business. To do that he had to stake his claim to the farm. Miguel told him he needed a certificate of non-residence from the municipal government. He also had to find out if there was any truth in what Montserrat Cases said, that there was a question mark over his title to Can Castanyer. These were things, he imagined, that could easily be achieved. He looked up Morín in the phone book; there were seventy-two entries. As a last resort he'd phone each one and ask if they'd ever been to Sant Martí dels Moixoness, but he'd wait to see if Carmen turned up anything first.

The civil government offices were beside the Estació França, one of a series of grand buildings around the palm-fringed Plaça del Palau. It put Alex in mind of Havana, although he only knew Havana from the movies. There were two queues at the entrance, one marked *Comunitarios*, for European Union citizens, and one marked *Non-Comunitarios*, for the rest of the world. About twenty *comunitarios* stood in line; the *non-comunitarios* – mainly Africans, Filipinos and Latin Americans – stretched round the block. Both queues converged at a door marked Information. Alex bypassed the queue and went up the steps into the main entrance. A uniformed attendant stopped him and told him to get back in line.

'But it's for information. I have the information, I called earlier. They told me what I needed over the phone.'

'Makes no difference,' the attendant said. 'Everyone has to go via Information.'

Alex joined the *non-comunitario* queue. After an hour he'd moved about thirty feet. He made friends with the couple in front who were amassing a series of papers from different departments so that she could apply for residency. They talked like veterans of a long campaign. He asked them to keep his place and he went and bought a newspaper. An hour and a quarter later the couple in front were at the information desk. They were arguing with the official. They didn't have the right papers. Alex felt sorry for them, and a little shamefaced because he knew that without the papers they'd have to leave sooner and then it would be his turn. There's nothing like a long queue to sour the milk of human kindness. The couple were reluctant to go, but the woman at the desk was politely unyielding and eventually they gathered up their papers and left. Alex gave them a look of solidarity and then the woman summoned him with a small nod. She had a face like Olive Oyl in the Popeye cartoon, with enormous cow-like brown eyes and a tiny mouth as small as a baby's. She studied the photocopy of his passport.

'Photos?' she said.

'Excuse me?'

'Photos, you must produce four of them, like passport photos. All identical.'

'No one said anything about photos on the phone,' he protested. She shrugged and handed him back the photocopy plus a form to fill in.

'There's a place that does them across the street,' she said.

'I bet there is,' Alex said. 'Does this mean I have to stand in line all over again? I'll be here all day.'

'We close in fifteen minutes,' she said by way of solace.

'That's great. Until when?'

'Until tomorrow.'

It was nearly one o'clock and too late to get the photos and finish the business of the certificate of non-residence. The land registry, however, was open until two. A black and yellow cab pulled away from the lights and Alex stepped into the road and flagged it down. It gave him a feeling of power, to stick out his hand and be whisked away from the line of weary petitioners outside the civil government offices. Taxis were his sister Pepa's only known vice. She used to say, If you're having a bad day, flag a cab. And it was true, it always produced a momentary sense of well-being. Crystal Gayle was singing 'Cry Me A River' on the car radio. A small statue of a black Virgin was glued to the dashboard. Alex thought of Montserrat Cases.

The land registry was just off Plaça d'Urquinaona. Alex liked the name, Urquinaona, it sounded like a Native American tribe. Every expense had been spared in kitting out the land registry office. The walls were bare, there was a ripped black plastic padded bench patched with gaffer tape, two strip lights on the ceiling, one of them flickering towards the end of its life, and at one end a high brown laminate counter that stretched the width of the room. Behind it sat a young man with cropped hair and a pencil moustache which matched his pencil thin sideburns. They were so thin they might have been drawn on with a stick of charcoal. He was writing in an old-fashioned bound journal with unlined pages which he covered with lines of unequal length. He appeared to be writing verse. He wrote with a large black fountain pen from which issued the most beautiful handwriting Alex had ever seen. He looked up at Alex as at an unexpected disturbance then, with the smallest of nods, indicated the ticket machine at the end of the counter.

He returned to his page and Alex sat down on the bench. His ticket was number 84 and the machine on the wall read 76. But there was no one else waiting. He daydreamed briefly about the poet with the pencil moustache. He dubbed him Virgil. He imagined he sat there every day, doing what he pleased, writing verse on a state salary. He pictured him coming in each morning and ripping the first eight tickets out of the machine and stuffing them in his pocket. After a few minutes of this Alex went back up to the counter and drummed on it with his fingertips until the poet looked up. His eyes swooped in a practised arc from the ticket in his hand to the machine on the wall to Alex's eyes before alighting back on the page of verse. The gesture said, 'It's not your turn.'

'Look Virgil,' Alex said, 'if you can show me who's holding tickets 76 to 83 I'll sit down and wait and leave you to write in peace. Otherwise, I'd appreciate some service.'

'Virgil?' the clerk said, as though considering a proposition. He looked at Alex, waiting to hear what else he had to say.

'I want to know who is the registered owner of a piece of land, and I had this whacky idea that maybe if I asked someone at the land registry office I might get an answer.'

Virgil screwed the top on the fountain pen, blotted the page and closed the journal. He took his time. Then, armed with a pencil and a notepad he asked Alex, in Catalan, where the land was.

Alex understood and told him where it was and who he was. Virgil said he'd be back in a moment and disappeared through the only door. He was back within seconds but only to move his journal so that Alex couldn't lean over the counter and read it. After a few minutes he returned and said something at length in Catalan. This time Alex didn't understand and knew he wasn't supposed to either.

'In Castilian, please,' he said, recalling some graffiti he saw scrawled on a Catalan advertising hoarding, to which someone else had added, in Catalan, the slogan: 'Bilingualism is genocide'.

Virgil let out a sigh of irritation.

'I'm afraid we have no record of this farm,' he said in Castilian. 'That is, I can't find a file.'

'Can't or won't?'

'We have no record here of a farm called Can Castanyer, or at least not in or near Sant Martí dels Moixones. Of course the main file may be in Tarragona, but even so we would have a copy of the deeds.'

'I'd like to speak to someone in charge,' Alex said, determined not to lose his temper. 'The manager, the director. Who would that be?'

Virgil looked sullen and fidgety, as though he'd already gone to a lot of trouble and anyway this wasn't information he was supposed to give out. He wet a fingertip on the tip of his tongue and drew it across his moustache, first to the right, then the left.

'Señor Busquets is in charge of the relevant sector,' he said.

'There, that didn't hurt too much did it? Would you get him for me please?'

The poet disappeared through the door again. His voice carried and now and again Alex could hear it above the low murmur of whoever he was talking to. Fifteen minutes passed. In another five the office would close. He was getting tight with anger. He remembered what a drummer once said after they'd been short-changed by a club owner: 'Don't get mad, get leverage.' Alex needed some leverage. Very quietly he climbed over the counter, picked up the journal and vaulted back to the other side. He opened the book. It was filled with verse; evidently work in progress, the pages dense with crossings out and marginalia, all in the same elegant, sweeping hand. The front of the book was inscribed with Virgil's real name: Ferran Llull. Alex tried to get his tongue round those double ls. A moment later Llull came back. Alex held the notebook down at his side, out of sight.

'I'm very sorry,' he said, trying to sound like he meant it, as though he'd been told to be nice. 'Señor Busquets is in a meeting.'

'It took him fifteen minutes to tell you that?'

'Señor Busquets is a very busy man. If you call later he might be able to arrange an appointment for next week.'

'I'm sure he's very busy. I can see this is a very busy office. What's Señor Busquets so busy with? No, let me guess, he works here but really he's a composer. He's writing a symphony back there and he's a bit stuck on the woodwind parts. Tell him I expect to see him tomorrow.'

'I'm afraid that won't be possible.'

Alex turned to leave. He already had a hand on the door by the time Llull saw he had his book. What little colour he had drained out of his face. He lunged against the high counter but Alex was already halfway out the door. He waved the book.

'Oh, I think it's possible. And I feel confident that file will turn up too, don't you? If I haven't heard from you within twenty-four hours this is going in the bin,' he said, waving the journal. 'I'm at the Hotel Dos Aguas in Princesa. Room seventeen.'

11

When Carmen arrived for the funeral, the church in Sarrià was already packed to the doors. Fèlix Grau was young, his friends were young, and death was still a shocking novelty so everyone showed up for the funeral. Carmen thought that maybe, given the circumstances of his death, some of the more strait-laced would have stayed away, but when the mourners filed out she spotted among them the editor of *Ara*, the paper he worked for, and a local MP, both God-fearing men of the old school. Fèlix came from a good family, solid Barcelona bourgeoisie; his father was a dentist and his mother taught law at the university. Perhaps to spare his parents' feelings and with the family reputation in mind, the coroner had recorded that Fèlix died as a result of a freak accident. But whatever the coroner said, the tale of the belt was already out there, the subject of sick jokes and gossip.

Fèlix Grau was found dead in a hotel room in Sants, one of those heartless places with no staff, where you put your credit card in the slot and out pops a room key and a receipt. That's it: no reception, no room service, no please and thank you. The machine takes your money and the key opens the door – what more could you want? When the morning cleaning staff found Fèlix he was naked except for a leather belt. The belt was round his neck and the buckle end hung from a coathook which, like everything else in the hotel, was firmly fixed to the wall. The police had two theories: suicide or a sex game gone tragically wrong. Fèlix's girlfriend Blanca had a third – she thought it was murder.

Fèlix was twenty-seven. He was a passionate Catalanist; to Fèlix, everything Catalan was good and anything that stood in the path of the Catalan people, culture or language was bad. He worked as a reporter on the Catalan-language daily *Ara*, which, despite its national and cultural credentials, stubbornly refused to outsell *El Mensajero*, its Castilian rival. To the editor, a second-generation Catalan but very much a champion of the cause, this represented a failure of national consciousness. The truth was more prosaic: *Ara* – the Catalan for now – didn't sell because it was too worthy, too dull and its sports pages had no bite.

Journalism has a way of turning young idealists into lazy cynics, but not Fèlix. He remained a true believer. He saw journalists as guardians of truth, whistleblowers in a wicked world and, because he broke a couple of major stories – about corruption among local officials – he had the grudging respect of his more jaded colleagues. But while Fèlix viewed the mechanics of power with a healthy scepticism, his girlfriend Blanca went a step further and saw conspiracies. Everything happened by design, each conspiracy part of a greater one. She was no fool and at her best she could deliver a savage exposition of the self-serving political establishment. But at her worst it was as though she'd reduced Aristotle's tinkling universe of spheres to a set of paranoid Russian dolls. Highly-strung by nature, she blunted her edginess with dope. She smoked a lot and, like anyone who rolls their first joint before ten in the morning and their last at bedtime, no longer realized she was stoned. The dope may have calmed her nerves but her conspiratorial fantasies thrived on it.

Carmen knew Fèlix slightly from press conferences and the like, although she never worked with him, but had known Blanca since university. They were good friends but not close.

It was one of those friendships that seems to consist less of a set of common interests than an accretion of time; they'd known each other so long they were de facto old friends, even though they met rarely and weren't in any way central to each other's lives.

After the service, the family went on to the burial at the small cemetery in Sarrià but Fèlix's friends were invited to join them later at the house for drinks. An hour later Carmen was at the Grau household. It was packed and noisy, with that supercharged atmosphere wakes often have, something between relief and hysteria. Carmen found Fèlix's parents in a corner of the dining room. She introduced herself and explained she hadn't known Fèlix well, more by reputation than anything else, and that he was a fine journalist. She said she was sorry, there was nothing she could say that would change anything, but that she was sorry for their loss. They thanked her and the unfeigned sincerity of their gratitude was heartbreaking; they were hungry for word of their son, whatever the source. Fèlix's mother squeezed Carmen's hand for a moment, clung to it, like she was clinging to Carmen's young life. She and her husband looked like people who had seen the abyss, people who knew something you hoped you'd never know.

Carmen took a beer on to the large terrace to get away from the noise and because, if she was going to cry, which she thought she might, she wanted to do it in peace. She watched the cars pass by below along the Passeig de la Bonanova. Her eyes pricked but the tears didn't come and she found herself thinking about Alex Nadal. Nothing in particular, just thinking. Someone touched her on the shoulder; it was Blanca. They had spoken briefly on the phone but this was their first real chance to talk since Fèlix died. She looked drawn but if she'd been crying it didn't show. Carmen put her arms round her and held her tight and said into her fine, fair hair, 'Blanca, I'm so sorry, so sorry.'

'You have to help me,' Blanca said, her face buried in Carmen's neck.

'Of course I will, I'm your friend.'

Blanca pulled out of the embrace and combed her hair back with her hands. Her eyes were dry. She looked over her shoulder to see who was in earshot.

'They killed him,' she said. 'He was on to something big this time, I know he was, so they killed him, the bastards.'

Carmen put an arm round her shoulder and they looked down on the traffic. If it had been her boyfriend, Carmen thought, she'd want an explanation too. Something better than believing he booked into a hotel in order to kill himself or that he was so bored with her sexually that he'd risk asphyxiation for the sake of a better than average wank. From that perspective, the idea that Fèlix might have been murdered was almost a relief. At least you didn't have to wonder if it was your fault. But it was absurd, Blanca's flailing attempt to make sense of her loss, the way people look around for someone to blame, or better still, to sue.

'This must be so terrible for you,' she said, giving Blanca's shoulder a squeeze, 'I can't imagine how you feel.'

Blanca accepted the affection but when she turned to Carmen the look in her eyes was clear and hard. She looked over her shoulder again but she didn't need to worry, people were giving them plenty of room, Carmen the woman friend consoling Blanca the sort of widow.

'Look, I know people think I'm paranoid and I know it's partly my own fault. I rant, I know that, but that's the way I am. Fèlix was murdered, I'm certain of it, but no one wants to know. I'm just a schoolteacher, but you have the resources, the contacts, the know-how. I don't know who else I can ask.'

Carmen's heart sank, but Blanca was her friend. What could she say?

'What do you know? What was Fèlix on to?'

'I don't really know. He was very secretive, well, not so much secretive as very professional. He didn't like to blab, not even to me. Not until he was absolutely sure. But I know it had something to do with Puig. I think Fèlix had something on him, something pretty damning.'

'Oscar Puig?'

'Of course, who else?'

Oscar Puig was the boss of the environment department of the Generalitat and a good man to know if you planned to build anything bigger than a hen-house. He was a bureaucrat, but a bureaucrat with star quality. He liked the media, he obliged them. He gave the papers interviews in which he said enough about nothing for a reporter to file the six hundred words he needed. As for TV, he gave them footage of him striding across Plaça Sant Jaume or whatever nonsense they required to pad out an otherwise drab to-camera piece delivered by some dowdy reporter standing in the rain in Martorell. He understood that what a reporter wants is one good quote and what TV needs is pictures. He gave them both and they loved him for it. He let them think he did it out of vanity, but the truth was he did it because he knew that was what they wanted. Oscar Puig liked people to feel they were getting what they wanted. That way he got what he wanted too.

'What do you think he had on Puig?'

'I don't know. All I know is Fèlix mentioned him in relation to this Roger de Flor thing. I think he thought he was mixed up in it.'

'Blanca, you're losing me. What Roger de Flor thing?'

Blanca smacked her hand on the parapet in frustration. Her lips were dry and stained from chain-smoking.

'I don't know, Carmen. That's the problem, I just don't know. Fèlix made a couple of trips down the coast recently. I checked his diary after he died and both times he went he wrote Roger de Flor. Maybe that had something to do with it. I don't know, I really don't know. But I know he didn't kill himself and I know it wasn't an accident. I know he wouldn't do something like that. I should know, shouldn't I?'

It was a plea as much as a statement. Carmen nodded, of course you would, of course. She could see her friend beginning to crumble. She took her in her arms again. Blanca started to sob. Slowly at first, whimpering, still holding on, keeping control, then deeper and deeper gasps, until she was crying in her throat, in her lungs, in her whole self. Carmen held her.

'It's OK, Blanca. Let it go, let it go. I'm here. I'm with you. I'm going to do everything I can.'

Maybe it was that Blanca's pain made it seem too cruel to doubt her, but just then Carmen thought perhaps there was something in it, something more than Blanca's inability to bear the unbearable.

12

When Alex made the crack that Busquets, Ferran Llull's boss at the land registry, was a composer he was half right – he wasn't a composer but he was a musician. He was a cellist, good enough to give amateur concerts with a pianist or in a string quartet. His dream was to play Bach's unaccompanied suites in public but he hadn't the nerve. Of his four children only the middle girl, Isa, showed any interest in music. She was already attracting attention as a violinist. She had talent, enough for one of the city's leading players to offer to take her under his wing. But these things cost money and Busquets couldn't keep up with the teaching fees. What he'd done seemed innocent enough, a bit irregular but nothing actually illegal. But now this Nadal fellow had turned up and cast everything in a different light.

Busquets lived with his family in a sixties block in L'Hospitalet. At eight thirty that evening, the day that Alex had come to the office, he was putting his key in the main door of the block when a voice behind him said, 'Señor Busquets, we need to talk.' He knew who it was without turning round. Narcís had a distinctive voice, with a pronounced sibilant s, like a snake talking. Narcís gestured Busquets inside with an ironic sweep of the arm. They took the lift to the fourth floor: neither spoke. The entrance to the flat led to a small hallway that opened out to all the other rooms. From one of them came the sound of someone practising the violin, running through arpeggios, first bowed, then pizzicato.

Busquets didn't invite him in beyond the hall. Narcís was a big man, solidly built, with a penchant for expensive suits. Today he had a on a sleek midnight-blue single-breasted Hugo Boss. He loomed over Busquets.

'Someone named Nadal called to see you,' he said.

'Yes, it seems there's been some mistake. Señor Nadal appears . . .'

'You don't have to worry about him.'

'That's easy to say, but I am worried about it. I have to protect myself, I can't afford to lose my job.'

His palms were sweating and he could feel a tremor coming into his voice. Narcís scared him, the whole business scared him. Losing his job would be a disaster. It wasn't just the financial implications, it was the shame; maybe the police would become involved. A watercolour of the monastery at Ripoll hung on the wall behind Narcís. In an effort to steady his voice, Busquets concentrated on the picture and the monastery's procession of Romanesque arches.

'Nobody will say anything, not if you do as you're told,' Narcís said.

'But it appears that this Nadal is genuine. He has a right.'

'I'll tell you who has a right,' Narcís shouted, suddenly angry.

The violin playing stopped and a door opened. A plump fair-haired girl of about fourteen stood in the doorway, holding the violin by the neck, the bow between her fingertips.

'Go back and practise, Isa,' Busquets said gently. 'We'll be through here in a minute.'

She turned to go but Narcís stopped her with a hand on her shoulder. She flinched.

'Isa, that's a pretty name,' Narcís said, the 's' whistling through his teeth. 'You play very well, Isa. How long have you been playing?'

The girl looked stricken with shyness. She glanced nervously at her father, who answered for her.

'Since she was five,' he said, looking at her, not at Narcís. 'Now run along.'

'Wait a moment,' Narcís said, gesturing at the violin. 'May I see it?'

Again the girl seemed paralysed and looked at her father, who nodded. Reluctantly, she handed Narcís the instrument, as though she was giving up her baby for adoption. He turned it in his large hands and stroked the wood.

'Very nice,' he said. 'Great craftsmanship. Still, I suppose it won't be long till all you want to play with is boys, not the violin. Isn't that so, Isa?'

He grinned at her and gave her a big, stagy wink. She looked mortified and blushed from the neck up. Narcís gave the peg on the thick G string a quarter turn. The girl winced.

'Come on now, don't be coy. You must get plenty of offers, pretty girl like you.'

He gave her an up and down and leered, then he gave the peg a sharp turn, making the thread creak. The girl looked imploringly at her father.

'Please,' he said. 'You'll damage it.'

Narcís looked at Busquets and turned the peg again. With a double thwack the string broke and the peg snapped off. Narcís's expression didn't change. He handed the girl the broken instrument and with his free hand stroked her hair. Inside she recoiled but her body wouldn't obey her and she stood rooted to the spot as the tears boiled out of her eyes.

'Say nothing, Señor Busquets,' he said to her father, dropping the broken peg into his hand. 'And do nothing. Better still, stay away from the office for a while.'

13

Miguel picked Alex up at the foot of la Rambla by the Columbus monument. He drove a mid-range, middle-aged Renault in need of a wash. Not much of a car for a lawyer, Alex thought. But then Miguel wasn't like the lawyers he knew in New York. He wondered if he was paying for Miguel's time. Someone had to be. In New York, if a lawyer took you out in his car for half a day he would bill you for his time, for the time of whoever was doing what he would be doing in the office had he not been driving you around, for the time of whoever was doing what the person who was doing what he would normally be doing normally did, for a proportion of the purchase price of the car, for the wear and tear entailed by the journey, for the extra premium on his health insurance and so forth. By the end of the day he'd have to sell the farm to pay the fees.

'Is the meter running?' Alex said. 'I feel I ought to know.'

'What?' Miguel raised one thick eyebrow. With his dolorous eyes safely hidden behind a pair of wraparounds he looked more droll than melancholy.

'Am I paying you for your time? Now, today?'

'Don't worry about it,' Miguel laughed. 'You can buy me a drink when we get back to the city.'

Which explained the crap, for a lawyer, car.

'There's something I'm not clear about,' Alex said. 'My aunt died in April, but I didn't hear from you till early September. Why was that?'

'I didn't know she was dead. It's not as though I phone my clients on a regular basis to check they're still alive. So I only found out when this Victor Sabadell came to see me, a few months after your aunt died.'

'A few months? Why so long?'

'He was a bit vague on that point. You'd better ask him yourself.'

'What's he like, this Victor?'

'Oh, just a regular country boy,' Miguel's eyes smiled over the top of his sunglasses. 'You'll see.'

Miguel's driving was erratic and Alex looked out the window rather than watch the road. The flat sea trembled like mercury under the weight of the afternoon.

'Ever been to the States?' he asked Miguel.

'No. I spent a weekend in Sitges with a guy from Buffalo, but that's as near as I got. God, he was a pain. Why?'

'I could swear the sky's bigger there.'

Miguel tutted.

'You Americans. Such size queens.'

They drove up the hill into the village. Alex tried to picture his father living here, a regular country boy himself. It was hard to reconcile that with the man he knew, the hardworking, brusque American patriot. His father wouldn't hear a word against America, he'd bought into the American dream completely, while his mother dreamed only that one day she would go home to Cuba. Miguel parked under the chestnut and they went round the side of the house. Someone was feeding the chickens. Alex's first thought was, Jesus, I'll have to kill the chickens if I want to eat them. He wondered if in these parts they wrung their necks or chopped their heads off, not that he'd ever done either. The man had his back to them. Miguel called out hello but he didn't seem to hear. As they got closer Alex could hear a strange scratching noise, like static, above

84

the sound of the chickens. Miguel said hello louder and this time Victor turned round. He was one of those smooth-skinned boyish types who never really have to shave, although he was doing his best to grow a goatee. Whatever Alex was expecting, it wasn't Victor. He was dressed in tight, sky-blue jeans, a faded black Jack Daniel's T-shirt with cut-off sleeves and white high-top trainers. He had straggly shoulder-length auburn hair and was plugged into a Walkman that was going full blast. Victor moved the bag of chicken feed from his right to his left hand and switched off the Walkman but left the earphones in.

He said hello with a shy and wary smile and held out his hand. Miguel introduced them.

'What's the music?' Alex said, nodding at the Walkman.

'*Love is for Suckers*', he said in heavily accented English. Then, seeing the blank look on Alex's face, added helpfully, 'Twisted Sister.'

The bucolic dream, Alex thought. Feeding the chickens to full-blast heavy metal.

'All this peace and quiet get on your nerves?' he said.

Victor met that with a shrug.

'Shall we take a look around?' Miguel suggested.

Victor led them round the back of the house. Alex followed and wondered how anyone could stand to do this kind of work in such tight jeans. As well as chickens there were a pair of geese, about half a dozen ducks, a young pig and, tethered in a small grove of olives, a solitary cow. The ground fell away behind the house in a long slope then rose again to where it dropped sharply down to the sea. The property was bounded on the seaward side by a line of small trees. Victor pointed out the crops between there and the house: six lines of hazel trees, the olive grove, a dozen almond trees, two rows of vines. They didn't make their own wine, he explained, but sold the grapes to the local cooperative. The rest was vegetables – tomatoes, aubergines, beans, courgettes, pumpkins and, on the far side of the house, fruit trees, mostly apples, but a couple of damsons, too, and a lemon tree. Again, Alex wondered what sort of a living could be made out of this. The ducks, for example: you could buy a whole duck in Mott Street for a few dollars, crispy fried, with pancakes and plum sauce.

'You keep the place really nice,' Alex said.

Victor gave a shy smile of pleasure.

'Most of my family's land is on the other side of the village. I come every day, do what I can to stop the place going to ruin. I've always loved this farm, for the past three years it's been 100 per cent organic too. No one else round here farms organically, they can't be bothered.'

'You obviously like the life. Never thought of moving to the city?'

'I go into Barcelona for gigs. Sometimes to buy records. My brothers live there, suit and tie jobs. Not the life for me.'

Then suddenly he struck a Freddy Mercury pose, feet splayed and one hand on an imaginary mike stand, and sang: 'I've got to break free.' He gave a shy, almost self-mocking grin. That was close to irony, Alex thought. Very post-modern for a country boy.

'And Núria, your sister, she's in Barcelona, I gather.'

Victor's face tightened. It was like the moment when a train pulls out, when all the slack between the cars is gathered up. Victor's sister weighed in his face.

'My aunt mentioned her in her will,' Alex explained. 'You too.'

Victor's features relaxed a little.

'She was very fond of Núria, very good to her,' he said in a quiet voice. 'And to me, ever since we were kids.'

'And so you repaid her kindness by looking after the place for her, is that right?'

Victor paused, looking for a trap in the question. He fiddled with the leather thong on his wrist.

'She couldn't manage it all by herself. She was too old.'

'So you did all the work?

'Eventually, yes. We had a deal: I did the work and kept two thirds of what the farm made. Not that it makes much,' he added quickly. 'A farm like this barely pays for itself.'

'I see. I'm sorry if it sounds like I'm interrogating you, I don't mean to. I'm just trying to get the picture. Didn't anyone else in the village help her out?'

Victor got that tight look in his face again. Alex guessed that Victor was honest by nature but mendacious through habit or necessity. But practice had not made perfect; too much showed in his face for him ever to be an accomplished liar. Victor raised his arms and pulled his hair back. He rolled an elastic band off his wrist and tied his hair back in a pony-tail.

'In general she was too proud to ask,' he said, adding with a flash of anger, 'I don't care about all that stuff, I'm not stuck in the past, not like a lot of people around here.'

For a moment Alex thought he was going to break into song again.

'My father betrayed some people here, three brothers, who were later shot. That's what they say, isn't it?'

Victor nodded.

'And my aunt?'

'She didn't talk about it and I didn't ask.'

'It seems to me that could be the opening line of the national anthem.'

'What?'

'Nothing. It doesn't matter.'

For a while no one spoke as the hens clucked around their feet.

'Shall we take a look at the house?' Miguel said.

Alex was puzzled by the house, it wasn't in any particular style and from the outside you couldn't even really say what shape it was. It seemed to be all over the place, two storeys in some parts, three in others. They went in through the low doorway and entered a long low room, whose main feature was a vast fireplace flanked by a pair of floral-patterned armchairs and a matching sofa. Victor opened the shutters and explained that this was the original part of the house and was about two hundred years old, no one was really sure. A plain wooden dining table ran half the length of the room; fifteen or twenty people could sit comfortably at the table. A black upright piano stood in a corner under a colourless bunch of dried flowers. Alex lifted the lid and played the opening bars of 'Round Midnight'. It was plain the piano hadn't been tuned in years.

'I never heard her play,' Victor said, anticipating his thoughts.

Alex opened the hinged seat of the piano stool and took out a small bundle of sheet music. Nearly all were short pieces or studies from which he guessed that his aunt had studied up to about Grade Eight, generally where someone of average talent could expect to get to by their mid-teens. Apart from the grade studies there were two pieces of music: a set of dances by Albéniz and, incongruously, Gershwin's 'Someone to Watch Over Me'. The sight of the songsheet made Alex shiver, despite the clammy heat. When he was seventeen he won a piano competition for his interpretation of 'Someone to Watch Over Me' and it remained one of his favourite songs. Until now he had no clear image of his Aunt Anna nor any real feeling for her, but now he felt a connection and a kinship with her, just knowing that she had sat at this piano playing his favourite Gershwin song made her less of a stranger.

'That's her,' Victor said, pointing to a picture on the wall.

Alex got up from the piano to take a closer look. It was a photograph of a teenage girl sitting at the piano. She had one hand on the lid while the other rested on her lap. She was fair-skinned and dark-eyed – like his father – and looked straight into the camera. Alex was trying to detect other family resemblances when he noticed something else. On top of the piano stood a carving of a horse. He recognized it immediately as his father's work. His father had been carving horses out of wood for as long as Alex could remember. Not many, probably two a year at most, and always and only horses. The carving seemed to be an outlet, the only thing his father did that was, in the strictest sense, unnecessary. Alex's father was pragmatic, careful and prudent; he lived life sparingly, and so these carvings seemed almost an indulgence, though clearly they were as necessary to his survival as food and drink. They expressed something otherwise unseen in the man. In artistic terms they were strictly representational, so much so – with webs of striated muscle showing through the flanks and veins bulging on the horses' necks – that they veered into super-realism. There was something distressing about these beasts; they were never placidly munching grass in a meadow like a Stubbs horse. His father's horses were active, rearing up or stretched out at a gallop, and always, it seemed, caught in a moment of terror. They were beautiful but afraid. Alex pointed to the carving in the photo.

'Where's that now?'

'I don't know,' Victor said. 'I've never seen it in the house.'

Victor led them up a series of staircases and it became clear that the house was added to piecemeal over the years, when-ever there was a little extra money or another mouth to feed. Nothing seemed planned. Whenever the need arose, someone knocked a hole in the wall and built a new landing or staircase and set off in another direction. The three of them stood on the roof terrace at the back, overlooking the property and the sea. Two freighters and a container ship were moored in a line, waiting to berth in Tarragona.

Victor explained various things about the land and pointed out the sprawling coastal town of Torredembarra and the castle on the hill at Altafulla. He was clearly uncomfortable in Castilian, like he'd put on another man's clothes, and when-ever he spoke directly to Miguel he reverted to Catalan with evident relief. Alex thought about his father, who said he hardly ever spoke Castilian till he arrived in Cuba. The poor man ended up with eccentric Spanish, clumsy English and a mother tongue that no one around him spoke. Whenever Miguel started speaking Catalan Alex gave him a look and he reverted to Castilian. Miguel offered Victor a Marlboro and they both smoked. It was stupid, but not smoking made Alex feel still more of an outsider. It seemed to him that, if he was going to have a friend in the village, then Victor, the local rebel, might be his best bet. But at the same time Victor clearly wanted the farm and so had every reason to want Alex to disappear.

'My aunt died six months ago, is that right?' Alex said.

'Yes, in April.'

'I hope you don't mind me asking, but why did you wait so long to inform Señor Montero?'

'I thought you would come. She wrote to you.'

'Wrote to me? Are you sure?'

'Yes, I'm sure. I took her to the post office in Torredembarra myself. She mailed two letters, well, packets really. One was addressed to you.'

'Who was the other one to?'

Victor looked uncomfortable.

'I don't remember, I mean I didn't notice.'

Lying again, Alex thought.

'Any idea what was in these packets?'

'No.'

Alex looked out over the farm. He noticed that to the south of Can Castanyer a large tract of land had been left to run wild.

'Whose is that land?' Alex said.

'My father's,' Victor said in a flat voice that conveyed more feeling than he intended. He couldn't dissemble to save himself, poor boy. 'It's separate from the rest of our land. We used to grow potatoes on it.'

'And now?'

Victor shrugged.

'Set aside?' Miguel asked.

'No, nothing like that,' Victor said, although he didn't know for sure, because his father wouldn't explain what he planned to do with the land.

'What's set aside?'

Miguel looked at Victor but Victor looked past him and picked at the frayed collar of his Jack Daniel's T-shirt.

'Set aside is when the commission in Brussels pays farmers to sit on their arses and not grow anything,' Miguel explained.

'To maintain demand, and to stop prices falling to a level where poor people could afford to eat.'

If Victor was irritated by Miguel's sarcasm it didn't show.

'Given the choice, I guess you'd like to carry on as you are,' Alex said.

Victor was the physical embodiment of tongue-tied. He fiddled with his leather thong and tugged at his wispy beard.

'I don't know, I mean, it's not up to me, is it? My father says I'm wasting my time keeping it going, that it's as good as sold already.'

'Does he really? And who's the buyer?'

'I don't know, it's just what he says.'

It wasn't hard to picture the relationship between Victor, the free spirit and organic farmer, and the garrulous Jaume Sabadell, or to see why Victor barricaded himself behind a wall of screaming guitars.

'What prompted you to tell Señor Montero here that my aunt was dead? You say you were waiting for me to show up, but when I didn't, why didn't you just let matters rest? The farm would have been yours effectively. From what you say, it probably should be.'

Victor looked both encouraged and embarrassed by what Alex said, as though he'd been caught out and let off in the one breath.

'A couple of months ago I found someone on the land. He had one of those things on a tripod, a thing you look through.'

'A telescope?'

'You mean a theodolite,' Miguel said. 'Was he a surveyor?'

'Yes, for the Generalitat. He said he was carrying out a survey of Can Castanyer for the Generalitat and when I asked him what for he wouldn't say.'

'So what happened then?'

'I got my shotgun and shooed him off. That's when I thought I should pay you a visit,' he said to Miguel. Alex imagined Victor travelling into Barcelona to see the lawyer, praying that his aunt had left him the farm.

'Good thing you did,' Alex said. 'And whatever your father says, the farm isn't as good as sold. In fact, it isn't even for sale at the moment and you have my word on that. Would you be willing to keep the same arrangement you had with Anna, but with me? You mind the farm and keep two thirds.'

Victor shook his hair back over his shoulders. He tried to look nonchalant but he couldn't pull it off. Whatever he felt, showed, and Alex could see he was pleased.

'I suppose so,' he said as sullenly as possible.

'And you?' Miguel asked Alex.

'Me? I'll move in, of course. Once I've done what I have to do in Barcelona.'

He hadn't planned to say that, but he was sure it was the right move. The easiest way to assert himself was by just being there and he needed to show a sense of purpose, even if he felt adrift. Miguel raised an eyebrow and the three of them went downstairs and stood at the front of the house. Victor was ill at ease and kept putting his hair in and out of a pony-tail.

'Something on your mind?' Alex said, afraid to push but aware that Victor was the nearest thing to an open door he'd come across here. Victor fiddled some more and looked over both shoulders. He wet his lips.

'Anna, your aunt, didn't drink,' he said finally. 'Not ever.'

There was a long silence, which Miguel broke.

'Perhaps it was her little secret,' he said. 'Lots of old ladies like a drink on the quiet.'

Victor ignored Miguel and looked at Alex.

'No, I'm certain. She had an allergy. Alcohol made her come up in itchy blotches like mosquito bites. So she never touched it.'

'But the coroner . . .' Alex began.

'I know,' said Victor.

14

Carmen was waxing her legs when he called. She took a sharp breath, ripped off a sheet of wax and picked up the phone.

'Any danger of lunch?' Angel said.

Pinpricks of blood sprang up on a stretch of newly hairless calf. Carmen didn't want any more afternoons in bed with Angel. She decided that before she met Alex, then she decided it all over again. But she had yet to pass this information on to Angel.

'Today? I don't know, I'm pretty busy. I've got to go to the library to do some background on Salvador Oriol, prepare for the interview.'

'I have a story for you, one I think you'll like very much.'

He'd done this before, played to her curiosity, and did it well. This time she tried to deflect him.

'And I have one for you: Roger de Flor. What does the name mean to you?'

He guessed this would happen from the moment she told him about Alex Nadal. He knew she wouldn't be able to keep her nose out.

'Is this a joke?' he said, trying to make it one. 'Or is it a quiz game? OK, for ten points: Roger de Flor, fourteenth-century explorer or pirate or mercenary, depending on which books you read, a hero from the golden age when Barcelona ruled the Mediterranean from the Côte d'Azur to the Bay of Naples. Next question.'

'I meant now, in a contemporary context. Does it ring any bells?'

'No, none. But enough questions, you said you had a story.'

'That was it. I may not know what it is, but it's still a story. What sort of story have you got for me?'

'The kind that can only be told over lunch.'

Angel could sense her at the other end of the phone, nibbling at the bait. He had a nose for human frailty, each had its own peculiar smell. Greed was metallic, like cold water in a new zinc bucket. Jealousy was briny, like a saltwater swamp. Mendacity had a used-up smell, like a bar just after it closes. As for Carmen, she smelled of ambition, an odour of raw steak.

'Well, OK. So long as it's just lunch.'

In the silence that followed she had the opportunity to say, 'I don't want to sleep with you any more.' But she didn't, and as he didn't want her to, he wasn't going to make her say it.

'I'm sorry,' she said. 'I didn't mean it to sound like that.'

Except she did. Angel let it pass.

'Do you know Can Ramonet?' he said.

'Heard of it, never been. In Barceloneta, right?'

'That's it, in the Carrer de la Maquinista. I'll book it for two o'clock.'

El Mensajero's cuttings file on Salvador Oriol went back more than thirty years, beginning in the early sixties with his arrest and subsequent five-year prison sentence after he and a handful of others had assembled beside the Canaletes fountain in la Rambla and sung Els Segadors, the banned Catalan national anthem, as Franco's motorcade passed. Then there was a short item on his release from jail, after serving barely a year, during an unexplained amnesty. After Franco died in 1975 he was everywhere. Oriol the firebrand addressing an outdoor meeting in the Plaça Sant Jaume, Oriol the statesman espousing Catalan autonomy at the Cortes in Madrid, shaking hands with Felipe González, shaking hands with the king. Oriol the patriarch opening a new children's ward in the Hospital Del Mar, Oriol the traditionalist wearing a big white bib and munching *calçots* in a restaurant in Valls, Oriol the populist with his arm around the goalkeeper Zubizareta after el Barça's victory over Sampdoria in the European Cup Final, and there in his Big Daddy Catalunya role posing with Peret, the *rumbero*, at the opening ceremony of the Olympics. Oriol was not a man to miss a photo-opportunity. He even opened the doors of his Tibidabo mansion to *Hello!* magazine. Carmen flipped through the glossy photostudy of his over-decorated, over-furnished house, full of ornaments and stuffed animal heads and bucolic paintings hung in heavy gilt frames. It was like Angel said, he was a complete invention. He never held or campaigned for public office. It seemed that by the time anyone thought to ask the what and the why of who he was it was too late; he was an institution, a Teflon-coated sacred cow.

When she finished with the cuts, Carmen skimmed his official biography. It was pretty nauseating, sycophantic stuff, breathless PR at its worst. The book recounted his humble beginnings in a village near Vilafranca del Penedès and how while still in his teens he took up arms for the republican cause, spending the last six months of the Civil War as a prisoner in a nationalist camp near Vinaròs. Among the many pictures in the book, one caught her eye: it was a studio photograph of Oriol dated 1940, a very stylized portrait of a bare-headed young man in an open-necked shirt, looking past the camera into the middle distance. Quite an extravagant indulgence for a country boy in 1940, Carmen thought, going to a photographic studio, right after the war. She photocopied a handful of the cuts and, on a whim, took a copy of the studio portrait of the young Oriol.

As she passed back through the newsroom, Enric Luna, the

news editor, was standing at his desk in his trademark pose, phone clamped against his shoulder, one hand cupping the back of his head, the other bunched in his trouser pocket. Luna was a prick, and in that respect he was no different from most news editors – he just covered his arse with whoever came to hand. What set Luna apart wasn't that he was a prick but that he enjoyed being a prick. He was good at it, he was a prick of the first water. He was a lean, bony man with a small, mean face, pinhead eyes and a gunslit mouth. He looked like he'd been conceived during a shortage of facial features. He was good at his job, Carmen had to give him that, but he was a bully, gratuitously unpleasant, especially to women. He took particular delight in reducing the young female trainees to tears, which wasn't difficult. And he believed that wherever else it might be, a woman's place was not in the newsroom. On arts and features, maybe, but not on news; news was men's work. Luna's low opinion of women was matched by the belief that they had a high opinion of him and struggled to resist his charms. Carmen, however, had no trouble resisting and so, as he didn't want women in the newsroom anyway, Luna had her shunted off to arts. She fought it, of course, but she was outgunned.

Luna's eyes followed Carmen as she passed. She gave him a forty-watt smile which he acknowledged with a flick of his narrow eyebrows. 'Yes,' he was saying to Narcís, 'she's one of ours. Arts reporter, no, not on news, no, nothing like that.' Narcís thanked him. Enric watched Carmen as she pushed out the door. 'Great arse,' he added under his breath as he put down the phone.

Can Ramonet was noisy and busy, it was always busy. They'd been cooking *suquet*, *paella* and *arròs negre* since 1763 and they were very good at it. This was the sort of food Angel wanted his restaurant to produce, food that came out of a tradition. None of this seared flim-flam served on a bed of marinated lah-di-dah with some weird coulis on the side. Sure you could improvise a bit, but food had to mean something, it couldn't just come out of your head. Angel thought about what Oriol said, that people were saying he'd lost his touch. Oriol probably made that up but it bothered him just the same, because he knew it was partly true. He didn't have the same hunger for the game that he did, and without the hunger he knew the first thing that happens is you make mistakes and then you start to lose control. All he wanted was to get his restaurant started and kick back for a while. Then this Nadal turned up. Angel would have played along with Oriol – it would be easy enough to scare the American off without resorting to the sort of rough stuff Narcís went in for – if he hadn't dragged his son Josep into it. As far as Angel was concerned, that was against the rules.

Several heads turned when Carmen walked in and Angel's ego sunned itself in the looks that followed her to his table. She was wearing a smoke-grey suit over a plain white top. She usually wore a suit to work. She explained to him once: in a suit you look respectable, you look like you know what you're talking about, and no one looks at your tits. You're sort of passing for a man, but you can still use what you've got going for you as a woman. Look at women newsreaders, she said, hair just so, make-up perfect. But have you ever seen a woman read the news in a dress? Never, always a suit.

They ordered Galician oysters and *esqueixada* to start with, bream baked in salt to follow. They drank Viña Sol and talked about this and that. Carmen told him about the *Bernarda Alba* at the Sala Beckett, said it was brilliant. Angel said he'd spent the morning with a German property dealer who was buying up Catalan farmhouses. Germans were crazy about Catalunya, he said, they felt an affinity with Catalans.

'You ever fucked a German, Angel?' she said. It was a way of fending him off, by acting ugly herself, because she knew he hated that kind of vulgarity.

'What? No, as a matter of fact. Have you?'

'No, but you know I'm not the collector you are. Isn't that a bit of a gap, no Germans? What about Finns? Taiwanese?'

'I like Mediterranean women; dark-skinned, black-eyed women with sharp tongues and moist lips.'

His words hung between them for a moment, then fell. Carmen didn't pick them up.

'So tell me about your American,' Angel said, feeling a little exposed. 'Was he what you expected?'

'Seems a nice guy, quite droll. I even detected a little irony there, so he has potential.'

'Potential as what?'

'Surely you're not jealous,' she said. This was another part of her withdrawal strategy, to deny that there was anything of substance between them, anything that might justify jealousy. Angel responded with cold amusement, a look that said, 'Don't flatter yourself, girl.' But when she talked about the American having potential a little fist of nausea gripped his stomach from within, a sick, angry feeling that, as far as he could remember, was very like jealousy.

'He's not getting much of a welcome,' Carmen went on. 'I think maybe he imagined it would be like the prodigal's return but it seems other people have designs on the farm he's inherited. They're leaning on him pretty heavily.'

'Is that so?' Angel said. 'Does he have any idea who's doing the leaning?'

'No, but he seems very determined, quite steely underneath.'

'Underneath what?'

Carmen gave him an inscrutable smile and lit a cigarette. The waiter brought the bream on an oven tray, magnificent in its baked salt overcoat. They admired it and he took it away. He returned a few minutes later with the salt removed and the fish served up on two plates.

'I'll never understand why this works,' Angel said. 'How baking a fish in a couple of kilos of salt makes the flesh sweeter. You like it?'

Carmen wasn't a sensualist about food the way Angel was. She appreciated good food, but it wasn't a passion. Eating was something she did between cigarettes.

'It's delicious,' she said absently. 'Did you see Oriol on TV the other day, talking about his eightieth birthday? He says he's going to make a gift to the nation. What do you think it will be?'

'I expect he's worried that he'll be upstaged by the Infanta's wedding, which is the weekend before his birthday.'

'So what's he planning?'

Carmen pushed her half-eaten fish away and lit a cigarette. Angel looked at her reprovingly. He wasn't blind, he could see her pulling away from him, maybe because of the American, maybe not. In any case, Angel was accustomed to being the dumper, not the dumped. In other circumstances he would devise some small but stinging punishment and walk away with his pride intact. But with Carmen he was torn between wanting to punish her and wanting to win her back. Ideally he'd manage both.

'Are you familiar with a company called Mallobeco?' he said.

'Vaguely, that is, I've heard the name. What do they do?'

'Mostly what they do is keep what they do very quiet. They finance things, construction projects as a rule, mostly but not exclusively in the city, hence the name.'

Carmen looked blank.

'What surrounds Barcelona? The sea in front of us, the two rivers – the Besòs to the north, Llobregat to the south, and the Collserola hills behind: Mar, Llobregat, Besòs, Collserola – Mallobeco.'

'And what's Mallobeco got to do with Salvador Oriol's gift to the nation.'

'That's for you to find out.'

'That's the story you brought me here to tell?'

'I didn't bring you here, Carmen, you came of your own accord. And yes, that's the story.'

'Why are you telling me?'

'Out of an overwhelming sense of civic responsibility. And because I know you're dying to break a good story so you can get back on the news desk.'

'How do you know that?'

'You told me, you've obviously forgotten. Perhaps you were in a swoon.'

Carmen pursed her lips and made eyes to the ceiling. What was she supposed to say? 'Oh thanks for the tip-off. By the way, did I tell you I don't want to fuck you any more?' But she felt bad. She liked Angel and she didn't want to hurt his feelings, and at the same time she couldn't believe she was worried about hurting a man like that. What if she had fallen in love with him? He'd have a run a mile.

'Shall we get the bill? I've tons of work on. I've got a piece to write this afternoon, then I've got to prepare for this interview with Oriol and then tonight I've got to review the new Carles Santos show at the Lliure.'

'You'd really like to get something on him, wouldn't you?'

'Who? Santos?'

Angel leaned across the table and gave her an 'Oh, come on' look. She gave him one back. Angel saw his face reflected in her black eyes.

'I suppose I could ask you what Oriol's got on you that makes you so keen for me to get something on him,' she said. 'Or maybe I should ask him.'

'I wouldn't do that,' Angel said, with just a touch of menace.

'You're right,' she said, with a playful smile. 'I wouldn't.'

15

Alex lay on his bed under the sacred heart of Jesus while the middle eight of 'Someone to Watch Over Me' played in his head. 'He may not be the man some/girls think of as handsome, but to my heart he'll carry the key.' He wondered if his aunt ever tried to sing it, or if she even played the tune; it seemed so out of place in that house. His father never told him Anna had studied piano, all he said was he had a sister who died of TB at sixteen. End of story, except it clearly wasn't. It was Alex's mother who encouraged him to play music. His father was grudgingly proud when he won prizes, and then just grudging when he went on to make a living but not a name for himself. There was always a bit of the peasant in his father; he saw life as a task to be accomplished, not a gift to be unwrapped. He was wounded by his father's suicide; so was Pepa, but she dulled the hurt with anger. Alex just felt the hurt, the inescapable fact that he and his sister weren't a good enough reason for their father to go on living.

The bedside phone rang. It was Carmen. Her voice went straight into his bloodstream. 'I think I've found your Captain Morín,' she said. 'There's a Guillermo Morín with an address on Passeig del Born, only I don't know which number. You'd have to ask around. El Born's just round the corner from your hotel. This Morín is eighty-four and he was a captain in the Civil War. On the nationalist side. Still draws his army pension, which is how I know all this.'

'Thanks, that's great, I'll go down there right away. How was the funeral, if that's not a stupid question?'

'Pretty heartbreaking, actually. How was your trip to the country?'

'Not quite what I expected. Victor, the guy who works the farm, is a bit eccentric. He implied fairly strongly that my aunt had some help falling downstairs.'

'Wow. What do the police say?'

'I haven't asked them yet. I'm going to move out there in a couple of days. Any chance of meeting up before then?'

'Oh, there's a always chance.' He could hear her smile. 'I'll call you. And be careful.'

Alex called Miguel to arrange to buy him the drink he was owed. He said he was going to be in the area around el Born.

'There's a place on el Born itself,' Miguel said. 'It's called Miramelindo.'

'That's what the bar's called, Miramelindo?'

'That's it. And it's not a gay bar, despite the camp name. There's no sign outside, just a little notice by the door. It's on your left if you've got your back to Santa María del Mar.'

Alex made two more calls, one to the Tarragona police, who said he could discuss his aunt's case with Detective Foix on Friday, which was the day after tomorrow. The other call was to a piano tuner. After that he lay down on the bed again and considered his options. He wanted to get Pepa to go round to his old address on Avenue B and see if the package Victor said his aunt had sent was still there, although it was a slim chance. He knew Pepa was out of town until the weekend but he left a message on her machine. Then there was Ferran Llull, the poet at the land registry. Llull left a message saying he thought he had what Alex wanted and would call back as soon as he was sure. Lluisa the concierge demonstrated how to say the name Llull – basically you said the l twice – like in the English word million. But when Alex tried his tongue seemed to stick to the roof of his mouth. Then there was Núria, Victor's sister, who, according to his aunt's will, knew things he wanted to know, if only he knew where to find her. Which left Captain Morín, the man who might know what drove his father to suicide.

Alex sensed there was someone outside his door. He slid off the bed and padded across the cool tiled floor. When he opened the door, there was Xavi, the concierge's plump and *seny*less son, putting on a bad imitation of nonchalance.

'Was there something?' Alex asked. The boy snuffled and waddled off down the corridor. Alex went back into the room and looked out the window. An American couple in matching turquoise tracksuits passed below him. Across the street was the junkie in the leather jacket, whose air of nonchalance was no more convincing than Xavi's. Alex whistled and the junkie looked up. When he caught Alex's eye he swivelled his shoulders inside the leather jacket in a James Dean meets Robert De Niro gesture of tough guy contempt and swaggered off in the direction of Via Laietana.

One hour, two beers and a talkative barman later Alex knew two things: first, that half the cops in Spain were being drafted into the city for the Infanta's wedding in case ETA tried to pull off something spectacular and, second, that old man Morín went for a walk every morning at the same time in Ciutadella park.

'You can't miss him,' the barman said. 'He wears a brown Homburg. How many people do you see in a Homburg these days? How may people do you see in any sort of hat? And I don't count baseball caps. Not long ago you'd no sooner leave the house hatless than you would naked. Now if you wear a hat, you look eccentric, like that old man Morín.'

Miramelindo was cool and chic. The customers were young and arty, they wore a lot of black and had look-at-me haircuts.

103

Alex and Miguel drank *mojitos* at a corner table. Alex told him about Morín.

'I worry about you,' the lawyer said. 'I mean, let's just say there's something in what Victor said, let's say your aunt was pushed . . .'

'Precisely, let's say she was. Wouldn't you want to know who did it and why?'

'Part of me would, of course. But a bigger part doesn't want to end up like her.'

'So you're saying if you were me you'd just let it ride. I thought lawyers were supposed to want to get at the truth.'

'Where did you read that? We want what's best for our clients, that's all, which means keeping them alive and out of jail. There's nothing lofty about it.'

'So what would you do?'

Miguel stirred the mint in his *mojito* and took a scrap of paper out of his pocket.

'That's the address of Montserrat Cases, the lawyer who talked to you in Barceloneta. I'd go and see her and tell her I'd changed my mind and decided to sell. It's not the heroic option, I grant you, but cowardice has its place.'

His eyes twinkled for a moment, then settled back into their natural melancholia. Alex drained his drink and ordered another.

'A few years ago,' he said, 'I went to look at an apartment. Because of some legal dispute no one had set foot in the place for two or three years. I went through the hall and into the living room, a distance of about fifteen feet, and by the time I reached the far wall I was covered in fleas, crawling with them. It happened in a few seconds. I discovered later that fleas can remain dormant for years. When I arrived at the apartment they hadn't yet hatched, they were eggs, programmed to hatch at the vibration of footsteps, a vibration that tells them lunch has arrived. That's all it takes; a couple of footsteps and they're out of the egg and biting your ankle. Amazing, isn't it? Anyway, that's how I feel, that my arrival here has aroused some slumbering beast. All I want is to know what it is.'

'This one could bite more than your ankle.'

Alex shrugged.

'You're right,' he said, 'I'm not a hero. But I don't like being pushed around. I told you my father was stubborn and bullies just made him more so. I'm a bit like that: heroic, no, but stubborn, oh yes.'

They stood in the street outside the bar breathing in the powerful odour of drains.

'How come they don't do something about that?' Alex said.

'Like what? Tear the city down? For centuries people have been building on top of buildings. Lots of the houses in the old city are medieval at street level but by the fifth floor you're in the early twentieth century. Some are built on Roman ruins, some even on Iron Age camps. Whenever they got a chance, people built another floor on top without really thinking about what was underneath. So now the drains can't cope. But you can't just go up to someone who's lived in one of these old houses all their life and say, "Terribly sorry, but we're going to tear your home down because there's an appalling smell of shit coming from underneath it."'

'This is another one of your allegories, isn't it?'

'Yes and no. It is literally true that that's how the city grew up, but I'm also trying to say that's how we live, on top of our past, layer upon layer. We can smell the shit, same as you, but we've got used to it. You have to if you want to live here. You say you want to get to the bottom of things, well, I'm telling you it's a long way down.'

It was around eleven thirty when Alex got back to the hotel. The hotel reception was unusually busy. There was Lluisa, looking tight-lipped, and fat Xavi, with his doggy eyes and shiny nose. And a young Japanese tourist Alex had bumped into once on the landing, and finally someone he'd not seen before: a slim, black-haired man, with sleek good looks, like a

105

Hollywood leading man from the fifties, a Mediterranean Clark Gable or Cary Grant. He looked at Alex, then at Xavi.

'This him?' he said. Xavi's head wobbled yes. The matinée idol produced a police badge from his pocket. He spoke in a gruff Barcelona accent, the words scrunched together, grumbling impatiently from the back of his throat like a crowd elbowing its way up out of a metro station.

'Alex Nadal,' he said. 'Hernández, Barcelona police. I'm arresting you on suspicion of theft.'

'Theft?' Alex said. 'Of what? Who from?'

He smiled at Luisa, looking for support, but she sniffed, pursed her lips and folded her arms self-righteously. The Japanese tourist managed to look upset, angry, remorseful, humiliated and embarrassed all at the same time.

'From this gentleman here,' Hernández said, consulting his notebook to make sure he got the name right. 'From Señor Asahi.'

16

The police station was on Via Laietana but it could have been anywhere. It had the same atmosphere of resignation and defeat of police stations everywhere, with a who-cares-anyway decor to match. Detective Hernández took him into an interview room and motioned Alex to a chair at a metal table. Hernández sat opposite at an ancient manual Underwood. The detective loaded a form into the machine banged the letters out one by one. It occurred to Alex that policemen must be the last people on Earth who still used typewriters.

'Your full name?'

'I want a lawyer.'

'This is not America, Señor Nadal. Though even there I'm sure a policeman is allowed to ask a person their name.'

Alex told him his name, then his occupation and finally his New York address.

'Mother's name?'

Alex sighed with irritation and said nothing. The detective sat with his fingers suspended over the keyboard, like a pianist poised to dive into the next movement. 'Mother's name?' he said again, without looking up. Alex sighed.

'Delfín,' he said. 'María Consuelo Delfín.'

'Is there any lawyer in particular you'd like me to call?' the detective said when the form was complete. Alex noted that he spoke in exactly the same tone of well-mannered hostility as a New York cop. Miguel wouldn't be at his office at this hour, so he gave him Carmen's mobile number and hoped she knew where to find her brother. Hernández wrote down the number and called out the door. A heavy-set, dark-skinned uniformed cop came in and took the detective's seat. Hernández left the room and the cop sat with his arms folded and his gaze fixed on a point somewhere above Alex's head. He didn't speak. An hour passed. Alex looked at the initials scratched into the metal table and wondered what drove people to make their mark in this way – on trees, in public toilets, in jail cells.

'This is all a stupid mistake,' Alex said.

The cop said nothing, as if no one had spoken. Another hour passed. Alex's boredom was fermenting into anger; he tried not to let it. The cop sat there like Buddha. Didn't say a word. Didn't read the paper. Didn't even smoke. Just sat.

'Do you think you could find out if my lawyer's on his way?' Alex said it nicely, trying hard to keep the irritation out of his voice. Nothing registered in the cop's face. Another thirty minutes passed. Alex was clenching up with rage.

'I suppose I'll just have to find out for myself,' he said. He stood up and took one step towards the door. The cop made two movements, blurred into one. The first brought him to his feet, the second delivered a straight left to the solar plexus. Alex crumpled to the floor. The tears swam up to his eyes and his bowels turned to water. He lay on the concrete with his knees pulled up to his chest and said to himself, 'Two things I forbid you to do, Alex Nadal: burst into tears or shit yourself. Anything else is permitted.' He lay there till his breathing was almost back to normal, got to his knees, then to his feet and then sat back in the chair. The cop was already back in his, impassive, as if nothing happened.

Half an hour later Hernández appeared with Miguel. Miguel was dressed in tight black trousers, a midnight-blue T-shirt made of some shiny fabric and a black leather bomber jacket. He asked for a few moments alone. The cops left the room.

'You look a bit green,' Miguel said.

'I got punched in the guts. But we'll let that pass.'

'I expect we will, we generally have to. So, I hear you've been robbing Japanese tourists.'

'I haven't stolen a thing. It's either a mistake or I've been fitted up.'

'That's what they all say.'

'You don't believe me?'

'Of course, I do. It's my job to believe my clients. That's what they buy – my credulity.'

'I'm sorry to drag you out in the middle of the night. And I will pay you, cash, not cocktails.'

'It's not the middle of the night, it's only two a.m. I was in a club in Gràcia, having a nice time with a nice man, or nice looking at least. The music was too loud to find out what he had between his ears, but then I didn't go there to discuss European monetary union. Carmen found me and made me leave, she said she was worried about you. Heaven knows, we're all worried about you. Isn't that touching?'

Alex rubbed his sore abdomen.

'Don't think I don't appreciate it. What's the situation here? It seems like some stupid joke?'

'Joke? Does Detective Hernández strike you as a practical joker. The situation here, as you put it, is that certain items of value disappeared from your Japanese friend's room and reappeared in your room. Now that in itself doesn't prove you stole them, so naturally they'll want your prints.'

'Fine. I'm not the thief and I've never touched any of the Japanese guy's things, so they won't find my prints on his stuff.'

'Quite. But they've thought of that and they've got some insurance.'

'Insurance?'

'Yes, the concierge's son, a boy called Xavi. He says he

confronted you outside the victim's room and asked you what you were doing.'

'I caught him hanging around outside my room this afternoon. I asked him what he wanted but he just slunk off.'

'His version is a little different. He says you told him to get lost and when he said he was calling the cops you said, "Go ahead, see if I care." Your precise words, according to his statement, were, "Sure, that really makes my dick droop."'

'I said what?'

'It's a Catalan expression, a macho way of telling someone you're not scared of them.'

'He said I said that, fat Xavi? He said he was calling the cops and I said, "That really makes my dick droop"? In Catalan? I don't speak Catalan, Miguel. Case closed.'

'I thought of that, but they could always say he'd only put it like that because he gave his testimony in Catalan, which is his right, and he was translating what you had said in Castilian. Of course in Castilian you wouldn't say, "That makes my dick droop," you'd say, "Oh yeah, my dick's really sweating now." Very sarcastically. It's real *chulo* talk, you know, mouthy little tough guy, doesn't take any shit from anyone. You threaten him and he juts out his chin and says, "Oh yeah, my dick's really sweating now."'

'This is all very edifying. But I wouldn't say that either, I've never heard that expression.'

'You have now, and it's your word against his.'

Hernández came in and said he wanted a word with Miguel. Through the open door Alex caught a glimpse of someone familiar. It was the man with the sad fish-eyes. The silent cop with the big punch came back to keep an eye on him. Alex imagined him at home, parked in front of a kung-fu movie while his wife worked her way through a puzzle magazine. Miguel returned five minutes later.

'There's been a slight change in the weather,' he said.

'You mean they realize they don't have a case.'

'I don't think they care. I get the impression from Hernández that he doesn't feel he has to care. But I don't think he wants this to go before a judge.'

'What then?'

'He's changed tack. When I arrived it was all routine, Hernández was doing what cops do, putting one foot after the other until the shift ends. Now suddenly he wants to make a deal.'

'Did you see that guy out there, very tall, with funny eyes?'

'Yes, he was talking to the detective. Why?'

'It's the man who paged me at the airport and followed me to the hotel, I'm sure of it. And I've just realized why he did that, why he had me paged: he knew I was on the plane but he didn't know what I looked like. Why else? I'm sure he's the reason Hernández is having a change of heart. So what's the deal?'

'The deal is they hand you over to immigration. You get the picture? That way you don't go to court, you just get deported. That appears to be the object of this whole exercise. Ever get the feeling you're in somebody's way?'

17

Alex told Miguel he wasn't prepared to negotiate. He said if they had a case, they should charge him. So at around half past three in the morning Hernández took his prints and his passport and let him go on condition that he signed on at the station the next day at seven p.m. Miguel offered him his sofa for what was left of the night and they caught a cab uptown to his place, a grand flat in the Eixample. Alex was prepared for a camp palace of lava lamps and pink velvet drapes, but the flat was very plain. Some family photos hung on one wall, including one of Carmen as a small child and another as a teenager. Alex studied them.

'You've taken a bit of a shine to my sister Carmen, haven't you?' Miguel said, appearing with a quilt and a pillow under his arm.

'I don't know her,' Alex demurred, using the same line Carmen had used on him.

The flats looked on to a large central courtyard planted with palms, canna, oleander and hibiscus. Miguel went to bed but Alex was too hyped up to sleep. He sat on the balcony and watched the light come up over the palms. His stomach still ached where the cop had hit him. At seven o'clock he scribbled a note for Miguel and left to find another hotel.

Exhausted but wide awake on adrenaline, he walked down Pau Claris as Barcelona banged and shouted its way into a new day. Was there a noisier people on Earth? Too bad for anyone who wanted a lie-in; the attitude seemed to be, I'm up so you can get up too. Little two-stroke bikes were kicked screaming into life then revved up like angry wasps; steel storefront roller shutters were thrown open with a crash that made Alex jump; and people shouted across the street or up to third-storey flats, clearing their lungs for another day of high-octane talk. Alex was hungry; he didn't remember the last time he ate. He stood at a bar and ate a huge plate of *churros* washed down with coffee. The other men at the bar drank coffee laced with anis or cognac and talked in brief phrases, harsh and guttural like Hernández, like bursts of gunfire. Alex staggered back into the street under the onslaught of fat, sugar and caffeine. He found another hotel around the corner in Argentería and went to Princesa to collect his things. They were packed and waiting in reception in the care of a disdainful Lluisa, now more Mother Superior than rumba queen. He made a big show of going through his cases to make sure nothing was missing. Lluisa presented him with the bill. They didn't speak. He paid, ostentatiously checked his change, and left.

In his new room there was no sacred heart of Jesus, just an amateurish gouache of Port Lligat, the Costa Brava fishing village where Dalí lived. The shower was a fat dribble, like a bad roof leak, but the street was quieter than Princesa.

He was outside the civil government building half an hour before it opened but a dozen others were there first. Never mind, he thought, a dozen shouldn't take more than an hour. He had the photos, the form was filled in, and he armed himself with *El Mensajero* to pass the time. He read Carmen's Lorca review twice and looked at her byline and said her name aloud. By the time he got to the sports pages he was at the front of the queue. There was a different woman behind the desk, not Olive Oyl. She cut up the strip of photographs and stapled them to the various duplicates of the form. Alex repressed a small surge of optimism.

'There's a fee of ninety pesetas,' she said.

He stuck his hand in his pocket and pulled out some change.

'You can't pay here,' she said.

His heart sank. These people have a way, he thought, of crushing you completely. So politely inflexible. Arguing with them was like beating a jelly with a stick.

'You have to buy a token and then bring it here,' she continued, gesturing in the general direction of the outside world. 'You can get them at the Banco d'España or Banco de l'Argentería.'

Ninety pesetas? He had to go to a bank to get a chit for ninety pesetas? Ninety pesetas was nothing, the price of a loaf of bread. Alex looked at the woman and then turned to the people behind him in the queue. The ones further back looked blank or impatient, those next in line made sympathetic gestures. They could afford to; they could see he'd hit a brick wall and in a moment it would be their turn. Alex picked up his papers and left. After half an hour he found a suitable bank and paid ninety pesetas for what looked like a cloakroom ticket and went back to the civil government office. The *non-comunitarios* were there in numbers. He didn't go to the back of the queue but went straight up to the desk. A small, middle-aged man was showing the woman some documents. Alex pushed in front and put his papers and the ninety-peseta chit on the counter.

'I'm sorry,' he said to the man. 'Believe me, this is totally out of character.'

There was some grumbling and comments from the people behind him but the man himself was so startled he gestured to Alex to go ahead. The woman went through his papers again, as though it was the first time she'd seen them.

'Where is this?' she said, pointing to the section where he'd filled in his address.

'It's in New York City, not far from the Williamsburg Bridge. They say the area's up and coming.'

'You can't put this,' she said. 'You must have an address in Spain.'

'On a certificate of non-residence?'

'Yes. We cannot accept an address in a foreign country.'

'Even though the point of this form is to certify that I don't live here?'

'That's correct.'

Alex took the form from her, crossed out the New York address and wrote Can Castanyer, Sant Martí dels Moixones, Provincia de Tarragona. The woman studied the form again.

'That's fine,' she said. 'We'll send the certificate to this address. It normally takes about three months.'

'Really? So soon?'

Alex almost skipped back to the hotel. For the first time since he arrived he felt like he'd achieved something, however paltry. There was a message for him to call Ferran Llull at the land registry. He had to say the name three times before they understood; evidently he needed to work on his double ls.

'You have my book, my work,' Llull said, with genuine distress. 'You have no right to read it.'

'I haven't read it. OK, I read enough to see it's in Catalan, which I can barely understand. Don't worry, your work is my hostage, but it's safe with me. Found anything out?'

Llull said his boss Busquets had phoned in sick and yes, he had some information about Can Castanyer. They arranged to meet at lunchtime in a bar near Llull's office in Urquinaona. Better and better, Alex thought. First I take on the state and win, now I'm a successful hostage-taker. Morín was next on his list.

At quarter to ten he was in Ciutadella Park looking for an old man in a brown Homburg. He didn't see him. He positioned himself at what seemed a vantage point beside the vast fountain with its rampant griffins and heroic statues. Like the absurd Columbus monument, or Mercè poised to fly off from her dome, this attempt at grandeur had come out as high camp. The fountain in Ciutadella wouldn't have looked out of place in the grounds of the mansion of some millionaire

115

Hollywood drag queen. Alex loved it. Then he saw him, shuffling along beside the duck pond. He walked with the slow measured step of someone who's followed the same route a thousand times. He rounded the little boating pond and was walking straight at Alex when he turned to his left. He went up to the small drinks kiosk that stood in the thin shade of a laburnum. Alex could see from the way the woman in the kiosk greeted him that this, too, was part of the daily routine. She put a glass of coffee on the bar. He left it there to cool and turned to face the fountain.

He was a shrunken little man with a small head, made smaller by the hat and a large pair of rectangular seventies-style amber-tinted glasses, like a couple of televisions framing his face. Alex was excited; here was his quarry, the man his father said had saved and ruined his life. He went over to the kiosk and ordered a *cortado*, then changed his mind, he'd had enough coffee and his mouth was dry. He asked for a beer instead and turned to Morín. Alex was of average height but a foot taller than the old man.

'Lovely morning,' he said.

Morín looked up at him and nodded, more it seemed in recognition that Alex had spoken than at what he said. His glasses were thick, his eyes milky blurs magnified by the strong lenses. Alex sipped his beer.

'I was hoping you might be able to help me with something,' he said, offering his hand. 'My name's Nadal, Alex Nadal.'

'*Bon Nadal*,' Morín said, a bit nonplussed, and apparently unaware of the outstretched hand.

Nadal is Catalan for Christmas. The old man was wishing him a happy Christmas. Alex chuckled, going along with the joke. He hadn't thought this through, hadn't thought of how he might work his way round to the subject, so he waded right in.

'I believe you knew my father long ago. I wonder if we could talk about those times.'

Morín said nothing, but his face took on a look of concentration, as though he was processing this information.

116

'Marta has gone to the market to buy mushrooms,' he said to no one in particular. 'The *rovellós* are in season.'

His face lit up and he clapped his hands together. Alex tried another tack.

'Perhaps you don't recall my father. I realize it was a long time ago. Maybe you remember the village, Sant Martí dels Moixones. I believe you were in command when the village fell in the Civil War.'

Morín stirred two lumps of sugar in to his coffee and drank it down in one slow swallow, sucking the sugary dregs through his teeth. He looked at Alex.

'Marta fries them in oil, very hot, whole, not sliced. With a sprinkling of thyme.'

Alex caught the eye of the kiosk woman. She had a hook nose and lonesome eyes and a skein of dyed black hair pinned up in a loose chignon. Behind the old man's back she tapped her temple with a finger and rolled her eyes. Morín adjusted his Homburg, touched the brim, and walked off towards the bandstand.

'Marta died ten years ago,' she said when he was out of earshot. 'It's like he died too, poor soul, only he went on living. It's all he talks about, Marta this and Marta that, as if talking could keep her alive.'

Alex sighed. The adrenaline abruptly stopped pumping and he felt dizzy with exhaustion. He watched the old man shamble off in the direction of el Born, paid for the drink and turned to go.

'You could try talking to Raul, his son,' the woman said. 'He's a mechanic. He has a garage in Poblenou, near the swimming pool. I'm not saying he'll talk to you but at least he's playing with a full deck.'

18

Ferran Llull was already there when Alex arrived, hunched over a beer, looking miserable. Alex took a stool next to him and set the journal down on the bar where Llull could see but not reach it. The look on the poet's face was a mixture of relief and panic. He stroked his pencil moustache with the tip of his index finger. Alex ordered a beer and looked at the stuff on the shelf above the bar; he was becoming a bit of an aficionado of bar bric-à-brac. This one had the obligatory team photo of el Barça, a flamenco doll, a black china poodle, a royal wedding pennant and a fox, stuffed and mounted and wrapped in sulphur-yellow Cellophane.

'Why would you wrap a fox in Cellophane,' he wondered aloud.

Llull looked up at the shelf.

'The yellow filters out the UV light, stops things fading,' he said, as though displaying a fox wrapped in yellow Cellophane was the most natural thing in the world.

'So, what have you got for me?' Alex said.

Llull looked around to see who was in earshot but the radio was playing loud flamenco pop so it was unlikely anyone could hear.

'Señor Busquets is still off sick, supposedly something to do with his nerves. But I found the file in his office. This farm you say is yours is, or was, on the point of becoming state property, because the owner was presumed to have died without heirs.'

That would explain why Victor found a surveyor from the Generalitat on the land.

'So they made a mistake. Why all the secrecy?'

'I'm not sure. I mean, there's nothing that unusual about it, although not that many people with anything worth leaving die without making a will. But if they do, there's a procedure, normally a very slow procedure, because every effort must be made to trace any possible heirs. Not in your case, however. This has been a bit of a rush job, a lot of corners have been cut. Nothing technically illegal, but definitely not by the book. Also, the village isn't in our domain, it's in the province of Tarragona and normally that's where it would be dealt with, but for some reason all the paperwork was moved here to Barcelona.'

'Is that all?'

'Not quite. A tract of land adjoining yours was sold recently. It was owned by someone called Sabadell. Provisional planning permission has been granted to develop the land.'

Alex remembered the field he could see from his terrace that had been left to go wild.

'To develop it? As what? I thought there was supposed to be a blanket ban.'

'There is, but the application is to build a school. Educational establishments are exempt.'

The flamenco came to an end and the radio segued incongruously into Dinah Washington singing 'Mad About the Boy'.

'There's more,' Llull said, eyeing his journal anxiously. 'The same people who bought Sabadell's land have filed an option on your farm.'

'That's a lot of land for a village school. Any idea who's behind this?'

'A company called Mallobeco. They're pretty big around here. That's all I know. They haven't filed any plans, which is unusual, just the application. Normally you wouldn't get even provisional permission without submitting detailed plans. I find it hard to believe that plans don't exist, but there aren't any copies in the file. That's all I could find out.'

Alex handed him the notebook.

'Ever get any of these published?'

Llull clutched the book and eyed him with suspicion.

'A few, in magazines,' he said with the faintest of blushes. 'But I won a prize at the Jocs Florals. It's a poetry competition held here every year. Quite prestigious.'

Alex nodded by way of congratulation. Two or three minutes passed. Behind them a fruit machine beeped and whirred. The radio station, which apparently ran a random-selection playlist, played Talking Heads' 'Psycho Killer'. Llull slipped off the bar stool and put his hand in his pocket.

'I'll pay,' Alex said. 'Look, I'm sorry I had to do this, really I am. Come on, let me buy you another beer, just to make amends.'

'No thanks,' he said, but stayed standing by the stool.

'So, do you plan to sell?' he said after a while.

'No,' Alex snapped. 'I'm sorry, I'm very tired. What I mean is no, not in the immediate future.'

'I'm sorry, I didn't mean to presume. It's just you don't strike me as the farming type.'

'I'm not, I'm a musician, a pianist. Jazz, mostly.'

'Looks like it's a bit of a poisoned chalice, this inheritance of yours. I don't suppose these Mallobeco people will be too pleased if you refuse to sell.'

'I've never really understood what that means, a poisoned chalice.'

'It's from Shakespeare, *Macbeth*. It means something that's good or a privilege but dangerous too. Like if some mad dictator appoints you as his prime minister. Or like walking the lions.'

'Like what?'

'It's nothing,' Llull said, turning away. He left the bar without another word.

'Hey, wait,' Alex called after him. He left some money on the bar and hurried out to the street. Llull was a fast walker and Alex had to break into a jog to catch up with him as he strode down Carrer de les Jonqueres, a street dedicated to the bedroom – every shop along its length sold mattresses and sheets and pillows and beds. Llull hurried along, wrapping his arms around the journal which he clutched to his chest.

'What lions?' Alex said.

'It doesn't matter.'

'I think it does. Tell me about the lions.'

'It's just a story my mother told me,' Llull said, striding along, eyes front. 'She's descended from *conversos*, do you know what they are?'

Alex put a hand on his shoulder and Llull stopped and turned to him.

'*Conversos* are Jews who were forced to convert. After 1492 even most of the *conversos* were kicked out of the country but my mother's people managed to stay. Some of the greatest figures of Spanish history are the descendants of *conversos*, even King Ferdinand, who ordered the expulsion, and, so they say, Torquemada, the Grand Inquisitor. So was Saint Teresa of Ávila, patron saint of Spain. Not surprisingly, the idea that the champions of Catholic Spain were Jewish retreads doesn't sit too well with the received wisdom, which is a pack of lies, of course.'

'So I gather,' Alex said, fearing another history lesson. 'Tell me about the lions.'

'Well, up until the end of the fourteenth century, which was when the real persecution started, the Jews were protected by the king, and they paid for this protection by paying higher taxes than the Christians. So as long as the king liked money more than he hated Jews, the Jews were more or less allowed to get on with their lives in peace. Then King Jaume the Conqueror had a problem with his lions. People kept bringing lions back from Africa as presents to impress the king and the poor beasts were kept cooped up in cages in Plaça del Rei. So Jaume decreed that one of the special duties of Barcelona Jews was that each day some of their number had to walk his lions. Now that's what I call a poisoned chalice. In those days riff-raff weren't allowed to set foot in the Plaça del Rei, so in that respect the Jews were privileged. Plus it was a service to the king, which was in itself an honour. But walking the lions, even the king's lions, well, that's not much of a career.'

Alex thought about this for a while.

'And you think that's the situation I'm in?' he said.

'I know nothing about your situation, Señor Nadal, I'm just telling you a story.'

Alex went back to the hotel. He didn't look to see if he was being followed and he didn't bother to check if the junkie was hanging around outside. He didn't care, he just wanted to sleep. He lay down on the bed but his brain wouldn't shut up. It didn't make any sense. Why would anyone go to such lengths to build a village school? Was it possible that his Aunt Anna had been murdered because it was believed she hadn't made a will and so the land would revert to the state? But to build a school? It was crazy. Alex assumed that Mallobeco was the mystery buyer who hired Montserrat Cases to badger him into a sale, which made her next on his list.

The address Miguel gave him was on the Carrer de Mallorca, close to Gaudí's Sagrada Família. Alex was too hot and too tired to walk, so he took the metro, which was air conditioned. It reminded him of New York, one moment slumped on a sweaty platform, the next freezing on an overcooled train. He picked up a copy of *El Periódico* that was lying on the seat. On page one there was a picture of the Infanta Cristina leaving her flat. She looked like an ordinary young prettyish blonde, dressed in a polo shirt and jeans. The papers seemed to play on this angle, that she was just like anyone else, as though this was supposed to endear people to her. Alex didn't get it: what was the point of being a princess? Anyone could be ordinary; B-list Hollywood stars looked more like princesses than the Infanta did.

A small black plaque next to the bell read: M. Cases, Advocat. Alex rang the bell and waited. After three more rings a woman's voice said: 'I'm sorry the office is closed until tomorrow.' He rang twice more. When she picked up the intercom he said: 'Alex Nadal to see Señora Cases.' There was a pause and then the woman repeated: 'I'm sorry, we're closed.' He rang twice more but got no answer. He was about to give up when a skinny boy arrived on a moped with a delivery of pizza.

'Thank God,' Alex said. 'I've been ringing for ages. It's my father, he's practically deaf. I know he's sitting up there with Verdi or Rossini on full blast. He'll never hear me unless I manage to catch him between arias.'

Someone buzzed the pizza boy in and Alex followed him. He took the lift to the third floor and rang the bell until she answered the door. Montserrat Cases stood in the doorway without any make-up, dressed in a faded pair of loose trousers of the sort you might wear to the beach and a beige blouse. There was a fresh stain on one shoulder of the blouse. She looked exhausted and harassed.

'As you can see,' she said. 'The office is closed. Phone tomorrow for an appointment if you wish.'

'Who is your client?' he said, sounding more aggressive than he intended.

'You know I can't tell you that. Now please go, I really can't see you now.'

'Is it a company called Mallobeco?'

He couldn't read her reaction because just as he said it there was a strange cry, more of a gurgle, from the next room, followed by the sound of a china plate or cup smashing to the floor. Cases took a step back towards the direction of the noise. She was so tense her movements were robotic.

'Please, you really must go.' She took another step back. Alex followed her across the room.

'Just tell me: Mallobeco, yes or no.'

There was another gurgling cry from the next room. Cases had her hand on the handle. She had a look of desperation about her, unrecognizable from the cool businesswoman in the violet suit who approached him in Barceloneta. There was another, louder cry and she turned and went into the next room. Alex followed her. He knew he shouldn't, he knew he was intruding, that it was none of his business, but he followed her anyway, into a living room crowded with dark, heavy pieces of old-fashioned furniture. A man in his early fifties, though it was hard to be certain, was propped up in a vinyl covered armchair. He had uncontrollable tremors in his hands and feet and every few moments his head jerked back in a semi-circle as he shouted something unintelligible. Bits of food stuck to his hair and clothes. The room had the dirty dishcloth and urine odour of long-term illness. Cases picked up the broken plate and put one hand on the man's shoulder.

'Pascal, this is Señor Nadal from New York. You must excuse us, Señor Nadal, my husband and I were just having lunch.'

The look she gave him was humiliated and humiliating; her eyes stung with hatred, hatred of her life and hatred of him for witnessing it. But there was no sarcasm in her voice, not a trace, and that made it worse. Never in his life had he felt so diminished. Now he knew what he saw in her that afternoon by the sea, the thing he thought was regret. He backed out of the room.

'I'm so sorry, so sorry,' he mumbled.

'Never mind, Señor Nadal,' she said. 'Some other time perhaps. You could make an appointment.'

Again her tone was polite and controlled, without nuance; the voice of someone so close to the edge they know if they let go for even one second they'll fall and never stop falling. As he turned to leave she called out to him.

'Señor Nadal, just for the record, I was not hired by Mallobeco. The truth is I was never allowed to know the identity of my client. I dealt with a go-between, an American. That's all I can tell you.'

Alex nodded his thanks and left. He went into the first bar he came to and ordered a cognac.

'You look like you've seen a ghost,' the barman said.

Alex drank the cognac down in one and asked for another.

*

124

When he presented himself at the police station at seven o'clock he was physically and emotionally drained and somewhere between a half and three-quarters drunk. Detective Hernández was waiting for him. He put Alex's passport on the desk and pushed a form and a pen towards Alex.

'What's this?' Alex said.

'The Jap dropped the charges.'

Whatever Hernández felt about this, he wasn't showing it. He wasn't showing anything. Alex signed and pocketed the passport.

'You took my prints,' he said. 'I want them back, seeing as I'm not charged with anything.'

'That won't be possible right now. A security alert is in force until after the royal wedding. Naturally we are keeping a close watch on all visitors to the city.'

'Do I look like an assassin?'

'You tell me, Señor Nadal. If you could tell what people are simply by looking at them, I'd be out of a job.'

As he left he saw the junkie in the leather jacket across the street. He was talking to a thin young woman with chestnut hair. Alex went over to them. The woman was small and pale with a pointed face and angry amber eyes. She had a junkie look about her too. She looked oddly familiar, but that was probably just the drink. The junkie adopted a tough-but-casual pose.

'I'm moving out to the country,' Alex said. 'So you won't have to follow me around any more. I hope I haven't put you out of a job. Pop by any time you fancy it. We could go out dancing some night. Do you rumba?'

'You better watch yourself,' the junkie said.

Alex clasped his head in his hands in mock horror.

'Oh my God,' he said in a loud whisper. 'My dick's really sweating.'

'What was that all about, Kiko?' Núria said after Alex had gone.

'Nothing,' Kiko said. 'Just someone I'm keeping an eye on.'

19

Guillermo Morín's mind was gone but the information of a lifetime was still there, it just didn't make sense any more. It was as though he'd been rewired by an amateur; the power was on but the connections were wrong and the circuits incomplete. So when he met Alex in the park he did know what he was talking about, he did know who Alex was, only it wasn't Alex he saw but Alex's father, Ignasi. He thought he'd seen a ghost and he believed his time had come. He mouth tasted of earth and he could smell his own breath. He thought he was dying. He was sure of it when the priest called that evening. Except it wasn't a priest, it was his son Raul, the car mechanic.

Sometimes he knew his son and sometimes he didn't. Raul was wearing a white T-shirt under black overalls and what Morín saw was a priest. He must be dying – why else would a priest come to the house? Raul came every night, either him or one of his sisters – his brother had washed his hands of the old man – to make sure his father was clean and to put him to bed. They paid a woman to clean the little flat on el Born and cook his lunch. But he was deteriorating. It began when their mother died and got worse when Morín was forced out of his home in Poblenou, so that it could be torn down to make way for the

Olympic village. Every week he got worse, not dramatically, and some weeks he even seemed to have improved, but Raul knew it was a one-way street. The time would come when they'd have to put him in a home; how they'd pay for it was another matter.

When he arrived his father was agitated, pacing the room and talking to himself. He hardly seemed to notice his son. That was fairly normal. Then the old man started rummaging in the sideboard and pulled out what looked like a handwritten manuscript which he rolled up and used to hit himself repeatedly on the side of the head. Raul didn't try to stop him, he was used to this and his father wasn't going to come to any harm beating himself up with a roll of papers. After a few minutes he calmed down and stood quietly in the middle of the room. That was normal, too, the sudden change of mood.

There was an old folding screen in the corner of the room which was never used except for drying sheets. Morín dragged the screen into the middle of the room and then put two chairs, one on either side of it. He looked at his son then bowed his head.

'Father, I want you to hear my confession,' he said, and then sat down behind the screen with the manuscript on his lap.

For a moment Raul didn't move. When his father first started going off the rails he resisted it and tried to argue some sense into him, as though he was still rational. But after a while it was plain that he might as well play along, and now wherever his father's mind wandered he tried to follow. It was a game, a sad, crazy game. So now he was a priest. He sat on the other side of the screen and waited.

'I'm not long for this world, Father,' his father said.

Even as his mind fell apart, whole traits of his character remained intact, like veins of minerals through crumbling rock. He always was a hypochondriac, every little twinge the harbinger of some terminal illness. Now he said he was dying. Raul humoured him.

'Then you must make a full confession, my son,' he said, getting into character. 'God is merciful.'

There was a pause of several minutes and then he began. 'Father, I have sinned.'

What followed was a lucid though haphazard confession of a lifetime of minor transgressions, spoken in a monotone, as though he'd rehearsed it a hundred times. Most of it was a catalogue of small frailties: unkindness, pride, an unwillingness to forgive, some small acts of dishonesty, a couple of flights of sexual fancy grounded by guilt before they got anywhere near the runway. Then he started talking about the Civil War, about firing squads and summary executions, about torture, about people taken at random and hanged or shot to set an example. He said all this in the same toneless voice, as if he was saying the rosary. Raul listened, fascinated and appalled. Then his father told him a terrible story, so terrible Raul could hardly bear to listen.

20

Carmen had a recurring dream that she was hit by a car and lay dying on a wet road. The road wasn't in Barcelona but some northern city, Paris perhaps, or London; in any case, a long way from home. She knew she was dying because everything was cold except the blood trickling from her ear. Her last thought was, 'What a shitty way to die,' and the last thing she was conscious of was the faraway sound of an ambulance siren, so far away it could never get to her in time. She always woke up before it arrived.

She stood outside the anonymous box of boxes in Sants where Fèlix Grau was found hanging from his belt. It wasn't much of a place to die. She wondered if that mattered, if at that moment of realization, when you know for certain this really is the end, it made any difference where you were or if anyone else was there with you. She imagined it did.

As there was no reception at the hotel, and no staff, there was no one to ask if they remembered anything about the night Fèlix died. There didn't seem to be anyone around at all and she couldn't even tell if the hotel had any guests. But there was a CCTV camera covering the check-in point where patrons inserted their credit cards. She assumed that, as the camera was probably the last thing to see Fèlix alive, even the laziest detective would have watched the tape of the night in question, but she wanted to see it for herself, which was where having a cop in the family came in handy. Her cousin Eduardo was a low-ranking detective in the drug squad. He had two major weaknesses – women in general and Carmen in particular. Eduardo had had a crush on her since childhood and, though she found it tiresome, her cousin's desire to please her had proved useful on a number of occasions when she needed some inside dope for a story. If he got too amorous, she said: 'Come on, Eduardo, we're first cousins, we'll burn in hell.' To which he invariably replied to the effect: 'I know, but what's eternal damnation compared to a night of pure passion?' The game was a little played out but it seemed to keep him amused.

Eduardo walked her through the drug squad's big open plan office. He liked to show off his gorgeous cousin, as he called her. Carmen felt like a trophy but she played along and rolled her eyes as if to say, 'What a dickhead of a cousin I've got', and they all loved her for it. Eduardo led her into a side office and shut the door. He took a video out of an evidence bag and pushed it into the machine.

'This is unofficial and strictly off the record,' he said, wagging a finger at Carmen.

'Of course. It never happened, I was never here.'

'Business was pretty slack that day and most of the tape is of the empty terrace outside the hotel, so we don't need to watch that.'

He fast forwarded until he hit a marker and pressed play. The tape showed Fèlix Grau approaching the building. He took a credit card out of his wallet and put it in the machine. Carmen hadn't anticipated how much it would upset her, seeing him like that, doing something so ordinary, on the very day he died. Eduardo froze the tape. On Fèlix's right there was a blur.

'What's that? It looks like someone's arm.'

Eduardo sighed and gave her a long look, a real cop's look.

'Before we go any further, Carmen, let me remind you of something: the case is closed. There is no case and never was.

Death by misadventure, the coroner said. No suspicious circumstances, no investigation. Do you hear me?'

'Loud and clear.'

He rewound for about fifteen seconds and pressed play. Once again Fèlix was approaching the hotel, but this was earlier in the sequence and this time he wasn't alone. He was with another man, a tall man in a white short-sleeved shirt. The tall man walked with a slight stoop, so the camera caught the top of his head and his thinning hair. The pair of them stopped and then turned away, as though they were having second thoughts. Then the tall man tugged on Fèlix's elbow and they turned back towards the hotel. The tall man glanced to his left and for a second his face was visible in half-profile.

'Pause it there,' Carmen said.

Eduardo rewound the tape, played it up to the profile shot and froze it. Carmen put her face up to the TV but the features blurred in close-up. She turned to look at her cousin.

'They did a video-grab and had it blown up but you couldn't ID anyone from it, it could be thousands of guys.'

'But you and I don't think it's thousands of guys, do we? We think it looks strikingly like one guy in particular, yes?'

'You think you know who it is, but I'm telling you that as an ID it's useless. Now you've seen the tape and so you know everything I know, which is nothing.'

Carmen left Eduardo and hurried down Carrer d'Avinyó to see if she could catch Francesc before he finished lunch. Francesc was a friend from her schooldays who was also briefly her brother Miguel's lover. He worked for the environment department of the Generalitat de Catalunya. His boss was the media-friendly Oscar Puig, who Blanca had implicated in Fèlix's supposed murder. Francesc lived for food and gossip and he knew a lot about who doing what in Barcelona. He was at his usual table in Pitarra, an old restaurant in Avinyó that had once been a theatre, his face in a book, with an espresso and a cognac on the table. He gave Carmen a big smile. They kissed and she sat down.

'What are you reading?' she said.

131

'*The Theory and Practice of Tomato Bread* by the venerable Leopold Pomés. Would you believe someone could write a whole book on the subject of rubbing tomato, oil and salt into bread?'

'Let alone read it,' Carmen said, calling to a waiter to bring her a *café con leche*.

Francesc was obsessed with food and cooking. He read cookbooks from cover to cover. He drooled over catalogues of kitchen equipment the way other men looked at pornography and an array of stainless steel whisks and bain-maries in a kitchen supplier's sent him into a swoon. The last time Carmen saw him he was engrossed in a fat volume called *The Story of Rice*.

'You seem to be glowing several watts above your usual output,' Francesc said, his eyebrows climbing up almost to his hairline. 'Are you in love?'

Carmen laughed a don't-be-so-silly laugh but she could feel herself colouring up. Francesc was practically her oldest friend. She told him about Alex and said she found him amusing.

'Amusing is good. What's he look like?'

'Nice, you know, not drop-dead gorgeous or anything.'

'Nice? How eloquent,' Francesc said archly. 'Could we have a little more information? Is he tall, thin, short, fat, bald?'

'Tallish. For here, anyway, but he's not some American giant. Slim but not skinny.'

'Something to grab hold of then. Hair?'

'Short, dark brown. A little grey at the temples.'

'Skin?'

'Darker than yours, lighter than mine.'

'Eyes?'

'Nice eyes. Greenish, like olives.'

'Green?'

'Well, brownish-green, the colour of those little olives you get in Tarragona.'

'Arbequines.'

'Those. But he has a strange way of looking at you sometimes. He makes you feel, I don't know, judged somehow. But maybe that's just how he looks. He's a musician and I haven't met one yet who wasn't basically weird.'

She said she'd been thinking of doing a little human interest story for the Saturday paper on his homecoming, something along the lines of, 'From Manhattan to Sant Martí dels Moixones', except his homecoming wasn't working out too well.

'There's that name again,' Francesc said. 'Sant Martí. I keep hearing it. Down by Torredembarra, right? Do you believe in coincidence?'

'I was brought up to believe in the immaculate conception and papal infallibility, same as you. No one mentioned coincidence. Why?'

'I don't know, nothing that specific. But you get a feel for it after a while, especially since the Olympics. It's the sound of backs being scratched. The last time I got that feeling was just before they did the deal to build that so-called shopping village outside Terrassa. I can't believe they got away with it. It's incredible really. For centuries we struggle for national self-determination, we fight to keep our language alive, we brag that the Catalan flag is the oldest in Europe, that we had a bill of rights centuries before anyone else, and then what do we do? We turn the place into some kind of American suburb. Is that what it was for? So some fat-faced kid in a baseball cap can stuff his face with a four seasons in a Pizza Hut in Granollers?'

'But the great thing is now he can order it in Catalan.'

'Very funny, Carmen. Look what's happening to Barcelona, every time you go out there's another McDonald's. Don't you hate that? My grandfather would have firebombed them, but no one's got the balls anymore.'

'Easy now, Francesc, you know I hate all that stuff too. Tell me about Sant Martí.'

'This all happened a few months ago. Like I say, it's just a feeling. Like the head of planning asking for detailed maps of the Sant Martí area. Nothing unusual in that. But then a while later you hear that the parliamentary deputy from down there is up in Barcelona and is getting the full champagne and lobster treatment from the department. Then I hear my boss Puig and the head of planning having a huge row and when I go into the office, after the planning boss has stormed out, there's the Sant Martí maps on the desk. See what I mean? Little things. Then a guy pays Puig a visit and after he's gone the quarrel with the head of planning is patched up just like that and they go out for a four-hour lunch.'

'What guy?'

'You ever come across someone called Angel Domènech?'

'Rings a bell,' Carmen said, as offhand as possible. She hadn't told anyone, not even Miguel, about her trysts down by the marina. Not that she felt ashamed, it just wasn't something she wanted to shout about.

'Domènech's what you'd call a fixer. Pretty shifty guy, but he comes from an old Catalan family, so he's got that cachet. All the big shots know him, and the older ones knew his dad before him. Domènech knows people and he knows about people. If you've got a mole on your arse he'll know. And he'll know who else knows you've got one, and whether they're supposed to know. You follow?'

Carmen had a mole on her right breast which Angel found curiously exciting.

'You're saying Oscar Puig was upset about something to do with Sant Martí until he received a visit from this Domènech and suddenly he realized he wasn't nearly as upset as he imagined?'

'Something like that. Now I've got to go.'

'I'll walk with you.'

She took his arm and they walked along Avinyó. Two girls in black with shaved heads sat on the steps of the School of Fine Art smoking a joint. The aroma of grass wafted along the street along with the smell of someone slow cooking onions and tomatoes for a *sofregit*.

'The aroma of Catalunya,' Francesc said reverently.

'What? Marijuana?'

'No, the simple *sofregit*. And yet, can you imagine, we'd

134

never heard of a tomato until the conquistadors brought them back from America. Imagine Mediterranean cuisine without the tomato. Or peppers and potatoes, for that matter. Anyway, what can I do for you? I know you only come to see me because you want something,' he sniffed in a show of faux martyrdom. Carmen squeezed his arm.

'A couple of things. Does the name Roger de Flor mean anything to you?'

'Medieval adventurer. The man who subdued . . .'

'I know the history, I mean now. I don't know what, maybe as the codename for something.'

'No, nothing, I'm afraid. Next question.'

'OK, what do you know about a company called Mallobeco?'

'Developers, mostly hotels, blocks of flats. Functional stuff, nothing that's going to win any architectural prizes. They did well out of the Olympics, of course, but what developer didn't? Will you be going to the wedding?'

'What wedding?'

'My dear, there's only one.'

'Am I invited? Of course not, I'm much too far down the food chain.'

'Sweetheart, I never imagined you were invited. By "going" I meant along the route, waving a handkerchief and hoping to catch her bouquet.'

'Only if the paper pays me to. One last thing, Francesc. Do you know anything about Oscar Puig's sex life? I mean, any rumours?'

'This is my boss you're talking about, Carmen. Oscar Puig is a married man. He has a devoted wife and three lovely children. He attends Mass at least four times a year, which is more than you and I can say. The answer is no, I have never heard such rumours, and if I had I wouldn't dream of passing them on.'

'Of course you would; you'd tell everyone.'

Francesc put on a look of mock indignation.

'Are you trying to get me sacked?'

135

'Oh sure, from the Generalitat, the ultimate job for life. What would you have to do to get sacked, Francesc, murder someone?'

'No, you'd probably just get a written warning for that. It would have to be more serious, something that undermined the dignity of the Generalitat or the integrity and honour of the Catalan nation. Maybe if you were caught humming in Castilian perhaps.'

21

Narcís waited in the car outside Rocío Roldán's house in Vallvidrera, flipping through *GQ* magazine. There was a four-button Versace blazer he liked but the trouble with Versace clothes there was always the danger that people would take you for a faggot. His Uncle Salvador had been coming to see Rocío once a fortnight for fifteen years. It was a fixed point in his diary, the one thing he never cancelled. She had a place in Sagrera before but a few years ago she moved up the hill to Vallvidrera so business was obviously good. You had to be making good money to live up here with all the football stars and gynaecologists.

Narcís called her the Gypsy, though never to the old man's face. Rocío wasn't a Gypsy and, as Oriol once grumpily made clear, she wasn't a fortune teller either. She described herself as a spiritual adviser, although she didn't give advice as such. Once a fortnight she did Oriol's Tarot and felt the pulse in his neck and feet and spent long stretches of time with her eyes closed, holding his hands, feeling his energy, as she put it. Then she offered her interpretation and sometimes, on the basis of this interpretation, a forecast. It was up to him what he did with the information. It was like a psychic traffic report. This is where you are now, she said, and this is what lies on the road ahead. If you choose to take that road. If you have a choice.

Today Rocío seemed agitated. Something unnerved her and at one point she shivered visibly.

'What is it?' Oriol said. 'What do you see?'

'I don't know, it's not clear, there's not enough light.'

'But you must see something. Something's making you afraid.'

Rocío closed her eyes in concentration but said nothing.

'Should I be afraid?' Oriol said.

'Only if you fear the dead,' she answered, without opening her eyes.

Oriol came out of Rocío's house looking older than when he went in. He didn't say anything and they drove off in silence. It was the not knowing that was so corrosive. Not knowing if there was anything still out there at Can Castanyer, any proof. Narcís didn't find a thing, or at least he said he didn't. Oriol had a fantasy of the farm being flattened, obliterated. He pictured a squadron of F16s swooping over the place and blasting it out of his life for ever. They were almost home before he spoke to Narcís.

'Do you know anything about our American being arrested?'

Narcís looked in the rearview mirror, trying to read the old man's face.

'Apparently a Jap in his hotel had some stuff stolen and the finger pointed at our American. Then the Jap dropped the charges. You know what they're like, they don't like to draw attention. Now this Nadal is starting to get cocky.'

He looked in the mirror again. His uncle appeared satisfied with this account. The idea of getting Nadal deported was a bit of improvisation that didn't come off, that's all. Hernández called him and said they had the American in the station and what did he want to do. He should have guessed the Jap wouldn't want to go through with it, but you have to take your chances as they come. It was like trying to score from thirty yards out; if you miss you look a fool, but if it goes in the net you're a god.

'Anyway, I thought Domènech was supposed to be dealing with this,' Narcís said.

'Maybe he is. He'd better be.'

Narcís didn't trust Angel and didn't like him either, the way he acted so superior. The way Narcís saw it, all the American needed was a good fright and they'd never hear from him again. No one's easier to frighten than an American, for all their tough guy movies. Look at the Gulf War, even Mr Rambo himself, Sly Stallone, was too scared to go to London for the weekend in case a bomb blew off course from Baghdad. It was pathetic. No, this Nadal character needed a scare. It wouldn't take much; just a little taste of terror and let his imagination do the rest.

'I have a job for you,' Oriol said wearliy. 'Some bastard's trying to blackmail me.'

'What do they want?'

'What do you think?' Oriol snapped. 'Money. What does anyone ever want?'

'I meant, what's it all about? What's the angle?'

The old man looked at his nephew in the mirror. He trusted him, he supposed, after a fashion. He trusted him the way you trust a pet Alsatian; you know it's loyal but you also know it's a domesticated wolf and could turn on you at any moment. You could never breed the bad blood out of a dog like that. As far as he was concerned, the less Narcís knew the better. For his part, Narcís was sick of being kept in the dark. And he was sick of being patronized by the old man's sons, the soulless pair of accountants who ran the business. He called them the grey death. Not to his uncle, of course; in his eyes they could do no wrong. But to Narcís they were just a couple of number-crunchers, journeymen with no imagination, no audacity.

'So who's the blackmailer?' he said.

'Some nobody, the world's full of them. A car mechanic from Poblenou. I'll give you the details when we get back to the house.'

'And?'

'And I don't want to hear from him again.'

22

The taxi drove off towards Torredembarra and Alex stood under the chestnut and flapped at flies in the hot whirr of the morning and sang quietly: 'There may be trouble ahead, but while there's moonlight and music and love and romance, let's face the music and dance.' Victor appeared from the side of the house, the fizz of his Walkman audible at fifty feet. He was dressed in the same tight jeans and high-top trainers and a black Megadeth T-shirt. He switched off the machine and waved to Alex, doing his best to act cool, but his awkwardness poked through like a broken bone.

'How are things?' Alex said.

'Oh, the usual,' Victor said, picking up a suitcase and turning towards the house. But Alex felt sure it wasn't the usual at all; Victor was the worst liar he'd ever met and plainly something was up. Victor reached under the potted rosemary bush beside the front door and produced a set of keys which he gave to Alex. He followed Alex in and opened the shutters.

'The piano tuner's been. He said to tell you he did his best.'

Alex felt a little surge of joy, as though he'd bumped into a friend in a strange town.

'He wasn't blind,' Victor added. 'I thought they were always blind.'

'It's not obligatory,' Alex laughed. 'Just as long as they're not deaf.'

He sat down at the piano and ran his fingers up and down the keyboard. The tone was a little harsh and some of the strings could do with being replaced, but it was in tune. He played 'Let's Face the Music', first with an urgent, pulsing figure on the left hand, then syncopated in a cross-hands stride piano style, throwing in seconds and fourths to give it a modern feel. It was good to be playing again, to feel in control of something. He was thinking of Carmen and wanted to play for her, to woo her with music. And he knew he had more important things to think about. He wrapped the tune up in a showy, high-kicking, Broadway walk-down fashion. Victor clapped with apparently genuine enthusiasm and went back outside to work.

Alex looked around the house, opening cupboards and drawers, looking for clues to the sort of person his aunt had been. But Anna Nadal lived a life without embellishment. Virtually everything at Can Castanyer was of practical use, the things you need to cook and eat and keep a house: cooking pots and utensils, china, a broom, a mop, needle and thread. There was almost nothing of monetary or sentimental value: scarcely an ornament or picture, no china for special occasions, and no sign of his father's carving. And there was little trace of Anna. In her bedroom he found a silver hairbrush and some hand cream, bottles and packets of prescription medicines, an unused sachet of hair dye. Her clothes were neatly folded in a chest of drawers which gave off a sweetly acrid smell of lavender and talc. There was nothing else in the room: just the chest, the bed and bedside table and a chair. The walls were bare except for a small plaster relief, about eight inches square, depicting Christ throwing the money-changers out of the temple. There were no documents of any kind, no official record that she lived and died here in this house. Alex didn't throw anything out. There was a chest of blankets in the room across the landing. He took the blankets out and replaced them with his aunt's things. All her worldly goods didn't fill

141

the chest. When he was done he sat on the stairs and thought about his father growing up in this house. There was no trace of him either. Alex thought he might find some letters from his father, something that explained how Anna found him, but there was nothing.

After he unpacked he went up on to the terrace and looked out over the farm. Victor was hoeing a row of tomatoes, chipping and scratching at the stony, red earth. Aside from the hoe and the crickets and the flies, the only sound was the thrumming of the hot midday air. He could barely see the sea through the heat haze. He leaned against the hot brick parapet wall and thought about his aunt; lonely, whether through choice or by default. Her parents died when she was still a girl, she never married, her brother had disappeared – he could see why people might assume she had nobody to leave the farm to. They waited for her to die, but then they couldn't wait any longer, so they killed her. That's what Alex thought, and Jaume Sabadell, Victor's father, was a part of it. Why else would he have sold land to this company Mallobeco? But to build a school? He kept coming back to that and it made no sense at all. Alex wasn't looking forward to tackling Sabadell. But before he did, he had a date with Detective Foix of the Tarragona police.

As well as the farm, Anna left him an old Seat 127. He sluiced the dust off it, got it started and drove the ten or so kilometres down to Tarragona, the capital of Roman Spain. Detective Foix was a big-boned, dark-skinned woman who wore her black hair clawed back in a bright pink butterfly clip. Although she was dark, she had the palest of blue eyes, the milky blue-white of mussel shells. The room smelled of black tobacco and a packet of Ducados lay on the table. Foix lit one up. She explained that she and a uniformed officer had been called to the scene early in the morning after Victor discovered Anna's body. There were no signs of a struggle and no suspicious circumstances. Her view was that it was an accident in which alcohol had played a part and that view had been borne out by the post-mortem examination.

'Were the usual scene of crime investigations carried out? Fingerprints and so forth? I'm not trying to tell you how to do your job, I'd just like to know.'

'We recovered various sets of fingerprints,' Foix said with just a trace of haughtiness. 'Three sets to be exact. One belonging to the deceased, one to the young man who reported the death.'

'And the third?'

'As I said, there were no suspicious circumstances. I wasn't about to fingerprint the entire village just to satisfy my curiosity as to who else might have been in her house.'

'According to my information,' Alex said, 'she didn't drink. She had an allergy which brought her out in itchy lumps.'

'She may well have had an allergy, and the coroner's report does mention some swellings that may have been caused by an allergic reaction. But that doesn't mean she didn't drink. Have you never persisted in doing something that made you feel bad?' she said with a wistful smile, waving the cigarette as a case in point. When she smiled her lips formed an s-shape, like the sound hole of a violin. 'Besides, your aunt may have been willing to put up with a few itchy lumps if the drink helped dull another, bigger pain.'

'What do you mean?'

'Anna Nadal had lung cancer,' Foix said, stubbing the cigarette out with sudden distaste. 'According to the coroner it was inoperable. If she'd gone to the doctor she could have got some morphine for the pain, but she didn't, so maybe the cognac helped.'

'She knew she was dying?'

'Almost certainly.'

'So there's a chance she might have . . .'

'Taken her own life? It's possible but not likely. Your aunt was a good Catholic, she attended Mass regularly. From what I gather her life on Earth wasn't a bed of roses, so I doubt that she would have added to her sorrows by knowingly choosing an afterlife of eternal damnation.'

23

Miguel had said something to the effect that there weren't any answers, only questions, and Alex was beginning to see what he meant. Every stone he turned revealed two more underneath. He wandered around Tarragona until he found himself in the indoor market in the Plaça de Corsini. At a *xarcuteria* he bought a variety of sausages – *fuet*, *chorizo* and *botifarra negra* – and was on the point of choosing a chicken when he realized Victor would laugh at him for buying something they already had on the farm.

Then the *peixateras* started on him. All the *peixateras* were women and to get you to buy their fish they came on like hookers. Each wore a frilly white apron and had dyed hair – either jet black or platinum blonde. All were in full make-up, with a pronounced penchant for bright blue and turquoise eye shadow. They called out to passing trade, men and women alike: 'Hey, good looking, Over here my love, Oh, my queen, how gorgeous you are, come see what I have here.'

'Hey, handsome,' a blonde in her fifties called out to him with her hand on her hip, 'look at these lovely clams I have here for you.'

Alex smiled but didn't buy and the next one along, also blonde but twenty years younger, took over.

'What a nice smile, what a gorgeous beast. You don't want clams, my sweet. Here, look at these *calamars*. Have you ever seen any more beautiful?'

And so it went on down the aisle, a dozen *peixateras* on each side, all vying for his attention and his money. It was sweet and funny and sexy and shameless and at the same time curiously chaste. He loved it, he answered back and flirted with them and for a few minutes he forgot about everything else. At the last stall, more out of gratitude than hunger, he bought a dozen brick-red prawns from a black-eyed, coral-lipped blonde who in the course of this brief transaction called him my darling, my love, my heart, my life and my dear heaven. Alex felt loved.

On the way home he called into the village shop on the pretext of buying the newspaper. The *patrona* was dressed in a respectable fawn ensemble and wore the same gold shell earrings as before. She offered Alex one of her thin professional smiles.

'How are things?' she said.

'Good. I've moved into Can Castanyer,' he said, certain she knew but equally certain she wouldn't ask. 'Victor Sabadell's helping me out, but I don't think his father's too pleased.'

She made a face that was as pleasant as it was expressionless. If it said anything it said, 'I may gossip from time to time, but not with you.' Alex looked at the videos above her head. *Toy Story* had replaced *Alice in Wonderland* but there'd been no takers as yet for *Fantasias Lesbianas*.

'So I guess everyone's really excited about the new school,' he said with a foolish grin.

That furrowed her brow. Her make-up stood out in creamy-pink ridges along her frown lines. She looked genuinely perplexed.

'The school they're building beside Can Castanyer, on Sabadell's land. You didn't know?'

She unfurrowed and slipped back behind her affable shopkeeper's mask.

'You must be mistaken. Why would anyone build a school

here? There are barely a dozen children in the village and they all go to school in La Nou de Gaia,' she said, gesturing in the direction of the next village.

Alex gave a self-deprecating shrug.

'You're probably right. I must have got my signals crossed.'

As he got into his car he reflected that if she didn't know about the school then no one else in the village did. And if no one knew, it almost certainly wasn't a school.

As he drove up past the cemetery on the way to the house who should he run into but Jaume Sabadell, Victor's father, coming along the road. He carried a shotgun under his arm and had a pair of rabbits slung around his neck. Alex stopped the car and got out. Sabadell stopped and made a big show of spitting at the side of the road. Fresh blood dripped from one of the rabbits. In the field to the left of them three men were shaking black olives from a tree on to a blue plastic sheet. Alex and Sabadell stood facing each other on the road.

'There's something I'd like to know,' Alex said.

'I've nothing to say to you.'

'Not even about the land you sold? Does anyone else know you sold it?'

That rattled him. He tried to hide it, but it showed.

'It's none of your business.'

'But I live next door, it's very much my business. Are they really going to build a school?'

'You won't be living next door for long,' Sabadell said, waving the shotgun at Alex.

'I see. I'll take that as a threat. By the way, where were you the night Anna died?' He hadn't planned to say that, he just blurted it out.

Sabadell raised the shotgun and aimed just above Alex's head. The gesture was entirely casual – until he pulled the trigger. Alex felt the whoosh of buckshot over the top of his head and staggered back in surprise. The men under the olive tree stopped their work and looked across but Sabadell was already stalking down the road. Alex leant against the car and stayed there until he stopped shaking.

As soon as he got back to Can Castanyer he phoned Detective Foix and told her what happened.

'Do you want to press charges?' she said.

'I'm not sure. I'm certainly not going to pretend it never happened. And I think he may have played a role in Anna's death.'

Foix said she'd come over as soon as she could. When Alex went outside Victor was repairing the mesh on the hen-house. That, it seemed to Alex, was what life consisted of on a farm like this, an endless succession of small tasks – milking the cow, tying up the tomatoes, watering the beans, pruning the fruit trees, tending the vines, collecting the eggs. Victor didn't work hard, but then he didn't stop working either. It was like looking after a small baby; not backbreaking work, but relentless. There was a sweet smell in the air. Victor took a spliff out of his mouth and offered it to Alex.

'Home-grown,' he said, pointing to a tall clump of marijuana at the back of the house.

Alex took up a couple of draws on the joint, thinking it might calm his nerves. Victor turned off the Walkman.

'I've just bumped into your father. He doesn't much like me.'

'He doesn't much like anyone.'

'Do you two get along?

He handed him the joint. Victor pulled on it and squinted at Alex.

'After a fashion. He's like the weather, you can't change it, so what's the use in complaining? But we had a big fight the other day.'

'Over what?'

'Over you, really. He doesn't want me to work the farm. He says it will only encourage you to stay.'

'And why is he so keen to see the back of me.'

'He says you don't belong here, that the farm shouldn't go to an outsider.'

This from a man who had sold his own land to a property developer, Alex thought. He wondered if Victor knew and, if he didn't, whether he should tell him.

'But he doesn't want you to look after it either,' Alex said.

'I told him as long as there was a chance of keeping Can Castanyer going I would. And he said if that was the case there was no room for me under his roof.'

'He threw you out? Where are you staying?'

Victor pointed to the small olive grove. A couple of blankets hung from a tree.

'It's OK for now. I just hope he calms down before the weather turns.'

'There's no need for that, you can stay in the house.'

He knew he'd regret it, that he didn't want to live with Victor; above all he didn't want to live with his music. But the dope was making him soft and fuzzy and big-hearted. What's more, Victor was taking his side, he was an ally, and he could do with one of those.

'Thanks,' Victor said. 'Maybe if it gets cold at night. Can I ask you something? Do you really plan to live here, or is it just sort of a holiday?'

'I really don't know. What I am clear about is I want to find out what happened here, even if I don't like what I find. I need to know. I know people say let sleeping dogs lie, but it depends whose dogs they are.'

Victor ground the roach out in the dust.

'A long time ago, when she was still at school, my sister Núria wanted to write a history of the village. Not just the Civil War, but all of it, since Roman times. People didn't want to talk about the war. Like you say, they said let sleeping dogs lie. My father told her to stop making trouble. He threatened her with a beating if she didn't drop it. But Núria never cared what anyone thought.'

Victor said this in a tone of admiration.

'So what did she find out?'

'I don't really know. I told you, I don't care about all that history and politics stuff.'

'Do you see much of Núria?'

'Not recently. I tried to find her when Anna died but no

luck,' he said sorrowfully. 'Anyway, I'm going for lunch. See you later.'

After he left, Alex realized Victor must have gone to the bar for lunch, as he could no longer go home. Alex was hungry too. Smoking dope had never put him in touch with his spiritual side, the way other people claimed it did; maybe he didn't have a spiritual side, because all dope ever did to Alex was swamp him with a desire for food and sex. He went inside and dropped the prawns into a hot pan and cooked them in garlic and salt. 'Sweethearts,' he said to the prawns as he flipped them over. 'My darlings, my loves, my life.' He ate them standing up, the whole dozen, washed down with cold beer. Then he wiped his hands and sat down at the piano. For a moment he sat with his hands on his thighs, staring at the wall above the piano. Then he started to play 'Someone to Watch Over Me'. There was always a temptation to milk it, to go for the lush and gush, but the melody didn't need any help; it soared of its own accord. He made the middle eight spare, almost austere, because however much you held back, the sweetness of the melody came through. He hung off the back of the beat, then soared back up with the melody, like a dreamy roller-coaster ride. He put his foot on the pedal for the last note and let it hang in the cool gloom of the old house.

'That was beautiful.'

Alex practically jumped out of his clothes. It was Carmen. She was wearing a loose black sun dress and very little else. Small silver lizards dangled from her ears. Having slaked his hunger on the prawns, the dope immediately set to work on Alex's other appetite. Carmen dropped her bag on the table and kissed him on each cheek. She smelled of sunned skin and tobacco. The dope threw Alex into primordial gear and reversed him about fifty thousand years down the evolutionary road. He'd come down from the trees but he was still walking on his knuckles. The words seduction and romance had not yet entered the human vocabulary. He was man, she was woman. He wanted her. He wanted her now. On the floor, on the sofa, on the table. He was getting an erection and he was afraid she'd notice. He turned away from her and started rubbing tomato into a slice of bread, just for something to do with his hands, then salted it and drizzled the bread with oil, Catalan-style.

'Oil before salt,' Carmen said. 'Tomato, oil, salt.'

'Is that the rule?'

'That's the law,' she smiled. She studied the photograph of Anna sitting at the piano.

'Is this your aunt?'

'That's her.'

Something about the picture made her uneasy, it seemed to stir some uncomfortable memory that she couldn't retrieve.

'So how's it going, country life?'

Alex's mouth was so dry from the dope it was virtually stuck shut. He took a swig from the half-drunk can of beer on the table, took a deep breath and tried not to think about sex.

'Well, I've learnt how to milk a cow,' he said. 'Quite proud of myself. But to be honest I don't think I want to spend the rest of my life sitting under a shit-streaked cow when I can buy all the milk I want in a supermarket. Would you like me to show you around?'

They stood on the top terrace and looked out over the farm. She stood close to him. Her brown shoulders gleamed in the sun and he tried not to look at her breasts which were clearly visible through the dress. He had regained some evolutionary ground during the tour of the house. Now he no longer wanted to throw her to the floor and pump her full of his seed. Now he wanted to kiss her as well.

'That detective who arrested you, Hernández, he has problems.'

'What kind of problems?'

'Disciplinary ones, plus he's a gambler. And like most gamblers he owes bad people good money. I have a cousin in the force, he says Hernández is on thin ice.'

'And therefore open to manipulation.'

'Quite.'

'But you didn't come all the way out here to tell me that.'

'I wanted to see how you were getting on. And I was wondering if you were free tomorrow afternoon. I've got two tickets for el Barça's game against Bilbao. Good seats. I think you might enjoy it.'

'Bill's beer hall in Bilbao, Bilbao, Bilbao,' Alex sang.

Carmen looked at him like he was mad.

'Sorry,' he said. 'It's a song by Kurt Weill. My head's full of them. There are days when almost anything is the cue for a song.'

Alex remembered why he hadn't smoked dope in a long time; as well as turning him into a glutton and a sex fiend it made him babble like an idiot.

'Yes I'd love to go to football with you,' he said, feeling his way in the luminous darkness of her eyes. It was late afternoon, heavy like an August day, but with a whiff of autumn nostalgia. He moved a fraction closer to her and studied her face. All she needed to do was make that let's-kiss face, a slight upward tilt of the chin and sideways tilt of the head. He needed a sign; he didn't dare make a move without one because he was stoned and he didn't trust himself not to grab her in some clumsy grope. Below them the gate smacked shut. It was Victor, back from lunch already. Somebody must have told him a strange car was parked outside the house so he came back early to find out whose. The metallic frothing of his earphones buzzed up to the terrace. He looked up, grinned, played a quick blast of air guitar then set about sharpening the hoe with a whetstone.

'That's Victor,' Alex said. 'A free spirit. In his head, he's an outlaw, born to run, a Stratocastaway in his own private road movie. In real life he's a country boy; his mother tongue may be Catalan but he dreams in American. You see that field over there, the one that's not being worked? It belongs to Victor's father, or did. He's sold it to a company called Mallobeco who claim they're going to build a school on it. And they've declared an interest in doing something similar on my land, if they can get their hands on it.'

151

'A school? Why would anyone build a school here? Who for? And I don't know much about Mallobeco but hotels, flats and leisure centres are their usual line of business, not schools. Corporate developer muscles in to build village school – sounds pretty far-fetched. I'll see what I can find out.'

'Why? What's in it for you?'

'A good story, I hope, especially if it involves Mallobeco. Besides, you said you needed a friend. Anything else I can do for you?'

She gave Alex a smile that seemed to say, I dare you to answer that. Below them Victor picked tomatoes and shouted along to the chorus of 'Bring your Daughter to the Slaughter'.

The dope was starting to wear off. The libidinous beast slunk back into the woods and the sentimental fool returned. Alex wanted to stroke the black hair on her brown forearms.

'A kiss would be nice,' he said, feeling as soon as he said it like he'd stepped off a cliff.

Carmen laughed and turned to go inside. Alex's heart sank. Then she turned in the doorway, now out Victor's sight, and said: 'OK, it's a deal. You kiss me, I'll kiss you back. Just out of curiosity of course.'

'Of course. It doesn't mean anything. How could it?'

Alex was a kissing aficionado. He was of the opinion that kissing is the most intimate form of human contact. That's why prostitutes don't, as a rule, kiss their clients. There is something especially human about kissing, much more so than fucking. Animals fuck, but although they nuzzle a bit, they don't kiss. With kissing, you enter and are entered all at once. It's reciprocal in a way that other sexual acts needn't be. You can fuck or be fucked and not let it show that you're not really interested, but kissing's harder to fake. To kiss you have to make an effort. Alex believed that, however dazzling a person might be between the sheets, if they couldn't kiss, or if as kissers you were incompatible, you might as well call the whole thing off. Carmen could kiss. She was good, she kissed slow and soft and like she meant it. He felt her kiss in his stomach, warm, glowing, like the sun was rising behind his abdominal wall. They kissed all the way up to the danger signs. Carmen gave him a wet smile and squeezed his hand.

'You kiss the way you play the piano, nice light touch. I'll see you tomorrow, after lunch. Meet me in Boadas, it's a sweet little cocktail bar on la Rambla, on the corner of Carrer de Tallers. Now I've got to go and see if I can make some trouble.'

Alex put his arm round her and squeezed her bare shoulder.

'I think you already have.'

The dope had worn off by the time Detective Foix arrived. They stood in the shade of the chestnut, the sharp smell of black tobacco smoke bitter in the green afternoon.

'Señor Sabadell denies everything. He even denies seeing you today.'

'What about the men harvesting the olives?'

'I tracked two of them down. They have no memory of the incident you describe. You seem to have made yourself rather unpopular in the village.'

'It's an hereditary condition.'

Foix looked out to sea, her blue-white eyes ghostly against her dark face.

'I got his prints,' she said, as though she was talking to someone else. Alex must have looked surprised.

'We're not entirely stupid, you know. I had a can of Coke. I asked him to hold it while I wrote something down in my notebook. Coke cans arc very good for getting prints.'

24

Salvador Oriol wasn't accustomed to being told what to do, but when Señor Williams summoned him to a meeting at the Meridien he made it clear, without actually saying so, that Oriol wasn't in a position to say no. Williams had taken a modest suite, just a bedroom and a room large enough to serve as an office, of which the only sign was a slim briefcase and slimmer laptop. A bottle of Vichy Catalan mineral water and two glasses stood on a tray on the coffee table. He didn't offer Oriol a drink, not even water. Williams wasn't like any man Oriol had dealt with; in fact he wasn't like a man at all. With him there was only business – no preamble, no lunch, no chat about one another's children or where to get the best *botifarra blanca* or Stoichkov's latest red card. Williams went straight to the main dish – no canapés, no aperitifs, and no coffee and cognac to follow.

'Our problem doesn't appear to be going away,' he said.

'Problem? Oh him, your fellow countryman,' Oriol said, trying to laugh it off. 'I don't think you need to worry about him.'

'I'm not worrying, but you should,' Williams said coldly.

Oriol was used to deference; people didn't speak to him like that. But he had no choice but to take it from Williams.

'I can assure you that the problem is being dealt with,' he said. 'But naturally it requires a light touch. We don't want to attract attention, after all.'

'Why can't he simply disappear? Would anyone go looking for him? And if they did, well, he's gone, vanished. In the meantime the process could continue as if he'd never existed.'

He said it as if it was nothing, as though killing a man was like knocking down a partition or scrapping a car. Oriol didn't say anything, he wasn't about to incriminate himself, and you never knew with Americans that there wasn't a tape running somewhere. He gave Williams a sideways nod that wasn't yes or no.

'It appears that this Nadal believes he's here to settle some old score, something to do with his father and the Civil War. You wouldn't know anything about that would you?'

Oriol shivered inwardly and suddenly had a powerful need to urinate. He clenched his bladder and looked Williams in the eye.

'I can't imagine what that's about,' he said. He chest was tightening with panic. In the beginning it was Williams who needed him; now the tables were turned and he needed the American. If Williams walked away he was in a hole, a big hole. This Nadal was ruining everything. He was like some useless relic washed up from history, like that time when they were digging the foundations for a hotel and everything had to stop because they uncovered some stupid Roman baths. Nadal had to be stopped.

'The wedding's on Saturday,' Williams said. 'That gives you a week. If it's not fixed by then it's off. Let me remind you that under our agreement, if these conditions aren't fulfilled, my client is not liable.'

Meaning I'll be left high and dry, Oriol thought.

Angel was flipping through *El Mensajero*'s Saturday magazine when Oriol called. His son Josep lay on the sofa and, as he was never up this early, Angel assumed he'd lain there all night. The shutters were closed and the room was sour with cigarettes and fried takeaway food. Josep, shirtless in a pair of jeans, was watching a video of an action movie. The American hero was running across a square in some vaguely Central American town with one hand on a huge automatic and the other gripping the elbow of a wild-eyed, tousle-haired Latina in a T-shirt two sizes too small for her. Josep flicked his ash in the direction of an empty Coke can without taking his eyes off the screen. Angel slid an ashtray noisily across the tiled floor with his foot. His son made no acknowledgement.

'You don't seem to be making much progress,' Oriol said, adopting the no frills Williams style.

'More than it might appear. But it doesn't help having amateurs muddying the waters. I'm talking about him being arrested. Whose stupid idea was that?'

'I was hoping you might be able to tell me,' Oriol said.

Angel thought about that. Oriol would never admit to being involved in something so incompetent, but if he knew nothing about it, he wasn't going to admit that either. On the TV a Mercedes exploded in a fireball, blowing the hero and the Latina off their feet. When the dust settled he had a black mark on his forehead and a cut lip but he still had the automatic in his hand. The force of the blast tore some nasty rips in his companion's T-shirt.

'I'm having lunch with Judge Mestres on Monday,' Oriol said.

It was a typical Oriol gambit. Judge Mestres was due to preside at Josep's trial. Josep's hand flapped on the floor beside the sofa, fishing for a cigarette. The hand found an empty packet. Angel picked up his own cigarettes off the table and tossed them on to the sofa. Josep took one out and lit it, eyes glued to the film. Again he made no acknowledgement of his father. It depressed Angel to see his son smoking. But he needed some point of contact with the boy and the only things he'd accept from him were cigarettes and money. Never advice and certainly not love. Josep's mother had washed her hands of him. This is a father's job, she said. Angel was a master at manipulation. Throughout his life he'd been able to cajole, goad or simply unnerve people into giving him what he wanted. Now he was defeated by his own son. He tried every approach, but every one was as blind an alley as the last.

'I can assure you the business is in hand,' Angel said, echoing what Oriol said to Williams.

'It's going too slowly. Saturday is the deadline, otherwise all bets are off. You may not think that matters to you, that you've had your share, but believe me you're wrong.'

Angel was struck once more by Oriol's apparent obsession with the deal. He wondered if the old skinflint actually had some of his own money tied up in it. He knew he said he faced ruin but that was just a manner of speaking. Whatever else he'd become, Oriol would always be a peasant, and if you ask a peasant how things stand he'll always tell you he's facing ruin.

The hero with the cut lip shoved the barrel of the huge automatic into the mouth of a sweaty Latino bad guy. 'Don't fuck with me, you fuck,' he said. Angel lip-read the words through the dubbed soundtrack and mouthed them down the phone.

'Our friend has developed a romantic attachment to a young woman,' Oriol said. 'She's a journalist. I believe you're acquainted. Use her.'

25

Carmen drove back to the city with Arrested Development playing loud on the car stereo. She felt happy in a girlish way and sexy in a way that was all grown up. And she had a story, she was sure of it; she could smell it. Right now she didn't have much more than that – the smell of corruption, but the facts would come. It was the sort of story Fèlix Grau would have liked – maybe even the one he was on to when he died – and she could do it for him, and for Blanca. She didn't tell Blanca about the video from the hotel camera because she knew Blanca would go off at the deep end and ruin everything. Blanca would have to be the last to know, if there was anything to tell. Carmen drummed her nails in time to the music. Her mind kept going back to the photograph of Alex's aunt; something about it nagged at her memory. Then her mobile trilled on the seat beside her. It was the editor's secretary; the editor wanted to see her immediately.

The editor leaned forward in his chair and took off his gold-framed reading glasses. He laid them on the old-fashioned leather-topped desk and picked up another, rimless pair. It was a curious habit. He changed his glasses continually in the course of a discussion, as though for emphasis, although the ritual in fact distracted from what he was saying. He looked down from the desk to where Carmen sat with Enric Luna, the news editor of *El Mensajero*, on a small leather sofa, like naughty children in the headmaster's office. Luna smelled of aftershave, a lemon-leather masculine scent. Carmen felt self-consciously female in the skimpy sun dress; not the sort of thing she'd dream of wearing to the office.

The office was designed for maximum gravitas, with sombre wood panelling and deep red floor tiles. The brass desk lamp had a green glass shade. The walls were hung with framed front pages and photos of the editor shaking hands or raising a glass with leading citizens: with Pujol, the Catalan president; with Nuñez, president of el Barça; with Samaranch of the Olympic committee; with the king of Spain himself, Juan Carlos, and of course, with Salvador Oriol. That was the kind of company he liked to keep. He wasn't a hands-on, shirt-sleeves sort of an editor and Carmen doubted if he knew the names of most of his junior staff. He was remote, aloof, the sort of editor who phones the newsdesk from a restaurant after he's seen the first edition and says, 'I don't like page seven', but doesn't say why or what he'd prefer, leaving the night editor second guessing. Sometimes the page was ripped out and done afresh, sometimes it was left untouched. The editor never commented either way; the phone calls were just to let everyone know who was the boss. The paper was more or less a family business. The editor's father was editor before him. The family was old money and hadn't found the Franco years too distressing.

'I have received a personal complaint about your conduct, from Salvador Oriol,' the editor said. He swapped the rimless glasses for the gold-framed pair. 'He says he acceded to an interview on the subject of the arts in Catalunya and then discovered that you were investigating his business affairs. Naturally I have to take this seriously.'

Naturally, Carmen thought, trying to steady her nerves. She wasn't afraid of the editor – he was just yet another pompous, puffed-up man, a Catalanist with a Falangist heart, like a sugar-coated bullet – but the atmosphere was intimidatingly male in the mahogany office with its smell of leather and varnish and cigars. Added to which she didn't know what the editor was talking about.

'I'm sorry, I don't understand,' she said, hoping he'd say more.

The editor pursed his lips and tapped a sheet of paper on his desk.

'Yesterday you ran a database search on a company called Mallobeco. You also made inquiries at the registrar of companies. And you called the company secretary of Mallobeco and asked for a list of directors, a request which the secretary not only refused but referred to Salvador Oriol.'

'But why?'

The editor swapped his glasses and leaned forward.

'Please don't play the ingenue. Jordi and Joaquím Oriol, Salvador's sons, are executive directors of Mallobeco, as I'm sure you're well aware.'

This was news to Carmen, very interesting news, but with Enric Luna sitting there she wasn't going to let on that she hadn't made the Oriol link.

'I was tipped off about a shady and possibly illegal property deal involving a company called Mallobeco, with which I later discovered Señor Oriol has a family connection. That's all. I wasn't investigating Señor Oriol.'

She tried to get the tone right, neither defensive nor abrasive. Men often used that word about her – abrasive. She never knew what they meant, but supposed she wasn't pliant enough for their tastes.

'If you thought you had a news story, why didn't you inform the news editor?' he said, nodding at Luna. Luna gave her a sideways look and raised one of his meagre eyebrows then looked down at her breasts in the flimsy sun dress. He didn't say anything; she knew not to expect any help from him.

'I didn't want to waste his time until I was sure I had something, that it wasn't just rumour.'

The editor swapped his glasses round and tapped his lower incisors with the rim of the spare pair.

'And is it?'

'I believe there really is something to it, but I can't stand it up yet.'

'Then don't try to. I shall do what I can to smooth this over, but if I hear any more about it things will go badly for you here, do you understand? Now in the meantime you're to forget about arts and help Enric here with our coverage of the Infanta's wedding.'

That was that. The backs of her knees were stuck to the leather sofa and when she stood up they peeled away from it with a small tearing sound. The editor affected not to notice. Downstairs in the newsroom she lit a cigarette and propped herself against Luna's desk.

'Thanks for the show of solidarity,' she said. 'You could have said something.'

'Like what? I didn't know what it was about until he gave you the lecture. If you thought you had a story why didn't you talk to me about it?'

Carmen laughed.

'Because three things would have happened: one, you would have rubbished it to my face; two, if you thought there was anything in it you'd have given it to someone else, preferably a man; and three, you'd have run a mile when you found out Oriol was involved.'

'My, you are pissed off. Beautiful when angry, though.'

'Oh, for God's sake.'

'OK, OK, I'm sorry I said that. But don't accuse me of running a mile from a good story just because it's going to hurt some big shot. You know how it is here.'

It was true, *El Mensajero* preferred not to make waves, not where big fish were concerned. When they did, it was usually because one of the Madrid papers broke the story and they had no choice but to follow it up.

'So what have you got?' Luna said.

'Well, I might just have a development scam that flies in the face of all the environmental and zoning protocols and involves Oriol, directly or indirectly, and at least one senior official at the Generalitat, another at the land registry and takes in along the way one and possibly two murders. Oh, and a bent cop. On the other hand, maybe I have nothing. In the meantime, do tell me how I can help with spreading the joyful tidings of the darling Infanta's wedding.'

'How about a vox pop?'

'You have such a good memory, Enric. You know I loathe vox pops: our reporter takes to the streets to ask how the great event touches the lives of the common people. And amazingly, when you read the paper you'll find they all said how thrilled they are; there won't be a single dissenting voice, no one who said, "Why doesn't she piss off back to Madrid where she belongs?" Not in *El Mensajero*, oh no.'

'I can see we're going to have great fun working together. OK, do a vox pop, seeing as it was your idea. But take a photographer with you so we can put faces to the names. That way we'll know you didn't just sit in a bar and make it up.'

'As if I'd do such a thing.'

26

Detective Foix rang just before Alex left the house to go to Barcelona. Victor was sitting at the kitchen table drinking coffee from a blue bowl. He hadn't exactly moved in, but on the sideboard there was now a small stack of cassettes and two packets of spare batteries for the Walkman, Victor's version of an overnight bag.

'I checked Señor Sabadell's prints against the ones we found in your aunt's house,' Foix said. 'They don't match. I thought you'd like to know.'

It was another hazy, heavy morning and the blue-white sea lay flat beneath the cliffs at Garraf as Alex drove north. Ahead of him the ochre smog hung between the hills above the city. He felt strangely comforted by the sight, like an animal returning to its natural habitat. He liked Can Castanyer and he liked living in the country. It was all the things it was supposed to be – clean air, tranquil days, starry nights. He liked it but he didn't understand it. Maybe Barcelona wasn't his city, but it was a city nevertheless; he knew the rules, he knew how it functioned. It was simple: you went to work and you made money. It didn't matter whether you sold insurance or played the piano: people gave you money and you passed the money on to other people and so it went on and around. No one really understood where the money came from – it wasn't as though the city produced anything of tangible value, like wheat or steel – but it didn't seem to matter, as long as money kept passing from hand to hand everything worked fine. Everything was clear, it made sense. All you needed was money and there are a million ways of making money. Being paid to play the piano seemed more natural to Alex than milking a cow or shaking olives from a tree. That's how much of a country boy he was.

He thought about Carmen; he thought about her a lot. He knew he was in trouble. He'd been in this kind of trouble before, so he knew the signs. When you wake up in the morning and your first thought is of a certain person, that's trouble. Or if you go out of your way to drive down their street in case they might just happen to be coming out of the house at that moment, that's trouble. When you discover by chance that the certain person is a fan of, say, early soul music, and you stay up all night crafting the most perfectly sequenced compilation tape of great but obscure soul numbers just to please them, that's trouble too. And when you look at them and, rather than fantasize about tearing their clothes off and fucking until you slump in a swamp of sweat and hormones, you think about how nice it would be to feel their hair on your face or to kiss the soft down on their neck, you're in trouble. And when a powerful development company is trying to muscle you off your ancestral home and there you are driving into the city with a hand on the wheel and an elbow out the window thinking about a black-eyed woman with crooked teeth and love-me lips, you are indeed in deep trouble. Not in love, but most definitely in trouble. Alex knew that sometimes he could wake up a few days later and it would be gone, just like a cold, and that other times it wasn't so easy to shake, even if he wanted to. He passed the weird vertical cemetery on the seaward slope of Montjuïc, like a high-rise development in Lilliput, and plunged under the city on the

Cinturó del Litoral. When he surfaced again he was in Poblenou. He was looking for Raul, the son of Captain Morín.

Raul was nervous. He was starting to think he didn't have the sang froid or whatever it took to be a successful blackmailer, but he needed the money. How else was he going to pay for full-time care for his father? Besides, he couldn't stop what he'd started now. He sat at an outside table of a large bar near the Olympic pool. As agreed he was wearing a mauve shirt and there was an A4 envelope and a copy of *Ara* on the table. He heard someone behind him mention his name; they were asking the waiter where his garage was. The waiter must have pointed him out because a moment later the man, younger than Raul expected, was standing at his table asking him if he was Raul Morín. He introduced himself as Alex Nadal and sat down opposite. This wasn't the arrangement; there was an agreed password, Romeu, and no names were to be used. Raul was confused, uneasy.

Alex could see that Raul was anxious, either that or he had a fever; he was sweating heavily even though the table was in the shade. He put out a half-smoked cigarette then immediately lit another. His eyes flitted across his face like moths.

'The reason I want to speak to you,' Alex began, 'is I was hoping your father might throw some light . . .'

'Read it for yourself,' Raul interrupted in a hoarse whisper. He pushed the envelope across the table. 'It's only a photocopy, mind. You get the original after I get the money.'

Alex decided to play along, he didn't know with what, but he was going to see where it led, even if it turned out that Raul was just another fruitcake. He opened the envelope and took out the document. There were five pages of text, written in close, old-fashioned sloping script, in Catalan. Alex understood the first sentence, which said this was Guillermo Morín's confession, but he found the rest hard to follow, because of the handwriting and because of the Catalan. Many words were so like Castilian it was clear what they meant, but then he'd

165

come to a word he didn't recognize, often a word that was key to the sense of the sentence. He scanned the first three pages, faking it, trying to get some sort of gist. Then on page four the words Can Castanyer jumped out at him, and lower down the page his father's name and that of Salvador Oriol. He read the top half of the page twice but couldn't make sense of it. He turned the document towards Raul, who was looking more and more ill at ease.

'What's this mean?' Alex said, pointing to a word. 'I'm sorry, but I don't know Catalan.'

Raul started to answer then grabbed the paper from Alex and got to his feet.

'What do you mean? We spoke in Catalan on the phone. Who are you? What are you doing here?'

He pushed past Alex, knocking over a chair and someone's beer in his haste. The other customers all looked up. The man who lost his beer shouted at him. Alex followed Raul into the street but the mechanic shouted at him to go away. He turned and pushed Alex back on his heels and shouted that if he didn't leave him alone he'd call the police. He turned away again and as Alex started off in pursuit the waiter joined in, shouting after them that Raul wouldn't be the only one calling the cops if someone didn't pay for the drinks. Alex didn't want any more trouble with the police. He paid for Raul's coffee and the beer he spilt and then left, wondering why all the people whom he imagined knew what he thought he wanted to know were either crazy or lying or both.

Narcís watched the whole episode from his car parked across the street. He chuckled. Two birds with one stone, he said to himself, two birds with one stone. He couldn't believe his luck.

27

Carmen was naked when Angel called. She was standing in front of the bedroom mirror rubbing in body moisturiser. It was uncanny how he managed to catch her at these intimate moments. She felt vulnerable, being naked with him, even if it was just on the phone. Something about Angel made her acutely aware of her sex. She clenched the phone between shoulder and ear and squirted a glob of liquid into her hand.

'Can we talk?' he said.

'I'm listening,' she said, massaging the cream into her breasts.

'Not on the phone. Can we meet this afternoon? I have something to tell you.'

Blobs of moisturiser lay in the shallow pools formed by her clavicle. She smeared it up into her neck. Her skin shone.

'I'm sorry, but I'm busy this afternoon.'

'Wouldn't you like to know more about this school?'

She'd said nothing to him about the school but she did nothing to break the silence; she wasn't going to let him play her like a fish. She put moisturiser into both hands and started working it into her lower back.

'What are you doing?' Angel said. 'I mean right now.'

'None of your business. Have you got something for me or not?'

There was another silence. This time Angel wasn't going to speak, he was going to wait until she choked on her curiosity. It was like holding your breath under water; he knew she had to come up for air eventually.

'I'm meeting someone in Boadas around four thirty,' she said irritably. 'I could meet you there a little earlier.'

'As long as I'm gone before this someone shows up, right?'

'It's not an issue.'

But as it turned out, it was, because someone threw themselves on the metro line, which meant there were no trains, so she had to walk all the way from Carrer de Provença and arrived at Boadas half an hour late. They were both there, at opposite ends of the little bar, half facing it and half facing the room, and they both turned towards her and smiled. She smothered the urge to burst out laughing and smiled back at each of them, and they in turn looked along the bar to see who else she was smiling at. They both came over to her with the same faux nonchalance, as if to say: She's nothing to me, just a woman. She kissed Alex first, introduced them, then kissed Angel.

Behind the bar Señora Boada was mixing a Manhattan. She could have been sixty but dressed like she was twenty-five and got away with it. Today she wore a silver mini-skirt, silver eye shadow and a tight black chiffon top decorated with black sequins. She was flanked behind the bar by two expressionless barmen in evening dress who mixed and shook and poured the cocktails with an equal measure of theatrical flourish and studied indifference. The three of them were quite a show. La Boada smiled at Carmen.

'Got the fan club in, Carmencita,' she said with a silver wink. 'Singapore Sling?'

Carmen winked back and nodded. Alex and Angel were busy trying to look relaxed in each other's company. Carmen weighed them up. Angel, she thought, was a fundamentally nice guy. Not the sort you'd want to take home to Mum and Dad, perhaps, but he was fun and attentive and flattering and generous in bed. No complaints there. As a woman, with Angel you knew you were in the hands of a professional. People said he used women. Probably he did, but what man didn't? Better to be well used by one man than to thoroughly wasted on another, she reckoned. So Angel was fine but with Alex it was different. Alex was soft without being weak. He was attentive too, but there was real feeling behind it, a sincerity that Angel could only fake. Angel had been too nice to too many women. He might think it was genuine, but he didn't know the difference any more. However much he enjoyed you, you knew he could never stop thinking of all the other women he hadn't enjoyed yet. Angel was entertainment. He was fun to be with, but when she wasn't with him she didn't think about him much. But she had been thinking about Alex.

'Carmen tells me you play the piano,' Angel said.

'Anything to avoid having a real job,' Alex said with a forced laugh. 'How about you?'

'Me? No, sadly I have no musical talent.'

'I meant, what do you do?'

Now it was Angel's turn for the forced laughter. He looked at Carmen, as though asking her for help .

'Don't look at me, Angel. I never have figured out what it is you do.'

There was something in the mood of the exchange that told Alex these two were lovers, or had been. Something in her teasing tone; Alex didn't imagine Angel was the sort who would take teasing from just anyone. He swallowed hard on the sour bilge of jealousy that rose in his throat and reminded himself it was none of his business what Carmen did with her time. Angel sipped his margarita.

'I guess you could say I'm sort of a facilitator,' he said with a look of mischief. 'I like to help people out, help them see things from a different angle. It can be quite liberating.'

There was something very likeable about him, Alex thought, though he was sure he was a shit. But he had charisma, as shits often do. He was never sure whether shits got more than their fair share of charisma or if having charisma made it easier to get away with being a shit.

'How does that work?' Alex said. 'This facilitating.'

'It's all about knowledge. Fundamentally there are only two things you need to know about people: what they dream of and what they dread.'

'What do people dream of?'

'Oh, it's always the same, any other life than the one they have. Which means they always want money because they believe it's the passport to this other life they think they want.'

'And what do they dread?'

'Well, death of course, or that their loved ones should suffer any sort of harm. Aside from that, I'd say the biggest fear is a reversal of fortune. People who have made something of themselves fear nothing more than a return to their origins: wealth dreads poverty, celebrity dreads obscurity, respect-ability dreads shame. Just about everyone dreads shame, in fact.'

'What do you think Salvador Oriol dreads?' Carmen asked casually, holding her drink up to the light.

Angel wore a thin smile of admiration and raised his glass in salute to her.

'I'm not going to make it easy for you,' he said.

'Make what easy?' The way he said it, she thought he meant her decision to end things between them.

Alex felt like they'd forgotten he was there.

'You're a journalist,' Angel said. 'How do I know what's on or off the record?'

Carmen was surprised by the edge of hostility in his voice, and stung by it too.

'What's that look supposed to mean?' Angel laughed. 'Why don't I trust you? OK, you tell me – what, aside from money, is Oriol's single greatest asset?'

'His reputation,' Carmen replied without hesitation.

'That's right.' He looked around the noisy bar. 'You like riddles?'

'No, as a matter of fact I hate them.'

'Too bad. Here's your riddle: if you want to know what Salavador Oriol dreads you must learn to dance the *sardana*. Roger de Flor can teach you. And when you dance the *sardana* in public you will be dancing on Oriol's toes.'

28

Narcís followed Raul back to the garage and watched from the corner of the street as the mechanic opened the side door and locked it behind him. After about twenty minutes Raul rolled up the steel shutter. A big Peugeot, both its rear wheels removed, was up on a jack. Raul, now in his overalls, picked up a couple of socket spanners, lay down on a low, wheeled trolley and rolled himself under the car where he started loosening the nuts around the differential. After a moment he became aware of someone standing at the back of the car. He twisted his head round and saw a pair of navy-blue linen trouser cuffs resting on a pair of ox-blood brogues. He heard the jack handle click and before he could slide out from under it the car came down, pinning his chest under the bulge of the differential. The garage door rolled shut with a crash and a face appeared at ground level.

'Romeu,' Narcís said. 'I believe that's the password we agreed.'

Raul was sweating. He could hardly breathe under the weight of the car.

'What the fuck are you doing?' he gasped. 'Take the jack up, you're going to kill me.'

'There is that possibility. But first I think you have something for me. Where's the envelope?'

'What envelope?'

Narcís reached one hand up to the jack handle and let it down another notch. Raul cried out but his voice made no sound. The blood was pumping in his ears.

'Where?' Narcís said.

Raul mouthed something inaudible. Narcís took the jack up a fraction and waited while Raul gulped at the air. His eyes bulged.

'The workbench,' he whispered. 'In the drawer.'

Narcís left him pinned under the car while he retrieved the envelope. He leaned against the bench and read Captain Morín's confession, skimming it till he got to the part about Salvador Oriol. It was so interesting he read it twice. Now he not only knew the blackmailer, he knew the blackmail too. He put the confession in his pocket and bent down to look at Raul. His face was purple. He was barely conscious.

'Who wrote this? Who's this Guillermo Morín?'

Raul's tongue filled his mouth. Narcís had to lip-read.

'Your father? Where is he?'

Raul shaped the word, 'Dead', amazed that he could still tell lies out of the darkness that was clouding his brain.

Narcís rose to his feet. He pumped the jack fast, until the car was a foot above Raul's chest. Raul gasped for breath but before he could move Narcís clicked the release and let the car drop. The trolley under Raul's back snapped. One half skittered out on two wheels from under the Peugeot and clattered into an oil can.

29

'Who is Salvador Oriol?' Alex said. They were walking up la Rambla to the metro station. Carmen gave him a brief account of the life and times of the grand old man of Catalunya.

'He's sort of – and I hate the word – talismanic. What he symbolizes matters more than what he actually does or says.'

'So what was Angel talking about, that stuff about the *sardana* and dancing on his toes?'

'Salvador Oriol's gift to the nation is to be a school for *sardana*, built on your neighbour's land, at least I think that's what he was trying to tell me; Angel likes to keep people guessing. And I suppose the plan is to name the school after Roger de Flor, a sailor and all-round Catalan hero from the fourteenth century. Again, it's only a guess.'

'What's *sardana*?'

'It's the traditional dance and music of Catalunya.'

'Like flamenco?'

Carmen grimaced. 'It's more Bavarian than that. I don't mean it is Bavarian, it just looks and sounds it, to me at least. I'm not much of a fan, but it's a bit of a nationalist sacred cow, so I keep my thoughts to myself.'

Alex remembered the discordant wind band in Plaça St Jaume.

'So why all the secrecy? It can't be just that he wants it to be a surprise.'

'Oh, I'm sure he does, but not in the way you think. You have to ask yourself, why are they so desperate to get their hands on your land? With that much land you could build a university, never mind a little school dedicated to folk dancing.'

'So, what then?'

'The school must be a front. You couldn't make money out of it and there wouldn't be all this pressure if it didn't involve money. These kind of people don't get this excited about anything else.'

'What about their reputations? What if they were trying to cover up some nasty secret?'

He told her about his encounter with Raul and about Morín's confession.

'It said that Oriol was at Can Castanyer with Morín in 1938. I got that much. Then there was something about someone called Romeu, and I think it said they were Germans.'

'Brothers,' Carmen said. '*German* is Catalan for brother. Didn't you say the whole incident revolved around the execution of three brothers? Maybe that was their name, Romeu.'

'If Oriol was there in 1938 and now plans to build a school on the same spot sixty years later that's quite a coincidence.'

'I agree, especially as according to the official record Oriol was nowhere near St Martí at the time.'

'So, with all this going on, why are we going to a football match?'

Carmen gave him an astonished look.

'Well, for one thing, because we have tickets. And for another, so you can get a look at Salvador Oriol. He hasn't missed a home game in forty years, or so he says.'

They climbed up the steps and landings of the concrete exoskeleton of the Camp Nou stadium and emerged above a pitch of impossible green, walled in by noisy, steeply-raked stands, like an encircling cliff of nesting gulls. It reminded Alex of when he used to go to Yankee Stadium. The stadium was in walking distance from where he grew up at 168th Street and Broadway, on the quasi-respectable northern fringe of Harlem. It was a bleak walk down 155th Street, across the Harlem River to the South Bronx, and he never got over the surprise of the dazzling baseball diamond – the green grass, the red dirt, the thousands of people filling the blue seats – all so improbably bright after the brown, hopeless streets. It was like dreaming in colour in a monochrome world.

Their seats were almost on the halfway line, just above and to the right of the executive enclosure. The people around Carmen and Alex were munching and spitting out sunflower seeds, but in the executive box every other man, the moment he took his seat, lit up a huge cigar. The sweet smoke wafted over the sunflower seats.

'The cream of Barcelona society, I presume?' Alex said, nodding towards the cigars.

'The cream and the dregs. Businessmen, politicians, hoodlums: anyone who's anyone is a *soci* of el Barça – the mayor, the president of Catalunya, the archbishop, the Pope – they're all paid-up members.'

'The Pope? You're kidding.'

'It's true.'

'But he's Polish.'

'He's a big football fan. He used to play. I read somewhere he even considered turning pro.'

Alex took out his notebook and added, *soci* = member, to his brief Catalan vocabulary. Carmen looked over his shoulder.

'All very blunt, she said. *Seny, vermut, tancat, soci.*'

She took the book from him and wrote *enyorança*.

'I love that word,' she said. 'It means longing, a sense of deep longing.'

Alex raised his eyebrows.

'There's no need to read anything into it. I just like the sound of it. It sounds like the feeling.'

'I didn't speak,' Alex said.

'You didn't need to.'

'How do you pronounce the words that begin with x?' he said.

'The x is like the ch of chocolate,' she said. 'She took the notebook and wrote *xocolata, xampany, xarnega.*'

'Chocolate, champagne and what?'

'*Xarnega*, it's what I am, an outsider in Catalunya.'

'I thought you were Catalan.'

'Depends who you ask. To foreigners I'm Spanish, of course, because they don't know any better. Personally, I regard myself as Catalan. But to diehard Catalans, because only one of my parents is Catalan, I'm an immigrant, what they call a *xarnega.*'

'Is that an insult?'

'The way some people say it, yes. It makes no difference that I speak and write better Catalan than most of them, I'll always be a *xarnega*. In Madrid or Seville, of course, I'm a *polacca.*'

'A Pole?'

'That's what they call Catalans in the rest of Spain. Because they can't understand what we're saying. What about you? Cuban mother, Catalan father, what does that make you?'

'It makes me an American.'

Carmen pulled on his sleeve.

'There he is.'

An old man with over-long grey hair, dressed in a cream safari suit made his way down the stairs towards the front of the enclosure. He was accompanied by someone Alex hadn't seen in a while: the big fish-eyed man. Fish-eyes wore a beautifully cut midnight-blue blazer over a collarless white shirt, an ensemble in which he looked oddly and brutishly camp. As they descended the steps, the men nearest the aisle rose to greet the old man, shaking his hand or patting his shoulder. He smiled and nodded and now and then rewarded one of these courtiers with an embrace or a squeeze of the arm. He and fish-eyes sat down in the front row of the box.

'So that's Oriol. Who's the clothes horse?'

'Oriol's gofer – he's also his nephew – Narcís Valls.'

Oriol lit up a cigar the size of a goal post.

The moment the match kicked off Carmen seemed to forget about everything else. She gave Alex a running commentary on the match, the players, the offside rule, how many goals Ronaldo had scored, why the referee was showing his name-sake Nadal the yellow card. All of this information was delivered on a tide of insults directed at the Bilbao players, the referee, and most of all at her own side. Alex looked around and everyone else was the same, smoking and spitting out sunflower husks and shouting about whores and faggots and sons of bitches. Everyone except the big cheeses in their enclosure. They seemed more interested in whether their neighbour had a bigger cigar or a smaller mobile phone than in anything happening on the pitch. Alex, too, as he didn't really understand the game, was more interested in the men with the big cigars. El Barça lost the match two-one after a disputed penalty late in the second half. Carmen was caught up in an animated discussion with two other fans about the penalty, the Basque penchant for diving in the eighteen-yard box and the sexual orientation of the referee. The air was stiff with tinny static as thousands of fans tuned into the post-match analysis on the radio. This was an opportunity Alex didn't want to miss.

'I'll see you outside,' he said to Carmen. 'By the VIP entrance.'

Carmen didn't register at first that he'd spoken. He was several seats away when she called out to him.

'Wait. Where are you going?'

'I'm going to have it out with him. With Oriol.'

'Jesus, Alex, wait. You're crazy.'

It was impossible to push through the dense crowd until he got outside. Then he zigzagged through the fans and souvenir sellers until he got to the door where the BMWs and Mercs were lined up. Carmen caught up with him.

'Maybe it would be better if you weren't seen with me.'

'I'll take my chances,' she said, giving his elbow a squeeze.

A variety of businessmen, sportsmen and local celebrities came down the steps. A blonde emerged on the arm of a man who modelled himself on Alain Delon. They had celebrity written all over them. Carmen said they were stars from *Nissaga de Poder*, a soap opera about *cava* and money. Narcís and Oriol were right behind them. Alex waited until they were nearly at the foot of the stairs then stepped up with his notebook and pen outstretched, as though he wanted the actors' autographs. The Alain Delon character reached graciously out for the pen but Alex went straight past him and stood in front of Oriol.

'Excuse me, señor,' he said. 'I'm trying to clear up some facts about an incident that happened long ago, in 1938, at a farm in the village of Sant Martí dels Moixones. I believe you were present when these events took place. I would really appreciate . . .'

Narcís pushed him aside and hustled the old man towards the car.

'I'd also really like to talk about the *sardana* school,' Alex said as the car door slammed.

Oriol's hands were shaking and the blood drained from his face.

'This is intolerable,' he said. He was so upset for a moment Narcís thought he was going to cry. 'Absolutely intolerable. He must be dealt with. Immediately and finally.'

Narcís looked at the old man in the mirror.

'Don't worry,' he said. 'It's all arranged.'

30

After the match they went for a drink in Gràcia.

'They seem to open another one every day,' Carmen said with some venom as they passed a McDonald's. 'It's cultural imperialism, like carpet bombing with junk food.'

'I don't see any tanks parked outside, do you?' Alex said.

'What's that supposed to mean?'

'Well, I agree with you that they seem to be taking over the world, all I'm saying is no one's forcing it on you. It's like Irving Berlin said: "Popular music is popular because a lot of people like it." You can't argue with that.'

She took him to a stylish bar in Carrer de l'Olla, all stainless steel and white pine and pale-green frosted glass. They took a table and ordered olives, *chipirones*, *patatas bravas* and beer. A Celine Dion album was playing in the background.

'I can't bear that woman's voice,' Alex said. 'It makes my fillings vibrate. I can't imagine why anyone buys her records, let alone millions of them.'

'I guess she's popular because a lot of people like her,' Carmen said, mimicking Alex's accent.

Alex reached over and took one of her Marlboros with a 'May I?' look.

'I didn't think you did.'

'I don't, or I didn't. I don't know.'

'If you don't know, then don't.'

She said it quite firmly, but in a nice way, as though she cared. He froze, the cigarette halfway to his lips. He was already primed to smoke it but she put her hand on his and gently slid the cigarette from his fingers and put it back in the packet. The action was tender, intimate and a touch maternal. Carmen took a toothpick and speared a *chipirón* into her mouth. It left a smear of oil on her lower lip.

'You know, they've been waiting for me all along,' he said. 'I thought it was Sabadell who was behind all the harassment, but I don't think he's anything more than a canny peasant; he saw a chance for some easy money and he took it, or he would if he could get me out of the picture. But I can see now that Oriol has been on to me from the start, that guy at the match, his nephew, he was there at the airport when I landed.'

'So how did he know you were coming, if up till then they thought your aunt hadn't made a will?'

'The only people who knew were your brother Miguel and the Sabadells. One of them, presumably old man Sabadell, must have tipped them off. Oriol's nephew was there again when I was arrested. Or at least he turned up later. I don't think he started it, I think it was that goofy kid Xavi trying to scam me, but then someone – probably the cops, specifically Detective Hernández – tipped off Narcís that I'd been arrested. These people are well connected.'

'That's a bit of an understatement if it's Salvador Oriol we're talking about, it's like saying the Pope has good connections in the Church. So what next?'

'Oriol thinks I know something he doesn't want me or perhaps anyone else to know. Only I don't really know what it is, except I'm sure it's bound up with whatever happened at Can Castanyer in 1938. Raul knows, and so probably does Núria, Victor's younger sister. Finding her is my priority.'

'Are you sure you're not getting a bit stuck in the past? Think like an American.'

'And how do I do that?'

181

'Follow the money.'

'I thought we'd done that; it leads to Salvador Oriol.'

'But why the big secret? If this Roger de Flor project was what it seems, a nice little school for folk-dancing, it would already be in the public domain.'

'That's what I mean, there must be something else, something he wants to hide.'

'Well, we agree about that much, if not what it is he's so desperate to conceal.'

Alex sipped his beer. In the background Celine Dion tortured a tuneless kitchen sink ballad; she sounded like a spoilt child throwing a crying fit.

'Why do think your friend Angel gave the game away about the school?'

Carmen heard that 'your friend'. Even though he didn't say it any sort of way, he didn't have to say it at all. Her teeth clenched in irritation.

'He'll have his reasons. He's using me, of course, to his own ends, that's how he is, but it doesn't mean there's nothing in it for me.'

'So does he often give you tip-offs? I mean, are you close?'

Alex was annoyed with himself for asking and she was annoyed he asked, but at the same time she wanted to level with him.

'Alex, there are two answers to your question: the one you deserve, which is that it's none of your business, and the one I'm going to give you, which is no, Angel and I are not close.'

Which was true; fucking someone doesn't mean you're close, certainly not someone like Angel. And she wasn't fucking him any more anyway.

It was gone midnight. They paid up and left and stood in the street, each waiting for the other to make a move, both knowing the other was waiting. The air was warm and heavy as a midsummer night. Carmen stood so close to him that her breast just lightly touched his upper arm, touching it in a just-so-happened-to-be-touching way. Alex knew there was no such thing. If a woman doesn't want her breast to be in

182

contact with your body she will very soon remedy the situation, but Carmen did nothing to remedy it.

'I'd offer you a lift home if I could remember where I parked my car,' he said, using the self-deprecating joke as a safety net if the come-on fell flat. 'I'd really like to see where you live. You know, from a strictly architectural point of view.'

'I'm afraid it's not open to the public,' Carmen said with grande dame haughtiness. 'We don't do tours.'

She hadn't taken a man home since she split up with Antoní after the abortion.

'Not even private ones, by appointment?' Alex said.

She put her arm round him and kissed him just below the ear.

'I could make an exception in your case. Seeing as you're a stranger in town.'

'Please won't someone take pity,' Alex sang. 'I'm all alone in this big city.'

Carmen stuck out her hand and hailed a taxi.

The driver belonged to some elite commando of cab drivers. He didn't so much drive as attack. He'd internalized with alarming precision the timing and sequence of the Barcelona traffic lights and sped down across Eixample running at all the reds in top gear, without so much as a tap on the brake pedal, confident that each light would turn green before he hit the junction. Which it did, as if it was a magic taxi that could trigger traffic lights. The driver talked non-stop about what a disgrace el Barça were this season and what an even bigger disgracc it was that they were probably going to win the league playing such crap football and suggested a variety of people associated with the club who should be shot at dawn if not earlier. Alex and Carmen sat in the back, clutching the seat and clenching their buttocks, too awestruck by his driving to speak.

Carmen's flat in Provença was of the same era as her brother Miguel's but not as grand. It didn't tell Alex much more about her than he knew already. She had a lot of books, mostly novels and plays, and a number of feminist texts. There was a print of *Garotte Vil* by Ramón Casas on the wall, which told him something, as not everyone would choose to hang a picture of a public execution in their home. There was a photograph of her and Miguel and another of what he took to be her parents but there were few personal touches. It was a little austere, though not forbiddingly so. Still, at least there were no teddy bears. Not long ago Alex went home with a waitress from a club where he had a week's residency. The waitress, who was in her thirties, had four teddy bears and a tiger tucked up in bed and before they could go to bed she had to apologize in baby talk for moving them, explaining to the toys that Mummy had a boy to visit.

'Shower?' Carmen said, offering a towel. She showed him the bathroom. Then she opened another door and said casually, 'And this is the bedroom.' After he showered he lay on her bed in his boxer shorts and listened to the sound of water running and Carmen brushing her teeth. She came into the bedroom wearing a T-shirt that was longish for a T-shirt but very short for a dress. She looked over at Alex, then glanced at the boxer shorts.

'Feeling shy?'

'I didn't want to assume.'

She pulled off her rings and silver bangle and dropped them on the dressing table.

'That's a nice piece of semantics,' she said, smiling with her eyes. 'Surely assumptions are made involuntarily, regardless of whether we want to make them.'

'What I meant to say is I had decided, were the possibility of an assumption to arise, that I would not make it.'

'Very commendable,' she said, pulling the T-shirt over her head and throwing it on a chair.

She climbed on to the bed and sat astride his legs, just above his knees, with her hands resting on her thighs and a sweet but sardonic smile on her face. Evidently she wasn't feeling shy. She leaned forward and they kissed. Carmen was usually content to let the man do the running so long as he was running in her general direction, but now she decided that she was going to take charge. Her skin was soft against his legs. He started to get hard. She touched his cock through his boxer shorts and made a hhhmm sound. She lifted the elastic of his boxer shorts over his cock and slid them down his thighs, raised herself on her knees and pulled them under her and off over his ankles. She bent down and ran her cheek along the side of his cock, like a cat. Her breath was soft on his stomach. He stroked her hair and neck and he was swept up in a wave of lust and tenderness. She slid her tongue the length of his cock and on to his stomach, wriggling her body up slowly until her labia touched the base of his cock. She was very wet. Just for a second he thought maybe this was a big mistake, that ever since he got off the plane everything that happened to him happened because someone else wanted it to, even this, that he wasn't taking control and maybe it was time he did. Then she kissed him and he didn't think about anything. Her mouth was a hot pool and he dived in.

She pulled back and sat up. She eyed him with amused curiosity. Alex ran his hand over her stomach and thighs. When you've been away from the sexual front line for a while the prospect of any sort of relationship seems impossibly complicated, precisely because it's the simple things that are so hard to recall: the smoothness of a woman's skin, the smell of her neck, the hair on her forearms, the smallness of her hands. Basic, uncomplicated, friendly animal stuff. She lifted her hips and settled herself gently on his cock, like a nesting bird, then moved slowly back and forth, his cock in the hot groove of her lips.

'How you doing?' she said, with a half-smile and one raised eyebrow.

Alex moaned and motioned for her to come down and kiss him again. She did. He really did want to kiss her, but he was also so excited that he thought he might come at any second. If he lay there looking up at her sliding against his cock with that whimsical what-do-you-think-of-this look on her face, he'd lose it. So he kissed her and did what he always did to stop himself coming: he imagined he was up a ladder in a bare room, hanging anaglypta wallpaper. He hung one drop and now he was hanging the second, trying to match up the embossed pattern across the join. It did the trick, it always did. Worked in seconds. He never had to hang more than the two drops to get out of the come-too-soon danger zone.

Carmen sat up again and took his cock in her hand and started moving it against her clit and the mouth of her cunt.

'I haven't got any condoms,' Alex said. 'I hadn't been thinking of having sex.'

'Liar,' she said, leaning across him to rummage in the drawer of the bedside table. She sat up and slowly tore open the foil packet. Her breasts were small and pointed, with long, dark nipples. The colour of black grapes, Alex thought. Alex arched his neck to kiss them and as the tip of his tongue touched her nipple she took him inside her. They both gasped, the feeling was so raw, so close to pain. It was plain this wasn't going to be a long ride, they were both too hungry for release. Alex hung some more anaglypta. Carmen moaned. He held her head while she moved on him, he held her breasts, her buttocks. After a few minutes he slid his hand down his stomach so that her clit rode on his middle finger and right away her eyes popped wide and she started to come. She came in a long slow arc, very quiet, very intense, gone inside herself, rolling over him like a wave, ending with a thin plangent cry, like a seagull caught in her throat. He held her head, stroking her while the last of the wave washed out of her. He drew the fingers of one hand slowly down over her nipple, hard and shining from his kisses, and held her hip with the other. He started to come. He was coming from way back, from every direction, from the basement up. All over the house the shutters and cupboards flew open, drawers spilled out on to the floor, pipes burst, fuses blew, banisters shook, ceilings collapsed, the smoke alarm went off. The house was on fire. He let it burn.

Carmen leaned forward, planting her hands either side of his head, her face shining with sweat. Alex drew his fingertips along the edge of her lips and looked into her black eyes. She looked different. Alex had forgotten that, too, that once someone's let you in for a closer look they never look quite the same again. He could feel his pulse beating in his neck. His blood was awash with whatever it is that sex releases – endorphins, dopamine, honeybees. He opened his mouth to say something but she silenced him with a kiss then slid off him and lay on her back holding his hand.

'So,' she said, lacing her fingers with his.

'Well,' he said, squeezing her hand.

31

Alex woke to the aroma of coffee and the chemical bite of nail varnish. Carmen sat on the end of the bed in the long white T-shirt with cotton wool balls between her toes, painting her toenails violet. In the kitchen the espresso pot plup-plupped on the stove.

'Good morning,' she said, keeping her eyes on her work.

'Hello. What a sleep. I feel like I've been drugged.'

'All natural ingredients, I assure you.'

Alex sat up and leaned over to kiss her but she held him at bay with the nail brush.

'Artist at work. Take the coffee off the heat before it burns.'

While he was in the kitchen her mobile rang. He took it in to her, still ringing, relieved her of the jar of nail varnish and the brush and handed her the phone. It was as if they'd been together for years.

'Blanca,' Carmen said. 'I was going to call you. What's up?'

Blanca looked terrible. Her skin was dry, her hair looked like it hadn't been washed in a month and the only light in her eyes was a paranoid flicker as though someone trapped behind them was desperately signalling with a torch. She insisted that, for security, they meet on the westbound platform of the Entença metro station but that Carmen should act as if they didn't know each other. When Carmen arrived Blanca acknowledged her with the slightest of nods then boarded the next train. Carmen followed, one car behind. At Verdaguer, Blanca switched to the orange line as far as Maragall. The cloak and dagger game tried Carmen's patience but she could see that Blanca was really on the edge and she felt guilty that she hadn't been in touch since Fèlix's funeral, so she didn't complain. At Maragall, Blanca boarded a blue line train heading east. She got off where they started, at Entença, except they were now on the eastbound platform. The trip had taken nearly an hour and put Carmen in a bad mood. Blanca sat on a bench at the far end of the platform and motioned with her head for Carmen to join her. They sat there in the spongy secondhand air as two trains came and went. When there was no one left in the station Blanca reached into her bag and handed Carmen a rolled up piece of paper and stood up to go.

'I found this among Fèlix's things,' she said bitterly. 'Now maybe you'll believe he was murdered.'

32

It was a long shot, looking for someone he'd never met in a city of two million people. Alex spent the morning in the old city – the Barri Gòtic, Raval and Barri Xino – where most of the urban castaways seemed to wash up. He told whoever would listen that he was looking for Núria Sabadell, that it was important, that he wasn't a cop and was willing to pay for good information. He said the same to anyone selling *La Farola*, the homeless people's newspaper. He said he could be found that afternoon between five and six o'clock in Cervecería Judas, a bar he chose because the name amused him; even by Barcelona standards naming a bar after Judas seemed eccentric. By then it was lunchtime, too late to look for Raul. Still, if no one showed up at Judas, Raul would be his next port of call. He had a late lunch of *fideus* in Plaça Reial where a Gypsy with flayed vocal cords serenaded the tourists. He sang, 'I'm a poor Gypsy and what I need is money, I'm a poor Gypsy and what I need is money,' with all the passion of a man lamenting a great and unrequited love, clearly confident that few in his audience understood what he was actually saying.

Cervecería Judas was close to Plaça George Orwell in the Carrer de Escudellers, a gloomy, piss-drenched street cheered only by the aroma of chickens spit-roasting on a wood fire outside Los Caracoles restaurant. The chicken smell drew the tourists who posed for pictures in front of the spit until the passing whoosh of a bag snatcher ruined their day. Judas was a narrow, grubby room with a worn Formica bar, half a dozen spindly stools with torn vinyl seats, a TV on a high shelf and a blue neon fly killer on the wall. The clientele ranged from sad to hopeless and no one stayed longer than it took to down a beer or a cup of coffee. The barmaid was a young, dark-skinned Gypsy who might have been pretty if only she had a smile to match her scowl. She was letting her rounded sensuality run to fat in a way that said, What do I care? In fact, everything about her said, What's it to you? Alex nicknamed her La Desdeñosa, the disdainful one. She poured him a sloppy beer and he took it to one of the two tables of the same rag-worn Formica and sat facing the street, waiting. A woman with a high-pitched voice was singing a Spanish cover of Madonna's 'Like a Virgin' on the radio. La Desdeñosa mouthed the words.

At five fifteen someone familiar came in. It was the skinny junkie-looking guy who was following him before he moved out to Can Castanyer. He was dressed in his habitual black jeans and black leather jacket and wore a mobile on his hip. La Desdeñosa said, 'Hello Kiko,' with little feeling. He replied, 'Hello gorgeous,' with less. They had a brief conversation that Alex caught snatches of, enough only to notice that they both spoke with the same accent, with the letters s and d stripped out, so that entire sentences bubbled out in one long, guttural, modulated vowel.

Alex caught Kiko's eye. Kiko held his gaze but continued his conversation with the barmaid. After a minute or so he swaggered slowly over to the table, flipped a chair round and parked himself with his forearms on the back of the chair.

'So, back on surveillance duties,' Alex said.

'No.' Kiko took out a Zippo lighter and flipped it open and shut. He did this five or six times, then took a cigarette from behind his ear and lit it.

'I hear you're looking for someone.'

'That's correct.'

'What for? Are they in trouble?'

'No.'

'What's it worth?'

'That depends on what it is.'

'An address.'

Alex told him what it was worth.

'Double it.'

'No.'

Kiko played with the lighter some more. He rolled it expertly across the back of his hand, knuckle to knuckle, then back again, the sort of trick you get lots of time to perfect in jail. Alex took some bills out of his wallet, counted them, then folded them away in his shirt pocket. If Kiko was a junkie, he needed money, junkies always need money as a matter of urgency. Which also meant he'd lie to get it; addiction has a corrosive effect on people's integrity.

'Half now, half when I find her,' he said, knowing that half was enough to tempt Kiko, even if he didn't trust Alex to pay the balance. 'And while we're here having this chat, why were you following me?'

Kiko leaned his head back and blew a thin stream of smoke at the ceiling.

'Because someone asked me to,' he said in the same weary go-fuck-yourself manner as the barmaid.

'And they're not asking you to now?'

'I expect it's passed that stage,' he said, the menace in his voice just a little too secondhand. Too many gangster movies, Alex thought. La Desdeñosa was throwing someone out of the bar, a tiny, grubby old street bum. She stood, one hand on her hip, the other pointing to the door, blasting the poor man into the street with a gale of the vilest insults.

'So,' Alex said, taking the cash from his shirt pocket, 'Núria Sabadell, where can I find her?'

Kiko looked at the money. Alex peeled off a bill and gave it to him.

'Carrer dels Carders,' Kiko said. 'Follow Carrer de la Bòria, off Via Laietana, and keep going till it becomes Carders.'

Kiko paused. Alex peeled off another bill.

'I don't know the number but halfway along on the left there's an old-fashioned shop, sells ladies underwear, old ladies underwear. Núria has a place above the shop, top floor.'

Alex gave him the rest of the money.

'You going to be in here tomorrow with the other half? Same time?'

'Sure, assuming I find her.'

They both knew he was lying. Alex stood up to go. Kiko flipped the Zippo open and shut.

'You do know you're in deep shit, don't you?' he said, not bothering to look up.

'I appreciate your concern, I really do,' Alex said sarcastically, thinking, If you've seen enough movies, anyone can play this tough guy role, even me.

Out in the street two young, burger-fattened American women in large pastel shorts and bumbags were waving their arms about and shouting in English in an effort to interest two Policía Nacional in the fact that a dark-haired man in jeans and red shirt had just that moment snatched their Nikon from outside Los Caracoles. The cops listened with grave faces, understanding nothing and everything. The women were red in the face, they shouted that it had just happened, that if the cops ran they could probably catch the thief. They flapped their plump arms and the cops nodded sympathetically. The more agitated the women became, the more impassive the cops. They didn't budge; it was like beating a mule.

33

Carmen was holding a summit meeting at a corner table in Pitarra. Francesc from the environment department was there, along with Enric Luna, the news editor of *El Mensajero*, and Carmen's brother Miguel. Francesc and Miguel had a tendency to banter that verged on sniping when they were together, but in the presence of the resolutely heterosexual Luna they formed a tacit united front. Carmen told them what she knew about Roger de Flor and showed Francesc the plan Blanca had found among Fèlix's things. It showed a series of developments, not only on the land that Jaume Sabadell sold to Mallobeco, but also on Can Castanyer. The drawings had the imprimatur of the Generalitat de Catalunya.

'What we really need to see is the elevation,' Francesc said. 'All you can tell from this is the footprint, you know, how many square metres the buildings occupy, but not how tall they are or what they look like. They could be single or multi-storey, there's no way of telling. But taking everything at face value, if this building here on the Sabadell land is the school – and it would be big enough – then these others could be, say, student facilities, a cafeteria, dormitories even. Pretty big ones, mind you.'

Carmen looked at Luna. She knew he was hot for the story

but he wasn't about to show it, not in front of her and certainly not in front of these two.

'So what do you think?' she said. Luna narrowed his narrow eyes and clasped his hands under his chin.

'Well, it's one of those stories that looks good from a distance, it has all the right elements, especially if Oriol really is involved. Nothing about him has ever seemed right, not to me anyway. But when you hold it up to the light it looks pretty threadbare. Some drawings, some threats, some rumours – most of it can't be substantiated and all of it's deniable.'

'Except Mallobeco did buy that plot of land.'

'Our only fact, I'm afraid, and not something that in itself demands an explanation. And Oriol would have no trouble asserting that he knew nothing about it, that he isn't involved in Mallobeco's day-to-day business. So what we have is a story that we don't believe – I mean we don't really think it's a *sardana* school, do we? – which is obscuring the true story about which we know nothing. And we can't stand either of them up.'

Luna was making a real effort not to be patronizing, which showed an awareness Carmen didn't think he had. It showed he could behave if he chose to, that being a bully wasn't entirely involuntary. Maybe it was the presence of the two gay men; maybe he was afraid of them in some way.

'What I'm thinking,' Carmen said, 'is if we try to stand up the story we don't believe in, maybe the true story will crawl out by default.' She turned to Francesc. 'Let's say you've just been handed this drawing. You've never heard of any plans for a *sardana* school or any such thing, and you have to guess what kind of a development is being proposed, what would you say?'

Francesc sat back and sipped his wine, savouring being the centre of attention. 'Well,' he said theatrically holding his forehead as though he had a sudden headache.

'Oh Lord,' Miguel said. 'Queen for a day. Get on with it, Xeco.'

195

'Not just a day, sweetie,' Francesc said airily.

Luna studied his plate and waited for the game to end. He didn't like fags. He didn't think they should be burnt at the stake, he just didn't like them or their company. And he always suspected they were laughing at him.

'All right,' Francesc said, 'this smaller building, the one we've been calling the school, it could be anything from a pigsty to an art gallery. But these three large ones, if I had to guess, I'd say they were apartment blocks.'

'Apartments? Why?'

'Because they all face the sea and they're staggered in such a way so as not to get in each other's light. That would be my first reaction, but then I'd have to think again, because even God couldn't get permission to build apartments in this zone.'

'Why not?' Carmen said. 'The rules are there for bending. Look at some of the stuff that's gone up since the restrictions came in.'

'Not here. Every application that's been put in for this zone over the past six or seven years has been knocked back, every single one.'

Luna looked at Carmen and shrugged as if to say, 'See what I mean, no story.' Not that she trusted him, but she knew *El Mensajero* wouldn't touch it. But *Ara*, Fèlix's old paper, would. *Ara* wasn't any more anxious than her own paper to rock the Catalan establishment's boat, but its circulation had fallen to break-even point and looked set to fall further. It desperately needed something more to justify its existence than the fact that it was written in Catalan. Carmen would give it to them as a straight story, no side, nothing sinister. Salvador Oriol is building a school for *sardana* as a gift to the nation. What a wonderful guy. You heard it first here in *Ara*. It wasn't going to make her famous, but she didn't care any more, she was doing it for Fèlix. And for fun too. She could hardly wait to see Oriol's face as the great citizens of Catalunya lined up on the TV3 lunchtime news to thank him for his generosity.

After the others left, Miguel and Carmen sat over their coffee. They talked about family things, their mother's osteo-

196

porosis which it was too late now to do anything about. And their father's deafness and how the more of a problem it became the more he pretended there wasn't a problem.

'How's lover boy?' Miguel said. 'And don't make that face, I know you too well.'

Carmen knew it was pointless to protest, she and Miguel could never hide anything from each other. The day she came back from the abortion he left three messages on her machine because he knew something was wrong. And at the very moment he broke a leg skiing in Andorra she got such bad cramp in her leg she couldn't stand up. They weren't twins but they had twin-like telepathy.

'He's nice,' she said. 'Sort of strange, but soft without being wet. He stayed the night.'

'At your place? Good God, a man has finally scaled the forbidding ramparts of Casa Carmen. The siege has ended, the *alcázar* has fallen at last. How was it?'

'It was good, very good. Except he fell asleep when I could have gone another round.'

'I'm jealous, seeing you glide down the gilded river of romance while I seem to be sinking ever deeper into the swamp of fuck-me-and-forget-it sex. I live in a world where long-term relationships are measured in hours.'

'Oh, please.'

'Really. And guess what? I've been invited to join a club, a very exclusive sex club, which says a lot about how other people see me.'

'What club? Where?'

'Listen to you, Miss Hotpants. Do you want to join too? It's not a club in the usual sense, I mean it doesn't have an address, it meets here and there. It's more of a salon, except I suppose a salon implies a certain minimum of conversation. This group see themselves as sexual adventurers, exploring the outer limits of pleasure. They call themselves Ultrapassa.'

'A step beyond. What do they do exactly?'

'I'd have to join to find out, and I'm not sure it's really my thing. As you know, as poofs go I'm really rather conventional.

But of course I'm curious. The person who invited me is a rather illustrious lawyer, and no, I'm not going to tell you his name, but everyone knows he's destined to be a judge, or a notary at the very least. It seems there are quite a few high-flyers in Ultrapassa. So maybe it's a good place to network, though I don't know quite what sort of networking you'd do in a leather gag with a bullwhip up your arse.'

Carmen put her hand on her brother's.

'Don't join, Miguel. It's dangerous, that stuff. Things can get out of hand.'

He patted her hand. 'Don't worry, I don't think it's really me. But it's nice to be asked, don't you think?'

34

Alex felt like Alice; everyone talked in riddles or could only answer a question with another question. So now he was pinning his hopes on Núria. Why? Because of what Victor said, that she didn't care whose feathers she ruffled, which made Alex think that if she knew something she'd tell him. And he wanted to find her because she was elusive and mysterious and because he liked her name.

Along Laietana workmen were unloading crush barriers in readiness for the royal wedding procession. Alex found Carrer de la Bòria, a well-heeled little street that rapidly slid down-market as it became Carrer dels Carders and slouched gloomily into the flaking graffiti and fried fish of Plaça de la Acadèmia. The shop was exactly as Kiko described: the window was cluttered with torso mannequins dressed in heavy duty bras and corsets, flesh-coloured or greying white, that looked like they'd been there since the fifties. He pressed the top buzzer. Across the street two Policía Nacional were running an ID check on a young Arab. Alex buzzed again. Another Arab came up the street beating a trolley of butane *bombonas* with a spanner. A frazzled-looking woman with a child in her arms shouted down from a third floor balcony for a refill. The Arab slung a *bombona* on to his shoulder. The muscles stood out on his skinny brown arms as he trudged wearily over to her door. Alex rang a third and fourth time. No one answered.

The next bell down had a name beside it, Sánchez. He rang it and when someone answered he mumbled something of which only the name Sánchez was intelligible. The person at the other end said, 'What?' and he mumbled something about Sánchez again. They buzzed him in. There was no lift, just a steep tiled staircase with a wobbly iron balustrade. The stair-well was dim, painted maroon up to shoulder height, then ochre up to the ceiling. From the look of it, it hadn't been repainted for decades. As he reached the second floor landing an elderly woman looked out of the door of the Sánchez residence. Alex wished her a pleasant hello and carried on upstairs. She muttered an insult and shut the door. The top floor buzzer didn't work so he knocked. The silence wasn't the silence of an empty flat. He could sense someone in there. So he knocked again and waited and then again, each time a little louder, until he heard the shuffle of steps on the other side of the door.

'What?' a small voice said, the voice of someone who hasn't spoken for some time.

'Núria? My name's Alex, I'm a friend of your brother Victor.'

'Victor doesn't have friends.'

'Alex Nadal, Anna Nadal's nephew. From New York. I need to talk to you.'

After a full minute's silence she slid back the bolt and opened the door. She was small and sparrow-frail, dressed in a long, baggy man's shirt. Her forearms and hands were childishly small and her pale, pointy face was framed by a thick mess of chestnut hair. Her amber eyes glowed inside dark rings and she looked like she'd been living on a diet of cigarettes. It was the girl who was with Kiko outside the police station in Laietana and he understood why she looked fam-iliar, because she was unmistakably Victor's sister.

'Hello Núria. Good to meet you at last. Can I come in?'

'To do what? You lay a hand on me I'll cut your fucking throat.'

She had an angry scared look like a cornered animal.

'Please, I'm not going to harm you. I just want to talk.'

'What about?'

'About Anna, and about her brother Ignasi, my father.'

Nuria flicked the hair off her face. Her lips were dry and cracked, her nails were bitten to the quick. She hesitated, then opened the door a few inches and stood aside to let him in.

He entered a large, unexpectedly bright room furnished with a worn sofa, a small table and two blue plastic chairs. Unlike Núria, the room was immaculately clean and tidy. There were a dozen or so drawings on the walls, stuck up with map pins, pencil drawings of Barcelona street scenes. They were good, very good.

'You do these?'

'How is Anna?' she said, ignoring the question and fixing a cigarette between her lips. 'I haven't seen her for weeks.'

Alex took a deep breath.

'She died more than six months ago. She had an accident, she fell down the stairs. It turns out she also had cancer. Inoperable.'

Núria looked completely deflated. The fight went out of her eyes and the cigarette drooped unlit from the side of her mouth.

'Dead? Shit. I didn't even know she was sick. God, I'm so fucking useless. Auntie Anna dead? Shit, shit, shit,' she said, beating her chest with her small fist for emphasis.

'I'm sorry. Victor said you were close. I know . . .'

'You don't know shit,' she said, her amber eyes back on high beam.

He held her gaze. He could see behind the angry eyes that she was crumbling and he wanted to put an arm around her shoulders to comfort her. He thought she'd probably knee him in the balls, but he tried anyway. He put a hand on her bony shoulder. She didn't react. Gently he took the cigarette from her mouth and held her head against his chest. Her hair was dirty and rank with sweat and tobacco. Her shoulder blades were sharp bumps under the baggy shirt. She didn't shake or sob, he didn't even know she was crying until he felt the tears soak through his shirt. They flowed out of her in a steady, silent stream. Time passed, crying time. Her arms hung by her side. Then she detached herself and took the cigarette from his hand and lit it. She stood with her back to him, smoking, silent. She smoked the cigarette down to the butt and ground it out in an ashtray advertising Veterano brandy.

'They hate me there, you know,' she said, staring at the ashtray. 'In the village. My father, my family. I can't go back there, I can't.'

Alex thought, No one's suggesting you should, no one except you, that is.

'You can stay at Can Castanyer. Victor's staying there now, for a while anyway. We can take care of you.'

'I can fucking well take care of my fucking self,' she said, pushing away the last of a tear with her fist.

'I only meant you'd have a place to stay. And since you raise the subject, you don't seem that good at taking care of yourself. How long since you had a hit?'

'What the fuck's it got to do with you?' she said, lighting another cigarette. Then, more softly, 'A week.'

'Are you doing it cold?'

'I had some methadone first day, then cold. I'm nearly through now, I think. How do you know all this shit? You don't look like a user?'

'Me, no, but we do have a couple of junkies in New York City. I think maybe we invented junkies. One of my best friends became a junkie. He's dead now.'

'Better off fucking dead,' she said.

'That wasn't how I felt at the time,' Alex said, very quietly.

'I'm sorry,' she said, softening a little. 'It was your friend, I'm sorry, it was a stupid thing to say. But that's me, stupid. Fucking useless in fact.'

'No one's useless. And your drawings are really good.'

'What do you know? Are you an art critic or something?' she said, sulky but flattered.

'No, I'm a piano player. And you don't have to be a critic to know what's good.'

'There's a piano at Can Castanyer. No one never played it.'

'They do now. I had it tuned.'

Núria paced around the room smoking. Then she stopped in the bedroom doorway and stood with a hand on her hip, like she was standing guard.

'I don't get you,' she said. 'What's your angle? Are you trying to fuck me?'

Alex laughed. 'Do you mean literally?'

And she did mean it literally, but because he said it like that, straight, with no nuance at all, and because he laughed but not at her or at the idea that someone might want to fuck her, she suddenly felt embarrassed, ashamed even. Alex caught a glimpse of the unhappy girl she might once have been before she became an unhappy woman.

'Last year my father killed himself because of something that happened at Can Castanyer in 1938, something he could no longer bear to live with. Maybe he did something terrible, or maybe he didn't but everyone else believed he did. All I want to know is what happened and then maybe the whole business can be laid to rest. That's my angle.'

Núria went into the tiny kitchen and appeared with a bottle of vodka and two glasses. They clinked glasses. Alex took a sip but she threw hers down in one and refilled the glass.

'It's a nasty story,' she said, draining the second glass. 'An ugly, nasty, cruel story. But no one's ever going to believe it, and of course there's no proof. I'm a bit freaked out right now, I really don't know if I can talk about it. It tears me up even to think about it.'

'I understand,' Alex said, impatient but determined not to let her out of his grasp. 'We could talk about it tomorrow. Why don't I take you to Can Castanyer? No one needs to know you're there, just me and Victor. You can get some rest, and there'd be no temptation, you know, from people like Kiko.'

'You know Kiko?'

'Not really. He told me where I could find you, for a price of course.'

'There isn't anything Kiko wouldn't do for money.'

'He was following me, for several days. Does he belong to a gang of some sort?'

'Kiko? No, Kiko wouldn't join anything. He's just generally for hire. He's your basic all-purpose whore. Now I'm going to take a shower.'

Half an hour later she reappeared, with clean hair, dressed in a short black skirt and a leopardskin-pattern shirt. She looked pretty in an urchinesque way.

'You look nice,' Alex said, without thinking, then braced himself for the reaction. All he got was a quick flash of the amber warning lights.

'Have you got any cash? I haven't eaten for days,' she said. Her speech was a bit slurred from the vodka. She took him to a pizza place down the road where they ate a couple of greasy pizzas washed down with Estrella. She did everything with the same compulsive urgency: she stuffed the pizza in as though someone might take it away, she drained the beer in three long gulps, and smoked each cigarette down to the filter.

Alex was twenty minutes late for his date with Carmen when he introduced her to a tipsy Núria in Boadas. By now it was plain that Núria couldn't hold her drink and Alex's sense of foreboding deepened when she ordered a vodka martini. La Boada was resplendent in an ultramarine mini-dress with a silver belt. Her hair was tied back in a loose pony-tail above bright blue glass earrings that matched the dress. Her deadpan sidekicks were in their customary tuxedos. She gave Alex a disapproving look, as though it was his fault Núria was drunk, then set about mixing the drinks. Núria smoked and ran her tongue over her dry lips. She looked at Carmen, then Alex, then Carmen again.

'You're his girlfriend, aren't you?' she said, swaying a little.

Carmen gave Núria a sweet smile that said absolutely nothing.

'I suppose he's quite cute,' Núria said, 'I can see why you'd go for him.'

Carmen looked at Alex with a mixture of amusement and irritation.

'I've never come across the name Núria before,' Alex said, trying to change the subject. 'It's nice. Is it Catalan?'

'Some fucking virgin,' Núria said in a loud voice as she downed the martini. A couple of heads turned. She signalled to one of La Boada's sidekicks for a refill but La Boada told him no with a flash of her blue-shadowed eyes.

'Catalan girls,' Núria went on, 'if they're not called Núria, they're fucking Montserrat. Pair of fucking virgins, so to speak. Black virgins, as a matter of fact. All Spanish girls are named after some fucking virgin, usually María. What about you, Carmen? I bet your full name is María Carmen, isn't it?'

Carmen nodded and gave her a thin smile, but Alex was relieved to see that she seemed more amused than annoyed.

'See what I mean? Got to get that fucking virgin in there somewhere. María Teresa, María Dolores, María Angustias, María Belén, María Pilar, María De Los Fucking Reyes – a nation of fucking virgin Marys. You know what my two best friends at school were called? Imma and Resu. Can you believe that? Immaculada and fucking Resurrecció. What kind of a fucking name is that to give a girl, Resurrecció?'

People were giving them dirty looks. If Núria noticed she didn't care, the vodka had gone straight to her head. She turned to La Boada.

'How about you? I bet you're a María something or another.'

The *patrona* didn't dignify Núria with a reply. She turned to the cash register, rang up the bill and handed it to Alex with a contemptuous look that said, 'Don't bring her in here again.'

Out in the street Núria warmed to her theme, calling out to

passersby with a litany of latter-day Marías: María of the Supermarkets, María of the Low Dosage Pill, María of the Stock Options, María of the Recycled Waste. She thought she was hilarious. The wave of vaguely paternal affection Alex felt for her ebbed away. He picked up her case.

'Come on,' he said, 'let's find the car.'

He kissed Carmen on the cheek.

'So, did she tell you what you want to know?' she said.

'No, but I know she knows,' he said, kissing the other cheek. He studied her face. Your fabulous face, he thought, but couldn't remember what song that was from. He wanted to say what? Something more than I like you but not as declamatory as I love you. But there isn't much, either in English or Spanish, so he cupped her head in his free hand and kissed her on the mouth and she kissed him back. They seemed to be saying the same thing to each other. Núria circled round them like a naughty child, chanting 'María of the Sloppy Kisses, María of the Illicit Affairs, María of the Stiff Dicks.'

The kiss dissolved into giggles.

'You'd better take her home before she gets arrested,' Carmen said, laughing. 'And be careful, and I don't mean of her. Oh, and be sure to pick up a copy of *Ara* tomorrow morning. The fun's really starting now.'

35

It's customary, when a newspaper is about to publish some damaging revelations, to forewarn the subject of the revelations on the eve of publication. It's done as a matter of courtesy, with just a hint of compassion, like letting a condemned man smoke a cigarette before the blindfold's tied. The editor of *Ara* waited until the first edition was biked around to his home in Sarrià before he made the call. He was savouring the moment, and with good reason. For a start, it was a good story in its own right, and what's more, an exclusive. Better still, an exclusive given to them by a disgruntled employee on a rival paper. But the editor was well aware that this wasn't the whole story and possibly wasn't the story at all; that while the piece they were running appeared to be completely straight, it was pure mischief. Even the headline – 'Oriol's secret gift' – was ambivalent. He was ninety-nine per cent certain it wasn't what Salvador Oriol wanted to read in his morning paper.

Salvador Oriol, self-appointed mascot of the Catalan nation, regularly featured on the pages of *Ara* and was invited as a matter of course to any function the paper sponsored. Shortly after the editor took over the job of running *Ara* he met Oriol at the private view of an exhibition at the Picasso museum.

Oriol shook his hand and said, 'Who would have imagined that a paper such as *Ara* would one day be edited by an African.' It was classic Oriol – a slight so vulgar that by the time the editor felt composed enough to respond the moment had passed. He was not, of course, an African, but although his mother was a *Catala de sempre*, his father came from Cartagena in the south, and the more racist Catalans regularly dismissed people from the south as Africans, though not usually to their face. So that was the other reason for savouring the moment before he made the call – revenge. Before he picked up the phone he poured himself a glass of Gran Juvé y Camps and watched the bubbles stream to the surface.

'I'd just like to say we all think it's a marvellous gesture,' he said breezily to a bemused Oriol. 'I can't imagine how you managed to keep it a secret for so long. Of course if a man doesn't want to broadcast his good works to the world, that's only to be admired. But in this instance we felt there was an overriding public interest, so we've put it on page one.'

'What are you talking about?'

It was clear from the near panic in his voice that he knew exactly what he was talking about.

'The *sardana* school. I know you wanted to keep it a secret a little while longer but if I know, then who knows who else does. We have to think of the competition. And we wanted to be the first to express our thanks, on behalf of the people.'

The editor listened to Oriol breathing; he was not breathing easily.

'But you can't, you've got it all wrong,' Oriol spluttered. 'You've no idea, I insist . . .'

'Wrong? Oh no, that can't be possible, we've seen the plans. Are you saying there is to be no school, no Roger de Flor?'

The editor sipped his *cava*. It was very good; cold and very dry.

'No, I'm not saying that.'

'So it's true. What a relief. Maybe there's still time to get your confirmation into the final edition. I'll call the night editor right away.'

'No, you mustn't do that.'

'Fine, fine, I understand that sometimes it's inappropriate to comment. We can just say that Señor Oriol declined to confirm or deny the story.'

'No, no. You must not print anything.'

'I'm so sorry, I had no idea you'd feel so strongly about this. But it's like I say, if it ever came out – and it would, believe me, journalists are the worst gossips – if it came out that I had this story and didn't run it, well I'd be out of a job and quite rightly too.'

'But you must not print it, you've no idea.' Oriol was trying to pull rank, but his desperation undermined his authority.

'It's too late, I'm afraid, it's already printed. The first edition will be on the trucks to Girona and Tarragona by now. I'm so sorry, I never imagined you'd be so put out, otherwise I would have spoken to you first.'

Oriol started to say something, then hung up. The editor drained his glass and wondered if he'd still have a job in the morning. *Ara*'s proprietor was, inevitably, a big pal of Oriol's.

Angel lay on the sofa watching TV. His son Josep had gone out but there was a lingering smell of marijuana and young male in the room. Angel made a couple of calls, just a couple, but he knew it would be enough. He put the mobile on the floor beside the sofa and waited. The phone started ringing within three minutes.

'It's just a rumour,' he said. 'But that's what I hear, he's really in the shit.'

As soon as the call ended the phone rang again.

'That's right,' Angel said. 'Seems like the old man's over-extended himself, fronted up for an American deal that's about to collapse. I don't know the details, but the word is he could be ruined, but then you know how people exaggerate.'

After that it rang every few minutes; Angel spread the word of Salvador Oriol's misfortune. Then he made one more call, to a courier service. He told them to collect an early edition of *Ara* from the newspaper's offices and bike it to a Señor Williams at the Hotel Meridien.

36

Alex was woken at three in the morning by Núria climbing into his bed. She was naked and she stank of booze.

'Hey, Núria, what do you think you're doing?'

But she was barely awake. She lay her cheek on his shoulder and flung an arm across his chest and went straight back to sleep like a child. Alex let his arm fall across her back and stroked her skinny shoulders. Núria's breath came slow and wheezy. In her sleep she slid her leg between his. Everything about her was sharp and bony except the flesh on the inside of her thighs. Alex's cock started to get hard. It was involuntary, it didn't mean anything, he didn't want her. It was just his cock talking; a cock has its own agenda. He thought about Carmen, but that only made it worse.

In the morning, when he went downstairs Victor was burning toast. It occurred to Alex that until his father threw him out Victor probably never made so much as a cup of coffee. It was so much easier to be a rebel when you knew your mum would have lunch on the table. Victor and Núria were only a few years younger than him but Alex was beginning to feel like he'd acquired two children.

'I found your sister,' Alex said. 'She's upstairs, asleep in my bed.'

Victor dropped the piece of toast.

'It's not what it looks like.'

Victor whirled his arm in an arc and brought it down on the strings of an imaginary guitar. 'Hey man, it's cool,' he said in heavily accented American. 'It's a free country. How did you find her?'

'It's a long story. Right now she's not very well. She's been sick for a while, she needs rest and she needs to eat.'

Why, he wondered, was he protecting Victor from the fact that his sister was a junkie? It was exactly what he did with his sister Pepa, protect her from unpleasant truths.

'Right, well, we can take care of her, can't we?'

It wasn't a rhetorical question, Victor was asking for reassurance. I'm replacing his mother, Alex thought.

'Sure we can,' he said. 'She'll be OK. Right now she just needs to sleep. Victor, you remember you took Anna to Torredembarra to post a couple of packages? One was to me, right? What about the other one?'

Victor got that mixed-up look that came over him whenever he was working himself up to tell a lie.

'Come on, Victor. I'm letting you stay here, I found your sister, I think you owe me this much.'

Victor fiddled with his hair and looked at the floor.

'Salvador Oriol. You know who he is?'

'Yes, I know.'

Victor muttered something about going to Tarragona to get the chainsaw fixed. There wasn't anywhere nearer and it was time to start getting the firewood ready, though you wouldn't think so in this heat, he said. Alex asked him to bring a copy of *Ara* back with him and took a tray of coffee upstairs. Núria opened one eye then sat up, unselfconsciously naked, and had a coughing fit. Her breasts, the only real flesh on her, shook as she coughed. Alex took a T-shirt out of the chest of drawers and threw it on to her lap. She made a prim face and put it on. He poured the coffee and when she saw the tray she smiled a sweet, girlish smile he hadn't seen before. The tray was painted with a crude picture of the church in Sant Martí.

212

'I painted that, when I was about twelve. I gave it to Anna as a present.'

'I'm surprised your father let you and Victor spend so much time here, given that he seems pretty hostile to the Nadal family.'

Núria laughed bitterly.

'I used to think his hostility was political, but I found out it was because she turned him down.'

'Who? Anna?'

'Yes, he offered to marry her. This is years ago; he was pretty young, five or six years younger than her. Anyway, he offered, that's what she said – he didn't ask her, he offered, like he was doing her a favour.'

'Because she was older than him?'

'No, not because of that. Anyway, she refused.'

'But why would he be doing her a favour by marrying her?'

Núria downed the cup of coffee and shuddered.

'We'll get to that. It's funny, she mentioned her brother – your father – a few times, well, when she told me all about what happened. But she never said anything about him having children, maybe she didn't know about you.'

'My father pretended she was dead. He said she died of TB when she was sixteen. I've no idea why. And I don't know how Anna knew I existed or where to find me. It's weird, there are no papers in the house. Nothing. She made a will but no one ever found a copy.'

'Have you looked in her not very secret hiding place?'

Núria pointed to the plaster relief of Jesus and the money-changers. Alex felt round the edge of it. It was set into the wall but not fixed there. He levered it out with a teaspoon handle. Behind it was a small metal cupboard, like a money-box, built into the wall; it was locked.

'Now all we need is the key.'

'It won't be far away. Try somewhere obvious, like above the door.'

Alex ran his hand along the top of the frame and a small key fell to the floor. He opened the metal box. Inside there were three envelopes: one contained a copy of her will, in another there were some typed letters and and in the third there was an inch-thick bundle of cash.

'Fuck me,' he said, in English. He handed Núria the envelope. 'You want to count it?'

'Fuck me,' she said, thumbing the bills. Alex laughed.

'You can't say it like that. The emphasis is wrong. You can't say, "*Fuck* me."'

'Why not?'

'Because it's like you're ordering someone to fuck you.'

'And?' she said with a cheap smirk.

'Now don't start.'

'So how do I say it?'

'The emphasis is on the me, not the fuck.'

'Fuck *me*,' she said.

'That's too much stress on the me. Now you sound like you're saying, fuck me, don't fuck her. It's supposed to be an exclamation, not a demand.'

'Fuck me, fuck me, fuck me, fuck me,' she repeated, with varying degrees of emphasis, all of them wrong.

'Maybe it would be safer if you just said gosh or oh my God,' he said.

She counted the money on to the bed. 'Ten, twenty, thirty, forty, fifty. Fuck me, fuck me. Sixty, seventy, eight, ninety, a hundred. Fuck me, oh my God, fuck me.'

Alex took the letters out of the envelope. There was a brief letter from a television company, another from a detective agency in Barcelona and a photocopy of Alex's father's death certificate. There was also a handwritten note from someone called Franklin Xavier Martin, with an address in Poughkeepsie, New York. Núria finished counting and fanned the money out on the bedspread.

'How much?'

'Plenty. Not a fortune, but enough to live on for a couple of years without having to go to work. What have you got there?'

'Letters. What's *Sorpresa, Sorpresa*?'

He handed her the letter from the TV company.

'God that's pretty sad,' Núria said. 'Anna tried to find your dad through *Sorpresa, Sorpresa*. It's a really tacky programme. People write in who want to find someone, you know, missing brothers and sisters or old flames or kids, whoever, and the programme brings them together on TV. It's pretty sick-making usually.'

'Oh that. I watched it one night in the hotel. They arranged for a truck driver to meet his favourite pin-up from the girlie calendar in his cab. We have the same programme in the States.'

The letter from the TV company said they were sorry but they'd already filled all the slots for the next series and suggested she ask a detective agency to trace her brother. Obviously she took their advice because there was a letter from a Barcelona agency saying that they'd managed to trace Ignasi Nadal but unfortunately he was already deceased, a fact confirmed by the attached photocopy of the death certificate. The letter went on to list his mother's, Pepa's and his addresses in New York. It gave Alex's old address on Avenue B. The letters were dated from six months before Anna died. He sat on the bed and pictured his aunt trying to find her brother through some crap TV programme. The whole thing was pathetically sad. Alex picked up the handwritten letter from New York.

It read: 'Dear Anna Nadal, These memories have stayed with me like evil spirits. It is perhaps in a bid to exorcise them that I send you these photographs from that terrible time, but also so they might bear witness. Perhaps it will do some good, perhaps not. I hope that if this finds you at all, it finds you in good health. Yours, Franklin X Walker.'

The note was dated April 1996, a year before Anna died. And so that, Alex assumed, was what his aunt sent him and Oriol – photographs. But of what?

'So,' he said, giving Núria a searching look.

She patted the bed beside her.

'Come sit by me, and I'll tell you what Anna told me. Then maybe you'll understand why your father pretended she was dead.'

37

'This is ridiculous, how much longer are we going to be stuck here?' Oriol complained.

They were held up at a police checkpoint on the road to Vallvidrera. There seemed no end to the heatwave, each day was hotter than the last. The sun flashed off the metal and glass of the cars in front while Oriol and Narcís waited in the air-conditioned oasis of the big BMW.

'It's the wedding,' Narcís said. 'They've been stopping people all week. I suppose the cops have to show they're doing something. Maybe they think they'll get lucky and find ETA's top man with a box of Semtex in the back seat.'

Oriol looked at his nephew in the rearview mirror. He couldn't see his eyes through the dark glasses but he felt sure he was laughing at him. He didn't like his tone; it was flippant, disrespectful. But he needed him right now, more than ever, and worse still, he had to trust him. He read the *Ara* article for the fifth or sixth time. It was skilful piece of work, honeyed words poured over poisonous intent. He had no doubt Angel was behind it; it was too smart a move, too subtle for a journalist. And too well-informed. First thing that morning Oriol hit back, or tried to. He phoned Judge Mestres, the judge presiding over the case of Angel's son Josep. Mestres' secretary said he would call back at the first opportunity, but two hours later he still hadn't called. Then he phoned Oscar Puig at the environment department to tell him to deny at all costs the Roger de Flor story. His secretary said Puig was in a meeting. Oriol told her to tell him it was urgent and a few minutes later the secretary came on to say Puig couldn't leave the meeting but would call back. Then he called the proprietor of *Ara* but was told he was on the golf course and couldn't be contacted.

The car slid silently up to the checkpoint. Narcís rolled down the window and held out his ID. A sluggish gust of humid air lolled into the cool interior. The cop wore dark aviator glasses and the body-hugging uniform of the Policía Nacional. He had a pistol and handcuffs on one hip and a truncheon and mobile on the other. He looked at the ID then asked Narcís to step out of the car. Narcís gave him a look but the cop stood back from the car door in a gesture that said he wasn't interested in having a discussion. Narcís felt the full force of the hot morning as he got out of the car. The cop asked him to turn round and put his hands on the roof of the car.

'You're kidding, aren't you?' Narcís said. The cop's face said he was not.

Narcís turned and put his hands on the roof. The metal was too hot to touch so he stood in a lean without leaning on anything while the cop frisked him. He removed something from the inside pocket of his jacket; it was Guillermo Morín's confession. The cop fanned the pages and told Narcís he could turn round. He handed him back the confession.

'Do I look like a fucking *etarra*?' Narcís said, snatching the paper.

'Why not? You think no one in ETA drives a BMW?'

As he said this Oriol rolled down his window. He looked at the cop and didn't say a word. He didn't have to, because as soon as the cop recognized him his career flashed before his eyes. He made an awkward gesture that was half a salute, half a bow.

'I'm sorry, Señor Oriol, for the inconvenience. Most sorry,' he said, but Oriol had already pushed the button and the closing window cut short the cop's apologies. Narcís put Morín's confession into his inside pocket as nonchalantly as he could and gave the cop a contemptuous smirk.

'Linares,' he said, prodding the cop's name badge. 'Well, Officer Linares, I think you can forget about promotion for the next twenty years or so.'

'What was that paper he took from you?' Oriol said as they drove off.

'Nothing, just some bumpf from the bank. You know how they're always sending you crap.'

Oriol knew he was lying, not only that, he didn't seem to make much effort to pretend he wasn't. The old man felt he was surrounded by traitors. They parked outside Rocío Roldán's house in Vallvidrera. This wasn't his normal day to see her and he made the appointment specially that morning, a sure sign, Narcís thought, that his uncle was losing his grip.

'Let's hope Rocío can see a clear way out of this,' Narcís said cheerily.

'I've told you, she's not a fortune teller,' Oriol said, catching the note of sarcasm in his nephew's tone. 'What about Nadal, has he been dealt with?'

'It's set up for today. Do you still want it to go ahead?'

'Of course, why not? Nothing's changed.'

Narcís didn't comment, although as far as he could see, now the cat was out of the bag everything had changed and the Roger de Flor deal, surely, was off. It was bad but it wasn't a disaster; all Oriol had to do was deny the *Ara* story and walk away. He could come up with some other thing as his gift to the nation and then *Ara* would be left with egg on its face. But it would cost him, and that hurt. The old man was acting like he faced ruin, but Narcís was sure he was exaggerating. He was just so mean, he hated the idea of spending his own money. Tighter than Christ's grip on the nails, that's what they said about him. But this time Narcís knew it wasn't just about money, that wasn't why he was so obsessed with Can Castanyer. Narcís knew his day had come, he had the old man by the balls, or almost. There was just one thing missing.

38

Alex stood on the upstairs terrace in the cottonwool silence of a hot country day. The story Núria told him played and replayed until it made his head spin. Now he knew what his father never knew: that he was innocent, that all his life he believed he had betrayed the Romeu brothers, when in fact Captain Morín already knew when he came to Can Castanyer that the Romeus were hidden in the cellar and everything that followed was just a nasty charade. Alex knew the truth but he couldn't prove it. He went downstairs and phoned Pepa for the third time in as many days. So far all he had got was her machine but it was the middle of the night in New York so he hoped he'd catch her in. But the machine clicked on and all he could do was ask again if she'd been to look for the parcel Anna sent to his old place on Avenue B.

He sat at the piano with his hands resting on his thighs. It was one of those times when he didn't know what to play. He raised his hands each time a tune came into his head and then let them fall; nothing seemed right. He closed his eyes and let his left hand hover until it found a chord. His hand chose C sharp minor, a chord with an edgy melancholia. He put his foot on the pedal and sustained the chord, then played it again. Still with his eyes closed his right hand began to pick out a melody, a restless motif in a pattern of falling minor thirds that merged and overlapped and seemed perpetually on the point of a resolution that never arrived. He imagined the notes falling in a series of rings like rain falling on still water. When he opened his eyes Núria was standing next to the piano. He kept playing until he found a way out of the circle and back to where he began, on a sustained C sharp minor chord. Núria bent over and gave him a sisterly kiss on the cheek.

'That was nice. What's it called?'

'It isn't called anything, I just made it up. We could call it "Núria" if you like.'

She stuck out her tongue but he could see she was touched.

'Are you a secret romantic?' she said.

'It's no big secret, but it's not a particularly useful characteristic. When the going gets tough, I sit down and play a ballad. Not very James Bond, is it?'

'What would you do now, if you were James Bond?'

'That's easy. I land my helicopter on the baddie's patio and after I've kicked him downstairs and blown up his house I sail off on my yacht to drink martinis with a beautiful woman.'

'With Carmen, I suppose,' she said in a sarcastic nyah-nyah voice.

'Women on yachts don't have names. And Carmen's a different story; she has nothing to do with James Bond.'

'OK, so that's James Bond. What's Alex Nadal going to do?'

'First of all I'm going to get up from the piano stool but before that I'm going to give in to an urge to play this,' he said, then played a chord and sang: 'Sit there and count the raindrops falling on you, it's time you knew, all you can count on are the raindrops that fall on little girl blue.'

'Did you write that too?'

'No, Mr Lorenz Hart wrote that. He was a sad drunk who lived with his mother but he had a way with a song lyric.'

'And I'm a sad junkie who's no good at anything.'

'Don't say that. Like I said, your drawings are great and

besides, you're clean now. You can stay clean, I know it's hard.'

'You've no idea how hard.'

'One day at a time, sweet Jesus.'

'Sweet Jesus nothing, I've been through this before, lots of times. The worst of it is suddenly you seem to have so much time that you don't know what do to with. Too much time to think about stuff you've told yourself you're not going to think about. It sounds so stupid, I know, but being strung out, it sort of simplifies things.'

'I imagine killing yourself always does.'

'It isn't that, it's just that you don't really have to think because every day starts with the same problem: get some stuff. Which means get some cash. So every day's like this adventure; OK, it's a pretty sordid adventure and the truth is your life's a complete disaster, but it's like every day's a life and death struggle. It makes you feel important, because everyone else looks like they're just ambling along, like their lives are just so fucking easy. But you, you're in a state of emergency all the time. Which is how it's so easy to convince yourself that it's OK to rip people off. You feel righteous. Everything's so simple, so self-centred. You don't have to think about anything else, like what you might be doing with your life if you weren't hustling for the next hit. So when you come off, life suddenly looks so big, so far away. Suddenly there's all this time to fill. It scares the hell out of you.'

Alex put his arms round her. He felt fond of her again, fond and protective.

'Now I've got to go to Torredembarra. I have a theory that Anna tried to blackmail Oriol, or at least threaten him with exposure and I have another theory that this may have led to her falling down the stairs. Victor said she sent me a parcel and a smaller one to Salvador Oriol, yes, *the* Salvador Oriol. Let's say that what she sent was the evidence or a copy of the evidence that would expose him, a photograph perhaps – you said Anna told you a news photgrapher was here at the time – then perhaps she sent me the same thing, as insurance in case something happened to her. That's what I'm trying to get my sister to track down but she doesn't seem to be home which is why I'm going to Torredembarra, so I can send a fax to her school in New York. I won't be long, and Victor should be back soon. Then maybe we could eat; I'm so hungry I could cry.'

'I'll cook us a chicken if you like.'

'I don't think there's anything in the house.'

Núria laughed and jerked her thumb in the direction of the hen-house.

'Hear that,' she said. 'That's what a chicken sounds like before it's cooked.'

Just as he was leaving the phone rang. It was Carmen.

'Alex, you know that photo of your aunt sitting at the piano? That carving of a horse, I knew I'd seen it somewhere before. It's in Oriol's house.'

'What?'

'*Hello!* did a photo spread of his home. It's there, I'm certain of it, or one exactly the same.'

'The final insult,' he said, not sure if he said it aloud or not.

39

There was nowhere in Torredembarra to send a fax so he had to go further down the coast to Altafulla. When he got back to the house an hour and a half later there was a motorbike parked under the chestnut. He stood outside the front door and listened. He could hear someone moving around upstairs. It could have been Victor but he didn't think so. He opened the door inch by inch and went in. Núria sat in one of the flowered armchairs. At first he thought she was asleep, but when his eyes adjusted to the light he could see she was completely smacked out, so out of it that the skinny plastic syringe still drooped out of a vein. She looked up and gave him a dopey, junkie grin. He felt hurt, betrayed and foolish. He wanted to take her in his arms and beg her to stop and he wanted to slap her face and throw her out of the house. He tugged the needle out of her arm and dropped it in the sink.

He could hear furniture being moved around upstairs. Whoever was up there couldn't have heard the car and didn't know he was back. Alex thought about the bundle of money in Anna's secret cupboard. He looked around the kitchen for a weapon. There were knives, but stabbing whoever was upstairs or cutting their throat didn't seem like a good idea. Knifeplay, he imagined, was something best rehearsed before going straight to live performance. A chicken lay on chopping board, limply dead but unplucked, and next to it a half-full litre bottle of olive oil. He picked the bottle up by the neck and waited.

After a few minutes he heard footsteps on the stairs. He stood behind the door at the foot of the stairs, the bottle in his hand. He wasn't going to wait to see who it was; whoever came through the door was going to get it. He hoped it wasn't Victor. The footsteps stopped on the last step. Alex held his breath, the bottle raised above his head. A skinny man in black denim stepped into the room and as Alex brought the bottle down hard on the side of his head he recognized Kiko, the junkie from Cervecería Judas. Kiko half turned towards him with a look of surprise, olive oil and blood already dripping out of his hair. Then he dropped to the floor, out cold. He had a small calibre pistol stuck in the waistband of his jeans. Alex put it in his pocket, rolled Kiko over with his foot and went through his pockets where he found money, though not much, a small jackknife, keys, a Zippo lighter, a wrap of what Alex took to be smack, and an ID card.

After about a minute Kiko moaned and opened his eyes. His head lay in a pool of oily blood, but he didn't seem to be bleeding much. Alex took the gun out of his pocket and with his free hand unpicked the packet of smack and held it above Kiko. The powder floated down and stuck to the oil on his face. Kiko moaned again and moved his hand up to feel his head. Alex stamped on his hand, hard, and kept his foot on top of it. All his fear had turned to anger. After all the unseen, unnamed forces he faced, here at last was a real person and Alex had a gun on him. He felt like he'd taken a couple of steps outside himself. He'd never handled a gun before but he liked the feel of it. His head was a jumble of crazy thoughts: that he didn't know if the safety catch was on and didn't know where to find it; that the gun might not be loaded; that the beauty of a gun was you didn't have to worry about messing up your hands, that a gun was the perfect weapon for a piano player.

'Don't even think about moving,' he said.

'Go fuck yourself.'

Alex brought his foot down on Kiko's hand again, harder this time. He heard a crack and Kiko cried out.

'What were you looking for upstairs?'

Kiko's eyes were all hatred but he didn't look scared until Alex poked the barrel of the gun into his nostril.

'What?'

'Photographs,' Kiko said. 'He told me to find some old photographs.'

'What photographs?'

'I don't know, he just said photographs.'

'Who said?'

'I can't tell you, he'll kill me.'

Alex put the barrel of the gun next to Kiko's ear and squeezed the trigger. The noise was incredible, even from such a small gun, though he doubted anyone would hear it beyond the thick stone walls of the house. The bullet pinged off the floor and lodged in a kitchen cabinet. Núria didn't stir.

'You're fucking crazy,' Kiko said.

'It's beginning to look that way. Who?'

'Narcís Valls.'

'Big man with fishy eyes? Salvador Oriol's sidekick?'

'Yes. Him.'

'And what's he to you?'

Kiko made as if to move but Alex held the gun over his right eye. Kiko had a scorch mark on his ear from when Alex fired the shot

'Nothing. I get him some coke now and then. Girls sometimes.'

'Girls? Like her?' Alex said in Núria's direction.

'Her, never,' he snorted. 'She doesn't put out for anyone, not even when she's desperate. Too proud.'

Alex was grateful for this information; he felt relieved. He seemed to have adopted Núria as his kid sister so it was nice to know she wasn't a whore, just a junkie.

'So how does she fit in? You obviously know each other well.'

'She doesn't. I mean, yes I know her, but I didn't know she was here. Why would I? I know her from the barrio and that's the only place I expect to see her. I ride up to the house and there she is holding a chicken by the neck, like a country girl. I never expected to find her here.'

'And you just happened to have some stuff that you chose to share with her. How much did you give her?'

'She'll be all right. She loves the stuff, can't leave it alone. It's her life.'

That was when Alex came closest to shooting him, not even out of rage because the rage had already all but drained away, but with a weary disdain, the way he'd flick the TV off with the remote control. Instead, he raised his foot above the broken hand and backed away. The craziness was wearing off, like a drug, and he'd had enough of acting tough. Besides, Kiko was probably right about Núria; most of the junkies he'd known had been lying for so long they didn't know the difference. He motioned with the gun towards the door. Kiko slowly got to his feet, not for one moment taking his eyes off Alex. He slicked the oily hair away from his face and noticed the things Alex had taken out of his pockets lying on the table.

'Not the knife,' Alex said. 'Take the rest and get out of here.'

He followed him to the door and watched him wince as he tried to throttle up the bike with his broken hand. Alex had never resorted to physical violence before, not even in the playground. He didn't much care for the feel of it, though he had to admit he liked the result. He was hungry. He found some *fuet* and *manchego* cheese and a hunk of day-old bread which he resuscitated with tomato and oil. He sat in the chair opposite Núria with the food on his lap and a beer in his hand. Núria looked at him and through him and past him. She was where every junkie aims to go: absolutely nowhere. Alex's now dead friend Charlie used to call it Numb City – a place where nothing matters.

Victor came in with a chainsaw in his arms and a copy of *Ara* stuffed in his back pocket. His headphones spat and

226

sizzled like bacon in a skillet. He put the saw down by the back door and saw Núria spaced out in the flowery armchair. He looked scared.

'Is she OK?'

'No, Victor, she's not OK. She's a junkie and she's unhappy. She needs help and she needs love and I think she might even accept it if someone was prepared to make the effort.'

Victor played with his hair and took his pony-tail in and out of the elastic.

'I knew she was using some bad drugs,' he said. 'But I didn't think . . .'

You mean you didn't want to know, Alex thought. Like everyone else around here. No one wants to know. It could be the national motto: Say nothing, I'd rather not know.

Victor spotted the blood on the floor and the gun on the table.

'Heavy shit,' he said in mimicked English, staring at the pistol. 'This is some heavy shit.'

The phone was ringing.

'You could say that, Victor, you certainly could say that.'

He picked up the phone. The voice was familiar, but he couldn't place it.

'This is Raul,' the voice said. 'Raul Morín. I have the documents you want. Come to my garage this afternoon and you can have them.'

Alex listened to the silence on the line, as though he was trying to hear something unspoken. 'OK,' he said. 'I'll be there.'

40

Carmen and the photographer loitered around the fountain in Plaça Catalunya looking out for suitable people to buttonhole for their views on the Infanta's wedding. It wasn't going well. The first person she asked was a young Basque who professed to know nothing about the event.

'We can hardly print that,' Carmen said to the snapper.

'Why not? She's marrying a Basque, after all.'

'Too negative. We'll only get sacks of letters from Basque monarchists saying we're showing the Basque people in a bad light.'

'Basque monarchists?'

'They're out there, believe me.'

The next two people they stopped were German, then a Scot.

'This is stupid,' Carmen said. 'The place is full of tourists. We need local people. Let's try the arches.'

The arches was shorthand for the nearby Plaça Vincenç Martorell, a small square colonnaded on two sides with a playground in the middle and a bar in one corner in the shade of the colonnade. It was also a popular shortcut. All Carmen needed was ten people with an address in Catalunya who could utter two printable sentences about the Infanta's big day and were willing to have their picture printed above their opinion in the paper. Then she could get on with the real work of standing up the Roger de Flor story. On the way over to the square she called Blanca on her mobile.

'Did you see *Ara* this morning?' she said.

'Yes, I didn't quite get it though.'

'You're not supposed to. You're supposed to wonder why you don't get it. There's more to come. Tell me, did Fèlix ever mention an organization called Ultrapassa?'

'Sure, he went every week.'

Carmen wasn't expecting that; given the circumstances of Fèlix's death, she thought twice about mentioning Ultrapassa at all, or anything else to do with unorthodox sexual practices.

'Where? What exactly is it?'

'Where? Nowhere in particular, restaurants and bars, I think. Anywhere they could talk.'

'Talk about what?'

'Catalan stuff. Fèlix said they advised the Generalitat and the parliament, informally of course. On cultural issues – things like language laws, promoting the Catalan identity in Europe – that sort of thing. They were just a group of passionate Catalanists. You know what Fèlix was like.'

Better than you, Carmen thought, you poor deluded fool. Then she reminded herself that she had failed to spot what many other people had known for a long time, that the man she loved was having an affair. Love blinds, she sighed, pushing the thought of Alex to the back of her mind.

The first person Carmen stopped in the plaça was a young woman with a dozing baby in a pushchair. She spoke to her in Catalan, an easy ploy to weed out the foreigners and out of towners. The woman said she was happy the Infanta had chosen Barcelona and that she seemed nice and not at all stuck up. Then Carmen stopped an old man who said it was as good an excuse as any for a party and besides, the Infanta spoke Catalan, which was more than you'd expect from a Bourbon princess. Then she got two men in succession who said they couldn't care less either way. Then a woman who used words like wonderful and thrilling and another who said the Infanta was just an ordinary girl, just like the rest of us, and that was why everyone loved her. Basically, the women were all for it and the men weren't interested, which Carmen thought was pretty well par for the course on the subject of weddings. Her last interviewee was a middle-aged woman from Arenys de Mar who said she heard the Infanta was already pregnant by her fiancé but never mind, she added confidentially, it could be worse, he may be a Basque but least he's not a nigger. Then she said please not to put her picture in the paper because her husband wouldn't like it.

'We'll use it anyway,' Carmen told the photographer when the woman was out of earshot. 'Racist old bag.'

Then she saw a familiar figure watching her from the bar under the arches. It was Angel. She gave him a small wave.

'There's someone I need to speak to,' she said to the snapper. 'I think we've got enough now. Just leave the pictures on my desk after you've printed them up. And please double-check the captions, you know what happened last week.'

El Mensajero had been forced to print a grovelling apology after printing a picture of the deputy for Badalona above a caption saying she was being tried for the murder of her three children. Right caption, wrong person; these things happen.

Carmen sat down with Angel and ordered a vermouth. She felt nothing for him any more sexually. It puzzled her, how desire came and went, how one day you cheerfully put a man's cock in your mouth and the next you wouldn't touch him with gloves on. She took a black paper lace fan out of her bag and began fanning her face.

'This humidity's a killer, isn't it,' Angel said. 'Every day you think it's going to rain but it never comes.'

Carmen didn't feel like discussing the weather.

'Is this a happy coincidence or are you following me?'

'A bit of both. I was coming to see you in the office but then there you were walking down the street with your colleague, so I followed you here. What's the assignment?'

'The wedding. A nation bares its soul to our reporter.'

'I think it's all very revealing, it shows we still have a colonial mentality. The old enemy wants to marry off his daughter in our cathedral; we're being shown favour and we like it, we're flattered. It's a classic post-colonial symptom.'

'I'd no idea you had such strong feelings about it. Should I be taking notes?'

'No, and I don't have strong feelings about it. I couldn't care less about the royal family or where or who they marry. I'm just offering you my observations.'

'But that wasn't why you were looking for me.'

'No, I have something to show you.'

The arts desk secretary winked at Carmen when she came in with Angel. Carmen scowled back and took Angel into the side office and shut the door. Angel handed her a videotape and she put it in the machine and pressed play. The video was amateur but good quality. It showed a naked man, wearing only a purple silk sash and a bishop's mitre, bound to a cross with leather restraints. He had a black leather belt around his neck and a pair of hands, their owner out of shot, controlled the tension on the belt, easing off only when the man being strangled looked like he was losing consciousness. A pale-skinned woman in a pink baby-doll nightie, knelt at the bound man's feet, giving him a blowjob. Every time the crucified man started to moan with pleasure the woman paused and turned to leer at the camera; she didn't look a day over sixteen. Carmen happened to know that the man she was fellating was fifty-one, married with three children. It was Oscar Puig, the media-friendly director of the department of the environment.

41

Alex felt that, because he stood up to Kiko, Raul phoned. It wasn't a mystical thing, but the two things were connected. In his experience that was what happened, one good thing followed another – if you got the girl, you probably got the job too – in the same way that at other times things went from bad to worse. Them that's got shall have, them that's not shall lose – that's how the song went and that was how life was. Most of the important stuff wasn't in your hands, but there was a hairline crack in fate and that was where you made your own luck. So Raul phoned because he, Alex, was finally making things happen. That felt good, but he felt like he was in someone else's skin when he strapped Kiko's pistol to his ankle with surgical tape, like an actor getting into character, or a kid playing out something he saw on TV. When he left the house Núria was still in a smack nod, an open-eyed unseeing coma. Victor sat opposite her looking forlorn. For once his Walkman was silent.

'You going to be OK?' Alex said.

'I think so.'

'What are you going to do when she comes round?'

'I thought maybe we could have a *castanyada*, like when we were kids. I thought maybe that would cheer her up.'

'A *castanyada*? What's that?'

'It's for All Saints Day, well, really it's because the chestnuts are ripe now. You roast the chestnuts and eat them with *panellets*, little cakes. Núria used to make great *panellets*.'

'Sounds nice,' Alex said, touched by Victor's quaint approach to drug rehab.

Alex parked in Poblenou near the bar where he had his first meeting with Raul. A waiter was wiping down the outside tables. He gave Alex a funny look when he asked for directions to Raul's garage. He soon understood why: a length of police tape drooped across the garage door and half a dozen bunches of flowers with sympathy cards were stuffed into a green plastic bucket outside. Alex tried the door, although a voice inside his head was telling him to get away from there. It was open. He went in and felt his way along the wall for a lightswitch. He stood on something on wheels that sped from under his feet and he fell heavily against the side of a car, banging his elbow. Behind him the door crashed shut and the lights came on. As his eyes adjusted Alex recognized Detective Hernández, the matinée idol of the Barcelona police.

'Looking for something, Señor Nadal?,' he said. His low voice played a gruff counterpoint to his pretty boy looks. Alex recognized it as the voice on the phone claiming to be Raul.

'Someone, not something. I get the feeling I'm too late.'

Hernández walked around him, sizing him up, a slight man with a taste for the theatrical.

'When did you last see Raul Morín?'

'A few days ago. That was the first and last time.'

'What did you want from him?'

'It was a personal matter.'

'A personal dispute?'

'No, I have no quarrel with him.'

'Had. I have witnesses who say you argued, that Morín had to push you away. Half an hour later he was murdered.'

In Alex's mind suddenly everything was clear. It was the

clarity that comes when the car spins out of control and in a timeless moment of calm you see the options – the oncoming traffic, the line of poplars, the ditch bright with wildflowers – with an unruffled detachment as though you're not involved except as a witness. Only later do you realize that it was the same you who managed to turn into the skid, pump the brakes rather than slam them on, and change down to third; who calmly did, in fact, all the right things, while another part of yourself stood aside and watched. Raul had been murdered and Alex was going to be fitted up as the killer. It was all circumstantial but no doubt Hernández would be able to come by whatever evidence he needed to clinch the case. Hernández unholstered his gun and told him to turn round and put his hands against the wall. He frisked him. When he found Kiko's pistol strapped to his ankle he laughed but didn't take it off him.

'That makes my job so much easier,' he said. 'I imagined I'd have to shoot you when you tried to escape from custody, but now that you've pulled a gun on me, what choice do I have but to shoot first?'

Since his father's suicide a part of Alex had wished himself dead as well but now, with Hernández's pistol cooling the nape of his neck, all of him wanted very much to stay alive. How? was the question. If he was heroic, if he was James Bond, he'd spot that with a simple double back-flip he could swing from the engine hoist and kick the gun from the detective's hand. But being Alex Nadal he began to experience the emotion that always seems to be at its strongest when you least need it – fear. Just when you need a clear head and a spur to action, along comes fear to root you to the spot and make you want to pee in your pants. But Alex didn't want to die in this dingy garage in Poblenou, or anywhere else either; he wanted to live. He coiled up all the energy he could find and threw himself blindly backward. Hernández crashed against the wall with Alex's weight against him. The gun spun out of his hand and under the car and the detective, winded, gasped for breath as Alex ran into the street. A moment later

234

he heard the door bang as Hernández came after him. It was only fifty metres to the corner but it seemed to take for ever, like in a dream where the harder you try to escape the heavier your legs become. He pictured Hernández, down on one knee, taking aim, and wondered if he'd hear the shot before he felt the bullet or if it was simultaneous or if it wasn't anything remotely like that at all.

He didn't have a plan, unless running flat out could be called a plan. He didn't look back till he got to the car. As he fumbled for his keys, Hernández appeared around the corner, still struggling to catch his breath. He was limping a bit so Alex must at least have given him a dead leg. He turned the car round and drove back towards the sea. In the mirror he saw Hernández get into a dark-green Seat. Alex didn't know where he was going and, even if he did, he didn't know the city well enough to find his way there. So he turned right along the Avinguda D'Icària and headed for the part he knew best, the Old City. All along he could see the green Seat, about three cars back. At Colom he turned into la Rambla and immediately regretted it. He got stuck behind a bus unloading tourists outside the wax museum. In the mirror he saw Hernández getting out of his car. Alex abandoned his car and took to his feet. The humidity was suffocating. He turned to run down Escudellers but two Policía Nacional were coming towards him, their truncheons swaying from their hips as they passed a *pastisseria*. Alex ran across la Rambla, elbowing through a tight phalanx of Japanese tourists, and danced through the traffic into the Barri Xino. He sensed Hernández behind him but didn't look back. He zig-zagged along the gloomy streets as far as Carrer d'en Robador. He looked back; Hernández was there, barely seventy-five metres behind.

Barri Xino was like another city. Here the streets didn't smell of drains, they smelled of shit that hadn't got as far as a drain. There were piles of garbage and broken glass every-where and every balcony was draped with washed out, worn out clothes, drying in the gloom. Children threw stones at the hopeless drunks and junkies babbling in the street or numbed against the walls. Men stood on corners, smoking and waiting with an air of everyday menace. Pancaked whores of indeterminate sex called to Alex as he ran sweating up the street. It seemed that in every other doorway someone was throwing up or shooting up or jerking off while less than a hundred metres away, thousands of tourists shuffled and gawped down la Rambla, strapped into their Nikons and clutching guidebooks that advised strongly against straying into Barri Xino. And rightly so, it was a scary barrio, unless you were on the run from a homicidal cop.

At the top of Robador Alex doglegged along l'Hospital and Jerusalem until he was behind the Boqueria, the vast indoor food market. Here, maybe, among the crowds and the maze of stalls, he could shake Hernández. His clothes were soaked in sweat and he suspected he looked just like what he was – a fugitive. He paused for a moment beside a *xarcuteria*. The cured hams and strings of *chorizo* and *fuet* gave off a homely odour of preserved pig fat. Alex pushed into the crowd in a flurry of elbows and 'excuse me's', heading for a spot near the fish stalls where he hoped he could see but not be seen by Hernández when he entered the market. The smell of cured pork gave way to an odour of damp earth as he dodged past mounds of green-tinted *rovello* mushrooms. The Boqueria was packed with shoppers and with tourists taking pictures of food. It was impossible to move fast, so he pushed his way through as gently as he could, anxious not to leave an angry wake for Hernández to follow. At a stall that sold nothing but white slabs of salt cod, he turned around. The detective was in front of the *xarcuteria*, scanning the crowds. Alex didn't wait to catch his eye. He turned and tripped over a shopping basket, apologized and shimmied and sidestepped his way towards the fish stalls. The *peixateras* were just like the ones in Tarragona, in full make-up with their hair dyed blue-black or platinum blonde, calling out: 'Hey, good looking, Over here my love, Oh, my queen, how gorgeous you are.' Alex stopped by a stall and pretended to examine the heaps of purple-tinted cuttlefish.

The *peixatera*'s ash-blonde hair was piled high on her head above a pair of bright black eyes.

'What can I get you, handsome?' she said with open arms. She held a large, pointed cleaver in one hand.

Alex could see Hernández coming his way, like a dog following a scent. He bent down as if to tie his shoe and scrambled under the fish counter, nearly knocking the *peixatera* off her feet. She pointed her cleaver angrily at him. Please don't scream, Alex's eyes implored her. Please. He crouched at her feet and put his finger on his lips and poured everything he had into his eyes. He gave her a look that was all at once beseeching, helpless, flirtatious, pathetic, conspiratorial, mischievous and despairing. He tried to get into his eyes every and any thing that might soften the heart of a middle-aged cleaver-wielding platinum blonde in pink rubber gloves. She didn't shout or come at him with the cleaver; she did the most wonderful thing she could possibly have done – she winked. He crouched under the counter between two buckets of guts and scales. Fishy water dripped on to his head. The *peixatera* wore white plastic sandals. Her toenails were painted coral pink and her calves were waxed smooth as marble. Through the gap he saw a pair of feet he was sure belonged to Hernández. He held his breath. Above him the *peixatera* was saying, 'Hello, love of my life, what can I offer you?' Hernández moved off and a pair of female legs appeared in the gap and the *peixatera* was off again: 'Hello gorgeous, hello queen, how can I help?' Now and then she gave Alex a friendly kick under the counter. He stayed there for twenty minutes, steeped in the smells of the sea, his heart filled with love for a woman whose pink-gloved hands brushed his cheek each time she dropped a fish head or a handful of guts into the bucket at her feet.

42

'This is beginning to look like a vendetta.'

The editor held a pair of glasses in each hand, uncertain which to put on.

'I thought I made it clear there was to be no more poking around in Oriol's affairs,' he added.

Carmen looked at Enric Luna. The only way she could play this was through him.

'I can assure you there's no vendetta,' Luna said. 'No one's been digging around. The story more or less fell into our lap.'

Our lap, Carmen thought contemptuously, already Luna was taking credit. And it didn't fall, she got the story. That was classic Luna, to belittle her while acting in her defence. But she had no choice. It couldn't be done in a way where she got all the glory, that wasn't how it worked. What mattered was that Luna kept his word. She'd been buttering him up, flattering him, asking his advice on how best to do the story. It seemed to work but it was a risky game; Luna was the type who would win your trust just so he could shaft you from a better angle.

'Who or what was the source of the story in *Ara*?' the editor said to Carmen, selecting the rimless glasses.

The accusation was clearly there but she knew he couldn't prove anything.

'The fact is the story's out there now,' she said, dodging the question. 'Everyone's going to be digging to find out what's underneath the *Ara* story. As soon as they take a good look at Oriol's school for *sardana* they're going to uncover the rest. We have the chance to be first. It's not often a scoop like this comes along.'

The editor swapped his glasses round and gave Carmen the sort of look he gave his daughters when they first started to defy him.

'There's something vindictive about it that I don't like. He's nearly eighty, for God's sake. Who knows how people will react? It's very out of tune with the public mood, what with the wedding and everything. Our readers could turn against us.'

Carmen gave Luna a sidelong look that was part conspiratorial, part flirtatious. The stuff she was using on him was old-fashioned female stuff, coquettish, stuff she rejected on principle. On the other hand, why should she feel bad about it? If a man fell for a fluttering eyelash, that said more about the man than the eyelash. Luna fell for it; he gave her a half-lidded look that said, 'You really do fancy me, don't you.' He drew himself up in his chair.

'There is that risk, I agree,' he said in a tone that was part appeasement, part patronizing, which he invariably adopted with bosses. 'But as Carmen said, the story's out there now. Someone's going to run it. And if it ever came out that we'd been sitting on this story all along, well . . .'

He spread his arms, palms outwards, and hunched his shoulders. He didn't need to finish the sentence, it was finishing itself in the editor's head.

'I thought you said you couldn't stand it up,' he said, although he knew perfectly well they wouldn't be sitting here if that was still the case. He watched Carmen and Luna exchange looks. Luna cleared his throat.

'Carmen is sure we can,' he said. 'Given her role in this she

239

feels, that is, I feel she should be seconded from arts to the newsroom.'

'Transferred,' Carmen corrected him.

'Transferred to news,' Luna repeated, pursing his thin lips.

The editor tilted back in the oak and leather chair and folded his hands over his midriff. These two were twisting his arm, trying to make a name for themselves. The best thing was to let them carry on and see what they came up with. A little whistleblowing would be good for the paper's credibility – sword of truth and all that nonsense newspapers now and then liked to puff themselves up with. As for Oriol, well, he was a friend but not a personal friend. This would hurt him, of course, but that's how things were sometimes. The editor looked at Carmen and Luna. There was a subtext with them, it wasn't just about this story. Sex, he assumed. It usually was when a man and a woman appeared to be acting in concert.

'This is what you want?' he said to Luna, pointedly excluding Carmen.

'Yes. It would look a bit strange if this story emanated from the arts desk.'

'Very well. But so far what you have is mostly hearsay. Where's the proof?'

'I have every confidence that a very prominent public official will confirm the details of the story,' Carmen said acidly. 'And that his active participation in revealing the evidence will deflect some of the public criticism you anticipate away from the paper.'

'And why is this official going to be so helpful?'

'Because he's going to be presented with an alternative that is infinitely less attractive,' she said, throwing the editor an unreadable smile.

43

There was a message from Alex on Carmen's mobile. He said to meet him in Santa María del Mar; he sounded a little crazy. She found him sitting slantwise on a pew where he could watch both doors. Behind him a statue of the Virgin of Montserrat stood in her shrine, a tiny black-faced figure dressed from head to toe in gold leaf. At her feet votive candles flickered in red plastic cylinders.

'You look terrible,' she whispered. She bent down to kiss him then recoiled. 'Mother of God, you smell awful.'

'Thank you. Alex Nadal sleeps with the fishes. Well, almost, anyway. You remember I told you about that detective, Hernández? Well, it seems he's been hired to kill me, which sort of complicates things as it precludes the possibility of calling the cops.'

'Where is he now?'

'Out there looking for me. Right now I owe my life to a fishwife in the Boqueria. Do you think that would work as a song: I owe my life to a fishwife?'

Carmen squeezed his hand and kissed him on the neck, despite the smell.

'Maybe I'll stay here for the rest of my life. I like this church, there's something uplifting about it. I came in here shaking with terror and now I feel quite calm. It has a spirituality, which I know is what you expect a church to have, but most of them don't. Especially ones as big as this; they're usually more intimidating than uplifting. Maybe it's because it's so plain. There's no decoration at all.'

'You can thank the anarchists for that, they set fire to it during the Civil War.'

'They did a good job. That's why they're trying to kill me, you know, because of the Civil War, because of what it turns out my father didn't do.'

He told her what Núria told him, and about Kiko and that Oriol's nephew had hired him to find some photos he thought were in the house.

After he told her the story Carmen held his hand and sat with her free hand on the back of pew in front, gazing up at the stained glass above the altar. They sat like that for a several minutes.

'Photos of what?' she said eventually.

'I don't know. Except they must implicate Oriol or he wouldn't be so desperate to get his hands on them.'

'According to Oriol's biography he was locked up in a Nationalist jail in Vinaro's, a hundred miles to the south of Sant Martí, at the time you're talking about. I'm not saying it's true, just that that's the official story. But who on Earth in Sant Martí would have owned a camera in 1938?'

'A photographer, that's who. There was a photographer at the house, according to the story my aunt told Núria, an American called Franklin Martin. He was covering the war for a news agency. He'd latched on to the Nationalists as they advanced on Barcelona. He paid my aunt and my father to let him stay at the house so he could use the cellar as a darkroom. It must have been him who took the picture of Anna.'

'But if your aunt had pictures all that time why did she wait sixty years to do anything about it?'

'She didn't have them. This Martin guy only sent them to her last year. I found a letter from him – it had the tone of an old man putting his house in order before it's too late, so who knows if he's still alive.'

'So where are these pictures now?'

'At my old address on Avenue B. If someone hasn't already thrown them out.'

'Which is quite likely, isn't it? You must prepare yourself for the possibility that you'll never find them. You could drive yourself crazy over this, Alex. You know the truth now, you know your father was innocent. Proving it is another thing; it's sixty years ago. Look at the trouble they have convicting Nazi war criminals, even when they can find survivors to testify against them, their lawyers claim mistaken identity, they say it's too long ago for anyone to be sure. Besides, all this trouble you've been having since you got here, I don't think it's about the Civil War, it's about land and, ultimately, it's about money. That's why they're so desperate to get rid of you – money, big money. But after I've been to see Oscar Puig at the Generalitat the whole thing's going to blow up in their faces – Oriol's particularly – and then they'll have much bigger things to worry about than you.'

'I'm going to have it out with Oriol.'

'Have it out? Have what out? You expect him to admit it?'

'You think I should let it go, as though it was nothing?'

'I think you don't know when to stop asking questions.'

'That's a funny thing for a journalist to say. Why shouldn't these things be out in the open?'

'Ask yourself that. You said yourself your family was – how did you put it? – a paragon of mendacity. You seem to apply different standards over here.'

A couple in their fifties came towards them. He had a candle and a taper in his hand, she had her arm in his. It took Carmen a moment to realize where she knew them from; it was Fèlix's mother and father. The mother's face was a mask, tight and blank, of grief blunted by medication; the father looked the way he did at the funeral, like he'd peered down into the abyss. They'd both aged visibly in the couple of weeks since

Fèlix died. They added their candle to others at Montserrat's feet and for a few minutes they watched it burn.

Alex went over to the little stall close to the altar and bought two candles and took them back to the shrine to Montserrat. Fèlix's parents had gone and Carmen came and stood beside him. Alex lit the candles.

'In memory of Anna and Ignasi,' he said. 'It's a long time since they were together. If I believed in the afterlife I'd say they were together now, but I don't, so this is as close as they'll get.'

They had to bribe the taxi driver to take them after he complained about the smell of fish. Alex slumped in the back seat, trying to stay out of sight. He kept imagining he saw Hernández. At a shop near Carmen's flat Alex bought a pair of trousers and a couple of shirts. It was only when he tried the trousers on that he remembered the pistol strapped to his ankle. He didn't want Carmen to know about the gun. When they got back to her flat he hid it behind the bathroom water heater then tore the strapping off his ankle with one quick tug, the way his mother used to when he was a boy. Most of the hair on his ankle came with it. When he came out of the shower he found Carmen in the kitchen in her underwear stirring a pitcher of margaritas with a chopstick.

'I'm going to make you drunk and then I'm going to seduce you,' she said. 'So don't say you weren't warned.'

'It's your house. It would be bad manners to resist.'

Later, when they sat up in bed drinking, Alex said: 'I think I may be falling in love with you.'

Carmen giggled defensively then rested her cheek against his shoulder.

'You only think it? Is it a theoretical position?'

'It's more of a fall-back position. I don't want to scare you off.'

'You like a fall-back position, don't you?'

'It's not my favourite.'

'Ha, ha, very funny. Listen, what scares women about men is their propensity to lie and their apparent lack of conscience about doing so. You won't scare a woman off by being honest. She may die of shock, but she won't be scared. And it's nice that you said it after we fucked and not before. It gives it more weight, more credibility. A man with a stiff cock is capable of saying anything if he thinks there's a chance it will get his balls emptied.'

'So what do you think?'

'About you maybe falling in love with me?'

'You know that's not what I meant.'

'Ah ha. You want to know if your feelings are reciprocated. How touching, how sweet, how old fashioned.'

'Oh forget it, Carmen. I wish I'd never said it.'

'And already he feels remorse. A flutter of love, a twinge of doubt, a pang of remorse – all in the space of a few minutes. You have a very short emotional cycle.'

'Please, just drop it.'

'Don't you like being teased. OK, you think you might be falling in love with me. I'll see you and raise you one: I almost certainly am falling in love with you, but the jury is still out.'

'What do they want, more evidence?'

'Well, of course one can never have too much evidence in such cases, but it's more that they'd like some more time. So far all we've done together, apart from have sex and drink cocktails, is try to find out if someone's trying to kill you and if so who and why. It's interesting, and it beats the hell out of talking about your favourite TV programmes, but it's not exactly a textbook start to a relationship.'

The phone rang. The machine clicked on and Carmen waited to see who it was. It was Pepa, Alex's sister. He leapt out of bed to get the phone before she rang off.

'Pepa, hi, it's me. How did you get this number?'

'From Victor. You gave it to him. Where are you?'

'At a friend's. Did you get my messages? Have you been to my old apartment?'

'I've got it, Alex, the stuff Aunt Anna sent you. It's terrible, really too terrible. I can hardly bear to look at it.'

'I need it urgently, Pepa. There's a really quick courier service on Lexington, damn, what's it called?'

'Alex, calm down. We don't need a courier service. I'm here.'

'What do you mean?'

'I mean I'm here at the farm, Can Castanyer. Mum freaked out when I showed her the stuff. She made me catch the first plane over. She thinks you're going to get yourself killed.'

44

Everyone liked Oscar Puig, even people who didn't like him. He had some quality that made people want to please him: they picked up the tab at dinner, they gave him tickets to the opera, they loaned him their house in the country. People couldn't do enough for him and the more they did the more privileged they felt. It was something he had, charisma maybe, that made people want to be around him, to breathe in when he breathed out.

His secretary showed Carmen into his office and he greeted her with a smile and a warm handshake and gestured for her to take a seat. On the wall behind him were pictures of his wife and children, each in an oval frame, a certificate from the school of architecture and a large framed print of Cerdà's turn-of-the-century plan for the development of the Eixample, the extension of the old city. Carmen put her tape recorder on the desk and pressed 'Record'. Puig leaned over and pressed 'Stop'.

'Later, perhaps,' he said. 'Let's get to the point, shall we? I assume it was Angel who gave you the videotape.' His tone, which was warm and light, was at odds with the words. It was another part of his charm, this directness. It made it seem he had nothing to hide and as a result people found themselves being more open with him than they intended. 'Angel and I have been friends for over twenty years.'

'I'd hardly call it the act of a friend.'

'So it *was* him, thank you for clearing that up for me.'

He smiled at Carmen, knowing she was annoyed with herself for falling so easily into the trap.

'Now all I need to figure out is what he wants, that way I'll know what you want. That's how he is. When Angel presents you with something you must try to see beyond it because all he shows you is the means, not the end. So, let's see, you're here because you want to know about the Roger de Flor and because you think the tape means you can blackmail me into telling you what you want to know. I wasn't aware that blackmail had become standard journalistic practice, but there you are, times change. It follows that Angel must want you to know about Roger de Flor. Why else give you the tape? So the question is: what does he have to gain from this? With Angel it's always the same question: what's in it for him? He's a lovely man in many ways, and good company, but there's only ever one thing on his agenda and that's the well-being of Angel Domènech. So, Carmen, what's in it for him?'

Normally she found that sort of familiarity patronizing but with him she didn't mind. The fact that it seemed perfectly natural and appropriate was, in the circumstances, as disarming as his directness.

'That's what I can't quite figure out, I can't see what his role is in Roger de Flor.'

'Well, that much is quite simple. His role was to twist my arm. I was opposed to the project from the start, vehemently opposed. I was – am – opposed in principle and also because I grew up La Nou de Gaia, which is just up the road from Sant Martí dels Moixones. My mother still lives there, so I have personal reasons for not wanting the area vandalized any more than it already has been. But Angel had that video and that's how he twisted my arm.'

'She looks very young,' Carmen said. 'The girl in the video.'

'Does she? It's hard to tell someone's age from the top of their head.'

It was a pointedly amoral statement, as though he was saying, Go on, take the high road if you like, it doesn't bother me.

'So,' she said, getting back to the point, 'if Angel has nothing to gain directly, the question must be: who stands to lose the most?'

'Quite, although that still doesn't tell us why Angel would want to hurt them.'

Carmen lit a cigarette and started pacing the office. She looked out the window at the people criss-crossing Plaça St Jaume. Across the square a group of disabled people were staging a wheelchair protest outside the *ajuntament*.

'Look, before we go into that,' she said, turning to Puig, 'there's something else we have to discuss – Fèlix Grau.'

If Puig was thrown by this change of tack it didn't show.

'Another video,' he said. 'Soon our whole lives will be available on video. I've seen it and I know what it looks like: it appears that we go into the hotel together, I come out later and later still Fèlix is found dead. I've already been through this with the police. You're a journalist, which means you operate at even lower standards of veracity than the police. It also means you draw the obvious conclusion, because the obvious conclusion makes the best story, or at least a story that's easy to tell. Journalists are always in a hurry, always on deadline, they have no time for nuance or ambiguity and that – and I'll tell you this for free – is what makes them so easy to manipulate. So, let me see, what would be the best story? I suppose it would run something like this: Oscar Puig is a churchgoing family man but a closet homosexual. A young man lures him into an assignation then threatens to expose him. Puig panics and murders him. Is that what you think?'

'All I know is you were there and that makes you the last person to see Fèlix alive,' Carmen said, sitting down again. Puig poured a glass of water from a jug on the desk.

'Let's make one thing absolutely clear: Fèlix was poking around in the Roger de Flor business and sooner or later it was going to get him into trouble. Whatever he did, Fèlix eventually got into trouble – that's how he lived. Maybe he should have been a war correspondent. But his death was an accident and had nothing to do with Roger de Flor or anyone involved in it. I know how it looks, all very convenient, but you have to understand the sort of person Fèlix Grau was. He was one of life's extremists. Whatever he did, he did to the limit. When he drove a car, he drove as fast as he could; he didn't often drink but when he did he didn't stop till he passed out. When he was eighteen, he told me, he took LSD every day for three weeks just to see what would happen. Later on, when he decided to run the marathon, he trained so hard he was lucky not to end up crippled. The same with sex. When he discovered that it was exciting to take certain risks, being Fèlix, he had to explore it to the limit.'

'So what happened?'

'Fèlix wanted me to go to this hotel with him to play a game. I'm not gay, incidentally, not that it matters. But you have to understand that this sort of experimentation is pursued for its own sake, partners are only relevant in so far as they can help you reach the goal, which is almost exclusively about obtaining pleasure for yourself, not giving it to anyone else.'

'So fairly normal male behaviour then?'

Puig smiled and looked at her with amusement.

'Not really, no, because there's no pretence that it's anything other than the selfish pursuit of pleasure. Normal male behaviour consists of a man cajoling a woman into believing that she's going to enjoy giving him what he wants, wouldn't you say?'

'The stiffer the cock, the looser the tongue, as the saying goes. But we're straying again.'

'We went to the hotel, Fèlix and I, but it was just unbearably drab and sordid. No, sordid is the wrong word, sordid can have its own charms. This place was utterly sterile and soulless. Fèlix didn't care; all he was interested in was the physical experience and seeing how far he could push the boundaries. He would have been happy to do it in a garage. But I'm not like that. I like – well, you've seen that video – I enjoy a bit of theatre.'

'Oh, right, the bishop's hat.'

'Actually, it's a cardinal's. Anyway, I told Fèlix the place was too depressing and he said you can do what you like but I've paid for the room now so I'm going to get my money's worth. So I left and the rest is exactly what the police concluded, a sex game gone wrong. It was always going to happen with Fèlix; he never knew he'd had enough until he'd had too much.'

'Did you know he had a girlfriend?' Carmen said, and then felt foolish, because Puig had a wife and she no doubt knew as little about what he got up to as Blanca did about Fèlix.

Puig's only response was an eloquently raised eyebrow. He made Carmen feel naive, like some lace-collar girl from the suburbs who thinks sexual experimentation means doing it with the light on. She felt like she was being conned, but she couldn't see how it was being done. As a rule, politicians as experienced as Oscar Puig tell you nothing. You can interview them for an hour and it all seems to be going fine but later, when you look at your notes, you realize they've said absolutely nothing. But Puig was frankness personified, treating her like a confidante. And that's what it was, she thought, a confidence trick, but knowing that didn't stop it working.

'Are you always this frank?' she said.

'I can see you think you've missed something, that perhaps I'm taking you for a ride. OK, I'll tell you what's missing: you came here with that video expecting to shame me. You thought I wouldn't be able to look you in the eye and and say yes, that's me, enjoying being throttled on the cross. But I'm not ashamed. The video is of course shaming in terms of social convention, ruinously so, which is why Angel came to see me and why you're here now. But I myself, I'm not ashamed. That's what's bothering you. As for my apparent frankness, I'm negotiating from a position of weakness. For all its preten-

251

sions, Barcelona is a small town, reputation is everything here and you have the means of destroying mine.'

'The means but not the desire,' she said, without intending to be so frank herself. He had a way of making her reveal more than she meant to. 'Tell me about the Roger de Flor. Who's behind it?'

'Mallobeco are, but the money and the brains behind them is an American-based finance company called Pacific Bluefields. I say American-based because they're one of these companies where everything's in flux so no one can ever pin them down about paying taxes. They're in the business of making money; they've got lots of it and they put it anywhere it will make lots more. They own hotels, leisure parks, sports facilities, distilleries, a huge tomato cannery in Italy, some vineyards in Chile and a great deal of property. That seems to be their big thing, property. Their *modus operandi* is to get all the legwork done locally and keep their name out of things.'

'Legwork? Does Angel blackmailing you constitute legwork?'

'Precisely. They say to someone on the ground, what we have in mind is such and such a project, and that someone is encouraged to deliver them the whole package: land, planning permission, political acquiescence, technical expertise, whatever.'

'Encouraged how?'

'In the time-honoured way, with money. But not up front, or not much up front. It seems they like to stimulate commitment from their local agents by getting them to invest quite large sums of money in the scheme, with the promise of huge rewards once the project has been realized.'

'And if it's not realized? If something goes wrong?'

'To put it bluntly, you're in the shit and they won't pull you out. You see what I mean by encouragement – they make sure you have a stake in the thing, a very real reason for making sure nothing goes wrong.'

'So Oriol and or Mallobeco are in the shit if this doesn't come off.'

'There's no if about it; the Roger de Flor is a dead duck – I wouldn't be quite so forthcoming if it wasn't. It was sunk the moment *Ara* ran that story. The plan was to announce the scheme on Friday, the eve of the Infanta's wedding. The press would be too wrapped up in the wedding to take a proper look at anything except Oriol's *sardana* school, his gift to the nation, and by the time anyone did look at the detail, it would have gone through committee. That is, I would have ushered it through. But the *Ara* story has got everyone asking questions and there's no chance of it sailing through committee now.'

'So what is the detail? I assume the *sardana* school is just a front.'

'More of a sop than a front, a diversion. The school would really be built, at Pacific Bluefields expense – so much for Oriol's gift. Adjacent to it, on land that was supposed to revert to the state after the owner died intestate – except I gather now that this wasn't the case – there were to be three accommodation blocks for the students. These weren't a gift but would be financed in the usual way, with a view to making a profit.'

'But that's what I don't get. What's in it for Bluefields? How could they make a profit?'

'The three blocks would comprise two hundred and seventy apartments. The school itself could accommodate a maximum of thirty-five students at any one time. You see?'

Puig tilted his head to the left and raised his eyebrows.

'I'm beginning to. So the project would very quickly become unviable because – with a ratio of eight or nine apartments for every potential student – most of them would be unoccupied. It would be impossible to keep up with the payments and so some way would have to be found of bailing it out, otherwise the school would have to close down. Oh, I get it, the surplus would be rented out or sold as holiday apartments, exactly the sort of scheme that is forbidden in that zone. But it would be done in the name of Catalan culture, to save the precious school.'

'Precisely.'

Carmen resumed pacing around the room.

'Planning permission's been granted for the school, right?' she said, thinking aloud.

'There's no problem with the school.'

'And Mallobeco own the land for the school, so all that can go ahead. And it's been announced that's what Oriol plans to do, so everyone expects him to confirm that and build the school. Except now it will be at his own expense because Pacific Bluefields will have packed up and gone.'

Puig nodded. He gave her a smile of satisfaction, as though she were his prize pupil who had just mastered some difficult concept.

'So that's what Angel wants. Oriol is notoriously mean with money. Angel wants to make him do the thing he hates more than anything – spend his own money. So not only will Oriol have fronted up for the now defunct Roger de Flor, he's going to have to pay for the school out of his own pocket. He can't not do it. He has to in order to save face. Meanwhile someone's been spreading rumours that the old man's facing bankruptcy, so that's one more reason to build it, to prove that he's solvent. Whatever Oriol did to piss off Angel he's certainly being made to pay.'

Carmen sat down and took a notebook and a videotape out of her bag. She waved the video at Puig.

'This could destroy your reputation, Señor Puig, but it could enhance it too.'

'How might that be? And please call me Oscar.'

Carmen held out her hand for the tape recorder. Puig gave it to her.

'This is what we're going to do, Oscar. You are going to give me an exclusive interview. In it you will explain that after hearing about Salvador Oriol's planned *sardana* school – no need to mention that you read about it in a rival newspaper – you decided to take a closer look at the scheme. That was when you discovered to your horror that attached to the school, like some parasite on the back of Oriol's goodwill, was an entirely bogus scheme which circumvented planning restrictions in order to build nearly three hundred holiday apartments on a site adjacent to the school. You will say that a full-scale inquiry has now been launched into how these plans reached such an advanced stage without your knowledge and how your signature had appeared on certain documents that you would not under any circumstances have signed. Furthermore, a question mark now hung over Mallobeco and its trading practices, which would also be the subject of an inquiry that could lead to the suspension of its licence. You will add that you are aware that there is a family connection between Oriol and Mallobeco but that you don't believe for a moment that he was party to this nefarious scheme. Finally, you will welcome the proposed *sardana* school and emphasize that it has the full backing of the Generalitat and you hope that maybe one day your own children might attend classes there.'

Puig smiled. 'Nice move, very nice indeed. Do you have a script for me to read from or can I use some of my own words?'

'I wouldn't dream of putting words into your mouth,' Carmen smiled back. 'That would be unethical.'

'And when the interview is complete?'

'You get to keep the videotape.'

Puig sat back in the chair and clasped his hands behind his head.

'It's interesting, isn't it? That tape was used to get me into this hole, now it's getting me out. And yet if we weren't so uptight about these things, about sex, the tape wouldn't matter. Such is the power of taboo.'

Carmen put her finger on the 'Record' button.

'Maybe that's something you should discuss with your wife,' she said.

45

Alex watched from the top of the cascade in the Ciutadella park as Pepa climbed the steps. Seeing her out of context, away from New York, she looked so American, in her white ankle socks and pastel holiday clothes. Like a lot of American women, his sister had clung resolutely to girlhood in the way she dressed and carried herself. They embraced and then he pulled her into the corner of the arched landing from where he had a good view of the park and the cafe below without, he hoped, being visible from the ground.

'Why are we meeting like this, in secret? What's going on?'

'I'm sort of on the run. Not from the police, well, not in the normal sense. It's a long story. In the short version someone's trying to kill me.'

'I don't understand. You've been here two weeks and, I don't know what it is, you look so different.'

'Different how?'

'I don't know, there's something about you.'

'There's something about you, baby, that makes me keep lovin' you.'

Stop it, Alex, I'm worried about you.'

'OK, sorry. How are things at Can Castanyer? Who was there?'

'Victor and Núria. They're an odd pair, but they were very nice to me, very hospitable. Núria taught me how to make these funny little cakes out of marzipan and pine nuts.'

'*Panellets*,' Alex said absently. 'Is she OK, Núria?'

'I suppose so, aside from the fact that she's so skinny. Are you and Núria, you know, an item?'

'Is that what she said?' Alex laughed.

'No, but she can't stop talking about you. It's all Alex this and Alex that. She seems a little unstable.'

'She's not the happiest of souls. Did she tell you what happened, I mean with Dad back then?'

'No, she said to ask you.'

Alex took a deep breath and told her what he knew. He didn't spare her any details. Pepa was uncharacteristically silent when he finished.

'But if it's true, and I can hardly believe it,' she said eventually, 'why didn't Dad do anything about it, why didn't he come back to prove his innocence?'

Alex had asked himself that question too, and in the end decided to give his father the benefit of the doubt.

'Actually I feel that, for my part, I judged Dad unfairly,' he said. 'You know, the way he was closed and gruff and refused to discuss things that were obviously bothering him. But now I think that, given what he went through, and how young he was when it happened, it's a wonder he turned out as sane and decent a man as he did. And I can see why he tried to blot it out.'

'But he just dumped it all on us, and on Mum. All that unspoken stuff, it was so heavy, it's always weighed on us because he wouldn't deal with it.'

Alex wanted to say, And you're so like him, Pepa, but he could also hear himself in her, when he was haranguing Miguel about honesty and openness and the cleansing power of talk. What was it Miguel said to him?

'People live with what they can bear, Pepa,' Alex said. 'Truth isn't always an option.'

Below them a small boy tried to retrieve his football from

the fountain. He lay on his stomach on the parapet wall, stabbing at it with a stick. The ball bobbed out of reach. Pepa opened her handbag and handed him an A4 envelope.

'I don't know what you plan to do with these. They're so horrible, I very nearly threw them in the garbage. I wish I had.'

The envelope contained half a dozen photographs, black and white eight by tens. There was a note in ungrammatical Castilian from his Aunt Anna which read: 'Dear Alex, I'm sorry we were not fated to meet in this life, perhaps, God willing, we shall meet in the next. No one in this country can face the truth, but I send you these so that the truth is in your hands to do with as you wish. Yours, Anna Nadal i Sunyer.'

The note was attached to a document in Anna's hand but this time in Catalan. Alex scanned it and recognized a familiar story: it was an extraordinarily detailed account of the events that occurred at Can Castanyer over two days in 1938.

He looked at the photos. Aside from one, they depicted various stages of the execution of at first four, then only three young men. They stood under the chestnut at Can Castanyer, their hands tied behind their backs, blindfolded. The picture was shot from behind the backs of the four-man firing squad. To the left stood a teenage girl. Behind her stood a young man in a white shirt beside an officer in uniform, and behind them a small crowd of villagers. The photos continued in sequence: the smoke from the guns, the astonishment on the victims' faces, the three men falling to the ground. In the last picture the officer held two of the dead men by the hair, pulling their blindfolds off their eyes for the camera. The young man in the white shirt held up the third. He and the officer were smiling straight into the lens. And then there was one picture that must have been taken the day before: it showed six young people sitting round the table at Can Castanyer, five men and a girl, who he recognized as Anna. The caption on the back named the others as the three Romeu brothers, Alex's father Ignasi, and Salvador Oriol. There were jugs of wine on the table and they were all smiling for the camera.

Alex flipped through the pictures a second time. He had, of course, seen pictures of atrocities before; photographs like these were one of the hallmarks of the twentieth century. But he'd never before known any of the protagonists. The pictures were captioned on the back: the man in uniform was Captain Guillermo Morín, and the teenage girl was his Aunt Anna. Then there were the victims, initially four, then only three who were actually executed. The three were the Romeu brothers and the fourth was his father. Not many people have a picture of their father standing before a firing squad. For Alex it was as though he'd fallen down the well of his father's psyche, that he was understanding his father in ways that were almost unbearable. As for the young man in the white shirt, the caption said it was Salvador Oriol. Alex put the photos back in the envelope.

'Come on,' he said, putting an arm around Pepa's shoulders, 'we'd better find you a hotel.'

They took a taxi, because Alex felt nervous and exposed in the street. He was sure Hernández was out looking for him. There was scarcely a room left in the city because of the Infanta's wedding. Eventually he found her a place in the Hotel Peninsula, a converted nunnery on the Carrer San Pau.

'Are you hungry?' he said. He felt protective.

'Not yet. I'm still a bit jet-lagged. I think I need to lie down.'

'You know people here don't eat till late?'

'What, like around seven thirty?'

'More like ten. I'll pick you up. There's a big firework display this evening in Plaça d'Espanya, for the Infanta. She's getting married tomorrow. If I'm not back in time, see if they'll let you watch it from the roof.'

'Where are you going?'

'To finish some unfinished business, I hope.'

*

He met Carmen in a noisy tapas bar in Carrer de Jovellanos. He asked her to find the oldest possible photo of Oriol and she brought the studio portrait taken at the end of the Civil War which she'd copied from his biography. It was the man in the white shirt, without question. Carmen gave a low whistle.

'This is dynamite. According to Oriol, when these pictures were taken he was in jail.'

'I told you it wasn't just about land and money.'

'And I told you it wasn't just about history. So we were both right. On Monday *El Mensajero* blows the lid off the Roger de Flor. We won't accuse Oriol of anything directly, but the fact is he's been nailed. The grand old man of Catalunya kneels before the mighty dollar and sells part of our birthright to American corporate finance – it's a great story.'

'He hasn't been nailed for this yet,' Alex said, tapping the packet of photographs.

Carmen reached across the table and stroked the back of his hand. It was an affectionate but also a consoling gesture.

'Nobody will touch that. It's unusable. Trust me.'

'Unusable? But the proof is here, incontrovertible proof. Especially when you put the pictures alongside my aunt's account of what actually happened. I mean, why would the woman make something like that up?'

'It's not a question of no one believing it, but there's sort of an understanding that this can't be done, or not yet, anyway.'

'What can't be done?'

'This sort of recrimination, people aren't ready for it. Obviously nothing was going to come out while Franco was still alive but even since he died there have been no official indictments over the Civil War, no war crimes trials, nothing like that. I suppose the feeling is it's too soon, that we've only had democracy for twenty years and it's too painful and, well, too explosive.'

'Let sleeping dogs lie, is that it?'

Carmen put out her cigarette and immediately lit another.

She looked Alex in the eye and for once he felt he could see in to something beyond the black mirrors.

'Let me tell you something,' she said. 'I've never told anyone this before, that is, no one except Miguel. I'm telling you because it's something I have to live with. Not just that, it's what hundreds of thousands, millions of people in this country have been living with these past sixty years. During the Civil War my parents were only little kids but of course their families were involved. My father's family weren't very political, but in so far as they were, they were republicans. My mother's family, on the other hand, were all fascists. Her father was an officer in Franco's army, although that doesn't automatically make him a monster. In fact he was a lovely man, a real sweetheart. But then a few years ago a guy I know was researching a TV documentary and he discovered that my grandfather wasn't just any officer; he commanded a unit that specialized in hunting down and killing leftwingers – intellectuals, artists, trade unionists. This is my grandfather, Alex. He read me stories, he taught me how to swim, he showed me his trick for cutting *jamón serrano*, how you must move the knife back and forth as though you're playing the violin.'

'Oh please. And Hitler liked children and small animals.'

The barman opened the glass case in front of them and filled two small plates with *pulpo gallego* and *boquerones*. Carmen smoked and said nothing until the barman went away. When she turned to Alex he expected to see anger in her eyes but there were tears instead.

'How do you think it feels to discover that what I thought was a sweet old man was a member of a fascist death squad? What am I supposed to do with that? Spend the rest of my life in therapy because I sat on this killer's knee, because I trusted him and gave him my little girl's love? I haven't even told my mother, for God's sake. I've no idea if she knows. She knows what she wants to know and I'm sure that's plenty. So that's another lie I live with, but what good would the truth do my mother? For that matter, what good has it done me?'

'All I want is justice.'

'No, you don't, you want vengeance. So do a lot of people, and who can blame them. The thing is, once you start down that road, there's no end to it. Look at . . .'

'Don't tell me, look what happened in Sarajevo.'

'Well, look at it. You think that can't happen here? They didn't think it could happen there either. Everyone says Sarajevo was a model of tolerance, live and let live. It was one of the most civilized cities on Earth.'

'Evidently the cat got out of the bag. These things have to be faced.'

'And they have to be lived with. What happened to your father and your aunt was terrible, a terrible injustice they had to live with. And then when he couldn't bear it any longer your father killed himself. So now that's something terrible you have to live with. But live with it, Alex. Don't get stuck.'

'I've come this far, I can't just walk away.'

'So what then?'

'I'm going to see Oriol tonight. We're going to watch the fireworks together.'

46

Alex expected a maid or a butler to answer the door but it was Narcís.

'Señor Nadal,' he smirked, standing aside to let Alex into the hall.

The hall floor was beautifully tiled in blue and white and brick red. Narcís gestured to the stairs, which were tiled in the same pattern. The banister was mahogany, polished to a high shine, gleaming up the stairs on a line of balusters of the same wood, turned in a series of flattened spheres. Narcís led Alex up the stairs. The hall and the staircase set the theme for the house, intricately tiled floors and dark wood. The furniture was heavy and grand and the walls were hung with nineteenth-century oils of pastoral scenes set in elaborate gilt frames. There was a suit of armour on the landing, a pair of flintlock pistols in a glass case on one wall, a stuffed boar's head on another. The style was baronial nouveau riche. And there it was on a heavy oak dresser – the carving of the horse that had stood on the piano in his father's house. Alex picked it up. The object was by now so freighted with meaning he felt like he held something living in his hand. He turned it over and on the base were the initials I.N. above the date, 1937.

'You'd better put that back,' Narcís said. 'Señor Oriol doesn't like people handling his things.'

'It's not his,' Alex said.

Narcís shrugged and ushered him on to the balcony. Oriol was sitting with his back to him in a grand gilded chair upholstered in blue brocade. The view was stunning: below them the city glowed and thrummed like an overcharged circuit board. Alex rounded the chair and the spectacle of this tiny, goblin-like man with a Beethoven hairstyle all but swallowed up in his golden throne made him want to burst out laughing. Oriol fixed him with a look. There was nothing amusing about his eyes. On the blue-tiled table there was a bottle of *cava* in an ornate silver ice bucket. Narcís filled three glasses.

'I didn't come here to celebrate,' Alex said. Narcís held out a glass.

'To the Infanta de Borbón,' Oriol said.

Alex took the glass, raised it, then put it back on the tray untouched. Narcís laughed.

'It's not poison, you know,' he said.

'Not literally, perhaps,' Alex said. He felt light, easy, unafraid. Oriol brought his glass to his lips then changed his mind and held it in a way that told Narcís to take it away. Narcís did as he was bid. He seemed in two minds about his own drink, then shrugged and took a swig.

'Let's get to the point,' Oriol said. 'How much do you want?'

Alex turned away from him and took in the view, the twinkling foreshore that was Barcelona, and the dark beyond of the sea. Rich people always live in the hills, he thought. Either that or by the sea. Or both if they can. He turned back to face Oriol.

'We'll come to that. There are some things we have to clear up first. Anna Nadal tried to blackmail you, didn't she? That's why you had her killed, not just for the land. Because you must have known about the pictures somehow, why else would your nephew here send someone to Can Castanyer to find them?'

Oriol gave Narcís a sharp look. Alex recognized it immediately; it was exactly the look he got from horn players if he played a bum chord under their solos, a mixture of surprise and irritation. Alex sensed some discord between the two of them. Maybe Oriol didn't know that Narcís had sent Kiko to look for the pictures.

'You don't really know what this is all about, do you?' he said to Narcís.

'It's nothing,' Oriol said, with a dismissive wave of the hand. Narcís looked at Alex.

'Nothing? It's a lot more than nothing,' Alex said, again to Narcís. 'Let me tell you a story.'

'There's no need for that,' Oriol said, dismissive again but clearly alarmed. 'Just tell me how much you want.'

There was loud bang and the sky above Barcelona was lit by a shower of gold. The Infanta's fireworks had begun.

'I'd like to hear what he has to say,' Narcís said, a note of contempt in his voice. He already had Captain Morín's confession, but Nadal had the photos and he wanted to see them just as badly as the old man wanted to keep them from him. A fusillade of rockets whooshed up from Plaça d'Espanya then burst in a spray of red and yellow stars.

'I'd hate to think you'd been kept in the dark,' Alex said, picking up the glass of *cava*. 'Do feel free to butt in if you feel I've left anything out,' he said to the old man with heavy irony.

'Let me set the scene. It's 1938, the Civil War is nearly over and the republican forces are retreating from the Ebro north towards Barcelona. My father is a non-combatant. His parents are dead and he and his sister are left to manage the farm at Can Castanyer as best they can. They're both still in their teens. One day three young fighters, three brothers from Barceloneta by the name of Romeu, turn up at the farm. They're all exhausted and my father agrees to let them rest at the farm. There's already one visitor there, a young American photographer who's covering the war for a news agency. Really they're just a bunch of kids. The eldest of the three brothers is only twenty-one. That same day another young man, your Uncle Salvador, arrives. He claims to have been separated from his comrades but when the Romeus ask him where he's been fighting he's a bit short on detail. But everyone lets that slide; people get confused in wartime.'

Alex pulled out the photocopies he had made of the photos and showed Narcís the picture of Oriol holding one of the dead Romeus up by the hair.

'That's your uncle there,' he said. Then he showed him the picture from Oriol's biography. 'See, no doubt it's the same man, is there?'

Oriol started to speak but he was drowned out by a succession of green and gold starburst rockets.

'The Romeu brothers have been fighting from day one and their speciality is explosives,' Alex continued. 'So when, on their first morning in Sant Martí, a small nationalist force under the command of a Captain Guillermo Morín arrives in the village, the Romeus decide to mount an attack. But the attack goes wrong and all they succeed in doing is blowing up the fountain in the village square. Morín is determined to find the culprits and slaps a twenty-four-hour curfew on the village. No one is allowed to step outside their house. So picture the scene at Can Castanyer. Sitting round the table are my father, his sister Anna, the Romeu brothers, the photographer and your uncle – see, here they are all happy and smiling. That's your uncle there in the white shirt. Like I say, they're just kids. The Romeus are all flirting with Anna and none of them seems scared of the soldiers coming, even though they should be. As well as the main cellar there's a secret cellar that runs off it, no one can remember why it was built, but anyway my father says the Romeus can hide there if the house gets searched. They're all hungry. People have been hungry for months, even on the farms there's nothing to eat. All they have between them is a few scraps of bread and some apples. But what they do have is wine from the cellar. So they drink, everyone except my aunt that is, because she's allergic to alcohol – you didn't know that, did you,' he said pointedly, but Narcís's face betrayed nothing, 'and your uncle, who says he has a bad stomach. But the rest of them get drunk.

'The Romeus start telling stories about the war, what fronts they've fought on and so forth. And they start to brag a bit. Then the youngest one jumps up, goes over to their pile of stuff, and drags a bag into the middle of the room. He empties it on to the floor and out tumble gold candlesticks, incense burners and other stuff they've looted from churches. His brothers try to stop him but it's too late. So they explain that when they get back to Barceloneta they're going to melt down the gold and buy a fishing boat.

'This sound about right to you so far?' Alex asked Oriol. The old man's face was lit by a barrage of fireworks. Still there was nothing in his eyes.

'I expect you can guess the rest. After a while everyone goes to bed. The Romeus and their booty are tucked away in the secret cellar and everyone, except Anna and your uncle, sleeps late because of the booze. Anna sees Oriol slip out early in the morning. Somehow he gets to Morín, despite the curfew, and tells him where he can find the Romeu brothers, but of course he neglects to mention the bag of booty. And he makes a deal, so that no one will know he's the informer. Morín gives him time to get back to the house and back into bed. Then he and his men raid the place. They beat up my father and accuse him of harbouring the Romeus. My father says he doesn't know what they're talking about, so they beat him up some more. They don't need to, because they already know where to find the Romeus. They're just having fun.'

A succession of giant silver and gold chrysanthemums lit up the sky.

'They keep beating my father and he keeps saying he doesn't know anything. So then Morín goes over to my aunt – this is a girl of sixteen we're talking about – and tears off her nightdress, and she's forced to stand there naked in front of all these men. Morín says to your Uncle Salvador, "Fuck her, go on, she's yours." My aunt is weeping uncontrollably; she's so terrified she wets herself. And your uncle – who I'm told is a national treasure – what does he do, this national treasure?'

'Your generation knows nothing about war,' Oriol said. 'You know nothing about oppression, or what people will do under duress.'

'Duress?' Alex said, ignoring Oriol and speaking directly to Narcís. 'Duress. Tell me, do you find duress exciting? If someone puts a gun to your head, do you get an erection? I don't think so. So, under duress, your uncle pushes my aunt face down over the table and starts to undo his trousers. But at this point my father can't take any more; they could beat him to death and he wouldn't say a word but he couldn't bear to see this happening to his baby sister. So he gives up the Romeus – or that's what he thinks, and it's what he goes on believing for the rest of his life – even though Morín knew where they were all along. The soldiers go and get the Romeus and bring them upstairs. So now Morín has what he came for, but he's not satisfied, he hasn't done enough damage. He says to your uncle, "Now fuck her and we'll watch." So he does, under duress, of course. And Morín makes my father watch.'

Narcís looked at Oriol with amazement. He didn't look shocked or disgusted, just amazed. Oriol didn't look at his nephew, but at Alex. It was a look of contempt, as though the disgrace was not his for what he did, but Alex's for relating it.

'Now Morín has to make an example. He summons all the villagers to Can Castanyer to witness the execution. The Romeus and my father are brought out with their hands tied behind their backs and lined up blindfold under the chestnut, here they are in this picture. The one on the left is my father. Then my aunt is brought out, that's her there. Her life's already ruined – even though she's the victim she knows the shame will fall on her. After all, this is 1938. So then what happens? The firing squad presents arms and just when everyone expects the order to fire, Morín steps up to my father, takes off his blindfold, unbinds his hands and tells him – in front of the entire village – that, because he betrayed the Romeus to the forces of God and Spain, he's free to go.'

The storytelling made Alex restless. He paced the balcony and then started circling around Oriol's chair.

'Imagine that,' he said, holding the carved horse against the old man's head as though it was a pistol. Oriol stiffened and Narcís took half a step towards them. Alex walked on. It was plain that Narcís was enjoying the old man's discomfort. 'Imagine,' he went on, 'you're eighteen years old and there you are blindfold before the firing squad. Any moment now your short life is about to end. You've just stood by and seen your sister raped so maybe you'd just as soon die as have to live with that. Heaven knows what's going through your head. And then, just when maybe you're ready to die, you're reprieved. The blindfold comes off and there's life staring you in the face again. Except it's not much of a reprieve. Your new incarnation begins with a public denunciation of you as a traitor and in a few seconds three young men are going to pay for your treachery with their lives. Imagine that, you're eighteen years old and you're going to have to live with this for a long time. What a difference a day makes, eh?'

Narcís tapped a cigarette on the side of a gold lighter and waited for Alex to continue before he lit it.

'So that's about that. My father does the only thing he can, which is run. As for Catalunya's national treasure, he goes back into the house, rapes my aunt again, and makes off with the Romeu brothers stash of ecclesiastical gold. And so began the family fortune. Oh, and as a souvenir he stole this,' he said, holding up the horse. He turned to address Oriol directly. 'I don't suppose you gave it a second thought, did you? Not until last year, anyway, when my aunt sent you one of these photographs. What did she want in return? I can't believe it was money, she wouldn't have touched your money. Maybe she just wanted you to face the truth, or perhaps she threatened to expose you. But you didn't wait to find out, did you? You decided to have her silenced, and as soon as you did you saw another opportunity to cash in. You gambled on her not having a will so you could take not only her life but her land too, the ideal site you'd been searching for to set up this phoney *sardana* school. Oh yes, I know all about that too. And everything went according to plan, well, almost everything. You never did find the photos because they weren't at Can Castanyer, they were in New York. And so was I because, thanks to you, that's where my father wound up. Well, now we're back.'

The fireworks reached a multi-million peseta climax of exploding, cascading stars. As the last shower fell to Earth the sound of applause drifted up from Plaça d'Espanya. Alex thought, This is what money buys: down below, half a million people were crammed into the square to watch the fireworks; up here on the balcony, where they had a better view and none of the discomfort, the applause of the huge crowd was reduced to a distant crackle, like the sound of someone crumpling a Cellophane bag. Oriol adjusted himself on his throne. If Alex's story had stirred any feeling in him it didn't show.

'What do you want?' he said again.

Alex stood with his hands flat on the cool stone balcony rail and looked out over the city. He felt a sense of arrival that he didn't understand, but if he'd hoped for some catharsis from this encounter, it hadn't happened. He didn't feel unburdened. More than anything he felt utterly weary.

'What I want,' he said. 'is justice. People tell me I can't or won't get it – because you're such a big shot and because they say this country isn't ready for justice. Fine, we'll call it something else then, revenge, perhaps, or spite. Call it whatever you like, all that matters is I'm going to make sure that everyone here knows the truth about you. If they can't deal with it that's their problem, but at least they can't say they didn't know.'

There was a barely detectable change in Oriol's expression, from cold and indifferent to cold and menacing.

'So if there's nothing you want from me, why are you here?' he said in a flat voice.

'I just wanted to be absolutely sure that you knew it was

me; when all the things you dread most come to pass, I want you to know it was my doing.' Oriol got to his feet and stood in front of Alex.

'Goodnight, Señor Nadal, I don't imagine I'll be hearing from you again.' Alex held the old man's unfeeling gaze then, in a last act of bravado, tapped his thigh with the bundle of photocopies and nodded towards the city below.

'Nice view,' he said.

All the way down stairs and down the street he was waiting for the arm around his throat or the press of cold steel on the nape of his neck. But he guessed they didn't want any mess on their doorstep. Even after a taxi appeared, its for hire light glowing a gratifying green, he expected Narcis to appear at his side and redirect the cab to some stone quarry or woodland or whever they took you in this town when they didn't expect to be hearing from you again. He sank back against the taxi's cool leather seat, feeling that all he had achieved was to buy some time.

47

Pepa left a note in reception saying she ate early and had gone to bed and that she'd call him at Carmen's in the morning. Alex was relieved. He wasn't in the mood for Pepa right now. What he was in the mood for was a drink. He went into the Viena bar in la Rambla and ordered a J&B on the rocks. He also wanted to smoke but buying a pack of cigarettes was too deliberate a step and he couldn't bring himself to bum one off a stranger. So he downed the whisky and walked up to Carmen's place on Provença. She was waiting for him as he stepped out of the lift. She put her arms around his neck and kissed him.

'I've been worried about you,' she said.

'I've been worried about me too.'

She led him inside by the wrist and sat him down. She had another jug of margaritas on the go.

'So what happened?'

'God, I feel totally drained. It was like one of those rows where you're screaming your head off and the other person just sits there looking at you as calm as can be. I don't think he was indifferent, but he certainly doesn't appear to be ashamed or overcome with guilt. It was as though I was just another nuisance, someone to be paid off and forgotten. Until the end, that is. I'm pretty sure I got to him in the end.'

'And he'll do everything in his considerable power to get to you. He won't rest till he has those photos.'

'I know. But in the meantime I'm going to make sure as many people as possible know the truth, even if I have to leave photocopies of the pictures and Anna's testimony in every bar in Barcelona.'

'I've got a better idea how we can tell the world. But I'm not telling you now, first there's something I want you to do.'

'What's that?'

'I've got a terrible itch I want you to scratch.'

Every time they made love they went deeper, further, stronger. It was all feeling – no fancy tricks, no prizes for contortion. Alex never was interested in the sex-as-yoga-class approach. He liked a certain tender ferocity that he could only get with someone for whom he felt some affection. He got it with Carmen, each time a bit more tender, a bit more ferocious. Afterwards she got the margarita jug out of the fridge and poured them another.

'You really like drinking in bed, don't you?' he said.

'I like drinking in bed with you. Maybe it's because you're American. In American movies there's a point in every love scene where someone fills two glasses with ice and pours two of the biggest bourbons you've ever seen. That must be it, you're my American dream.'

She propped herself on one elbow and looked at him. She had her serious face on now.

'So are you going back to New York now you've got what you came for?'

'Have I got what I came for? What was it anyway: what did my father do that was so bad and did he really do it? OK, I know the answer to that, but it's not as though it's cleared the air. And besides, I still don't know if Anna was murdered, or at least I can't prove it. That's what really gets to me, that Oriol ruined her life and then when she tried to get some payback he had her killed. But no one knows and no one seems to give a damn.'

'And how do I figure in all this, as a little local colour?'

Alex stretched past her glass and kissed her.

'I told you I'm falling in love with you.'

'You told me you thought you were.'

'I stopped thinking.'

'You are falling, then, as in the present continuous. Is it a long way down?'

'I hope so, I forgot my parachute. And no, the plan, in so far as a plan exists, is to stay here.'

'Here being Can Castanyer?'

'No, I'll never be a farmer. I intend to lease it to Victor, sort of in perpetuity. I'll still own it but that's all, I won't make anything out of it. In effect it will be his, and Núria's if she wants to stay there. I haven't figured out the details, I'll have to talk to Miguel.'

'And what are you going to do?'

'Play music and make love with you.'

Carmen rolled over and sat astride him, setting the drink down on his chest.

'You'll never get a visa,' she said.

'You always nibble round the edge, like a fish, wary of the hook inside the bait. Do you never just close your eyes and bite?'

'I am as I am. Bait your hook.'

'I just did. You obviously weren't paying attention. Or you're too scared to bite.'

Carmen rattled the ice in her drink and wriggled forward until she was sitting on his sternum.

'Will I be your girlfriend, is that it? OK, let's give it a try. In fact, let's live dangerously, you can move in here and we'll see how long it takes before we kill each other.'

48

Carmen went out early. Her brief was to mingle with the crowds lining the royal couple's route. It was barely two months since Princess Diana died and everyone was talking up the Infanta as the next best thing, another people's princess. Carmen had to do a colour piece on the mood in the street. Enric Luna said it might even make page one, but she knew he was lying because she'd already seen a page one dummy and there wasn't any space for text, just a picture and a banner headline.

Alex phoned the hotel but Pepa had gone out for a walk. Twenty minutes later the phone rang and the machine clicked on. He picked it up expecting to hear Pepa's voice but it was a man's voice, sibilant and serpentine – Narcís.

'I've got your girl,' he said. There was a roaring sound in the background, as though he was calling from an airport. 'Listen carefully. Get the photographs and meet me here within an hour, alone. Do what I say and the girl will be unharmed. Any messing around and she's dead.'

'How do I know she's with you?' Alex said, stalling, though he didn't know what for. They had Carmen's phone number so they could easily get the address. And there were never many people in the street in this part of town. Easy enough to bundle her into a car as she came out of the building.

'You know because I'm telling you.'

'Where are you?'

'Montjuïc. The cemetery. Now get a piece of paper and write this down.'

Alex got his car from the parking building and joined the traffic crawling down la Rambla. The cathedral bells were ringing and there were cops everywhere, thousands of them lining the street and parked in vanloads on every other corner. The traffic was barely moving and he banged the wheel in frustration. It was half an hour before he rounded the Columbus monument and headed south towards Montjuïc, sweating from the heat and anxiety.

He parked at the gloomy wrought-iron gates at the main cemetery entrance and started up the hill on the Via Santa Eulalia. He'd never seen a cemetery like it. Almost the entire seaward face of Montjuïc had been cut into terraces so the mountain rose in a series of irregular steps of rust-coloured stone. The dead were buried in niches stacked several deep so the rising part of each step was faced with hundreds of memorial stones, some with a photograph of the deceased set behind glass, which sealed off the end of each niche. A number of graves had been broken into and he could see right in, like a drawer with the front torn off. The better off were housed on top of the terraces in elaborate mausoleums, some as big as a small house. There was a pervasive smell of cypress and feral cat. The metallic roar of traffic pounding along the coast highway and the clanging of dock cranes in the container port swept straight up the hillside. Alex recognized it as the background noise he heard when Narcís called. The noise didn't stop for a moment. It was strange, this deathly place hanging over the sea, its former tranquillity shattered by the clamour of the living racing past below. Not a place to rest in peace, Alex thought.

The cemetery was divided into sections, each named after a saint, and each subdivided by number. Via Santa Eulalia had become Via Sant Francesc. This was the place. Now he had to find section six. He left the path and started along the top of the terrace until he came to a sign that read Agrupació 6. The section was dominated by an oppressively large granite mausoleum which held the remains of various members of a family called Collaso. Narcís said to meet him there. Alex looked around. The Collaso tomb stood on a semi-circular terrace, crowded with tombs and shaded by acacia and cypress. To his left the sea and the din of the highway, to his right the next step up the hillside, and another wall of graves, some of them empty. The wall was split by a flight of stone steps, leading up to the next level and another huge mausoleum, for the Familia del Rio, capped by a grey stone cross. Alex waited, he hadn't seen another soul in the cemetery. The smell of cats was overpowering.

Narcís appeared from behind the Del Rio mausoleum and stood at the top of the steps. Despite the heat he wore a black suit over a black polo shirt. Dressed to kill, Alex thought.

'Put the photos there,' he said, pointing to a white marble tomb, then take ten paces back and stay there.'

'Where's Carmen?'

'The photos first.'

'Where is she? I'm not giving you anything till I see her.'

'For God's sake, Alex, it's not Carmen, it's me. Just do what he says. He's got a gun.'

It was Pepa. For a moment Alex was so surprised his mind went completely blank. He couldn't figure out where her voice was coming from.

'Pepa, where are you?'

'Here, right in front of you.'

He could hardly hear her above the road noise. He looked at the wall, Pepa's face appeared at the opening of an empty grave, then disappeared, as though she'd been dragged back.

'Pepa, are you all right?'

He looked at Narcís and saw an awful symmetry – Oriol with Anna, Narcís with Pepa.

'I'm OK. I'm OK, just do what he tells you.'

Alex held the envelope with the photographs above his head where Narcís could see it, and walked slowly towards the white tomb. He put the envelope down and took ten steps back.'

'Now let her out.'

Narcís came down the stone steps, taking his time. When he reached the bottom step a gun appeared in his hand. He motioned with the barrel towards the open grave.

'Get in,' he said.

Alex was surprised at how calm he felt. He was terrified, but normally terror ran through him like water, washing away his resolve, but this fear was like ice. He stopped sweating and his heart was still, so still it hardly seemed to beat at all. He took a few steps forward and stopped. Narcís waved him towards the grave with the gun. It was a neat little automatic, almost a fashion accessory. Alex took a few more steps. There was now only about ten feet between them.

'You murdered Anna Nadal, didn't you? You forced her to drink and then shoved her down the stairs to make it look like suicide.'

Narcís shrugged, as much to say, So what? He waved the pistol towards the niche again.

'I'm not getting in there,' Alex said.

Narcís laughed and pointed the gun into the open tomb.

'I don't think you're in a great position to tell me what to do. Now get in or I'm going to close my eyes and pump a few rounds in here and see what happens.'

Alex knew he had only one chance and he had to take it. The opportunity would barely last a second. He knew that, and the worst of it was waiting for the moment to come. He couldn't force it.

'OK, OK,' he said. 'I'm coming. Don't worry Pepa, everything's going to be all right.'

He put one leg into the tomb and steadied himself with his hand as he swung the other one up. It was like climbing through a bathroom window. He couldn't feel the bottom with his feet.

'There's a drop of about three feet,' Pepa said from the darkness beneath him.

He lowered himself down, braced with one hand, the other one ripping Kiko's .32 from the tape around his ankle. As soon as his feet touched bottom he turned round to face the opening. Immediately, Narcís's face appeared. He had just started to crack a smile when Alex fired. Point blank. Twice. Into his left eye. For a moment Pepa thought that she'd been shot, then she thought Alex had. She started to whimper.

'Come on, let's get out of here,' Alex said. He hauled himself out of the grave and half fell, half climbed headfirst out on top of Narcís. A wisp of blue smoke rose out of his left eye socket. He helped Pepa out. She was filthy with grave dirt and stank of tomcat. Narcís' jacket was open and a document poked out of the inside pocket. It was Guillermo Morín's confession. Alex took it and grabbed Pepa by the wrist and started off towards the path. He picked up the envelope from the white tomb and put the confession inside. There was no one around. Pepa was shaking and sobbing.

'Stop, Alex, what's happening? Where are we going?'

'Anywhere but here. Come on.'

He dragged her down the hill towards the car.

'But we can't just run off. We have to get the police. There must be somebody here, a caretaker or something.'

Alex stopped. He still had the gun in his hand. He wiped it carefully on his shirt then scanned the wall of graves. A corner of the headstone sealing the opening to a niche was broken off. Alex dropped the gun through the hole. It landed with a small tap.

'We are not calling any cops. Do you want me to spend the rest of my life in jail?'

'But it was self-defence, he was going to kill us both.'

'So what, they'd still call it murder. You know who that guy is? He's the nephew of one of the most powerful men in Catalunya.'

'But he kidnapped me and then he was going to kill us. Alex, you've just killed a man. You can't just walk off like it was nothing.'

'I don't think it's nothing, but you have to try to understand. Imagine I've just killed a Kennedy. Imagine, we're on Martha's Vineyard, a couple of foreigners, and we've just blown away a Kennedy. What chance have we got?'

They got to the car without passing anyone. Pepa pulled on her seatbelt and gave him a long look. Her face was streaked with grave dirt. Her hair stuck to the sweat on her cheeks.

'Where are we going?'

'To the beach. We're filthy and we stink, and you can't go back to the hotel like that. We can wash our clothes in the sea, they'll be dry in twenty minutes.'

'This is scary Alex, you're scary. I don't know you. You're my brother but I look at you and I just don't know who you are any more.'

As the adrenaline wore off the enormity of what he'd done began to hit him. He was seized by an overwhelming desire to vomit. He swallowed hard and crunched the car into reverse.

'I hardly know myself these days,' he said.

He drove south, away from Montjuïc and away from the city, with no real idea where he was going. The journey took on a metaphysical quality. He had, after all, just killed a man, and wondered if it showed, if people would look at him and know. It was the beginning of a journey from one self to another, but it was more prosaic than the road to Damascus; as it turned out, it was the road to El Prat de Llobregat, the wilderness of warehouses that surrounds Barcelona airport. El Prat was an international nowhere that could have been the perimeter of any big airport anywhere in the world: a low-rise sprawl of storage barns, transit hotels and, inevitably, a brewery. Alex tried to find a way out of this featureless town that wasn't a town and pointed the car in the general direction of the sea. Neither of them had spoken since they left the cemetery. The car stank of cats and some clinging graveyard must that it seemed nothing would wash away. They came to a beach which, although still in sight of the container port and directly under the flight path, was evidently used by someone, as it had a push-button shower for bathers.

Alex parked and they walked over to the shower, each

understanding what had to be done, but neither saying a word. The only other people on the beach were a couple who appeared to be trying to have sex while fully clothed. Alex and Pepa stripped down to their underwear. Pepa was thin-lipped with anger, or anger was how it came across, but it could have been fear, it could have been almost anything right then. Alex kept the shower knob pressed in while she methodically and thoroughly washed her clothes, holding each item up to the light before wringing it out. When she was finished they changed places while he washed his clothes. Even then the stench of the cemetery clung to them. They picked up their things and carried them to the water's edge and laid them out where the beach sloped down to the sea, where they'd get the most sun. The fully-clothed couple writhed in the distance, apparently unaware of anyone but themselves.

Alex and Pepa walked into the sea and when the water was up to their waists dived in. It wasn't the cleanest corner of the Mediterranean but Alex felt instantly cleansed – not in any spiritual or moral sense – but of the sweat and stink of everything that had gone before. He rolled over on to his back and floated, eyes slitted against the bright sky. Pepa floated beside him.

'That guy, the guy I shot. He murdered Aunt Anna, you know.'

A plane took off directly overhead. As it turned and banked over the sea and the noise started to subside, Alex added: 'Not that that justifies anything.'

Pepa said nothing. Another plane screamed into the air. After it had gone Alex said:

'You know, it's funny, I mean not funny but strange, this is exactly the point where I should run away to America.'

Pepa still didn't speak but she turned her face to him as if to say, 'What do you mean?'

'Well, we always think of America as a refuge for the poor huddled masses, fleeing poverty and persecution. But there must have been thousands, millions maybe, who were running away from something else, a crime they'd committed, a debt they couldn't pay, or maybe they'd got some girl pregnant. Imagine if right now I could jump on a boat and get off at Ellis Island – new name, new identity and, above all, no history. A whole new beginning. Who wouldn't choose that rather than stay put and face the music?'

'Like Dad?' she said.

'Except it turns out Dad was innocent, even if he didn't think he was.'

'What about Anna? What about what happened to her – abused, outcast, stained for ever by what was done to her and what people believed her brother had done. Dad was no saint you know,' she said.

'I never said he was. What's that got to do with anything?'

Pepa didn't answer.

'I know what a difficult man he was,' Alex said, 'but knowing what we know now, don't you think you've been a little hard on him?'

Pepa turned over on to her front and trod water. They had lain head to head, addressing their remarks to the sky. Now they were face to face.

'Knowing what we know now, you could say he abandoned his sixteen-year-old sister who'd just been raped, aware that, given the moral code of the time, she was the one who'd be punished, who would, if you like, pay with her life.'

'But what choice did he have?'

'Everyone has choices.'

Pepa could be very black and white, he was used to that. But there was a steeliness about her now he hadn't seen before.

'He never tried to find her, to find out if she was OK. We know she looked for him, eventually, but as far as we know he never looked for her.'

'He could hardly come back.'

'Alex, Franco died in 1975. I know you think I don't know anything, but I know that much. That gave him twenty-two years in which he could have come back.'

'I don't think you don't know anything, it's just . . .'

282

'It's just you think I'm a naive girl who has to be shielded from the rough world. That's a joke – you try bringing up two kids on your own, or as good as on your own. And the bigger joke is you're the one everyone's always protected. It's always been, "Don't tell Alex, he'll only get upset." '

The light off the water turned her eyes, which were the same olive brown as his, to clear hazel. Another plane roared up into the sky and Alex laughed. He didn't know what else to do. To him this was so like Pepa, so Pepacentric, to take something that was uncomfortably true about herself and transfer it someone else.

'For instance,' he said. 'Don't tell Alex what?'

'What's it matter, you know everything anyway, or you think you do,' she said, and turned to swim away. Alex swam after her and grabbed her shoulder.

'What?'

She had that hard look in her eyes again.

'OK, you think Dad was a wronged man, and in some respects he was. But there's more to it than that. You think you know everything, well, here's something you didn't know: Dad has, or had, another family, two kids, about fifteen years younger than us.'

Alex was too shocked to speak. When he did, all he could think of saying was, 'Where?'

'Oh, just up the road from Mum and Dad's house, up on Amsterdam. Dad never ventured far. OK, he went to Cuba but that was more or less an accident, and once he got to Manhattan he scarcely left the neighbourhood. Manhattan does that to people, as you know.'

'How do you know about this?'

'I've known for years.'

'Does Mum know?'

Pepa rolled her eyes. 'Mama made me promise not to tell you.'

'But why?'

'Shame. It's a woman thing, I wonder sometimes if men really know what shame is. Look at Anna, a whole life defined by shame. As for Mama, she was ashamed that she'd been betrayed by her husband, ashamed of herself and of him. She didn't want you to find out because she didn't want you to think badly of him.'

Alex was stunned. This really pulled the rug from under everything; it was like finding out that you're adopted.

'If you ever let on to Mama that you know I'll kill you,' Pepa said, then started swimming ashore. They showered and turned their clothes over on the sand. The writhing couple had gone. They had no towels so they stood drying in the sun, facing out to sea, Pepa with her hands on her hips, Alex's arms folded across his chest. He felt like he'd been dropped into a centrifuge, a whirl of half-finished thoughts and half-formed emotion.

'Is there any reason why anyone should connect you to what happened back there at the cemetery?' Pepa said. She looked out to sea, not at him. There was nothing judgmental in her tone; it was the no nonsense now-don't-you-lie-to-me voice she used on her kids.

'Yes, I had a confrontation last night, me and that guy, Narcís, the guy I killed, and his uncle, the big shot. It was about the photographs.'

He struggled to say the words, 'the guy I killed'. They weren't words he'd ever imagined on his lips. He killed a man and it didn't feel good; when he looked the deed in the eye he was appalled. But not so appalled that he felt impelled to walk into the nearest police station and confess; nor that atonement should require him to spend the rest of his life in jail. His heart was hardening. It was a necessary thing. This country called for a degree of heartlessness, he could see that now. Beneath all the gabbling gaiety there was a brutality, something harsh and pitiless about the place and the people. In spite of which Alex was starting to feel he belonged here. He knew he didn't want to go back to New York, at least not yet. But nor did he want to go to jail.

'You'll be needing an alibi,' Pepa said, her eyes still fixed on the horizon.

'Look, I don't want you to get dragged into this, I hardly expect . . .'

Pepa turned to him. Her eyes still had that pale clarity they'd picked up from the sea.

'Alex,' she said. 'You're a murderer and, whatever the extenuating circumstances, there's no going back on that. But you're also my brother, and there's no going back on that either.'

49

At eleven o'clock, as Señor Williams boarded an Iberia filght to Miami, Carmen started working the crowd penned in behind the crush barriers on the Ribera side of Via Laietana which was on the route the Infanta would take after the service in the cathedral. Actually there wasn't that much of a crowd, they were only one or two deep and, aside from the tourists, it soon became clear that a number of them didn't want to be there at all but were trapped when the police suddenly closed off all the streets around the cathedral. The police lined both sides of Laietana, at three-metre intervals, legs apart, hands behind their backs, facing the crowd. All around her Carmen heard people pleading to be let through so they could get to the market or pick up their children or meet someone who was waiting for them. When the pleading failed, the abuse started, but the cops were impervious to pleas or insults; they had their orders and no one was going anywhere until the wedding was over and the guests had all been bussed up to Pedralbes. Later these same irritable people would see themselves on TV and hear the commentator describe them as an ecstatic crowd.

Carmen retreated into a bar, and over a gin and tonic, she wrote her piece in a little under half an hour. She made the whole thing up. That is, she described the scene in Laietana but left out the resentment, and all her interviewees were her own creations. Someone in the bar called out to Alicia, so she wrote: 'Alicia Valdes, a secretary in an insurance company, made the journey from Figueres in the hope of catching a glimpse of the Infanta.' The barman loaded the coffee grinder from a bag of Santos coffee, and she wrote: 'Joan Santos, a machinist from Sant Andreu, admitted that he'd had no interest in the wedding at first but had been carried away by what he called the irresistible tide of emotion.' And so she went on, picking up names from conversations around her and inventing lives and quotes to go with them. She wasn't proud of what she was doing but she knew what the newsdesk wanted and she had the choice of interviewing real people until she found enough of them willing to say what the paper wanted them to say or of making the whole thing up. One process was as dishonest as the other. If she went back to the office and said, 'Guess what, I couldn't find anyone who gives a shit about the wedding,' they'd send her back out until she did.

From the noise outside she guessed that the Infanta must be in sight. She wormed her way through to the front in time to see the newlyweds coming down Laietana in an open-topped car waving at the crowd who, Carmen had to admit, were now cheering enthusiastically and calling out *Viva los novios!* You could see that the groom was a commoner because he hadn't yet learnt the trick of the royal wave, a swivelling action, like unscrewing the lid of an upside-down jar, which enables you to wave for hours without tiring. The Infanta looked pretty, the way brides usually do, but more than that she looked really happy. Carmen surprised herself by feeling happy for her and as the car passed she too clapped and called out '*Viva los novios!*' And she meant it.

Then her mobile rang. It was Enric Luna.

'Where are you?'

'I'm on Laietana. She's just gone by but the cops aren't letting anyone move. I think I'll be stuck here for a while. How soon do you need copy? I could phone it through.'

'Get back here as soon as you can. Salvador Oriol is in hospital, he collapsed on his way to the wedding. They think he's had a stroke, no idea how serious. And there's a rumour that his nephew's been found with a bullet in his head.'

Carmen said nothing while the news sank in.

'You still there?' Luna said.

'Yes, I suppose this gives the editor the perfect excuse to put the Roger de Flor piece on hold. I can just hear him,' she said, mimicking the editor's grave tone. 'Nothing could be in worse taste than to attack a public figure such as Salvador Oriol when he's on his deathbed. Our readers would turn against us en masse.'

'Careful now, you could choke on all that empathy.'

'Oh boo-hoo, I wouldn't put it past Oriol to fake a stroke just to get the story pulled.'

'Well, whatever happens, it's not going into Monday's paper, that's for sure. Do you know anything about some photographs of Oriol?'

'What kind of photographs? Hey, the cops are letting us through, I'm on my way.'

'Old ones, from the Civil War, atrocity pictures. Oriol has a website set up for his eightieth birthday and someone's posted these pictures of him on the site, or at least a site with an almost identical address. The pictures are pretty damning.'

'Now who would do a thing like that? Have you seen the pictures yourself?'

'Of course. They're powerful stuff. So is the story that goes with them.'

50

Alex sat at an outside table at La Ribera in the Plaça de les Olles. The restaurant was almost opposite the municipal government offices where he queued for the certificate of non-residence all those years ago. Or that's how it felt; in fact he'd been here barely a month but a lot had happened in that month. Among other things, he'd got away with murder. That didn't sit too easily with him, at least the murder didn't; the getting away with it troubled him less than he would have imagined. Pepa concocted an alibi that put them in Sitges at the time of the murder. Once their clothes were dry they drove down to Sitges to scout it out and ate lunch in a small restaurant where they made sure they were remembered by leaving a large tip. To Alex they still stank of cats and death but Pepa insisted it was his imagination. For the next few days Alex waited for the police. They never came.

Soon after that Pepa went back to New York. The kids were with Greg, their useless father, and she couldn't help worrying about them. Alex drove her to the airport.

'Thanks for coming,' he said, not seeing the irony until the words were out. They both laughed.

'What's that line? I've had some great times and this wasn't one of them,' she said. 'But I suppose all in all, I'm glad I was here.'

'Tell me, this other family of Dad's, do you know . . .?'

'I went to see them.'

'Really? Are they all right, financially I mean.'

'Alex, they're fine, it's not your problem. I think you've done enough of Dad's housework for now, don't you?'

Before she went through to departures Alex handed her an envelope.

'It's a copy of Anna's testimony, plus a copy of Morín's confession. I leave it up to you whether you show them to Mama or not.'

'Like she needs to know,' Pepa said.

Carmen and Núria were meeting him for lunch in La Ribera. They'd gone to buy shoes. As soon as Núria got her head clear of smack and resolved to sort out her life, she said the first thing she needed was shoes. Alex didn't get it but Carmen did, as though it was the most obvious thing in the world that you couldn't start a new life without new shoes.

As for Victor, he jumped at the deal Alex offered him, of running the farm more or less as his own. That, plus his new role as Núria's saviour, had given him new confidence. He'd never dared argue with his father but he steeled himself and confronted him about selling land to Mallobeco which, it turned out, his father had done out of sheer greed and not because he was under a lot of pressure. The old man told Victor it was none of his business but Victor had the wit to time the confrontation for when his mother was in the room and she hit the roof. She'd put up with a lifetime of insults and belligerence from him, she told her husband, but she wasn't going to let him sell the farm from under them. For the first time ever she sided with Victor against the old man, telling him he was a disgrace to the family and that she was ashamed to be his wife. Victor felt almost heroic.

Someone cast a shadow over the table. Alex looked up

expecting the waiter but when he squinted up into the sun he saw Angel.

'Feel free to join me,' Alex said. Angel pulled out a chair and sat down.

'They say Salvador Oriol is going to pull through,' he said, a propos of nothing. 'Tough old bird.'

'So will he still be building his *sardana* school?'

'I doubt it,' Angel laughed. 'Not with his own money, anyway, he's lost enough of it already. I expect he'll use his illness to put it off and then it will just quietly be forgotten.'

Alex hadn't got the justice he wanted; publicly Oriol was still the man he was, the grand old man of Catalunya. But the truth was out, even if it wasn't being shouted from the rooftops, and Núria made sure everyone in Sant Martí knew that they'd been wrong all these years about Alex's father. Publicly, in the press and on TV, everyone was praying for Oriol's speedy recovery but in private they were agog at the pictures and the account of the atrocity at Can Castanyer and Oriol's role in it. Carmen had posted it all on the Internet and, although it was removed within twenty-four hours, by then it had been seen by thousands and downloaded by several hundred. It was the talk of the town. And however imperfect, Alex had to admit it was a victory.

'Does Oriol know it was you who exposed the Roger de Flor deal?' Alex asked, not for a moment expecting an answer.

Angel smiled his inward smile and ordered a glass of *cava*.

'Surely it was Carmen who blew the whistle,' he said.

'I thought it was more a case of you holding the whistle to her lips and telling her when to blow.'

'You underestimate her.'

'I've wanted to ask you,' Alex said, 'you remember we had a conversation about dread? What is it that you dread?'

'Oh nothing terribly original. Boredom, tedium, repetition, doing the same thing day in, day out. Any sort of prison, I suppose, literal or metaphorical. And you?'

'The usual – pain, loss, death. Plus, like all musicians, I have an almost neurotic dread of damaging my hands.'

'That's where a gun comes in useful,' Angel said with a cat-like grin. 'No risk of breaking a finger, you know, if you get into some sort of conflict.'

The sun was burning Alex's neck. He shifted his chair so he was under the parasol. Angel's tone was unsettling; Alex was pretty sure it was supposed to be.

'I know we Americans have a reputation as gun-crazies, but we're not all like that.'

Angel was still wearing the cat smile.

'I hear that you're pretty good, as a pianist, I mean. I was thinking, I'm opening a restaurant soon in the old city, and I thought it would be nice to have some music at the weekend, maybe Fridays too. A little jazz, nothing too wild; we don't want to put people off their food.'

'Thanks, but I don't really go for the supper club scene if I can avoid it.'

'But can you avoid it? I assume you only have a tourist visa, which means you're not allowed to work, and even that must expire soon. It would break Carmen's heart if you were deported,' he said with measured insincerity.

'I'm sure she'd be very touched by your concern. Are you suggesting that if I play in your restaurant illegally you'll turn a blind eye? That's very big of you, but really it's not my scene.'

'What I'm suggesting is that you won't last long here without a visa, but that maybe I could help you get one.'

'And why would you do that?'

Angel took off his jacket and hung it on the back of the chair. He lit a cigarette.

'I want those photos,' he said. 'The Oriol photos. And the old soldier's confession.'

'They're not for sale, but there are plenty of copies in circulation.'

'I have a weakness for originals.'

'Sorry, like I said, they're not for sale.'

'I can arrange for you to get residency, which is only a step away from citizenship. There are people who would kill for that.' He threw back his head and laughed. 'I don't mean that literally of course.'

Alex shook his head. His palms were sweating.

Angel slid his sunglasses up on to his head. Sometimes, he found, you could work better from behind dark glasses; other times you needed to bring your eyes into play.

'Have you ever found a bunch of keys?' he said, taking a long sip of *cava*. 'You know, in the street or a phone box or somewhere. It's funny how useless they are when you don't know who they belong to. You can imagine all sorts of doors or safes they might open, but you can look at those keys for a hundred years and they're never going to tell you their address. That's the problem the police often have with forensics – they've got the keys but not the lock. Take this murder in Montjuïc cemetery, Salvador Oriol's nephew, you must have read about it, the press loved it. Imagine, a man killed by someone already in their grave. But the cops are at a loss for motive and they haven't got a single suspect. But what they have got is forensic evidence – threads from clothing, fingerprints on some marble, and some flakes of skin, which means of course they've got some DNA. But they haven't a clue who it belongs to, and they can hardly take a sample from everyone in Barcelona in the hope that they'll find a match. So they've got enough forensic evidence to build a case but it's like that set of keys – they don't know who the DNA belongs to and until they do it's useless. You can imagine their frustration.'

Was he bluffing? About the forensics probably not; there was probably plenty. But why hadn't the cops questioned him? After the row on the evening of the fireworks with Oriol and Narcís he must have been a prime suspect. The only explanation was that Oriol had said nothing about their meeting. Maybe he was too ill. Maybe he wanted to forget Alex existed and had blanked him from his memory – or maybe the stroke was to blame for that. Angel might have been bluffing, but since Pepa dropped the bombshell about his father, Alex had lost faith in his judgment.

'I know what you're thinking,' Angel said, and he did. 'Salvador Oriol may mourn his nephew's passing but not that much, and certainly not enough for his desire for justice to overwhelm his instinct for self-preservation. At the moment he's the subject of gossip and he doesn't like it. But, as long as it's just gossip, no one's going to make a TV documentary about it. You see what I mean? What he doesn't want is for someone to stand up in a court of law and, as part of their defence, put the whole nasty tale into the public record. Then what is now unprintable gossip would become front page news. It appears the police have got the message: let the Montjuïc murder case slide, don't make waves.'

The trap was closing. All Alex could do was sit there and watch it close around him.

'Good news for murderers, then,' he said, resorting, as ever when he was in a tight spot, to irony.

'For one murderer. But what if someone, say a citizen who was upset that expediency appeared to be taking precedence over justice, pointed the police in a certain direction, what if they gave them the address that corresponded to that bunch of keys.'

'From what you say, the police would let it ride.'

'But the press is still hot for this story, they smell a rat, a cover-up. What if a newspaper reported that the police were inexplicably failing to follow up a lead, a very strong lead, in the case of the murder of a prominent Barcelona citizen. Oriol isn't the only one whose reputation is at stake – there are the newspaper editors, there's the chief of police, the mayor. Do you see? And the thing about forensic evidence is it's so damning; you may have a dozen witnesses ready to say you were on the moon at the time in question, but the forensics put you at the scene of the crime. It's like being caught in bed with another woman; an affair you can lie about, but *flagrante delicto* – one is a little lost for words.'

Alex drank his beer and wiped a slick of foam from his top lip.

'I imagine that this good citizen's principles have a price.'

'I believe we've already touched on that – the photos and the confession.'

Carmen and Núria arrived, both of them wearing that conspiratorial look of women who have been shopping together. Angel got to his feet.

'Well now, there's a surprise,' said Carmen. She kissed him on the cheek and introduced Núria, who greeted him with a suspicious nod. 'Are you joining us for lunch?'

'No, I've got to get going. We bumped into each other and I was just keeping Alex company until you arrived.'

'Angel thinks he can help me get a visa, a working visa,' Alex said, looking Angel in the eye.

'That's nice,' Carmen said, putting on one of her more enigmatic smiles. 'That's very sweet of you, Angel.'

'No one's all bad,' he said, giving Alex a wink. 'I'll be in touch.'

Alex nodded. After Angel left, Núria stood beside Alex's chair and kept poking his shoulder, jiggling about like an impatient child that isn't getting the attention it wants.

'Well?' she said. '*Well?*'

'Well what?'

Núria looked at Carmen and rolled her eyes and sighed theatrically.

'My shoes, dickhead. What do you think?'